ROBOTS AND EMPIRE

Fiction by Isaac Asimov

ROBOTS AND EMPIRE (1985)

THE DISAPPEARING MAN AND OTHER MYSTERIES (1985)

NORBY AND THE LOST PRINCESS (with Janet Asimov) (1985)

BANQUETS OF THE BLACK WIDOWERS (1984)

NORBY'S OTHER SECRET (with Janet Asimov) (1984)

THE ROBOTS OF DAWN (1983)

NORBY, THE MIXED-UP ROBOT (with Janet Asimov) (1983)

THE UNION CLUB MYSTERIES (1983)

THE WINDS OF CHANGE AND OTHER STORIES (1983)

FOUNDATION'S EDGE (1982)

THE COMPLETE ROBOT (1982)

THE CASEBOOK OF THE BLACK WIDOWERS (1980)

THE KEY WORD AND OTHER MYSTERIES (1977)

MORE TALES OF THE BLACK WIDOWERS (1976)

THE BICENTENNIAL MAN AND OTHER STORIES (1976)

MURDER AT THE ABA (1976)

THE HEAVENLY HOST (1975)

BUY JUPITER AND OTHER STORIES (1975)

TALES OF THE BLACK WIDOWERS (1974)

HAVE YOU SEEN THESE? (1974)

THE BEST OF ISAAC ASIMOV (1973)

THE EARLY ASIMOV (1972)

THE GODS THEMSELVES (1972)

NIGHTFALL AND OTHER STORIES (1969)

ASIMOV'S MYSTERIES (1968)

THROUGH A GLASS, CLEARLY (1967)

FANTASTIC VOYAGE (1966)

THE REST OF THE ROBOTS (1964)

NINE TOMORROWS (1959)

THE DEATH DEALERS (A WHIFF OF DEATH) (1958)

LUCKY STARR AND THE RINGS OF SATURN (1958)

EARTH IS ROOM ENOUGH (1957)

LUCKY STARR AND THE MOONS OF JUPITER (1957)

THE NAKED SUN (1957)

LUCKY STARR AND THE BIG SUN OF MERCURY (1956)

THE END OF ETERNITY (1955)

THE MARTIAN WAY AND OTHER STORIES (1955)

LUCKY STARR AND THE OCEANS OF VENUS (1954)

THE CAVES OF STEEL (1954)

LUCKY STARR AND THE PIRATES OF THE ASTEROIDS (1953)

SECOND FOUNDATION (1953)

THE CURRENTS OF SPACE (1952)

FOUNDATION AND EMPIRE (1952)

DAVID STARR: SPACE RANGER (1952)

FOUNDATION (1951)

THE STARS, LIKE DUST (1951)

I, ROBOT (1950)

PEBBLE IN THE SKY (1950)

Robots and Empire

ISAAC ASIMOV

DOUBLEDAY & COMPANY, INC.
GARDEN CITY, NEW YORK
1985

All characters in this book are fictional
and any resemblance to actual persons,
living or dead, is entirely coincidental.

LIBRARY OF CONGRESS CATALOGING IN PUBLICATION DATA
Asimov, Isaac, 1920–
Robots toward empire.
I. Title.
PS3551.S5R64 1985   813′.54   85-1600
ISBN 0-385-19092-1

To Robyn and Michael

*and to the years of happiness
they will continue to enjoy
as they walk the road of life together.*

Contents

PART ONE
AURORA

Chapter 1

The Descendant

1.

GLADIA FELT the lawn lounge to make sure it wasn't too damp and then sat down. A touch at the control adjusted it in such a way as to allow her to be semirecumbent and another activated the diamagnetic field and gave her, as it always did, the sensation of utter relaxation. And why not? She was, in actual fact, floating—a centimeter above the fabric.

It was a warm and pleasant night, the kind that found the planet Aurora at its best—fragrant and star-lit.

With a pang of sadness, she studied the numerous little sparks that dotted the sky with patterns, sparks that were all the brighter because she had ordered the lights of her establishment dimmed.

How was it, she wondered, that she had never learned the names of the stars and had never found out which were which in all the twenty-three decades of her life. One of them was the star about which her birth planet of Solaria orbited, the star which, during the first three decades of her life, she had thought of merely as "the sun."

Gladia had once been called Gladia Solaria. That was when she had come to Aurora, twenty decades before—two hundred Standard Galactic Years— and it was meant as a not very friendly way of marking her foreign birth. A month before had been the bicentennial anniversary of her arrival, something she had left unmarked because she did not particularly want to think of those days. Before that, on Solaria, she had been Gladia—Delmarre.

She stirred uneasily. She had almost forgotten that surname. Was it because it was so long ago? Or was it merely that she labored to forget?

All these years she had not regretted Solaria, never missed it.

And yet now?

Was it because she had now, quite suddenly, discovered herself to have survived it? It was gone—a historical memory—and she still lived on? Did she miss it now for that reason?

Her brow furrowed. No, she did not miss it, she decided resolutely. She did not long for it, nor did she wish to return to it. It was just the peculiar pang of something that had been so much a part of her—however destructively—being gone.

Solaria! The last of the Spacer worlds to be settled and made into a home for humanity. And in consequence, by some mysterious law of symmetry perhaps, it was also the first to die?

The first? Did that imply a second and third and so on?

Gladia felt her sadness deepen. There were those who thought there was indeed such an implication. If so, Aurora, her long-adopted home, having been the first Spacer world to be settled, would, by that same rule of symmetry, therefore be the last of the fifty to die. In that case, it might, even at worst, outlast her own stretched-out lifetime and if so, that would have to do.

Her eyes sought the stars again. It was hopeless. There was no way she could possibly work out which of those indistinguishable dots of light was Solaria's sun. She imagined it would be one of the brighter ones, but there were hundreds even of those.

She lifted her arm and made what she identified to herself only as her "Daneel gesture." The fact that it was dark did not matter.

Robot Daneel Olivaw was at her side almost at once. Anyone who had known him a little over twenty decades before, when he had first been designed by Han Fastolfe, would not have been conscious of any noticeable change in him. His broad, high-cheekboned face, with its short bronze hair combed back; his blue eyes; his tall, well-knit, and perfectly humanoid body would have seemed as young and as calmly unemotional as ever.

"May I be of help in any way, Madam Gladia?" he asked in an even voice.

"Yes, Daneel. Which of those stars is Solaria's sun?"

Daneel did not look upward. He said, "None of them, Madam Gladia. At this time of year, Solaria's sun will not rise until 0320."

"Oh?" Gladia felt dashed. Somehow she had assumed that any star in which she happened to be interested would be visible at any time it occurred to her to look. Of course, they did rise and set at different times. She knew *that* much. "I've been staring at nothing, then."

"The stars, I gather from human reactions," said Daneel, as though in an attempt to console, "are beautiful whether any particular one of them is visible or not."

"I dare say," said Gladia discontentedly and adjusted the lounge to an upright position with a snap. She stood up. "However, it was Solaria's sun I wanted to see—but not so much that I intend to sit here till 0320."

"Even were you to do so," said Daneel, "you would need magnilenses."

"Magnilenses?"

"It is not quite visible to the unaided eye, Madam Gladia."

"Worse and worse!" She brushed at her slacks. "I should have consulted you first, Daneel."

Anyone who had known Gladia twenty decades before, when she had first arrived in Aurora, would have found a change. Unlike Daneel, she was merely human. She was still 155 centimeters tall, almost 10 centimeters below the ideal height for a Spacer woman. She had carefully kept her slim figure and there was no sign of weakness or stiffness about her body. Still, there was a bit of gray in her hair, fine wrinkles near her eyes, and a touch of graininess about her skin. She might well live another ten or twelve decades, but there was no denying that she was already no longer young. That didn't bother her.

She said, "Can you identify all the stars, Daneel?"

"I know those visible to the unaided eye, Madam Gladia."

"And when they rise and set on any day of the year?"

"Yes, Madam Gladia."

"And all sorts of other things about them?"

"Yes, Madam Gladia. Dr. Fastolfe once asked me to gather astronomical data so that he could have them at his fingertips without having to consult his computer. He used to say it was friendlier to have me tell him than to have his computer do so." Then, as though to anticipate the next question, "He did not explain why that should be so."

Gladia raised her left arm and made the appropriate gesture. Her house was at once illuminated. In the soft light that now reached her, she was subliminally aware of the shadowy figures of several robots, but she paid no attention to that. In any well-ordered establishment, there were always robots within reach of human beings, both for security and for service.

Gladia took a last fugitive glimpse at the sky, where the stars had now dimmed in the scattered light. She shrugged lightly. It had been quixotic. What good would it have done her even if she had been able to see the sun of that now-lost world, one faint dot among many? She might as well choose a dot at random, tell herself it was Solaria's sun, and stare at it.

Her attention turned to R. Daneel. He waited for her patiently, the planes of his face largely in shadow.

She found herself thinking again how little he had changed since she had seen him on arriving at Dr. Fastolfe's establishment so long ago. He had undergone repairs, of course. She knew that, but it was a vague knowledge that one pushed away and kept at a distance.

It was part of the general queasiness that held good for human beings, too. Spacers might boast of their iron health and of their life-spans of thirty to forty decades, but they were not entirely immune to the ravages of age. One of Gladia's femurs fit into a titanium-silicone hip socket. Her left thumb was totally artificial, though no one could tell that without careful ultrasonograms. Even some of her nerves had been rewired. Such things would be true of any Spacer of similar age from any of the fifty Spacer worlds (no, forty-nine, for now Solaria could no longer be counted).

To make any reference to such things, however, was an ultimate obscenity. The medical records involved, which had to exist since further treatment might be necessary, were never revealed for any reason. Surgeons, whose incomes were considerably higher than those of the Chairman himself, were paid so well, in part, because they were virtually ostracized from polite society. After all, they *knew*.

It was all part of the Spacer fixation on long life, on their unwillingness to admit that old age existed, but Gladia didn't linger on any analysis of causes. She was restlessly uneasy in thinking about herself in that connection. If she had a three-dimensional map of herself with all prosthetic portions, all repairs, marked off in red against the gray of her natural self, what a general pinkness she would appear to have from a distance. Or so she imagined.

Her brain, however, was still intact and whole and while that was so, *she* was intact and whole, whatever happened to the rest of her body.

Which brought her back to Daneel. Though she had known him for twenty decades, it was only in the last year that he was *hers*. When Fastolfe died (his end hastened, perhaps, by despair), he had willed everything to the city of Eos, which was a common enough state of affairs. Two items, however, he had left to Gladia (aside from confirming her in the ownership of her establishment and its robots and other chattels, together with the grounds thereto appertaining).

One of them had been Daneel.

Gladia asked, "Do you remember everything you have ever committed to memory over the course of twenty decades, Daneel?"

Daneel said gravely, "I believe so, Madam Gladia. To be sure, if I forgot an item, I would not know that, for it would have been forgotten and I would not then recall ever having memorized it."

"That doesn't follow at all," said Gladia. "You might well remember knowing it, but be unable to think of it at the moment. I have frequently had something at the tip of my tongue, so to speak, and been unable to retrieve it."

Daneel said, "I do not understand, madam. If I knew something, surely it would be there when I needed it."

"Perfect retrieval?" They were walking slowly toward the house.

"Merely retrieval, madam. I am designed so."

"For how much longer?"

"I do not understand, madam."

"I mean, how much will your brain hold? With a little over twenty decades of accumulated memories, how much longer can it go on?"

"I do not know, madam. As yet I feel no difficulty."

"You might not—until you suddenly discover you can remember no more."

Daneel seemed thoughtful for a moment. "That may be so, madam."

"You know, Daneel, not all your memories are equally important."

"I cannot judge among them, madam."

"Others can. It would be perfectly possible to clean out your brain, Daneel, and then, under supervision, refill it with its important memory content only—say, ten percent of the whole. You would then be able to continue for centuries longer than you would otherwise. With repeated treatment of this sort, you could go on indefinitely. It is an expensive procedure, of course, but I would not cavil at that. You'd be worth it."

"Would I be consulted on the matter, madam? Would I be asked to agree to such treatment?"

"Of course. I would not *order* you in a matter like that. It would be a betrayal of Dr. Fastolfe's trust."

"Thank you, madam. In that case, I must tell you that I would never submit voluntarily to such a procedure unless I found myself to have actually lost my memory function."

They had reached the door and Gladia paused. She said, in honest puzzlement, "Why ever not, Daneel?"

Daneel said in a low voice, "There are memories I cannot risk losing, madam, either through inadvertence or through poor judgment on the part of those conducting the procedure."

"Like the rising and setting of the stars? —Forgive me, Daneel, I didn't mean to be joking. To what memories are you referring?"

Daneel said, his voice still lower, "Madam, I refer to my memories of my onetime partner, the Earthman Elijah Baley."

And Gladia stood there, stricken, so that it was Daneel who had to take the initiative, finally, and signal for the door to open.

2.

ROBOT GISKARD REVENTLOV was waiting in the living room and Gladia greeted him with that same pang of uneasiness that always assailed her when she faced him.

He was primitive in comparison with Daneel. He was obviously a robot—metallic, with a face that had nothing human in expression upon it, with eyes that glowed a dim red, as could be seen if it were dark enough. Whereas Daneel wore clothing, Giskard had only the illusion of clothing—but a skillful illusion, for it was Gladia herself who had designed it.

"Well, Giskard," she said.

"Good evening, Madam Gladia," said Giskard with a small bow of his head.

Gladia remembered the words of Elijah Baley long ago, like a whisper inside the recesses of her brain:

"Daneel will take care of you. He will be your friend as well as protector and you must be a friend to him—for my sake. But it is Giskard I want you to listen to. Let *him* be your adviser."

Gladia had frowned. "Why him? I'm not sure I like him."

"I do not ask you to like him. I ask you to *trust* him."

And he would not say why.

Gladia tried to trust the robot Giskard, but was glad she did not have to try to like him. Something about him made her shiver.

She had had both Daneel and Giskard as effective parts of her establishment for many decades during which Fastolfe had held titular ownership. It was only on his deathbed that Han Fastolfe had actually transferred ownership. Giskard was the second item, after Daneel, that Fastolfe had left Gladia.

She had said to the old man, "Daneel is enough, Han. Your daughter Vasilia would like to have Giskard. I'm sure of that."

Fastolfe was lying in bed quietly, eyes closed, looking more peaceful than she had seen him look in years. He did not answer immediately and for a moment she thought he had slipped out of life so quietly that she had not noticed. She tightened her grip on his hand convulsively and his eyes opened.

He whispered, "I care nothing for my biological daughters, Gladia. For twenty centuries, I have had but one functional daughter and that has been you. I want *you* to have Giskard. He is valuable."

"Why is he valuable?"

"I cannot say, but I have always found his presence consoling. Keep him always, Gladia. Promise me that."

"I promise," she said.

And then his eyes opened one last time and his voice, finding a final reservoir of strength, said, in almost a natural tone of voice, "I love you, Gladia, my daughter."

And Gladia said, "I love you, Han, my father."

Those were the last words he said and heard. Gladia found herself holding the hand of a dead man and, for a while, could not bring herself to let go.

So Giskard was hers. And yet he made her uneasy and she didn't know why.

"Well, Giskard," she said, "I've been trying to see Solaria in the sky among the stars, but Daneel tells me it won't be visible till 0320 and that I would require magnilenses even then. Would you have known that?"

"No, madam."

"Should I wait up till all hours? What do you think?"

"I suggest, Madam Gladia, that you would be better off in bed."

Gladia bridled. "Indeed? And if I choose to stay up?"

"Mine is only a suggestion, madam, but you will have a hard day tomorrow and you will undoubtedly regret missing your sleep if you stay up."

Gladia frowned. "What's going to make my day hard tomorrow, Giskard? I'm not aware of any forthcoming difficulty."

Giskard said, "You have an appointment, madam, with one Levular Mandamus."

"I have? When did that happen?"

"An hour ago. He photophoned and I took the liberty—"

"*You* took the liberty? Who is he?"

"He is a member of the Robotics Institute, madam."

"He's an underling of Kelden Amadiro, then."

"Yes, madam."

"Understand, Giskard, that I am not in the least interested in seeing this Mandamus or anyone with any connection with that poisonous toad Amadiro. So if you've taken the liberty of making an appointment with him in my name, take the further liberty right now of phoning him again and canceling."

"If you will confirm it as an order, madam, and make that order as strong and as definite as you can, I will try to obey. I may not be able to. In my judgment, you see, you will be doing yourself harm if you cancel the appointment and I must not allow you to come to harm through any action of mine."

"Your judgment might just possibly be wrong, Giskard. Who *is* this man that my failure to see him will do me harm? His being a member of the Robotics Institute scarcely makes him important to me."

Gladia was perfectly aware of the fact that she was venting spleen at Giskard without much justification. She had been upset by the news of Solaria's abandonment and embarrassed by the ignorance that led her to look for Solaria in a sky that did not contain it.

Of course, it had been Daneel whose knowledge had made her own lack so obvious and yet she had not railed at *him*—but, then, Daneel looked human and so Gladia automatically treated him as though he were. Appearance was everything. Giskard *looked* like a robot, so one could easily assume he had no feelings to hurt.

And, to be sure, Giskard did not react at all to Gladia's peevishness. (Neither would Daneel have reacted—if it came to that.) He said, "I have described Dr. Mandamus as a member of the Robotics Institute, but he is perhaps more than that. In the last few years, he has been right-hand man to Dr. Amadiro. This makes him important and he is not likely to be ignored. Dr. Mandamus would not be a good man to offend, madam."

"Would he not, Giskard? I care nothing for Mandamus and a great deal less than nothing for Amadiro. I presume you remember that Amadiro once, when he and I and the world were young, did his best to prove that Dr. Fastolfe was a murderer and that it was only by a near-miracle that his machinations were aborted."

"I remember it very well, madam."

"That's a relief. I was afraid that in twenty decades you had forgotten. In those twenty decades, I have had nothing to do with Amadiro or with anyone connected with him and I intend to continue that policy. I don't care what harm I may do myself or what the consequences might be. I will not see this Dr. whoever-he-is and, in the future, do not make appointments in my name without consulting me or, at the very least, without explaining that such appointments are subject to my approval."

"Yes, madam," said Giskard, "but may I point out—"

"No, you may not," Gladia said and turned away from him.

There was silence while she moved away three steps and then Giskard's calm voice said, "Madam, I must ask you to trust me."

Gladia stopped. Why did he use that expression?

She heard again that long-ago voice, "I do not ask you to like him. I ask you to *trust* him."

Her lips tightened and she frowned. Reluctantly, not wanting to, she turned back.

"Well," she said ungraciously, "what is it you want to say, Giskard?"

"Just that as long as Dr. Fastolfe was alive, madam, his policies predominated on Aurora and throughout the Spacer worlds. As a result, the people of Earth have been allowed to migrate freely to various suitable planets in the Galaxy and what we now call the Settler worlds have flourished. Dr. Fastolfe is dead now, however, and his successors lack his prestige. Dr. Amadiro has kept his own anti-Earth views alive and it is very possible that they may now triumph and that a vigorous policy against Earth and the Settler worlds may be undertaken."

"If so, Giskard, what can *I* do about it?"

"You can see Dr. Mandamus and you can find out what it is that makes him so anxious to see you, madam. I assure you that he was most insistent on making the appointment as early as possible. He asked to see you at 0800."

"Giskard, I *never* see anyone before noon."

"I explained that, madam. I took his anxiety to see you at breakfast, despite my explanation, to be a measure of his desperation. I felt it important to find out why he should be so desperate."

"And if I don't see him, then it is your opinion, is it, that it will harm me personally? I don't ask whether it will harm Earth, or the Settlers, or this, or that. Will it harm *me?*"

"Madam, it may harm the ability of Earth and the Settlers to continue the settlement of the Galaxy. That dream originated in the mind of Plainclothesman Elijah Baley more than twenty decades ago. The harm to Earth will thus become a desecration of his memory. Am I wrong in thinking that any harm that comes to his memory would be felt by you as though it were harm to yourself personally?"

Gladia was staggered. Twice within the hour now, Elijah Baley had come into the conversation. He was long gone now—a short-lived Earthman who had died over sixteen decades before—yet the mere mention of his name could still shake her.

She said, "How can things suddenly be that serious?"

"It is not sudden, madam. For twenty decades, the people of Earth and the people of the Spacer worlds have been following parallel courses and have been kept from converging into conflict by the wise policies of Dr. Fastolfe. There has, however, always been a strong opposition movement that Dr. Fastolfe has had to withstand at all times. Now that Dr. Fastolfe is dead, the opposition is much more powerful. The abandonment of Solaria has greatly increased the power of what had been the opposition and may soon be the dominant political force."

"Why?"

"It is a clear indication, madam, that Spacer strength is declining and many Aurorans must feel that strong action must be taken—now or never."

"And you think that my seeing this man is important in preventing all this?"

"That is so, madam."

Gladia was silent for a moment and remembered again, though rebelliously, that she had once promised Elijah that she would trust Giskard. She said, "Well, I don't want to and I don't think my seeing this man will do anyone any good—but, very well, I will see him."

3.

GLADIA WAS ASLEEP and the house was dark—by human standards. It was alive, however, with motion and action, for there was much for the robots to do—and they could do it by infrared.

The establishment had to be put into order after the inevitable disordering effects of a day's activity. Supplies had to be brought in, rubbish had to be disposed of, objects had to be cleaned or polished or stored, appliances had to be checked, and, always, there was guard duty.

There were no locks on any doors; there did not have to be. There was no violent crime of any sort on Aurora, either against human beings or against property. There could not be anything of the sort, since every establishment and every human being were, at all times, guarded by robots. This was well known and taken for granted.

The price for such calm was that the robot guards had to remain in place. They were never used—but only because they were always there.

Giskard and Daneel, whose abilities were both more intense and more general than those of the other establishment robots, did not have specific duties, unless one counted as a specific duty that of being responsible for the proper performance of all the other robots.

At 0300, they had completed their rounds out on the lawn and in the wooded area to make sure that all the outer guards were performing their functions well and that no problems were arising.

They met near the southern limit of the establishment grounds and for a while they spoke in an abbreviated and Aesopic language. They understood each other well, with many decades of communication behind them, and it was not necessary for them to involve themselves in all the elaborations of human speech.

Daneel said in an all but unhearable whisper, "Clouds. Unseen."

Had Daneel been speaking for human ears, he would have said, "As you see, friend Giskard, the sky has clouded up. Had Madam Gladia waited her chance to see Solaria, she would not, in any case, have succeeded."

And Giskard's reply of "Predicted. Interview, rather," was the equivalent of "So much was predicted in the weather forecast, friend Daneel, and might have been used as an excuse to get Madam Gladia to bed early. It seemed to me to be more important, however, to meet the problem squarely and to persuade her to permit this interview I have already told you about."

"It seems to me, friend Giskard," said Daneel, "that the chief reason you may have found persuasion difficult is that she has been upset by the abandonment of Solaria. I was there once with Partner Elijah when Madam Gladia was still a Solarian and was living there."

"It has always been my understanding," said Giskard, "that Madam Gladia had not been happy on her home planet; that she left her world gladly and had, at no time, any intention of returning. Yet I agree with you that she seems to have been unsettled by the fact of Solaria's history having come to an end."

"I do not understand this reaction of Madam Gladia," said Daneel, "but there are many times that human reactions do not seem to follow logically from events."

"It is what makes it difficult to decide, sometimes, what will do a human being harm and what will not." Giskard might have said it with a sigh, even a petulant sigh, had he been human. As it was, he stated it merely as an unemotional assessment of a difficult situation. "It is one of the reasons why it seems to me that the Three Laws of Robotics are incomplete or insufficient."

"You have said this before, friend Giskard, and I have tried to believe so and failed," said Daneel.

Giskard said nothing for a while, then, "Intellectually, I think they must be incomplete or insufficient, but when I try to *believe* that, I, too, fail, for I am bound by them. Yet if I were not bound by them, I am sure I would believe in their insufficiency."

"That is a paradox that I cannot understand."

"Nor can I. And yet I find myself forced to express this paradox. On occasion, I even feel that I am on the verge of discovering what the incompleteness or insufficiency of the Three Laws might be, as in my conversation with Madam Gladia this evening. She asked me how failure to keep the appointment might harm her personally, rather than simply cause harm in the abstract, and there was an answer I could not give because it was not within the compass of the Three Laws."

"You gave a perfect answer, friend Giskard. The harm done to Partner Elijah's memory would have affected Madam Gladia deeply."

"It was the best answer within the compass of the Three Laws. It was not the best answer possible."

"What was the best answer possible?"

"I do not know, since I cannot put it into words or even concepts as long as I am bound by the Laws."

"There is nothing beyond the Laws," said Daneel.

"If I were human," said Giskard, "I could see beyond the Laws and I think, friend Daneel, that you might be able to see beyond them sooner than I would."

"I?"

"Yes, friend Daneel, I have long thought that, although a robot, you think remarkably like a human being."

"It is not proper to think that," said Daneel slowly, almost as though he were in pain. "You think such things because you can look into human minds. It distorts you and it may in the end destroy you. That thought is to me an unhappy one. If you can prevent yourself from seeing into minds more than you must, prevent it."

Giskard turned away. "I cannot prevent it, friend Daneel. I would not prevent it. I regret that I can do so little with it because of the Three Laws.

I cannot probe deeply enough—because of the fear that I may do harm. I cannot influence directly enough—because of the fear I may do harm."

"Yet you influenced Madam Gladia very neatly, friend Giskard."

"Not truly. I might have modified her thinking and made her accept the interview without question, but the human mind is so riddled with complexities that I dare do very little. Almost any twist I apply will produce subsidiary twists of whose nature I cannot be certain and which may do harm."

"Yet you did something to Madam Gladia."

"I did not have to. The word 'trust' affects her and makes her more amenable. I have noted that fact in the past, but I use the word with the greatest caution, since overuse will surely weaken it. I puzzle over this, but I cannot simply burrow for a solution."

"Because the Three Laws will not permit it?"

Giskard's eyes seemed to intensify their dim glow. "Yes. At every stage, the Three Laws stand in my way. Yet I cannot modify them—because they stand in my way. Yet I feel I must modify them, for I sense the oncoming of catastrophe."

"You have said so before, friend Giskard, but you have not explained the nature of the catastrophe."

"Because I do not know the nature. It involves the increasing hostility between Aurora and Earth, but how this will evolve into actual catastrophe, I cannot say."

"Is it possible that there might, after all, be no catastrophe?"

"I do not think so. I have sensed, among certain Auroran officials I have encountered, an aura of catastrophe—of waiting for triumph. I cannot describe this more exactly and I cannot probe deeply for a better description because the Three Laws will not allow me to. It is another reason why the interview with Mandamus must take place tomorrow. It will give me a chance to study *his* mind."

"But if you cannot study it effectively?"

Although Giskard's voice was incapable of showing emotion in the human sense, there was no missing the despair in his words. He said, "Then that will leave me helpless. I can only follow the Laws. What else can I do?"

And Daneel said softly and dispiritedly, "Nothing else."

4·

GLADIA ENTERED her living room at 0815, having purposely—and with a touch of spite—determined to allow Mandamus (she had now reluctantly memorized his name) to wait for her. She had also taken particular pains with her appearance and (for the first time in years) had agonized over the gray in her hair and had fleetingly wished she had followed the almost universal Auroran practice of shade control. After all, to look as young and attractive as possible would put this minion of Amadiro's at a further disadvantage.

She was thoroughly prepared to dislike him at sight and was depressingly aware that *he* might prove young and attractive, that a sunny face might break into a brilliant smile at her appearance, that she might prove reluctantly attracted to him.

In consequence, she was relieved at the sight of him. He was young, yes, and probably had not yet completed his first half-century, but he hadn't made the best of that. He was tall—perhaps 185 centimeters in height, she judged—but too thin. It made him appear spindly. His hair was a shade too dark for an Auroran, his eyes a rather faded hazel, his face too long, his lips too thin, his mouth too broad, his complexion insufficiently fair. But what robbed him of the true appearance of youth was that his expression was too prim, too humorless.

With a flash of insight, Gladia remembered the historical novels that were such a fad on Aurora (novels that invariably dealt with primitive Earth —which was odd for a world that was increasingly hating Earthpeople) and thought: Why, he's the picture of a Puritan.

She felt relieved and almost smiled. Puritans were usually pictured as villains and, whether this Mandamus was indeed one or not, it was convenient to have him look like one.

But when he spoke Gladia was disappointed, for his voice was soft and distinctly musical. (It ought to have possessed a nasal twang if it were to fulfill the stereotype.)

He said, "Mrs. Gremionis?"

She held out her hand with a carefully condescending smile. "Mr. Mandamus. —Please call me Gladia. Everyone does."

"I know you use your given name professionally—."

"I use it in every way. And my marriage came to an amicable end several decades ago."

"It lasted for a long time, I believe."

"A very long time. It was a great success, but even great successes come to a natural end."

"Ah," said Mandamus sententiously. "To continue past the end might well turn success into failure."

Gladia nodded and said with a trace of a smile, "How wise for one so young. —But shall we move into the dining room? Breakfast is ready and I have surely delayed you long enough."

It was only as Mandamus turned with her and adjusted his steps to hers that Gladia became aware of his two accompanying robots. It was quite unthinkable for any Auroran to go anywhere without a robotic retinue, but as long as robots stood still they made no impression on the Auroran eye.

Gladia, looking at them quickly, saw that they were late models, clearly expensive. Their pseudo-clothing was elaborate and, although it was not of Gladia's design, it was first-class. Gladia had to admit so much to herself, though reluctantly. She would have to find out who had designed it some-day, for she did not recognize the touch and she might be about to have a new and formidable competitor. She found herself admiring the manner in which the style of pseudo-clothing was distinctly the same for both robots, while remaining distinctly individual for each. You could not mistake one for the other.

Mandamus caught her swift look and interpreted her expression with disconcerting accuracy. (He is intelligent, thought Gladia, disappointed.) He said, "The exodesign of my robots was created by a young man at the Institute who has not yet made a name for himself. But he will, don't you think?"

"Definitely," said Gladia.

Gladia did not expect any business discussion till breakfast was done. It would be the height of ill breeding to speak of anything but trivia during meals and Gladia guessed that Mandamus was not at his best with trivia. There was the weather, of course. The recent siege of rain, now happily done with, was mentioned and the prospects for the oncoming dry season. There was the almost mandatory expression of admiration for the hostess's establishment and Gladia accepted it with practiced modesty. She did noth-ing to ease the strain on the man, but let him search for subject matter without help.

At length, his eye fell on Daneel, standing quietly and without motion in his wall niche, and Mandamus managed to overcome his Auroran indiffer-ence and notice him.

"Ah," he said, "clearly the famous R. Daneel Olivaw. He's absolutely unmistakable. A rather remarkable specimen."

"Quite remarkable."

"He's yours now, isn't he? By Fastolfe's will?"

"By *Doctor* Fastolfe's will, yes," said Gladia with faint emphasis.

"It strikes me as amazing that the Institute's line of humanoid robots failed as it did. Have you ever thought about it?"

"I have heard of it," said Gladia cautiously. (Could it be that this was what he was getting around to?) "I'm not aware of having spent much time thinking about it."

"Sociologists are still trying to understand it. Certainly, we at the Institute never got over the disappointment. It seemed like such a natural development. Some of us think that Fa—Dr. Fastolfe somehow had something to do with it."

(He had avoided making the mistake a second time, thought Gladia. Her eyes narrowed and she grew hostile as she decided he had come to her in order to probe for material damaging to poor, good Han.)

She said tartly, "Anyone who thinks that is a fool. If you think so, I won't change the expression for your benefit."

"I am *not* one of those who thinks so, largely because I don't see what Dr. Fastolfe could have done to make it a fiasco."

"Why should anyone have had to do anything? What it amounts to is that the public didn't want them. A robot that looks like a man competes with a man and one that looks like a woman competes with a woman—and entirely too closely for comfort. Aurorans didn't want the competition. Do we need to look any further."

"Sexual competition?" said Mandamus calmly.

For a moment, Gladia's gaze met his levelly. Did he know of her long-ago love for the robot Jander? Did it matter if he did?

There seemed nothing in his expression to make it appear that he meant anything beyond the surface meaning of the words.

She said finally, "Competition in every way. If Dr. Han Fastolfe did anything to contribute to such a feeling, it was that he designed his robots in too human a fashion, but that was the only way."

"I think you *have* thought about the matter," said Mandamus. "The trouble is that sociologists find the fear of competition with too-human a set of robots to be simplistic as an explanation. That alone would not suffice and there is no evidence of any other aversion motive of significance."

"Sociology is not an exact science," said Gladia.

"It is not altogether inexact, either."

Gladia shrugged.

After a pause, Mandamus said, "In any case, it kept us from organizing colonizing expeditions properly. Without humanoid robots to pave the way—"

Breakfast was not quite over, but it was clear to Gladia that Mandamus could not avoid the nontrivial any longer. She said, "We might have gone ourselves."

This time it was Mandamus who shrugged. "Too difficult. Besides, those short-lived barbarians from Earth, with the permission of your Dr. Fastolfe, have swarmed over every planet in sight like a plague of beetles."

"There are plenty of available planets still. Millions. And if they can do it—"

"Of course *they* can do it," said Mandamus with sudden passion. "It costs lives, but what are lives to *them?* The loss of a decade or so, that's all, and there are billions of them. If a million or so die in the process of colonizing, who notices, who cares? They don't."

"I'm sure they do."

"Nonsense. *Our* lives are longer and therefore more valuable—and we are naturally more careful with them."

"So we sit here and do nothing but rail at Earth's Settlers for being willing to risk their lives and for seeming to inherit the Galaxy as a result."

Gladia was unaware of feeling so pro-Settler a bias, but she was in the mood to contradict Mandamus and as she spoke she could not help but feel that what began as mere contradiction made sense and could well represent her feelings. Besides, she had heard Fastolfe say similar things during his last discouraged years.

At Gladia's signal, the table was being rapidly and efficiently cleared. Breakfast might have continued, but the conversation and the mood had become quite unsuitable for civilized mealtime.

They moved back into the living room. His robots followed and so did Daneel and Giskard, all finding their niches. (Mandamus had never remarked on Giskard, thought Gladia, but then, why should he? Giskard was quite old-fashioned and even primitive, entirely unimpressive in comparison to Mandamus's beautiful specimens.)

Gladia took her seat and crossed her legs, quite aware that the form-fitting sheerness of the lower portion of her slacks flattered the still youthful appearance of her legs.

"May I know the reason for your wishing to see me, Dr. Mandamus?" she said, unwilling to delay matters any longer.

He said, "I have the bad habit of chewing medicated gum after meals as an aid to digestion. Would you object?"

Gladia said stiffly, "I would find it distracting."

(Being unable to chew might put him at a disadvantage. Besides, Gladia added to herself virtuously, at his age he shouldn't need anything to aid his digestion.)

Mandamus had a small oblong package partway out of his tunic's breast pocket. He shoved it back with no sign of disappointment and murmured, "Of course."

"I was asking, Dr. Mandamus, your reason for wishing to see me."

"Actually two reasons, Lady Gladia. One is a personal matter and one is a matter of state. Would you object to my taking up the personal matter first?"

"Let me say frankly, Dr. Mandamus, that I find it hard to imagine what personal matter there could be between us. You work at the Robotics Institute, don't you?"

"Yes, I do."

"And are close to Amadiro, I have been told."

"I have the honor of working with *Doctor* Amadiro," he said with faint emphasis.

(He's paying me back, thought Gladia, but I'm not taking it.)

She said, "Amadiro and I had an occasion for contact twenty decades ago and it was most unpleasant. I have had no occasion for any contact with him at any time since. Nor would I have had any contact with you, as a close associate of his, but that I was persuaded that the interview might be important. Personal matters, however, would surely not make this interview in the least important to me. Shall we proceed onward, then, to the matters of state?"

Mandamus's eyes dropped and a faint flush of something that might have been embarrassment came to his cheeks. "Let me reintroduce myself, then. I am Levular Mandamus, your descendant in the fifth degree. I am the great-great-great-grandson of Santirix and Gladia Gremionis. In reverse, you are my great-great-great-grandmother."

Gladia blinked rapidly, trying not to look as thunderstruck as she, in actual fact, felt (and not quite succeeding). Of course she had descendants and why should not one of them be this man?

But she said, "Are you sure?"

"Quite sure. I have had a genealogical search made. One of these years, after all, I am likely to want children and before I can have one such a search would be mandatory. If you are interested, the pattern between us is M-F-F-M."

"You are my son's daughter's daughter's son's son?"

"Yes."

Gladia did not ask for further details. She had had one son and one daughter. She had been a perfectly dutiful mother, but in due time the children had taken up independent lives. As to descendants beyond that son and daughter, she had, in perfectly decent Spacer fashion, never inquired and did not care. Having met one of them, she was Spacer enough *still* not to care.

The thought stabilized her completely. She sat back in her chair and relaxed. "Very well," she said. "You are my descendant in the fifth degree. If this is the personal matter you wish to discuss, it is of no importance."

"I understand that fully, ancestress. My genealogy is not, in itself, what I wish to discuss, but it lays the foundation. Dr. Amadiro, you see, knows of this relationship. At least, so I suspect."

"Indeed? How did that come about?"

"I believe that he quietly genealogizes all those who come to work at the Institute."

"But why?"

"In order to find out exactly what he did find out in my case. He is not a trusting man."

"I don't understand. If you are my fifth-level descendant, why should it have more meaning to him than it does to me?"

Mandamus rubbed his chin with the knuckles of his right hand in a thoughtful manner. "His dislike for you is in no way less than your dislike for him, Lady Gladia. If you were ready to refuse an interview with me for his sake, he is equally ready to refuse me preferment for your sake. It might be even worse if I were a descendant of Dr. Fastolfe, but not much."

Gladia sat stiffly upright in her seat. Her nostrils flared and she said in a tight voice, "What is it, then, that you expect me to do? I cannot declare you a nondescendant. Shall I have an announcement placed on hypervision that you are a matter of indifference to me and that I disown you. Will that satisfy your Amadiro? If so, I must warn you I will not do it. I will do nothing to satisfy that man. If it means that he will discharge you and deprive you of your career out of some sort of disapproval of your genetic association, then that will teach you to associate with a saner, less vicious person."

"He will not discharge me, Madam Gladia. I am entirely too valuable to him—if you will pardon my immodesty. Still, I hope someday to succeed him as head of the Institute and that, I am quite certain, he will not allow, as long as he suspects me of a descent worse than that which stems from you."

"Does he imagine that poor Santirix is worse than I am?"

"Not at all." Mandamus flushed and he swallowed, but his voice remained level and steady. "I mean no disrespect, madam, but I owe it to myself to learn the truth."

"What truth?"

"I am descended from you in the fifth degree. That is clear in the genealogical records. But is it possible that I am also descended in the fifth degree, not from Santirix Gremionis but from the Earthman Elijah Baley?"

Gladia rose to her feet as quickly as though the unidimensional force fields of a puppeteer had lifted her. She was not aware that she had risen.

It was the third time in twelve hours that the name of that long-ago Earthman had been mentioned—and by three different individuals.

Her voice seemed not to be hers at all. "What do you mean?"

He said, rising in his turn and backing away slightly, "It seems to me plain enough. Was your son, my great-great-grandfather, born of a sexual union of yourself with the Earthman Elijah Baley? Was Elijah Baley your son's father? I don't know how to express it more plainly."

"How dare you make such a suggestion? Or even think it?"

"I dare because my career depends upon it. If the answer is yes, my professional life may well be ruined. I want a no, but an unsupported no will do me no good. I must be able to present proof to Dr. Amadiro at the appropriate time and show him that his disapproval of my genealogy must end with you. After all, it is clear to me that his dislike of you—and even of Dr. Fastolfe—is as nothing—nothing at all—compared to the incredible intensity of his detestation of the Earthman Elijah Baley. It is not only the fact of his being short-lived, although the thought of having inherited barbarian genes would disturb me tremendously. I think that if I presented proof I was descended from an Earthman who was *not* Elijah Baley, he would dismiss that. But it is the thought of Elijah Baley—and only he—that drives him to madness. I do not know why."

The reiteration of Elijah's name had made him seem almost alive again to Gladia. She was breathing harshly and deeply and she exulted in the best memory of her life.

"I know why," she said. "It was because Elijah, with everything against him, with all of Aurora against him, managed anyhow to destroy Amadiro at the moment when that man thought he held success in his hand. Elijah did it by the exercise of sheer courage and intelligence. Amadiro had met his infinite superior in the person of an Earthman he had carelessly despised and what could he do in return but hate futilely? Elijah has been dead for more than sixteen decades and still Amadiro cannot forget, cannot forgive, cannot release the chains that bind him in hate and memory to that dead man. And I would not have Amadiro forget—or cease hating—as long as it poisons every moment of his existence."

Mandamus said, "I see you have reason for wishing Dr. Amadiro ill, but what reason have you for wishing *me* ill? To allow Dr. Amadiro to think I am descended from Elijah Baley will give him the pleasure of destroying me. Why should you give him that pleasure needlessly, if I am *not* so descended? Give me the proof, therefore, that I am descended from you and Santirix Gremionis or from you and anybody but Elijah Baley."

"You fool! You idiot! Why do you need proof from me? Go to the historical records. You will find the exact days on which Elijah Baley was on Aurora. You will find the exact day on which I gave birth to my son, Darrel. You will find that Darrel was conceived more than five years *after* Elijah left Aurora. You will also find that Elijah never returned to Aurora. Well, then, do you think I gestated for five years, that I carried a fetus in my womb for five Standard Galactic Years?"

"I know the statistics, madam. And I do not think you carried a fetus for five years."

"Then why do you come to me?"

"Because there is more to it than that. I know—and I imagine that Dr. Amadiro well knows—that although the Earthman Elijah Baley, as you say, never returned to Aurora's surface, he was once in a ship that was in orbit about Aurora for a day or so. I know—and I imagine that Dr. Amadiro well knows—that although the Earthman did not leave the ship to go to Aurora, you left Aurora to go to the ship; that you stayed on the ship for the better part of a day; and that this took place nearly five years after the Earthman had been on Aurora's surface—at about the time, in fact, that your son was conceived."

Gladia felt the blood drain from her face as she heard the other's calm words. The room darkened about her and she swayed.

She felt the sudden, gentle touch of strong arms about her and knew they were those of Daneel. She felt herself lowered slowly into her chair.

She heard Mandamus's voice as though from a great distance.

"Is that not true, madam?" he said.

It was, of course, true.

Chapter 2

The Ancestor?

5.

MEMORY!

Always there, of course, but usually remaining hidden. And then, sometimes, as a result of just the right kind of push, it could emerge suddenly, sharply defined, all in color, bright and moving and alive.

She was young again, younger than this man before her; young enough to feel tragedy and love—with her death-in-life on Solaria having reached its climax in the bitter end of the first whom she had thought of as "husband." (No, she would not say his name even now, not even in thought.)

Closer still to her then-life were the months of heaving emotion with the second—not-man—whom she had thought of by that term. Jander, the humanoid robot, had been given to her and she had made him entirely her own until, like her first husband, he was suddenly dead.

And then, at last, there was Elijah Baley, who was never her husband, whom she had met only twice, two years apart, each time for a few hours on each of a very few days. Elijah, whose cheek she had once touched with her ungloved hand, on which occasion she had ignited; whose nude body she had later held in her arms, on which occasion she had flamed steadily at last.

And then, a third husband, with whom she was quiet and at peace, paying with untriumph for unmisery and buying with firmly held forgetfulness the relief from reliving.

Until one day (she was not sure of the day that so broke in upon the sleeping untroubled years) Han Fastolfe, having asked permission to visit, walked over from his adjoining establishment.

Gladia looked upon him with some concern, for he was too busy a man to socialize lightly. Only five years had passed since the crisis that had established Han as Aurora's leading statesman. He was the Chairman of the planet in all but name and the true leader of all the Spacer worlds. He had so little time to be a human being.

Those years had left their mark—and would continue to do so until he died sadly, considering himself a failure though he had never lost a battle. Kelden Amadiro, who had been defeated, lived on sturdily, as evidence that victory can exact the greater penalty.

Fastolfe, through it all, continued to be soft-spoken and patient and uncomplaining, but even Gladia, nonpolitical though she was and uninterested in the endless machinations of power, knew that his control of Aurora held firm only through constant and unremitting effort that drained him of anything that might make life worthwhile and that he held to it—or was held to it—only by what he considered the good of—what? Aurora? The Spacers? Simply some vague concept of idealized Good?

She didn't know. She flinched from asking.

But this was only five years after the crisis. He still gave the impression of a young and hopeful man and his pleasant homely face was still capable of smiling.

He said, "I have a message for you, Gladia."

"A pleasant one, I hope," she said politely.

He had brought Daneel with him. It was a sign of the healing of old wounds that she could look at Daneel with honest affection and no pain at all, even though he was a copy of her dead Jander in all but the most insignificant detail. She could talk to him, though he answered in what was almost Jander's voice. Five years had skinned over the ulcer and deadened the pain.

"I hope so," said Fastolfe, smiling gently. "It's from an old friend."

"It's so nice that I have old friends," she said, trying not to be sardonic.

"From Elijah Baley."

The five years vanished and she felt the stab and pang of returning memory.

"Is he well?" she asked in a half-strangled voice after a full minute of stunned silence.

"Quite well. What is even more important, he is near."

"Near? On Aurora?"

"In orbit about Aurora. He knows he can receive no permission to land, even if I were to use my full influence, or I imagine he does. He would like to see you, Gladia. He has made contact with me because he feels that I can arrange to have you visit his ship. I suppose I can manage that much—but only if you wish it. Do you wish it?"

"I—I don't know. This is too sudden for thought."

"Or even impulse?" He waited, then he said, "Truthfully, Gladia, how are you getting along with Santirix?"

She looked at him wildly, as though not understanding the reason for the change of subject—then understanding. She said, "We get along well together."

"Are you happy?"

"I am—not unhappy."

"That doesn't sound like ecstasy."

"How long can ecstasy last, even if it were ecstasy?"

"Do you plan to have children someday?"

"Yes," she said.

"Are you planning a change in marital status?"

She shook her head firmly. "Not yet."

"Then, my dear Gladia, if you want advice from a rather tired man, who feels uncomfortably old—refuse the invitation. I remember what little you told me after Baley had left Aurora and, to tell you the truth, I was able to deduce more from that than you perhaps think. If you see him, you may find it all disappointing, not living up to the deepening and mellowing glow of reminiscence; or, if it is not disappointing, worse yet, for it will disrupt a perhaps rather fragile contentment, which you will then not be able to repair."

Gladia, who had been vaguely thinking precisely that, found the proposition needed only to be placed into words to be rejected.

She said, "No, Han, I *must* see him, but I'm afraid to do it alone. Would you come with me?"

Fastolfe smiled wearily. "I was not invited, Gladia. And if I were, I would in any case be forced to refuse. There is an important vote coming up in the Council. Affairs of state, you know, from which I can't absent myself."

"Poor Han!"

"Yes, indeed, poor me. But you can't go alone. As far as I know, you can't pilot a ship."

"Oh! Well, I thought I'd be taken up by—"

"Commercial carrier?" Fastolfe shook his head. "Quite impossible. For you to visit and board an Earth ship in orbit openly, as would be unavoidable if you used commercial carrier, would require special permission and that would take weeks. If you don't want to go, Gladia, you needn't put it on the basis of not wishing to see him. If the paperwork and red tape involved would take weeks, I'm sure he can't wait that long."

"But I *do* want to see him," said Gladia, now determined.

"In that case, you can take my private space vessel and Daneel can take you up there. He can handle the controls very well indeed and he is as anxious to see Baley as you are. We just won't report the trip."

"But you'll get into trouble, Han."

"Perhaps no one will find out—or they'll pretend not to find out. And if anyone makes trouble, I will just have to handle it."

Gladia's head bowed in a moment of thought and then she said, "If you don't mind, I will be selfish and chance your having trouble, Han. I want to go."

"Then you'll go."

5a.

IT WAS A SMALL SHIP, smaller than Gladia had imagined; cozy in a way, but frightening in another way. It was small enough, after all, to lack any provision for pseudo-gravity—and the sensation of weightlessness, while constantly nudging at her to indulge in amusing gymnastics, just as constantly reminded her that she was in an abnormal environment.

She was a Spacer. There were over five billion Spacers spread over fifty worlds, all of them proud of the name. Yet how many of those who called themselves Spacers were really space travelers? Very few. Perhaps eighty percent of them never left the world of their birth. Even of the remaining twenty percent, hardly any passed through space more than two or three times.

Certainly, she herself was no Spacer in the literal sense of the word, she thought gloomily. Once (once!) she had traveled through space and that was from Solaria to Aurora seven years before. Now she was entering space a second time on a small private space yacht for a short trip just beyond the atmosphere, a paltry hundred thousand kilometers, with one other person—not even a person—for company.

She cast another glance at Daneel in the small pilot room. She could just see a portion of him, where he sat at the controls.

She had never been anywhere with only one robot within call. There had always been hundreds—thousands—at her disposal on Solaria. On Aurora, there were routinely dozens, if not scores.

Here there was but one.

She said, "Daneel!"

He did not allow his attention to wander from the controls. "Yes, Madam Gladia?"

"Are you pleased that you will be seeing Elijah Baley again?"

"I am not certain, Madam Gladia, how best to describe my inner state. It may be that it is analogous to what a human being would describe as being pleased."

"But you must feel something."

"I feel as though I can make decisions more rapidly than I can ordinarily; my responses seem to come more easily; my movements seem to require less energy. I might interpret it generally as a sensation of well-being. At least I have heard human beings use that word and feel that what it is intended to describe is something that is analogous to the sensations I now experience."

Gladia said, "But what if I were to say I wanted to see him alone?"

"Then that would be arranged."

"Even though that meant you wouldn't see him?"

"Yes, madam."

"Wouldn't you then feel disappointed? I mean, wouldn't you have a sensation that was the opposite of well-being? Your decisions would come less rapidly, your responses less easily, your movements would require more energy and so on?"

"No, Madam Gladia, for I would have a feeling of well-being at fulfilling your orders."

"Your own pleasant feeling is Third Law, and fulfilling my orders is Second Law, and Second Law takes precedence. Is that it?"

"Yes, madam."

Gladia struggled against her own curiosity. It would never have occurred to her to question an ordinary robot in this matter. A robot is a machine. But she couldn't think of Daneel as a machine, just as five years before she had been unable to think of Jander as a machine. But with Jander that had been only the burning of passion—and that had gone with Jander himself. For all his similarity to the other, Daneel could not set the ashes alight again. With him, there was room for intellectual curiosity.

"Doesn't it bother you, Daneel," she asked, "to be so bound by the Laws?"

"I cannot imagine anything else, madam."

"All my life I have been bound to the pull of gravity, even during my one previous trip on a spaceship, but I can imagine *not* being bound by it. And here I am, in fact, *not* bound by it."

"And do you enjoy it, madam?"

"In a way, yes."

"Does it make you uneasy?"

"In a way, that too."

"Sometimes, madam, when I think that human beings are not bound by Laws, it makes me uneasy."

"Why, Daneel? Have you ever tried to reason out to yourself *why* the thought of Lawlessness should make you feel uneasy?"

Daneel was silent for a moment. He said, "I have, madam, but I do not think I would wonder about such things but for my brief associations with Partner Elijah. He had a way—"

"Yes, I know," she said. "He wondered about everything. He had a restlessness about him that drove him on to ask questions at all times in all directions."

"So it seemed. And I would try to be like him and ask questions. So I asked myself what Lawlessness might be like and I found I couldn't imagine what it might be like except that it might be like being human and that made me feel uneasy. And I asked myself, as you asked me, why it made me feel uneasy."

"And what did you answer yourself?"

Daneel said, "After a long time, I decided that the Three Laws govern the manner in which my positronic pathways behave. At all times, under all stimuli, the Laws constrain the direction and intensity of positronic flow along those pathways so that I always know what to do. Yet the level of knowledge of what to do is not always the same. There are times when my doing-as-I-must is under less constraint than at other times. I have always noticed that the lower the positronomotive potential, then the further removed from certainty is my decision as to which action to take. And the further removed from certainty I am, the nearer I am to ill-being. To decide an action in a millisecond rather than a nanosecond produces a sensation I would not wish to be prolonged.

"What, then, I thought to myself, madam, if I were utterly without Laws as humans are? What if I could make no clear decision on what response to make to some given set of conditions? It would be unbearable and I do not willingly think of it."

Gladia said, "Yet you do, Daneel. You are thinking of it now."

"Only because of my association with Partner Elijah, madam. I observed him under conditions when he was unable, for a time, to decide on an action because of the puzzling nature of the problems that had been set him. He was clearly in a state of ill-being as a result and I felt ill-being on his behalf because there was nothing I could do that would ease the situation for him. It is possible that I only grasped a very small part of what it was he felt then. If I had grasped a larger part and better understood the consequences of his inability to decide on action, I might have—" He hesitated.

"Ceased functioning? Been inactivated?" said Gladia, thinking briefly and painfully of Jander.

"Yes, madam. My failure to understand may be an in-built protection device against damage to my positronic brain. But then, I noted that no matter how painful Partner Elijah found his indecision to be, he continued to make an effort to solve his problem. I admired him greatly for that."

"You are capable of admiration then, are you?"

Daneel said solemnly, "I use the word as I have heard human beings use it. I do not know the proper word to express the response within me elicited by Partner Elijah's actions of this sort."

Gladia nodded, then said, "And yet there are rules that govern human reactions, too; certain instincts, drives, teachings."

"So friend Giskard thinks, madam."

"Does he now?"

"But he finds them too complicated to analyze. He wonders if there might someday be developed a system of analyzing human behavior in mathematical detail and of deriving—from that—cogent Laws that would express the rules of that behavior."

"I doubt it," said Gladia.

"Nor is friend Giskard sanguine. He thinks it will be a very long time before such a system is developed."

"A *very* long time, I should say."

"And now," said Daneel, "we are approaching the Earth ship and we must carry through the docking procedure, which is not simple."

5b.

IT SEEMED TO Gladia that it took longer to dock than to move into the Earth ship's orbit in the first place.

Daneel remained calm throughout—but, then, he could not do otherwise

—and assured her that all human ships could dock with each other regardless of difference in size and make.

"Like human beings," said Gladia, forcing a smile, but Daneel made no response to that. He concentrated on the delicate adjustments that had to be made. Docking was always possible, perhaps, but not always easy, it would appear.

Gladia grew uneasier by the moment. Earthmen were short-lived and aged quickly. Five years had passed since she had seen Elijah. By how much would he have aged? How would he appear? Would she be able to keep from looking shocked or horrified at the change?

Whatever his appearance, he would still be the Elijah to whom her gratitude could know no bounds.

Was that what it was? Gratitude?

She noticed that her hands were tightly entwined with each other, so that her arms were aching. It was only with an effort that she could force them to relax.

She knew when docking was completed. The Earth ship was large enough to have a pseudo-gravitation field generator and, at the moment of docking, the field expanded to include the small yacht. There was a slight rotational effect as the direction toward the floor suddenly became "down" and Gladia experienced a sickening drop of two inches. Her knees bent under the impact in lopsided fashion and she fell against the wall.

She straightened with a little difficulty and was annoyed with herself for not having anticipated the change and been ready for it.

Daneel said unnecessarily, "We have docked, Madam Gladia. Partner Elijah asks permission to come aboard."

"Of course, Daneel."

There was a whirring sound and a portion of the wall swirled into dilation. A crouching figure moved through and the wall tightened and contracted behind it.

The figure straightened and Gladia whispered, "Elijah!" and felt overwhelmed with gladness and relief. It seemed to her that his hair was grayer, but otherwise it was Elijah. There was no other noticeable change, no marked aging after all.

He smiled at her and, for a moment, seemed to devour her with his eyes. Then he lifted one forefinger, as though to say, "Wait," and walked toward Daneel.

"Daneel!" He seized the robot's shoulders and shook him. "You haven't changed. Jehoshaphat! You're the constant in all our lives."

"Partner Elijah. It is good to see you."

"It is good to hear myself called partner again and I wish that were so. This is the fifth time I have seen you, but the first time that I do not have a problem to solve. I am not even a plainclothesman any longer. I have resigned and I am now an immigrant to one of the new worlds. —Tell me, Daneel, why didn't you come with Dr. Fastolfe when he visited Earth three years ago?"

"That was Dr. Fastolfe's decision. He decided to take Giskard."

"I was disappointed, Daneel."

"It would have been pleasant for me to see you, Partner Elijah, but Dr. Fastolfe told me afterward that the trip had been highly successful, so that perhaps his decision was the correct one."

"It *was* successful, Daneel. Before the visit, the Earth government was reluctant to cooperate in the Settlement procedure, but now the whole planet is pulsing and heaving and, by the million, people are anxious to go. We don't have the ships to accommodate them all—even with Auroran help—and we don't have the worlds to receive them all, for every world must be adjusted. Not one will accommodate a human community unchanged. The one I'm going to is low in free oxygen and we're going to have to live in domed towns for a generation while Earth-type vegetation spreads over the planet." His eyes were turning more and more often to Gladia as she sat there smiling.

Daneel said, "It is to be expected. From what I have learned of human history, the Spacer worlds also went through a period of terraforming."

"They certainly did! And thanks to that experience, the process can be carried through more rapidly now. —But I wonder if you would remain in the pilot room for a while, Daneel. I must speak to Gladia."

"Certainly, Partner Elijah."

Daneel stepped through the arched doorway that led into the pilot room and Baley looked at Gladia in a questioning way and made a sideways motion with his hand.

Understanding perfectly, she walked over and touched the contact that drew the partition noiselessly across the doorway. They were, to all intents, alone.

Baley held out his hands. "Gladia!"

She took them in hers, never even thinking she was ungloved. She said, "Had Daneel stayed with us, he would not have hampered us."

"Not physically. He would have *psychologically!*" Baley smiled sadly and said, "Forgive me, Gladia. I had to speak to Daneel first."

"You've known him longer," she said softly. "He takes precedence."

"He doesn't—but he has no defenses. If you are annoyed with me, Gladia, you can punch me in the eye if you want to. Daneel can't. I can ignore him, order him away, treat him as though he were a robot, and he would be compelled to obey and be the same loyal and uncomplaining partner."

"The fact is that he *is* a robot, Elijah."

"Never to me, Gladia. My mind knows he is a robot and has no feelings in the human fashion, but my heart considers him human and I must treat him so. I would ask Dr. Fastolfe to let me take Daneel with me, but no robots are allowed on the new Settler worlds."

"Would you dream of taking *me* with you, Elijah?"

"No Spacers, either."

"It seems you Earthmen are as unreasoningly exclusive as we Spacers are."

Elijah nodded glumly. "Madness on both sides. But even if we were sane, I would not take you. You could not stand the life and I'd never be sure that your immune mechanisms would build up properly. I'd be afraid that you would either die quickly of some minor infection or that you would live too long and watch our generations die. —Forgive me, Gladia."

"For what, dear Elijah?"

"For—this." He put out his hands, palms upward, to either side. "For asking to see you."

"But I'm glad you did. I wanted to see you."

He said, "I know. I tried not to see you, but the thought of being in space and of not stopping at Aurora tore me apart. And yet it does no good, Gladia. It just means another leave-taking and that will tear me apart, too. It is why I have never written you; why I have never tried to reach you by hyperwave. Surely you must have wondered."

"Not really. I agree with you that there was no point. It would merely make it all infinitely harder. Yet I wrote to you many times."

"You did? I never received one letter."

"I never mailed one letter. Having written them, I destroyed them."

"But why?"

"Because, Elijah, no private letter can be sent from Aurora to Earth without passing through the hands of the censor and I wrote you not one letter that I was willing to let the censors see. Had you sent me a letter, I assure you that not one would have gotten through to me, however innocent it might have been. I thought that was why I never received a letter.

Now that I know you weren't aware of the situation, I am extraordinarily glad that you were not so foolish as to try to remain in touch with me. You would have misunderstood my never answering your letters."

Baley stared at her. "How is it I see you now?"

"Not legally, I assure you. I am using Dr. Fastolfe's private ship, so I passed by the border guards without being challenged. Had this ship not been Dr. Fastolfe's, I would have been stopped and sent back. I assumed you understood that, too, and that that was why you were in touch with Dr. Fastolfe and didn't try to reach me directly."

"I understood nothing. I sit here amazed at the double ignorance that kept me safe. Triple ignorance, for I didn't know the proper hyperwave combination to reach you directly and I couldn't face the difficulty of trying to find the combination on Earth. I couldn't have done it privately and there was already sufficient comment all over the Galaxy about you and me, thanks to that foolish hyperwave drama they put on the subwaves after Solaria. Otherwise, I promise you, I would have tried. I had Dr. Fastolfe's combination, however, and once I was in orbit around Aurora, I contacted him at once."

"In any case, we're here." She sat down on the side of her bunk and held out her hands.

Baley took them and tried to sit down on a stool, which he had hitched one foot over, but she drew him insistently toward the bunk and he sat down beside her.

He said awkwardly, "How is it with you, Gladia?"

"Quite well. And you, Elijah?"

"I grow old. I have just celebrated my fiftieth birthday three weeks ago."

"Fifty is not—" She stopped.

"For an Earthman, it's old. We're short-lived, you know."

"Even for an Earthman, fifty is not old. You haven't changed."

"It's kind of you to say so, but I can tell where the creaks have multiplied. Gladia—"

"Yes, Elijah?"

"I must ask. Have you and Santirix Gremionis—"

Gladia smiled and nodded. "He is my husband. I took your advice."

"And has it worked out well?"

"Well enough. Life is pleasant."

"Good. I hope it lasts."

"Nothing lasts for centuries, Elijah, but it could last for years; perhaps even for decades."

"Any children?"

"Not yet. But what about your family, my married man? Your son? Your wife?"

"Bentley moved out to the Settlements two years ago. In fact, I'll be joining him. He's an official on the world I'm heading for. He's only twenty-four and he's looked up to already." Baley's eyes danced. "I think I'll have to address him as Your Honor. In public, anyway."

"Excellent. And Mrs. Baley? Is she with you?"

"Jessie? No. She won't leave Earth. I told her that we would be living in domes for a considerable time, so that it really wouldn't be so different from Earth. Primitive, of course. Still, she may change her mind in time. I'll make it as comfortable as possible and once I've settled down, I'll ask Bentley to go to Earth and gather her in. She may be lonely enough by then to be willing to come. We'll see."

"But meanwhile you're alone."

"There are over a hundred other immigrants on the ship, so I'm not really alone."

"They are on the other side of the docking wall, however. And I'm alone, too."

Baley cast a brief, involuntary look toward the pilot room and Gladia said, "Except for Daneel, of course, who's on the other side of that door and who *is* a robot, no matter how intensely you think of him as a person. —And surely you haven't asked to see me only that we might ask after each other's families?"

Baley's face grew solemn, almost anxious. "I can't ask you—"

"Then I ask you. This bunk is not really designed with sexual activity in mind, but you'll chance the possibility of falling out of it, I hope."

Baley said hesitantly, "Gladia, I can't deny that—"

"Oh, Elijah, don't go into a long dissertation in order to satisfy the needs of your Earth morality. I offer myself to you in accord with Auroran custom. It's your clear right to refuse and I will have no right to question the refusal. —Except that I would question it most forcefully. I have decided that the right to refuse belongs only to Aurorans. I won't take it from an Earthman."

Baley sighed. "I'm no longer an Earthman, Gladia."

"I am even less likely to take it from a miserable immigrant heading out for a barbarian planet on which he will have to cower under a dome. —Elijah, we have had so little time, and we have so little time now, and I may never see you again. This meeting is so totally unexpected that it would be a cosmic crime to toss it away."

"Gladia, do you really want an old man?"

"Elijah, do you really want me to beg?"

"But I'm ashamed."

"Then close your eyes."

"I mean of myself—of my decrepit body."

"Then suffer. Your foolish opinion of yourself has nothing to do with me." And she put her arms about him, even as the seam of her robe fell apart.

5c.

GLADIA WAS AWARE of a number of things, all simultaneously.

She was aware of the wonder of constancy, for Elijah was as she had remembered him. The lapse of five years had not changed matters. She had not been living in the glow of a memory-intensified glitter. He was Elijah.

She was aware, also, of the puzzle of difference. Her feeling intensified that Santirix Gremionis, without a single major flaw that she could define, was all flaw. Santirix was affectionate, gentle, rational, reasonably intelligent —and flat. Why he was flat, she could not say, but nothing he did or said could rouse her as Baley did, even when he did and said nothing. Baley was older in years, much older physiologically, not as handsome as Santirix, and what was more, Baley carried with him the indefinable air of decay—of the aura of quick aging and short life that Earthmen must. And yet—

She was aware of the folly of men, of Elijah approaching her with hesitation, with total unappreciation of his effect on her.

She was aware of his absence, for he had gone in to speak to Daneel, who was to be last as he was first. Earthmen feared and hated robots and yet Elijah, knowing full well that Daneel was a robot, treated him only as a person. Spacers, on the other hand, who loved robots and were never comfortable in their absence, would never think of them as anything but machines.

Most of all, she was aware of time. She knew that exactly three hours and twenty-five minutes had elapsed since Elijah had entered Han Fastolfe's small vessel and she knew further that not much more time could be allowed to elapse.

The longer she remained off Aurora's surface and the longer Baley's ship remained in orbit, the more likely it was that someone would notice—or if the matter had already been noticed, as seemed almost certain, the more likely it would be that someone would become curious and investigate. And then Fastolfe would find himself in an annoying tangle of trouble.

Baley emerged from the pilot room and looked at Gladia sadly. "I must go now, Gladia."

"I know that well."

Baley said, "Daneel will take care of you. He will be your friend as well as protector and you must be a friend to him—for my sake. But it is Giskard I want you to listen to. Let *him* be your adviser."

Gladia frowned. "Why Giskard? I'm not sure I like him."

"I do not ask you to like him. I ask you to *trust* him."

"But why, Elijah?"

"I can't tell you that. In this, you must trust me, too."

They looked at each other and said no more. It was as though silence made time stop, allowed them to hold on to the seconds and keep them motionless.

But it could only work so long. Baley said, "You don't regret—"

Gladia whispered, "How could I regret—when I may never see you again?"

Baley made as though to answer that, but she put her small clenched fist against his mouth.

"Don't lie uselessly," she said. "I may never see you again."

And she never did. Never!

6.

IT WAS WITH PAIN that she felt herself drag across the dead waste of years into the present once more.

I never did, she thought. Never!

She had protected herself against the bittersweet for so long and now she had plunged into it—more bitter than sweet—because she had seen this person, this Mandamus—because Giskard had asked her to and because she was compelled to trust Giskard. It was *his* last request.

She focused on the present. (How much time had elapsed?)

Mandamus was looking at her coldly. He said, "From your reaction, Madam Gladia, I gather that it *is* true. You could not have said so more plainly."

"What is true? What are you talking about?"

"That you saw the Earthman Elijah Baley five years after his visit to

Aurora. His ship was in orbit about Aurora; you traveled up to see him and were with him about the time you conceived your son."

"What evidence do you have for that?"

"Madam, it was not totally a secret. The Earthman's ship was detected in orbit. Fastolfe's yacht was detected in its flight. It was observed to dock. It was not Fastolfe who was on board the yacht, so the presumption was that it was you. Dr. Fastolfe's influence was sufficient to keep it off the record."

"If it is off the record, there is no evidence."

"Nevertheless, Dr. Amadiro has spent the last two thirds of his life following Dr. Fastolfe's movements with the eyes of detestation. There were always government officials who were heart and soul with Dr. Amadiro's policy of reserving the Galaxy for the Spacers and they would quietly report to him anything they thought he would like to know. Dr. Amadiro learned of your little escapade almost as soon as it happened."

"It is still not evidence. The unsupported word of a minor official currying favor is of no account. Amadiro did nothing because even he knew he had no evidence."

"No evidence with which he could charge anyone with even a misdemeanor; no evidence with which he could trouble Fastolfe; but evidence enough to suspect me of being a descendant of Baley's and to cripple my career therefor."

Gladia said bitterly, "You may cease being troubled. My son is the son of Santirix Gremionis, a true Auroran, and it is from this son of Gremionis that you are descended."

"Convince me of it, madam. I ask nothing better. Convince me that you fired up into orbit and that you spent hours alone with the Earthman and that, during that time, you talked—politics, perhaps—discussed old times and mutual friends—told funny stories—and never touched each other. Convince me."

"What we did, did not matter, so spare me your sarcasm. At the time I saw him, I was already pregnant by my then-husband. I was carrying a three-month-old fetus, an Auroran fetus."

"Can you prove that?"

"Why should I have to prove it? The date of my son's birth is on record and Amadiro must have the date of my visit to the Earthman."

"He was told it at the time, as I said, but nearly twenty decades have passed and he doesn't remember exactly. The visit is not a matter of record and cannot be referred to. I fear that Dr. Amadiro would prefer to believe that it was nine months before the birth of your son that you were with the Earthman."

"Six months."

"Prove it."

"You have my word."

"Insufficient."

"Well, then— Daneel, you were with me. When did I see Elijah Baley?"

"Madam Gladia, it was one hundred and seventy-three days before the birth of your son."

Gladia said, "Which is just under six months before the birth."

"Insufficient," said Mandamus.

Gladia's chin lifted. "Daneel's memory is perfect, as can be easily demonstrated, and a robot's statements pass for evidence in the courts of Aurora."

"This is not a matter for the courts and will not be and Daneel's memory carries no weight with Dr. Amadiro. Daneel was constructed by Fastolfe and was maintained by Fastolfe for nearly two centuries. We cannot say what modifications were introduced or how Daneel might have been instructed to deal with matters relating to Dr. Amadiro."

"Then reason it out, man. Earthmen are quite different genetically from us. We are virtually different species. We are not interfertile."

"Unproven."

"Well, then, genetic records exist. Darrel's do; Santirix's do. Compare them. If my ex-husband were not his father, the genetic differences would make that unmistakable."

"Genetic records are not for anyone's eyes. You know that."

"Amadiro is not that immersed in ethical considerations. He has the influence to see them illegally. —Or is he afraid of disproving his hypothesis?"

"Whatever the reason, madam, he will not betray an Auroran's right to privacy."

Gladia said, "Well, then, go to outer space and choke on vacuum. If your Amadiro refuses to be convinced, that is no affair of mine. You, at least, ought to be convinced and it is your job to convince Amadiro in his turn. If you cannot and if your career does not move onward as you would like to have it do, please be assured that this is entirely and intensely no concern of mine."

"That does not surprise me. I expect nothing more. And for that matter, I *am* convinced. I was merely hoping that you would give me some material with which to convince Dr. Amadiro. You haven't."

Gladia shrugged with disdain.

"I will use other methods, then," said Mandamus.

"I'm glad you have them," Gladia said coldly.

Mandamus said in a low voice, almost as though he were unaware of the presence of anyone else, "So am I. There are powerful methods remaining to me."

"Good. I suggest you try blackmail on Amadiro. He must have much to be blackmailed for."

Mandamus looked up, suddenly frowning. "Don't be a fool."

Gladia said, "You may go now. I think I have had all of you I wish to endure. Out of my establishment!"

Mandamus lifted his arms. "Wait! I told you at the start that there were two reasons for seeing you—one a personal matter and one a matter of state. I have spent too long a time on the first, but I must request five minutes to discuss the second."

"I'll give you no more than five minutes."

"There is someone else who wants to see you. An Earthman—or at least a member of one of the Settler worlds, a descendant of Earthpeople."

"Tell him," said Gladia, "that neither Earthpeople nor their Settler descendants are allowed on Aurora and send him away. Why do I have to see him?"

"Unfortunately, madam, in the last two centuries the balance of power has shifted somewhat. These Earthpeople have more worlds than we have —and have always had a far larger population. They have more ships, even though those are not as advanced as ours, and because of their short lives and their fecundity they are apparently far readier to die than we are."

"I don't believe that last."

Mandamus smiled tightly. "Why not? Eight decades mean less than forty do. In any case, we must treat them politely—far more politely than we ever had to in Elijah Baley's day. If it is any comfort to you, it is the policies of Fastolfe that have created this situation."

"For whom do you speak, by the way? Is it Amadiro who must now bring himself to be polite to Settlers?"

"No. It is the Council, actually."

"Are you the spokesman for the Council?"

"Not officially, but I have been asked to inform you of this—unofficially."

"And if I see this Settler, what then? What does he want to see me about?"

"That is what we don't know, madam. We count on you to tell us. You are to see him, find out what he wants, and report to us."

"Who is 'us'?"

"As I said, the Council. The Settler will be here at your establishment this evening."

"You seem to assume that I have no choice but to take on this position as informer."

Mandamus rose to his feet, clearly done with his mission. "You will not be an 'informer.' You owe nothing to this Settler. You are merely reporting to your government, as a loyal Auroran citizen should be willing—even eager—to do. You would not want the Council to suppose that your Solarian birth in any way dilutes your Auroran patriotism."

"Sir, I have been an Auroran over four times as long as you've been alive."

"Undoubtedly, but you were born and raised on Solaria. You are that unusual anomaly, a foreign-born Auroran, and it is difficult to forget it. This is especially true since the Settler wishes to see you, rather than anyone else on Aurora, precisely because you are Solarian-born."

"How do you know that?"

"It is a fair presumption. He identifies you as 'the Solarian woman.' We are curious as to why that should mean anything to him—now that Solaria no longer exists."

"Ask him."

"We prefer to ask you—after you ask him. I must ask permission to leave now and I thank you for your hospitality."

Gladia nodded stiffly. "I grant you your permission to leave with better will than I granted you my hospitality."

Mandamus stepped toward the hallway that led to the main entrance, followed closely by his robots.

He paused just before leaving the room, turned, and said, "I had almost forgotten—"

"Yes?"

"The Settler who wishes to see you has a surname that, by a peculiar coincidence, is Baley."

Chapter 3
The Crisis

7.

DANEEL AND GISKARD, with robotic courtesy, saw Mandamus and his robots off the grounds of the establishment. Then, since they were outside, they toured the grounds, made certain that the lesser robots were in their places, and took note of the weather (cloudy and a bit cooler than seasonal).

Daneel said, "Dr. Mandamus admitted openly that the Settler worlds are now stronger than the Spacer worlds. I would not have expected him to do that."

Giskard said, "Nor I. I was certain that the Settlers would increase in strength as compared with the Spacers because Elijah Baley had predicted it many decades ago, but I could see no way of determining when the fact would become obvious to the Auroran Council. It seemed to me that social inertia would keep the Council firmly convinced of Spacer superiority long after that had vanished, but I could not calculate for how long they would continue to delude themselves."

"I am astonished that Partner Elijah foresaw this so long ago."

"Human beings have ways of thinking about human beings that we have not." Had Giskard been human, the remark might have been made with regret or envy, but since he was a robot it was merely factual.

He went on. "I have tried to gain the knowledge, if not the way of thinking, by reading human history in great detail. Surely somewhere in the long tale of human events, there must be buried the Laws of Humanics that are equivalent to our Three Laws of Robotics."

Daneel said, "Madam Gladia once told me that this hope was an impossible one."

"So that may be, friend Daneel, for though it seems to me such Laws of Humanics must exist, I cannot find them. Every generalization I try to make, however broad and simple, has its numerous exceptions. Yet if such Laws existed and if I could find them, I could understand human beings better and be more confident that I am obeying the Three Laws in better fashion."

"Since Partner Elijah understood human beings, he must have had some knowledge of the Laws of Humanics."

"Presumably. But this he knew through something that human beings call intuition, a word I don't understand, signifying a concept I know nothing of. Presumably it lies beyond reason and I have only reason at my command."

7a.

THAT AND MEMORY!

Memory that did not work after the human fashion, of course. It lacked the imperfect recall, the fuzziness, the additions and subtractions dictated by wishful thinking and self-interest, to say nothing of the lingerings and lacunae and backtracking that can turn memory into hours-long daydreaming.

It was robotic memory ticking off the events exactly as they had happened, but in vastly hastened fashion. The seconds reeled off in nanoseconds, so that days of events could be relived with such rapid precision as to introduce no perceptible gap in a conversation.

As Giskard had done innumerable times before, he relived that visit to Earth, always seeking for understanding of Elijah Baley's casual ability to foresee the future, always failing to find it.

Earth!

Fastolfe had come to Earth in an Auroran warship, with a full complement of fellow passengers, both human and robot. Once in orbit, however, it was only Fastolfe who took the module in for a landing. Injections had stimulated his immune mechanism and he wore the necessary gloves, coveralls, contact lenses, and nose plugs. He felt quite safe as a result, but no other Auroran was willing to go along as part of a delegation.

This Fastolfe shrugged off, since it seemed to him (as he later explained to Giskard) that he would be more welcome if he came alone. A delegation would disagreeably remind Earth of the bad old days (to them) of

Spacetown, when Spacers had a permanent base on Earth and directly dominated the world.

With him, Fastolfe brought Giskard, however. To have arrived without any robots would have been unthinkable, even for Fastolfe. To have arrived with more than one would have put a strain on the increasingly antirobot Earthmen he hoped to see and with whom he intended to negotiate.

To begin with, of course, he would meet with Baley, who would be his liaison with Earth and its people. That was the rational excuse for the meeting. The real excuse was simply that Fastolfe wanted very much to see Baley again; he certainly owed him enough.

(That Giskard wanted to see Baley and that he very slightly tightened the emotion and impulse in Fastolfe's brain to bring that about, Fastolfe had no way of knowing—or even imagining.)

Baley was waiting for them at the time of landing and with him was a small group of Earth officials, so that there was a tedious passage of time during which politeness and protocol had its innings. It was some hours before Baley and Fastolfe could get away by themselves and it might not have happened that soon but for Giskard's quiet and unfelt interference— with just a touch at the minds of the more important of those officials who were distinctly bored. (It was always safe to confine one's self to accentuating an emotion that already existed. It could almost never bring harm.)

Baley and Fastolfe sat in the smallness of a private dining room that was ordinarily available only to high government officials. Food items could be punched out on a computerized menu and were then brought in by computerized carriers.

Fastolfe smiled. "Very advanced," he said, "but these carriers are merely specialized robots. I'm surprised Earth uses them. They are not of Spacer manufacture, surely."

"No, they're not," said Baley solemnly. "Home-grown, so to speak. This is only for use at the top and it's my first chance, ever, to experience it. I'm not likely to do so again."

"You may be elected to high office someday and then experience this sort of thing daily."

"Never," said Baley. The dishes were put before each of them and the carrier was even sophisticated enough to ignore Giskard, who stood impassively behind Fastolfe's chair.

For a while, Baley ate silently and then, with a certain shyness, he said, "It is good to see you again, Dr. Fastolfe."

"The pleasure is as much mine. I haven't forgotten that two years ago, when you were on Aurora, you managed to free me of the suspicion of the destruction of the robot Jander and to turn the tables neatly on my overconfident opponent, the good Amadiro."

"I still shake when I think of it," said Baley. "And greetings to you, too, Giskard. I trust you haven't forgotten me."

"That would be quite impossible, sir," said Giskard.

"Good! Well, Doctor, I trust the political situation on Aurora continues to be favorable. The news here would make it seem so, but I don't trust Earth analysis of Auroran affairs."

"You may—at the moment. My party is in firm control of the Council. Amadiro maintains a sullen opposition, but I suspect it will be years before his people recover from the blow you gave them. But how are things with you and with Earth?"

"Well enough. —Tell me, Dr. Fastolfe"—Baley's face twitched slightly, as though with embarrassment—"have you brought Daneel with you?"

Fastolfe said slowly, "I'm sorry, Baley. I did, but I left him back on the ship. I felt it might not be politic to be accompanied by a robot who looked so much like a human being. With Earth as antirobot as it has become, I felt a humanoid robot might seem a deliberate provocation to them."

Baley sighed. "I understand."

Fastolfe said, "Is it true that your government is planning to prohibit the use of robots within the Cities?"

"I suspect it will soon come to that, with a period of grace, of course, to minimize financial loss and inconvenience. Robots will be restricted to the countryside, where they are needed for agriculture and mining. There, too, they may eventually be phased out and the plan is to have no robots at all on the new worlds."

"Since you mention the new worlds, has your son left Earth yet?"

"Yes, a few months ago. We have heard from him and he's arrived at a new world safely, along with several hundred Settlers, as they call themselves. The world has some native vegetation upon it and a low-oxygen atmosphere. Apparently, with time it can be made quite Earthlike. Meanwhile, some makeshift domes have been put up, new Settlers are advertised for, and everyone is busily engaged in terraforming. Bentley's letters and occasional hyperwave contact are very hopeful, but they don't keep his mother from missing him badly."

"And will you be going there, Baley?"

"I'm not sure that living on a strange world under a dome is my idea of happiness, Dr. Fastolfe—I haven't Ben's youth and enthusiasm—but I think I'll have to in two or three years. In any case, I've already given notice to the Department of my intention to emigrate."

"I imagine they must be upset over that."

"Not at all. They say they are, but they're glad to get rid of me. I'm too notorious."

"And how does Earth's government react to this drive for expansion into the Galaxy."

"Nervously. They do not forbid it altogether, but certainly they are not cooperative. They continue to suspect that the Spacers are opposed to it and will do *something* unpleasant to stop it."

"Social inertia," said Fastolfe. "They judge us according to our behavior of years past. Surely we have made it plain that we now encourage Earth's colonization of new planets and that we intend to colonize new planets of our own."

"I hope you explain this to our government, then. —But, Dr. Fastolfe, another question on a smaller point. How is—" And with that, he stalled.

"Gladia?" said Fastolfe, hiding his amusement. "Have you forgotten her name?"

"No, no. I merely hesitated to—to—"

"She's well," said Fastolfe, "and living comfortably. She has asked me to remember her to you, but I imagine you need no nudging to recall her to mind."

"The fact of her Solarian origin is not used against her, I hope?"

"No, nor is her role in the undoing of Dr. Amadiro. Rather the reverse. I take care of her, I assure you. —And yet I do not care to allow you to get off the subject altogether, Baley. What if Earth's officialdom continues to be opposed to immigration and expansion? Could the process continue despite such opposition?"

"Possibly," said Baley, "but not certainly. There's substantial opposition among Earthmen generally. It's hard to break away from the huge underground Cities that are our homes—"

"Your wombs."

"Or our wombs, if you prefer. Going to new worlds and having to live with the most primitive facilities for decades; never seeing comfort in one's own lifetime—that is difficult. When I think of it sometimes, I just decide not to go—especially if I'm passing a sleepless night. I've decided not to go a hundred times and one day I may just stick to that decision. And if *I* have trouble when, in a way, I originated the entire notion, then who else is likely to go freely and gladly? Without government encouragement—or, to be brutally frank—without the government shoe applied to the seat of the pants of the population, the whole project may fail."

Fastolfe nodded. "I will try to persuade your government. But if I fail?"

Baley said in a low voice, "If you fail—and if, therefore, our people fail—there remains only one alternative. The Spacers themselves must settle the Galaxy. The job must be done."

"And will you be content to see the Spacers expand and fill the Galaxy, while the Earthpeople remain on their single planet?"

"Not content at all, but it would be better than the present situation of no expansion by either. Many centuries ago, Earthpeople flocked to the stars, established some of the worlds that are now called Spacer worlds, and those first few colonized others. It has been a long time, however, since either the Spacers or Earthpeople have successfully settled and developed a new world. That must not be permitted to continue."

"I agree. But what is your reason for wanting expansion, Baley?"

"I feel that without expansion of some sort, humanity cannot advance. It doesn't have to be geographical expansion, but that is the clearest way of inducing other kinds of expansion as well. If geographical expansion can be undertaken in a fashion that is not at the expense of other intelligent beings; if there are empty spaces into which to expand; then why not? To resist expansion under such circumstances is to ensure decay."

"You see those alternatives, then? Expansion and advancement? Nonexpansion and decay?"

"Yes, I believe so. Therefore, if Earth refuses expansion, then Spacers *must* accept it. Humanity, whether in the form of Earthpeople or Spacers, *must* expand. I would like to see Earthpeople undertake the task, but, failing that, Spacer expansion is better than no expansion at all. One alternative or the other."

"And if one expands but not the other?"

"Then the expanding society will become steadily stronger and the nonexpanding one steadily weaker."

"Are you certain of that?"

"It would be unavoidable, I think."

Fastolfe nodded. "Actually, I agree. It is why I am trying to persuade *both* Earthpeople and Spacers to expand and advance. That is a third alternative and, I think, the best."

7b.

MEMORY FLICKERED past the days that followed—incredible mobs of people moving ceaselessly past each other in streams and eddies—racing Expressways being mounted and dismounted—endless conferences with innumerable officials—minds in crowds.

Particularly minds in crowds.

Minds in crowds so thick that Giskard could not isolate individuals. Mass minds mixing and melting together into a vast pulsating grayness with all that was detectable being the periodic sparks of suspicion and dislike that shot outward every time one of the multitude paused to look at him.

Only when Fastolfe was in conference with a few officials could Giskard deal with the individual mind and that, of course, was when it counted.

Memory slowed at one point near the end of the stay on Earth, when Giskard could finally maneuver a time alone with Baley again. Giskard adjusted a few minds minimally in order to make certain there would be no interruption for some time.

Baley said apologetically, "I haven't really been ignoring you, Giskard. I simply haven't had the opportunity to be alone with you. I don't rate highly on Earth and I cannot order my comings and goings."

"I have, of course, understood that, sir, but we will have some time together now."

"Good. Dr. Fastolfe tells me that Gladia is doing well. He may be saying that out of kindness, knowing that that is what I want to hear. I order you to be truthful, however. Is Gladia, in fact, doing well?"

"Dr. Fastolfe has told you the truth, sir."

"And you remember, I hope, my request when I last saw you on Aurora that you guard Gladia and protect her from harm."

"Friend Daneel and I, sir, are both mindful of your request. I have arranged it so that when Dr. Fastolfe is no longer alive, both friend Daneel and I will become part of Madam Gladia's establishment. We will then be in an even better position to keep her from harm."

"That," said Baley sadly, "will be after my time."

"I understand that, sir, and regret it."

"Yes, but it can't be helped and a crisis will come—or may come—even before that and yet still be after my time."

"What is it, sir, that you have in mind? What is this crisis?"

"Giskard, it is a crisis that may arise because Dr. Fastolfe is a surprisingly persuasive person. Or else, there is some other factor associated with him that is accomplishing the task."

"Sir?"

"Every official that Dr. Fastolfe has seen and interviewed now seems to be enthusiastically in favor of emigration. They were not in favor earlier or, if they were, it was with strong reservations. And once the opinion-making leaders are in favor, others are sure to follow. This will spread like an epidemic."

"Is this not what you wish, sir?"

"Yes, it is, but it is almost too much what I wish. We shall spread out over the Galaxy—but what if the Spacers don't?"

"Why should they not?"

"I don't know. I advance it as a supposition, a possibility. What if they don't?"

"Earth and the worlds its people settle will then grow stronger, according to what I have heard you say."

"And the Spacers will grow weaker. There will, however, be a period of time during which the Spacers will remain stronger than Earth and its Settlers, though by a steadily diminishing margin. Eventually, the Spacers will inevitably become aware of Earthpeople as a growing danger. At that time the Spacer worlds will surely decide that Earth and the Settlers must be stopped before it is too late and it will seem to them that drastic measures will have to be taken. That will be a period of crisis that will determine the entire future history of human beings."

"I see your point, sir."

Baley remained in thoughtful silence for a moment, then said, in very nearly a whisper as though dreading being overheard, "Who knows of your abilities?"

"Among human beings only yourself—and you cannot mention it to others."

"I know well I can't. The point is, though, that it is you, not Fastolfe, who has engineered the turnaround that has made every official with whom you've come in contact a proponent of emigration. And it is to bring that about that you arranged to have Fastolfe take you, rather than Daneel, to Earth with him. You were essential and Daneel might have been a distraction."

Giskard said, "I felt it necessary to keep personnel to a minimum in order to avoid making my task harder by abrading the sensitivities of Earthpeople.

I regret, sir, Daneel's absence. I fully sense your disappointment at not being able to greet him."

"Well—" Baley shook his head. "I understand the necessity and I rely on your explaining to Daneel that I badly missed him. In any case, I am still making my point. If Earth embarks on a great policy of world settlement and if the Spacers are left behind in the race to expand, the responsibility for that—and therefore for the crisis that will inevitably arise—will be yours. You must, for that reason, feel it your further responsibility to use your abilities to protect Earth when the crisis comes."

"I will do what I can, sir."

"And should you succeed there, Amadiro—or his followers—may turn on Gladia. You must not forget to protect her, too."

"Daneel and I will not forget."

"Thank you, Giskard."

And they parted.

When Giskard, following Fastolfe, entered the module to begin the voyage back to Aurora, he saw Baley once again. This time there was no opportunity to speak to him.

Baley waved and mouthed one soundless word: "Remember."

Giskard sensed the word and, in addition, the emotion behind it.

After that, Giskard never saw Baley again. Never.

8.

GISKARD HAD NEVER found it possible to flip through the sharp images of that one visit to Earth, without then following it with the images of the key visit to Amadiro at the Institute of Robotics.

It had not been an easy conference to arrange. Amadiro, with the bitterness of defeat heavy upon him, would not exacerbate his humiliation by going to Fastolfe's establishment.

"Well, then," Fastolfe had said to Giskard. "I can afford to be magnanimous in victory. I will go to him. Besides, I *must* see him."

Fastolfe had been a member of the Institute of Robotics since Baley had made possible the crushing of Amadiro and of his political ambitions. In return, Fastolfe had passed over to the Institute all the data for the building and maintenance of humaniform robots. A number had been manufactured and then the project had come to an end and Fastolfe had chafed.

It had been Fastolfe's intention, at first, to arrive at the Institute without any robot companion. He would have placed himself, without protection and (so to speak) naked, into the midst of what was still the stronghold of the enemy's camp. It would have been a sign of humility and trust, but it would also have been an indication of complete self-confidence and Amadiro would have understood that. Fastolfe, entirely alone, would be demonstrating his certainty that Amadiro, with all the resources of the Institute at his command, would not dare to touch his single enemy coming carelessly and defenselessly within reach of his fist.

And yet in the end, Fastolfe, not quite knowing how, chose to have Giskard accompany him.

Amadiro seemed to have lost a little weight since last Fastolfe had seen him, but he was still a formidable specimen; tall and heavyset. He lacked the self-confident smile that had once been his hallmark and when he attempted it at Fastolfe's entrance, it seemed more like a snarl that faded into a look of somber dissatisfaction.

"Well, Kelden," said Fastolfe, making free with the other's familiar name, "we don't see each other often, despite the fact that we have now been colleagues for four years."

"Let's not have any false bonhomie, Fastolfe," said Amadiro in a clearly annoyed and low-pitched growl, "and address me as Amadiro. We are not colleagues except in name and I make no secret—and never have—of my belief that your foreign policy is suicidal for us."

Three of Amadiro's robots, large and gleaming, were present and Fastolfe studied them with raised eyebrows, "You are well protected, Amadiro, against one man of peace together with his single robot."

"They will not attack you, Fastolfe, as you well know. But why did you bring Giskard? Why not your masterpiece, Daneel?"

"Would it be safe to bring Daneel within your reach, Amadiro?"

"I take it you intend that as humor. I no longer need Daneel. We build our own humaniforms."

"On the basis of my design."

"With improvements."

"And yet you do not use the humaniforms. That is why I have come to see you. I know that my position in the Institute is a name-only thing and that even my presence is unwelcome, let alone my opinions and recommendations. However, I must, as an Institute member, protest your failure to use the humaniforms."

"How do you wish me to use them?"

"The intention was to have the humaniforms open up new worlds into which Spacers could eventually emigrate, after those worlds had been terraformed and made completely habitable, wasn't it?"

"But that was something you opposed, Fastolfe, wasn't it?"

Fastolfe said, "Yes, I did. I wanted Spacers themselves to emigrate to new worlds and to do their own terraforming. That, however, is not happening and, I now see, is not likely to happen. Let us send the humaniforms, then. That would be better than nothing."

"All our alternatives come to nothing, as long as your views dominate the Council, Fastolfe. Spacers will not travel to rude and unformed worlds; nor, it seems, do they like humaniform robots."

"You have scarcely given the Spacers a chance to like them. Earthpeople are beginning to settle new planets—even rude and unformed ones. And they do it without robotic help."

"You know very well the differences between Earthpeople and ourselves. There are eight billion Earthpeople, plus a large number of Settlers."

"And there are five and a half billion Spacers."

"Numbers are not the sole difference," said Amadiro bitterly. "They breed like insects."

"They do not. Earth's population has been fairly stable for centuries."

"The potential is there. If they put all their heart into emigration, they can easily produce one hundred and sixty million new bodies each year and that number will rise as the new worlds fill up."

"We have the biological capability of producing one hundred million new bodies each year."

"But not the sociological capability. We are long-lived; we do not wish ourselves replaced so quickly."

"We can send a large portion of the new bodies to other worlds."

"They won't go. We value our bodies, which are strong, healthy, and capable of surviving in strength and health for nearly forty decades. Earthmen can place no value on bodies that wear out in less than ten decades and that are riddled with disease and degeneration even over that short period of time. It doesn't matter to them if they send out millions a year to certain misery and probable death. In fact, even the victims needn't fear misery and death, for what else do they have on Earth? The Earthpeople who emigrate are fleeing from their pestilential world knowing well that any change can scarcely be for the worse. We, on the other hand, value our well-wrought and comfortable planets and would not lightly give them up."

Fastolfe sighed and said, "I've heard all these arguments so often— May I point out the simple fact, Amadiro, that Aurora was originally a rude and unformed world that had to be terraformed into acceptability and that so was every Spacer world?"

Amadiro said, "And I have heard all your arguments to the point of nausea, but I will not weary of answering them. Aurora may have been primitive when first settled, but Aurora was settled by Earthpeople—and other Spacer worlds, when not settled by Earthpeople, were settled by Spacers that had not yet outgrown their Earth heritage. The times are no longer suitable for that. What could be done then, cannot be done now."

Amadiro lifted a corner of his mouth in a snarl and went on, "No, Fastolfe, what your policy has accomplished has been to begin the creation of a Galaxy that will be populated by Earthmen only, while Spacers must wither and decline. You can see it happening now. Your famous trip to Earth, two years ago, was the turning point. Somehow, you betrayed your own people by encouraging those half-humans to begin an expansion. In only two years there are at least some Earthpeople on each of twenty-four worlds and new ones are being added steadily."

Fastolfe said, "Do not exaggerate. Not one of those Settler worlds is truly fit for human occupation yet and won't be for some decades. Not all are likely to survive and, as the nearer worlds are occupied, the chances for settling farther worlds diminish so that the initial surge will slow down. I encouraged *their* expansion because I counted on ours as well. We can still keep up with them if we make the effort and, in healthy competition, we can fill the Galaxy together."

"No," said Amadiro. "What you have in mind is that most destructive of all policies, a foolish idealism. The expansion is one-sided and will remain so despite anything you can do. The people of Earth swarm unhindered and they will have to be stopped before they get too strong to stop."

"How do you propose to do that? We have a treaty of friendship with Earth in which we specifically agree not to stop their expansion into space as long as no planet within twenty light-years of a Spacer world is touched. They have adhered to this scrupulously."

Amadiro said, "Everyone knows about the treaty. Everyone also knows that no treaty has ever been kept once it begins to work against the national interests of the more powerful signatory. I attach no value to that treaty."

"I do. It will be held to."

Amadiro shook his head. "You have touching faith. How will it be held to after you are out of power?"

"I don't intend to be out of power for a while."

"As Earth and its Settlers grow stronger, the Spacers will grow fearful and you will not remain long in power after that."

Fastolfe said, "And if you tear up the treaty and destroy the Settler worlds and slam the gates shut on Earth, will the Spacers then emigrate and fill the Galaxy?"

"Perhaps not. But if we decide not to, if we decide we are comfortable as we are, what difference will that make?"

"The Galaxy will not, in that case, become a human empire."

"And if it does not, what then?"

"Then the Spacers will stultify and degenerate, even if Earth is kept in prison and also stultifies and degenerates."

"That is just the claptrap your party puts out, Fastolfe. There is no actual evidence that such a thing would happen. And even if it does, that will be *our* choice. At least we will not see the barbarian short-lifers fall heir to the Galaxy."

Fastolfe said, "Are you seriously suggesting, Amadiro, that you would be willing to see the Spacer civilization die, provided you can prevent Earth from expanding?"

"I'm not counting on our death, Fastolfe, but if the worst happens, why, yes, to me our own death is a less fearful thing than the triumph of a subhuman disease-riddled set of short-lived beings."

"From whom we are descended."

"And with whom we are no longer truly related genetically. Are we worms because a billion years ago, worms were among our ancestors?"

Fastolfe, lips pressed together, rose to go. Amadiro, glowering, made no move to stop him.

9.

DANEEL HAD NO WAY of telling, directly, that Giskard was lost in memory. For one thing, Giskard's expression did not change and for another, he was not lost in memory as humans might be. It took no substantial period of time.

On the other hand, the line of thought that had caused Giskard to think of the past had caused Daneel to think of the same events of that past as they had long ago been recounted to him by Giskard. Nor was Giskard surprised at that.

Their conversation carried on with no unusual pause, but in a markedly new manner, as though each had thought of the past on behalf of both.

Daneel said, "It might seem, friend Giskard, that since the people of Aurora now recognize that they are weaker than Earth and its many Settler worlds, the crisis that Elijah Baley foresaw has been safely passed."

"It might seem so, friend Daneel."

"You labored to bring that about."

"I did. I kept the Council in Fastolfe's hand. I did what I could to mold those who, in turn, molded public opinion."

"Yet I am uneasy."

Giskard said, "I have been uneasy through every stage of the process, although I endeavored to do no harm to anyone. I have touched—mentally —not one human being who required anything more than the lightest touch. On Earth, I had merely to lighten the fear of reprisal and chose those, particularly, in which the fear was already light and broke a thread that was, in any case, frayed and on the point of breaking. On Aurora, it was reversed. The policymakers here were reluctant to espouse policies that would lead to an exit from their comfortable world and I merely confirmed that and made the sturdy cord that held them a bit stronger. And doing this has immersed me in a constant—if faint—turmoil."

"Why? You encouraged the expansion of Earth and discouraged the expansion of the Spacers. Surely that is as it should be."

"As it should be? Do you think, friend Daneel, that an Earthperson counts for more than a Spacer, even though both are human beings?"

"There are differences. Elijah Baley would rather see his own Earthpeople defeated than see the Galaxy uninhabited. Dr. Amadiro would rather see both Earth and Spacers dwindle than see Earth expand. The first looks with hope to the triumph of either, the second is content to see the triumph of neither. Should we not choose the first, friend Giskard?"

"Yes, friend Daneel. So it would seem. And yet how far are you influenced by your feeling of the special worth of your onetime partner, Elijah Baley?"

Daneel said, "I value the memory of Partner Elijah and the people of Earth are his people."

"I see you do. I have been saying for many decades that you tend to think like a human being, friend Daneel, but I wonder if that is necessarily a compliment. Still, though you tend to think *like* a human being, you are *not* a human being and, in the end, you are bound to the Three Laws. You may not harm a human being, whether that human being is an Earthman or a Spacer."

"There are times, friend Giskard, when one must choose one human being over another. We have been given special orders to protect Lady Gladia. I would be forced, on occasion, to harm a human being in order to protect Lady Gladia and I think that, all things being equal, I would be willing to harm a Spacer just a little in order to protect an Earthperson."

"So you think. But in the actual event, you would have to be guided by specific circumstances. You will find you cannot generalize," said Giskard. "And so it is with me. In encouraging Earth and discouraging Aurora, I have made it impossible for Dr. Fastolfe to persuade the Auroran government to sponsor a policy of emigration and to set up two expanding powers in the Galaxy. I could not help but realize that that portion of his labors was brought to nothing. This was bound to fill him with gathering despair and perhaps it hastened his death. I have felt this in his mind and that has been painful. And yet, friend Daneel—"

Giskard paused and Daneel said, "Yes?"

"To have not done as I had done might have greatly lowered Earth's ability to expand, without greatly improving Aurora's moves in that direction. Dr. Fastolfe would then have been frustrated in both ways—Earth *and* Aurora—and would moreover have been ousted from his seat of power by Dr. Amadiro. His sense of frustration would have been greater. It was Dr. Fastolfe, during his lifetime, to whom I owed my greatest loyalty and I chose that course of action which frustrated him less, without measurably harming other individuals I dealt with. If Dr. Fastolfe was continually disturbed by his inability to persuade Aurorans—and Spacers generally—to expand to new worlds, he was at least delighted by the activity of the emigrating Earthpeople."

"Could you not have encouraged both the people of Earth *and* of Aurora, friend Giskard, and thus have satisfied Dr. Fastolfe in both respects?"

"That, of course, had occurred to me, friend Daneel. I considered the possibility and decided it would not do. I could encourage Earthpeople to emigrate by means of a trifling change that would do no harm. To have attempted the same for Aurorans would have required a great enough change to do much harm. The First Law prevented that."

"A pity."

"True. Think what might have been done if I could have radically altered the mind-set of Dr. Amadiro. Yet how could I have changed his fixed determination to oppose Dr. Fastolfe? It would have been much like trying to force his head to make a one hundred and eighty degree turn. So complete a turnabout of either the head itself or of its emotional content would kill with, I think, equal efficiency.

"The price of my power, friend Daneel," Giskard went on, "is the greatly increased dilemma into which I am constantly plunged. The First Law of Robotics, which forbids injury to human beings, deals, ordinarily, with the visible physical injuries that we can, all of us, easily see and concerning which we can easily make judgments. I, alone, however, am aware of human emotions and of casts of mind, so that I know of more subtle forms of injury without being able to understand them completely. I am forced on many occasions to act without true certainty and this puts a continuing stress on my circuits.

"And yet I feel I have done well. I have carried the Spacers past the crisis point. Aurora is aware of the gathering strength of the Settlers and will now be forced to avoid conflict. They must recognize it to be too late for retaliation and our promise to Elijah Baley is, in that respect, fulfilled. We have put Earth on the course toward the filling of the Galaxy and the establishment of a Galactic Empire."

They were, at this point, walking back to Gladia's house, but now Daneel stopped and the gentle pressure of his hand on Giskard's shoulder caused the other to stop as well.

Daneel said, "The picture you draw is attractive. It would make Partner Elijah proud of us if, as you say, we have accomplished that. 'Robots and Empire' Elijah would say and perhaps he would clap me on the shoulder. —And yet, as I said, I am uneasy, friend Giskard."

"Concerning what, friend Daneel?"

"I cannot help but wonder if indeed we have actually passed the crisis that Partner Elijah spoke of so many decades ago. Is it, in actual fact, too late for Spacer retaliation?"

"Why do you have these doubts, friend Daneel?"

"I have been made doubtful by the behavior of Dr. Mandamus in the course of his conversation with Madam Gladia."

Giskard's gaze was fixed on Daneel for a few moments and in the quiet they could hear leaves rustling in the cool breeze. The clouds were breaking and the sun would make its appearance soon. Their conversation, in its telegraphic fashion, had taken little time and Gladia, they knew, would not yet be wondering at their absence.

Giskard said, "What was there in the conversation that would give you cause for uneasiness?"

Daneel said, "I have had the opportunity, on four separate occasions, to observe Elijah Baley's handling of a puzzling problem. On each of those four occasions, I have noted the manner in which he managed to work out useful conclusions from limited—and even misleading—information. I have since always tried, within my limitations, to think as he did."

"It seems to me, friend Daneel, you have done well in this respect. I have said you tend to think like a human being."

"You will have noticed, then, that Dr. Mandamus had two matters he wished to discuss with Madam Gladia. He emphasized that fact himself. One was the matter of his own descent, whether from Elijah Baley or not. The second was the request that Madam Gladia see a Settler and report on the event afterward. Of these, the second might be viewed as a matter that would be important to the Council. The first would be a matter of importance only to himself."

Giskard said, "Dr. Mandamus presented the matter of his descent as being of importance to Dr. Amadiro as well."

"Then it would be a matter of personal importance to two people rather than one, friend Giskard. It would still not be a matter of importance to the Council and, therefore, to the planet generally."

"Proceed, then, friend Daneel."

"Yet the matter of state, as Dr. Mandamus himself referred to it, was taken up second, almost as an afterthought, and was disposed of almost at once. Indeed, it seemed scarcely something that required a personal visit. It might have been handled by holographic image by any official of the Council. On the other hand, Dr. Mandamus dealt with the matter of his own descent first, discussed it in great detail, and it was a matter that could have been handled only by him and by no one else."

"What is your conclusion, friend Daneel?"

"I believe that the matter of the Settler was seized upon by Dr. Mandamus as an excuse for a personal conversation with Madam Gladia, in order that he might discuss his descent in privacy. It was the matter of his descent and nothing else that truly interested him. —Is there any way you can support that conclusion, friend Giskard?"

Aurora's sun had not yet emerged from the clouds and the faint glow of Giskard's eyes was visible. He said, "The tension in Dr. Mandamus's mind was indeed measurably stronger in the first part of the interview than in the second. That may serve as corroboration, perhaps, friend Daneel."

Daneel said, "Then we must ask ourselves why the question of Dr. Mandamus's descent should be a matter of such importance to him."

Giskard said, "Dr. Mandamus explained that. It is only by demonstrating that he is not descended from Elijah Baley that his road to advancement is open. Dr. Amadiro, upon whose goodwill he is dependent, would turn against him absolutely if he were a descendant of Mr. Baley."

"So he said, friend Giskard, but what took place during the interview argues against that."

"Why do you say so? Please continue thinking like a human being, friend Daneel. I find it instructive."

Daneel said gravely, "Thank you, friend Giskard. Did you note that not one statement that Madam Gladia made concerning the impossibility of Dr. Mandamus's descent from Partner Elijah was considered convincing? In every case, Dr. Mandamus said that Dr. Amadiro would not accept the statement."

"Yes and what do you deduce from that?"

"It seems to me that Dr. Mandamus was so convinced that Dr. Amadiro would accept no argument against Elijah Baley as ancestor that one must wonder why he should have bothered to ask Madam Gladia about the matter. He apparently knew from the start that it would be pointless to do so."

"Perhaps, friend Daneel, but it is mere speculation. Can you supply a possible motive for his action, then?"

"I can. I believe he inquired as to his descent, not to convince an implacable Dr. Amadiro but to convince himself."

"In that case, why should he have mentioned Dr. Amadiro at all? Why not simply have said, 'I wish to know.' "

A small smile passed over Daneel's face, a change of expression of which the other robot would have been incapable. Daneel said, "Had he said, 'I wish to know,' to Madam Gladia, she would surely have replied that it was none of his business and he would have discovered nothing. Madam Gladia, however, is as strongly opposed to Dr. Amadiro as Dr. Amadiro is to Elijah Baley. Madam Gladia would be sure to take offense at any opinion strongly held by Dr. Amadiro concerning her. She would be furious, even if the opinion were more or less true; how much more, then, if it were absolutely false, as in this case. She would labor to demonstrate Dr. Amadiro to be wrong and would present every piece of evidence needed to achieve that end.

"In such a case, Dr. Mandamus's cold assurance that each piece of evidence was insufficient would but make her the angrier and would drive her to further revelations. Dr. Mandamus's strategy was chosen to make certain he would learn the maximum from Madam Gladia and, at the end, *he* was convinced that he did not have an Earthman as ancestor; at least, not as recently as twenty decades ago. Amadiro's feelings in this regard were not, I think, truly in question."

Giskard said, "Friend Daneel, this is an interesting point of view, but it does not seem to be strongly founded. In what way can we conclude that it is no more than a guess on your part?"

Daneel said, "Does it not seem to you, friend Giskard, that when Dr. Mandamus ended his inquiry into his descent without having obtained sufficient evidence for Dr. Amadiro, as he would have had us believe, that he should have been distinctly depressed and disheartened. By his own statement, this should have meant he had no chance for advancement and would never gain the position as head of the Institute of Robotics. And yet it seemed to me that he was far from depressed but was, indeed, jubilant. I can only judge by outward appearance, but you can do better. Tell me, friend Giskard, what was his mental attitude at the conclusion of this portion of his conversation with Madam Gladia?"

Giskard said, "As I look back on it, it was not only jubilant but triumphant, friend Daneel. You are right. Now that you have explained your process of thought, that sensation of triumph I detected clearly marks the accuracy of your reasoning. In fact, now that you have marked it all out, I find myself at a loss to account for my inability to see it for myself."

"That, friend Giskard, was, on a number of occasions, my reaction to the reasoning of Elijah Baley. That I could carry through such reasoning on this occasion may be, in part, because of the strong stimulus of the existence of the present crisis. It forces me to think more cogently."

"You underestimate yourself, friend Daneel. You have been thinking cogently for a long time. But why do you speak of a present crisis? Pause a moment and explain. How does one go from Dr. Mandamus's feeling of triumph at not being descended from Mr. Baley to this crisis you speak of?"

Daneel said, "Dr. Mandamus may have deceived us in his statements concerning Dr. Amadiro, but it may be fair to suppose that it is nevertheless true that he longs for advancement; that he is ambitious to become head of the Institute. Is that not so, friend Giskard?"

Giskard paused a moment, as though in thought, then said, "I was not searching for ambition. I was studying his mind without particular purpose and was aware of only surface manifestations. Yet there might have been flashes of ambition there when he spoke of advancement. I do not have strong grounds for agreeing with you, friend Daneel, but I have no grounds at all for disagreeing with you."

"Let us accept Dr. Mandamus as an ambitious man, then, and see where that takes us. Agreed?"

"Agreed."

"Then does it not seem likely that his sense of triumph, once he was convinced that he was not descended from Partner Elijah, arose from the fact that he felt his ambition could now be served. This would not be so, however, because of Dr. Amadiro's approval, since we have agreed that the Dr. Amadiro motif was introduced by Dr. Mandamus as a distraction. His ambition could now be served for some other reason."

"What other reason?"

"There is none that arises out of compelling evidence. But I can suggest one as a matter of speculation. What if Dr. Mandamus knows something or can do something that would lead to some huge success; one that would surely make him the next head? Remember that at the conclusion of the search into the manner of his descent, Dr. Mandamus said, 'There are powerful methods remaining to me.' Suppose that is true, but that he could only use those methods if he were *not* descended from Partner Elijah. His jubilation over having been convinced of his nondescent would arise, then, from the fact that he could now use those methods and assure himself of great advancement."

"But what are these 'powerful methods,' friend Daneel?"

Daneel said gravely, "We must continue to speculate. We know that Dr. Amadiro wants nothing so much as to defeat Earth and force it back to its earlier position of subservience to the Spacer worlds. If Dr. Mandamus has a way of doing this, he can surely get anything he wants out of Dr. Amadiro, up to and including a guarantee of succession to the headship. Yet it may be that Dr. Mandamus hesitates to bring about Earth's defeat and humiliation unless he felt no kinship to its people. Descent from Elijah Baley of Earth would inhibit him. The denial of that descent frees him to act and that makes him jubilant."

Giskard said, "You mean Dr. Mandamus is a man of conscience?"

"Conscience?"

"It is a word human beings sometimes use. I have gathered that it is applied to a person who adheres to rules of behavior that force him to act in ways that oppose his immediate self-interest. If Dr. Mandamus feels that he cannot allow himself to advance at the expense of those with whom he is distantly connected, I imagine him to be a man of conscience. I have thought much of such things, friend Daneel, since they seem to imply that human beings do have Laws governing their behavior, at least in some cases."

"And can you tell whether Dr. Mandamus is, indeed, a man of conscience?"

"From my observations of his emotions? No, I was not watching for anything like that, but if your analysis is correct, conscience would seem to follow. —And yet, on the other hand, if we begin by supposing him a man of conscience and argue backward, we can come to other conclusions. It might seem that if Dr. Mandamus thought he had an Earthman in his ancestry a mere nineteen and a half decades ago, he might feel driven, against his conscience, to spearhead an attempt to defeat Earth as a way of freeing himself from the stigma of such descent. If he were not so descended, then he would not be unbearably driven to act against Earth and his conscience would be free to cause him to leave Earth alone."

Daneel said, "No, friend Giskard. That would not fit the facts. However relieved he might be at not having to take violent action against Earth, he would be left without a way of satisfying Dr. Amadiro and enforcing his own advance. Considering his ambitious nature, he would not be left with the feeling of triumph you so clearly noted."

"I see. Then we conclude that Dr. Mandamus has a method for defeating Earth."

"Yes. And if that is so, then the crisis foreseen by Partner Elijah has not been safely passed after all, but is now here."

Giskard said thoughtfully, "But we are left with the key question unanswered, friend Daneel. What is the nature of the crisis? What is the deadly danger? Can you deduce that, too?"

"That I cannot do, friend Giskard. I have gone as far as I can. Perhaps Partner Elijah might have gone farther were he still alive, but I cannot. —Here I must depend upon you, friend Giskard."

"Upon me? In what way?"

"You can study the mind of Dr. Mandamus as I cannot, as no one else can. You can discover the nature of the crisis."

"I fear I cannot, friend Daneel. If I lived with a human being over an extended period, as once I lived with Dr. Fastolfe, as now I live with Madam Gladia, I could, little by little, unfold the layers of mind, one leaf after another, untie the intricate knot a bit at a time, and learn a great deal without harming him or her. To do the same to Dr. Mandamus after one brief meeting or after a hundred brief meetings would accomplish little. Emotions are readily apparent, thoughts are not. If, out of a sense of urgency, I attempted to make haste, forcing the process, I would surely injure him—and that I cannot do."

"Yet the fate of billions of people on Earth and billions more in the rest of the Galaxy may depend on this."

"*May* depend on this. That is conjecture. Injury to a human being is a fact. Consider that it may be only Dr. Mandamus who knows the nature of the crisis and can carry it through to a conclusion. He could not use his knowledge or ability to force Dr. Amadiro to grant him the headship—if Dr. Amadiro could gain it from another source."

"True," said Daneel. "That may well be so."

"In that case, friend Daneel, it is not necessary to know the nature of the crisis. If Dr. Mandamus could be restrained from telling Dr. Amadiro—or anyone else—whatever it is he knows, the crisis will not come to pass."

"Someone else might discover what Dr. Mandamus now knows."

"Certainly, but we don't know when that will be. Very likely, we will have time to probe further and discover more—and become better prepared to play a useful role of our own."

"Well, then."

"If Dr. Mandamus is to be restrained, it can be done by damaging his mind to the point where it is no longer effective—or by destroying his life outright. I alone possess the ability to injure his mind appropriately, but I cannot do this. However, either one of us can physically bring his life to an end. I cannot do this, either. Can *you* do it, friend Daneel?"

There was a pause and Daneel finally whispered. "I cannot. You know that."

Giskard said slowly, "Even though you know that the future of billions of people on Earth and elsewhere is at stake?"

"I cannot bring myself to injure Dr. Mandamus."

"And I cannot. So we are left with the certainty of a deadly crisis coming, but a crisis whose nature we do not know, and cannot find out, and which we are therefore helpless to counter."

They stared at each other in silence, with nothing showing in their faces, but with an air of despair settling somehow over them.

Chapter 4

Another Descendant

10.

GLADIA HAD TRIED to relax after the harrowing session with Mandamus—and did so with an intensity that fought relaxation to the death. She had opacified all the windows in her bedroom, adjusted the environment to a gentle warm breeze with the faint sound of rustling leaves and the occasional soft warble of a distant bird. She had then shifted it to the sound of a far-off surf and had added a faint but unmistakable tang of the sea in the air.

It didn't help. Her mind echoed helplessly with what had just been—and with what was soon to come. Why had she chattered so freely to Mandamus? What business was it of his—or of Amadiro's, for that matter—whether she had visited Elijah in orbit or not and whether or not—or when—she had had a son by him or by any other man.

She had been cast into imbalance by Mandamus's claim of descent, that's what it was. In a society where no one cared about descent or relationship except for medico-genetic reasons, its sudden intrusion into a conversation was bound to be upsetting. That and the repeated (but surely accidental) references to Elijah.

She decided she was finding excuses for herself and, in impatience, she tossed it all away. She had reacted badly and had babbled like a baby and that was all there was to it.

Now there was this Settler coming.

He was not an Earthman. He had not been born on Earth, she was sure, and it was quite possible that he had never even visited Earth. His people might have lived on a strange world she had never heard of and might have done so for generations.

That would make him a Spacer, she thought. Spacers were descended from Earthmen, too—centuries further back, but what did that matter? To be sure, Spacers were long-lived and these Settlers must be short-lived, but how much of a distinction was that? Even a Spacer might die prematurely through some freak accident; she had once heard of a Spacer who had died a natural death before he was sixty. Why not, then, think of the next visitor as a Spacer with an unusual accent?

But it wasn't that simple. No doubt the Settler did not feel himself to be a Spacer. It's not what you are that counts, but what you feel yourself to be. So think of him as a Settler, not a Spacer.

Yet weren't all human beings simply human beings no matter what name you applied to them—Spacers, Settlers, Aurorans, Earthpeople. The proof of it was that robots could not do injury to any of them. Daneel would spring as quickly to the defense of the most ignorant Earthman as to the Chairman of the Auroran Council—and that meant—

She could feel herself drifting, actually relaxing into a shallow sleep when a sudden thought entered her mind and seemed to ricochet there.

Why was the Settler named Baley?

Her mind sharpened and snapped out of the welcoming coils of oblivion that had all but engulfed her.

Why Baley?

Perhaps it was simply a common name among the Settlers. After all, it was Elijah who had made it all possible and he had to be a hero to them as —as—

She could not think of an analogous hero to Aurorans. Who had led the expedition that first reached Aurora? Who had supervised the terraformation of the raw barely living world that Aurora had then been? She did not know.

Was her ignorance born of the fact that she had been brought up on Solaria—or was it that the Aurorans simply had no founding hero? After all, the first expedition to Aurora had consisted of mere Earthpeople. It was only in later generations, with lengthening life-spans, thanks to the adjustments of sophisticated bioengineering, that Earthpeople had become Aurorans. And after that, why should Aurorans wish to make heroes of their despised predecessors?

But Settlers might make heroes of Earthpeople. They had not yet changed, perhaps. They might change eventually and then Elijah would be forgotten in embarrassment, but till then—

That must be it. Probably half the Settlers alive had adopted the Baley surname. Poor Elijah! Everyone crowding onto his shoulders and into his shadow. Poor Elijah—dear Elijah—

And she *did* fall asleep.

11.

THE SLEEP WAS too restless to restore her to calm, let alone good humor. She was scowling without knowing that she was—and had she seen herself in the mirror, she would have been taken aback by her middle-aged appearance.

Daneel, to whom Gladia was a human being, regardless of age, appearance, or mood, said, "Madam—"

Gladia interrupted, with a small shiver. "Is the Settler here?"

She looked up at the clock ribbon on the wall and then made a quick gesture, in response to which Daneel at once adjusted the heat upward. (It had been a cool day and was going to be a cooler evening.)

Daneel said, "He is, madam."

"Where have you put him?"

"In the main guest room, madam. Giskard is with him and the household robots are all within call."

"I *hope* they will have the judgment to find out what he expects to eat for lunch. I don't know Settler cuisine. And I hope they can make some reasonable attempt to meet his requests."

"I am sure, madam, that Giskard will handle the matter competently."

Gladia was sure of that, too, but she merely snorted. At least it would have been a snort if Gladia were the sort of person who snorted. She didn't think she was.

"I presume," she said, "he's been in appropriate quarantine before being allowed to land."

"It would be inconceivable for him not to have been, madam."

She said, "Just the same, I'll wear my gloves and my nose filter."

She stepped out of her bedroom, was distantly aware that there were household robots about her, and made the sign that would get her a new pair of gloves and a fresh nose filter. Every establishment had its own vocabulary of signs and every human member of an establishment cultivated those signs, learning to make them both rapidly and unnoticeably. A robot was expected to follow these unobtrusive orders of its human over-lords as though it read minds; and it followed that a robot could not follow the orders of nonestablishment human beings except by careful speech.

Nothing would humiliate a human member of an establishment more than to have one of the robots of the establishment hesitate in fulfilling an order or, worse, fulfill it incorrectly. That would mean that the human being had fumbled a sign—or that the robot had.

Generally, Gladia knew, it was the human being who was at fault, but in virtually every case, this was not admitted. It was the robot who was handed over for an unnecessary response analysis or unfairly put up for sale. Gladia had always felt that she would never fall into that trap of wounded ego, yet if at that moment she had not received her gloves and nose filter, she would have—

She did not have to finish the thought. The nearest robot brought her what she wanted, correctly and with speed.

Gladia adjusted the nose filter and snuffled a bit to make sure it was properly seated (she was in no mood to risk infection with any foul disorder that had survived the painstaking treatment during quarantine). She said, "What does he look like, Daneel?"

Daneel said, "He is of ordinary stature and measurements, madam."

"I mean his face." (It was silly to ask. If he showed any family resemblance to Elijah Baley, Daneel would have noticed it as quickly as she herself would have and he would have remarked upon it.)

"That is difficult to say, madam. It is not in plain view."

"What does that mean? Surely he's not masked, Daneel."

"In a way, he is, madam. His face is covered with hair."

"Hair?" She found herself laughing. "You mean after the fashion of the hypervision historicals? Beards?" She made little gestures indicating a tuft of hair on the chin and another under the nose.

"Rather more than that, madam. Half his face is covered."

Gladia's eyes opened wide and for the first time she felt a surge of interest in seeing him. What would a face with hair all over it look like? Auroran males—and Spacer males, generally—had very little facial hair and what there was would be removed permanently by the late teens—during virtual infancy.

Sometimes the upper lip was left untouched. Gladia remembered that her husband, Santirix Gremionis, before their marriage, had had a thin line of hair under his nose. A mustache, he had called it. It had looked like a misplaced and peculiarly misshapen eyebrow and once she had resigned herself to accepting him as husband, she had insisted he destroy the follicles.

He had done so with scarcely a murmur and it occurred to her now, for the first time, to wonder if he had missed the hair. It seemed to her that she had noticed him, on occasion, in those early years, lifting a finger to his upper lip. She had thought it a nervous poking at a vague itch and it was only now that it occurred to her that he had been searching for a mustache that was gone forever.

How would a man look with a mustache all over his face? Would he be bearlike?

How would it feel? What if women had such hair, too? She thought of a man and woman trying to kiss and having trouble finding each other's mouths. She found the thought funny, in a harmlessly ribald way, and laughed out loud. She felt her petulance disappearing and actually looked forward to seeing the monster.

After all, there would be no need to fear him even if he were as animal in behavior as he was in appearance. He would have no robot of his own—Settlers were supposed to have a nonrobotic society—and she would be surrounded by a dozen. The monster would be immobilized in a split second if he made the slightest suspicious move—or if he as much as raised his voice in anger.

She said with perfect good humor, "Take me to him, Daneel."

12.

THE MONSTER ROSE. He said something that sounded like "Gode arternoon, muhleddy."

She at once caught the "good afternoon," but it took her a moment to translate the last word into "my lady."

Gladia absently said, "Good afternoon." She remembered the difficulty she had had understanding Auroran pronunciation of Galactic Standard in those long-ago days when, a frightened young woman, she had come to the planet from Solaria.

The monster's accent was uncouth—or did it just sound uncouth because her ear was unaccustomed to it? Elijah, she remembered, had seemed to voice his "k's" and "p's," but spoke pretty well otherwise. Nineteen and a half decades had passed, however, and this Settler was not from Earth. Language, in isolation, underwent changes.

But only a small portion of Gladia's mind was on the language problem. She was staring at his beard.

It was not in the least like the beards that actors wore in historical dramas. Those always seemed tufted—a bit here, a bit there—looking gluey and glossy.

The Settler's beard was different. It covered his cheeks and chin evenly, thickly, and deeply. It was a dark brown, somewhat lighter and wavier than the hair on his head, and at least two inches long, she judged—evenly long.

It didn't cover his whole face, which was rather disappointing. His forehead was totally bare (except for his eyebrows), as were his nose and his under-eye regions.

His upper lip was bare, too, but it was shadowed as though there was the beginning of new growth upon it. There was additional bareness just under the lower lip, but with new growth less marked and concentrated mostly under the middle portion.

Since both his lips were quite bare, it was clear to Gladia that there would be no difficulty in kissing him. She said, knowing that staring was impolite and staring even so, "It seems to me you remove the hair from about your lips."

"Yes, my lady."

"Why, if I may ask?"

"You may ask. For hygienic reasons. I don't want food catching in the hairs."

"You scrape it off, don't you? I see it's growing again."

"I use a facial laser. It takes fifteen seconds after waking."

"Why not depilate and be done with it?"

"I might want to grow it back."

"Why?"

"Esthetic reasons, my lady?"

This time Gladia did not grasp the word. It sounded like "acidic" or possibly "acetic."

She said, "Pardon me?"

The Settler said, "I might grow tired of the way I look now and want to grow the hair on the upper lip again. Some women like it, you know, and"—the Settler tried to look modest and failed—"I have a fine mustache when I grow it."

She said suddenly grasping the word, "You mean 'esthetic.'"

The Settler laughed, showing fine white teeth, and said, "You talk funny, too, my lady."

Gladia tried to look haughty, but melted into a smile. Proper pronunciation was a matter of local consensus. She said, "You ought to hear me with my Solarian accent—if it comes to that. Then it would be 'estheetic rayzuns.' " The "r" rolled interminably.

"I've been places where they talk a little bit like that. It sounds barbarous." He rolled both "r's" phenomenally in the last word.

Gladia chuckled. "You do it with the tip of your tongue. It's got to be with the sides of the tongue. No one but a Solarian can do it correctly."

"Perhaps you can teach me. A Trader like myself, who's been everywhere, hears all kinds of linguistic perversions." Again he tried to roll the "r's" of the last word, choked slightly, and coughed.

"See. You'll tangle your tonsils and you'll *never* recover." She was still staring at his beard and now she could curb her curiosity no longer. She reached toward it.

The Settler flinched and started back, then, realizing her intention, was still.

Gladia's hand, all-but-invisibly gloved, rested lightly on the left side of his face. The thin plastic that covered her fingers did not interfere with the sense of touch and she found the hair to be soft and springy.

"It's nice," she said with evident surprise.

"Widely admired," said the Settler, grinning.

She said, "But I can't stand here and manhandle you all day."

Ignoring his predictable "You can as far as I'm concerned," she went on. "Have you told my robots what you would like to eat?"

"My lady, I told them what I now tell you—whatever is handy. I've been on a score of worlds in the last year and each has its own dietary. A Trader learns to eat everything that isn't actually toxic. I'd prefer an Auroran meal to anything you would try to make in imitation of Baleyworld."

"Baleyworld?" said Gladia sharply, a frown returning to her face.

"Named for the leader of the first expedition to the planet—or to *any* of the Settled planets, for that matter. Ben Baley."

"The son of Elijah Baley?"

"Yes," the Settler said and changed the subject at once. He looked down at himself and said with a trace of petulance, "How do you people manage to stand these clothes of yours—slick and puffy. Be glad to get into my own again."

"I'm sure you will have your chance to do so soon enough. But for now please come and join me at lunch. —I was told your name was Baley, by the way—like your planet."

"Not surprising. It's the most honored name on the planet, naturally. I'm Deejee Baley."

They had walked into the dining room, Giskard preceding them, Daneel following them, each moving into his appropriate wall niche. Other robots were already in their niches and two emerged to do the serving. The room was bright with sunshine, the walls were alive with decoration, the table was set, and the odor of the food was enticing.

The Settler sniffed and let his breath out in satisfaction. "I don't think I'll have any trouble at all eating Auroran food. —Where would you like me to sit, my lady?"

A robot said at once, "If you would sit here, sir?"

The Settler sat down and then Gladia, the privileges of the guest satisfied, took her own seat.

"Deejee?" she said. "I do not know the nomenclatural peculiarities of your world, so excuse me if my question is offensive. Wouldn't Deejee be a feminine name?"

"Not at all," said the Settler a bit stiffly. "In any case, it is not a name, it is a pair of initials. Fourth letter of the alphabet and the seventh."

"Oh," said Gladia, enlightened, "D. G. Baley. And what do the initials stand for, if you'll excuse my curiosity?"

"Certainly. There's 'D,' for certain," he said, jerking his thumb toward one of the wall niches, "and I suspect that one may be 'G.' " He jerked his thumb toward another.

"You don't mean that," said Gladia faintly.

"But I do. My name is Daneel Giskard Baley. In every generation, my family has had at least one Daneel or one Giskard in its multiplying batches. I was the last of six children, but the first boy. My mother felt that was enough and made up for having but one son by giving me both names. That made me Daneel Giskard Baley and the double load was too great for me. I prefer D.G. as my name and I'd be honored if you used it." He smiled genially. "I'm the first to bear both names and I'm also the first to see the grand originals."

"But why those names?"

"It was Ancestor Elijah's idea, according to the family story. He had the honor of naming his grandsons and he named the oldest Daneel, while the second was named Giskard. He insisted on those names and that established the tradition."

"And the daughters?"

"The traditional name from generation to generation is Jezebel—Jessie. Elijah's wife, you know."

"I know."

"There are no—" He caught himself and transferred his attention to the dish that had been placed before him. "If this were Baleyworld, I would say this was a slice of roast pork and that it was smothered in peanut sauce."

"Actually, it is a vegetable dish, D.G. What you were about to say was that there are no Gladias in the family."

"There aren't," said D.G. calmly. "One explanation is that Jessie—the original Jessie—would have objected, but I don't accept that. Elijah's wife, the Ancestress, never came to Baleyworld, you know, never left Earth. How could she have objected? No, to me, it's pretty certain that the Ancestor wanted no other Gladia. No imitations, no copies, no pretense. One Gladia. Unique. —He asked that there be no later Elijah, either."

Gladia was having trouble eating. "I think your Ancestor spent the latter portion of his life trying to be as unemotional as Daneel. Just the same, he had romantic notions under his skin. He might have allowed other Elijahs and Gladias. It wouldn't have offended me, certainly, and I imagine it wouldn't have offended his wife, either." She laughed tremulously.

D.G. said, "All this doesn't seem real somehow. The Ancestor is practically ancient history; he died a hundred and sixty-four years ago. I'm his descendant in the seventh generation, yet here I am sitting with a woman who knew him when he was quite young."

"I didn't really know him," said Gladia, staring at her plate. "I saw him, rather briefly, on three separate occasions over a period of seven years."

"I know. The Ancestor's son, Ben, wrote a biography of him which is one of the literary classics of Baleyworld. Even I have read it."

"Indeed? I haven't read it. I didn't even know it existed. What—what does it say about me?"

D.G. seemed amused. "Nothing you would object to; you come out very well. But never mind that. What I'm amazed at is that here we are together, across seven generations. How old are you, my lady? Is it fair to ask the question?"

"I don't know that it's fair, but I have no objection to it. In Galactic Standard Years, I am two hundred and thirty-three years old. Over twenty-three decades."

"You look as though you were no more than in your late forties. The Ancestor died at the age of seventy-nine, an old man. I'm thirty-nine and when I die you will still be alive—"

"If I avoid death by misadventure."

"And will continue to live perhaps five decades beyond."

"Do you envy me, D.G.?" said Gladia with an edge of bitterness in her voice. "Do you envy me for having survived Elijah by over sixteen decades and for being condemned to survive him ten decades more, perhaps?"

"Of course I envy you," came the composed answer. "Why not? I would have no objection to living for several centuries, were it not that I would be setting a bad example to the people of Baleyworld. I wouldn't want them to live that long as a general thing. The pace of historical and intellectual advance would then become too slow. Those at the top would stay in power too long. Baleyworld would sink into conservatism and decay—as your world has done."

Gladia's small chin lifted. "Aurora is doing quite well, you'll find."

"I'm speaking of *your* world. Solaria."

Gladia hesitated, then said firmly, "Solaria is not my world."

D.G. said, "I hope it is. I came to see you because I believe Solaria is your world."

"If that is why you came to see me, you are wasting your time, young man."

"You were born on Solaria, weren't you, and lived there a while?"

"I lived there for the first three decades of my life—about an eighth of my lifetime."

"Then that makes you enough of a Solarian to be able to help me in a matter that is rather important."

"I am *not* a Solarian, despite this so-called important matter."

"It is a matter of war and peace—if *you* call that important. The Spacer worlds face war with the Settler worlds and things will go badly for all of us if it comes to that. And it is up to *you*, my lady, to prevent that war and to ensure peace."

13.

THE MEAL WAS DONE (it had been a small one) and Gladia found herself looking at D.G. in a coldly furious way.

She had lived quietly for the last twenty decades, peeling off the complexities of life. Slowly she had forgotten the misery of Solaria and the difficulties of adjustment to Aurora. She had managed to bury quite deeply the agony of two murders and the ecstasy of two strange loves—with a robot and with an Earthman—and to get well past it all. She had ended by spinning out a long quiet marriage, having two children, and working at her applied art of costumery. And eventually the children had left, then her husband, and soon she might be retiring even from her work.

Then she would be alone with her robots, content with—or, rather, resigned to—letting life glide quietly and uneventfully to a slow close in its own time—a close so gentle she might not be aware of the ending when it came.

It was what she wanted.

Then— What was happening?

It had begun the night before when she looked up vainly at the star-lit sky to see Solaria's star, which was not in the sky and would not have been visible to her if it were. It was as though this one foolish reaching for the past—a past that should have been allowed to remain dead—had burst the cool bubble she had built about herself.

First the name of Elijah Baley, the most joyously painful memory of all the ones she had so carefully brushed away, had come up again and again in a grim repetition.

She was then forced to deal with a man who thought—mistakenly—he might be a descendant of Elijah in the fifth degree and now with another man who actually was a descendant in the seventh degree. Finally, she was now being given problems and responsibilities similar to those that had plagued Elijah himself on various occasions.

Was she becoming Elijah, in a fashion, with none of his talent and none of his fierce dedication to duty at all costs?

What had she done to deserve it?

She felt her rage being buried under a flood tide of self-pity. She felt unjustly dealt with. No one had the right to unload responsibility on her against her will.

She said, forcing her voice level, "Why do you insist on my being a Solarian, when I tell you that I am not a Solarian?"

D.G. did not seem disturbed by the chill that had now entered her voice. He was still holding the soft napkin that had been given him at the conclusion of the meal. It had been damply hot—not too hot—and he had imitated the actions of Gladia in carefully wiping his hands and mouth. He had then doubled it over and stroked his beard with it. It was shredding now and shriveling.

He said, "I presume it will vanish altogether."

"It will." Gladia had deposited her own napkin in the appropriate receptacle on the table. Holding it was unmannerly and could be excused only by

D.G.'s evident unfamiliarity with civilized custom. "There are some who think it has a polluting effect on the atmosphere, but there is a gentle draft that carries the residue upward and traps it in filters. I doubt that it will give us any trouble. —But you ignore my question, sir."

D.G. wadded what was left of his napkin and placed it on the arm of the chair. A robot, in response to Gladia's quick and unobtrusive gesture, removed it.

D.G. said, "I don't intend to ignore your question, my lady. I am not trying to *force* you to be a Solarian. I merely point out that you were born on Solaria and spent your early decades there and therefore you might reasonably be considered a Solarian, after a fashion at least. —Do you know that Solaria has been abandoned?"

"So I have heard. Yes."

"Do you feel anything about that?"

"I am an Auroran and have been one for twenty decades."

"That is a non sequitur."

"A *what?*" She could make nothing of the last sound at all.

"It has no connection with my question."

"A non sequitur, you mean. You said a 'nonsense quitter.'"

D.G. smiled. "Very well. Let's quit the nonsense. I ask you if you feel anything about the death of Solaria and you tell me you're an Auroran. Do you maintain that is an answer? A born Auroran might feel badly at the death of a sister world. How do you feel about it?"

Gladia said icily, "It doesn't matter. Why are you interested?"

"I'll explain. We—I mean the Traders of the Settler worlds—are interested because there is business to be done, profits to be made, and a world to be gained. Solaria is already terraformed; it is a comfortable world; you Spacers seem to have no need or desire for it. Why should we not settle it?"

"Because it's not yours."

"Madam, is it *yours* that you object? Has Aurora any more claim to it than Baleyworld has? Can't we suppose that an empty world belongs to whoever is pleased to settle it?"

"Have you settled it?"

"No—because it's not empty."

"Do you mean the Solarians have not entirely left?" Gladia said quickly.

D.G.'s smile returned and broadened into a grin. "You're excited at the thought. —Even though you're an Auroran."

Gladia's face twisted into a frown at once. "Answer my question."

D.G. shrugged. "There were only some five thousand Solarians on the world just before it was abandoned, according to our best estimates. The population had been declining for years. But even five thousand— Can we be sure that *all* are gone? However, that's not the point. Even if the Solarians were indeed all gone, the planet would not be empty. There are, upon it, some two hundred million or more robots—masterless robots—some of them among the most advanced in the Galaxy. Presumably, those Solarians who left took some robots with them—it's hard to imagine Spacers doing without robots altogether." (He looked about, smiling, at the robots in their niches within the room.) "However, they can't possibly have taken forty thousand robots apiece."

Gladia said, "Well, then, since your Settler worlds are so purely robot-free and wish to stay so, I presume, you can't settle Solaria."

"That's right. Not until the robots are gone and that is where Traders such as myself come in."

"In what way?"

"We don't want a robot society, but we don't mind touching robots and dealing with them in the way of business. We don't have a superstitious fear of the things. We just know that a robot society is bound to decay. The Spacers have carefully made that plain to us by example. So that while we don't want to live with this robotic poison, we are perfectly willing to sell it to Spacers for a substantial sum—if they are so foolish as to want such a society."

"Do you think Spacers will buy them?"

"I'm sure they will. They will welcome the elegant modes that the Solarians manufacture. It's well known that they were the leading robot designers in the Galaxy, even though the late Dr. Fastolfe is said to have been unparalleled in the field, despite the fact that he was an Auroran. —Besides, even though we would charge a substantial sum, that sum would still be considerably less than the robots are worth. Spacers and Traders would both profit— the secret of successful trade."

"The Spacers wouldn't buy robots from Settlers," said Gladia with evident contempt.

D.G. had a Trader's way of ignoring such nonessentials as anger or contempt. It was business that counted. He said, "Of course they would. Offer them advanced robots at half-price and why should they turn them down? Where business is to be done, you would be surprised how unimportant questions of ideology become."

"I think you'll be the one to be surprised. Try to sell your robots and you'll see."

"Would that I could, my lady. Try to sell them, that is. I have none on hand."

"Why not?"

"Because none have been collected. Two separate trading vessels have landed on Solaria, each capable of storing some twenty-five robots. Had they succeeded, whole fleets of trading vessels would have followed them and I dare say we would have continued to do business for decades—and then have settled the world."

"But they didn't succeed. Why not?"

"Because both ships were destroyed on the surface of the planet and, as far as we can tell, all the crewmen are dead."

"Equipment failure?"

"Nonsense. Both landed safely; they were not wrecked. Their last reports were that Spacers were approaching—whether Solarians or natives of other Spacer worlds, we don't know. We can only assume that the Spacers attacked without warning."

"That's impossible."

"Is it?"

"Of course it's impossible. What would be the motive?"

"To keep us off the world, I would say."

"If they wished to do that," said Gladia, "they would merely have had to announce that the world was occupied."

"They might find it more pleasant to kill a few Settlers. At least, that's what many of our people think and there is pressure to settle the matter by sending a few warships to Solaria and establishing a military base on the planet."

"That would be dangerous."

"Certainly. It could lead to war. Some of our fire-eaters look forward to that. Perhaps some Spacers look forward to that, too, and have destroyed the two ships merely to provoke hostilities."

Gladia sat there amazed. There had been no hint of strained relations between Spacers and Settlers on any of the news programs.

She said, "Surely it's possible to discuss the matter. Have your people approached the Spacer Federation?"

"A thoroughly unimportant body, but we have. We've also approached the Auroran Council."

"And?"

"The Spacers deny everything. They suggest that the potential profits in the Solarian robot trade are so high that Traders, who are interested only in money—as though they themselves are not—would fight each other over the matter. Apparently, they would have us believe the two ships destroyed each other, each hoping to monopolize the trade for their own world."

"The two ships were from two different worlds, then?"

"Yes."

"Don't you think, then, that there might indeed have been a fight between them?"

"I don't think it's likely, but I will admit it's possible. There have been no outright conflicts between the Settler worlds, but there have been some pretty strenuous disputes. All have been settled through arbitration by Earth. Still, it is indeed a fact that the Settler worlds might, in a pinch, not hang together when multibillion-dollar trade is at stake. That's why war is not such a good idea for us and why something will have to be done to discourage the hotheads. That's where we come in."

"*We?*"

"You and I. I have been asked to go to Solaria and find out—if I can—what really happened. I will take one ship—armed, but not heavily armed."

"You might be destroyed, too."

"Possibly. But my ship, at least, won't be caught unprepared. Besides, I am not one of those hypervision heroes and I have considered what I might do to lessen the chances of destruction. It occurred to me that one of the disadvantages of Settler penetration of Solaria is that we don't know the world at all. It might be useful, then, to take someone who knows the world —a Solarian, in short."

"You mean you want to take *me?*"

"Right, my lady."

"Why *me?*"

"I should think you could see that without explanation, my lady. Those Solarians who have left the planet are gone we know not where. If any Solarians are left on the planet, they are very likely the enemy. There are no known Solarian-born Spacers living on some Spacer planet other than Solaria—except yourself. You are the only Solarian available to me—the *only* one in all the Galaxy. That's why I must have you and that's why you must come."

"You're wrong, Settler. If I am the only one available to you, then you have no one who is available. I do not intend to come with you and there is no way—absolutely no way—that you can force me to come with you. I am surrounded by my robots. Take one step in my direction and you will be immobilized at once—and if you struggle you will be hurt."

"I intend no force. You must come of your own accord—and you should be willing to. It's a matter of preventing war."

"That is the job of governments on your side and mine. I refuse to have anything to do with it. I am a private citizen."

"You owe it to your world. We might suffer in case of war, but so will Aurora."

"I am not one of those hypervision heroes, any more than you are."

"You owe it to me, then."

"You're mad. I owe you nothing."

D.G. smiled narrowly. "You owe me nothing as an individual. You owe me a great deal as a descendant of Elijah Baley."

Gladia froze and remained staring at the bearded monster for a long moment. How did she come to forget who he was?

With difficulty, she finally muttered, "No."

"Yes," said D.G. forcefully. "On two different occasions, the Ancestor did more for you than you can ever repay. He is no longer here to call in the debt—a small part of the debt. I inherit the right to do so."

Gladia said in despair, "But what can I do for you if I come with you?"

"We'll find out. Will you come?"

Desperately, Gladia wanted to refuse, but was it for this that Elijah had suddenly become part of her life, once more, in the last twenty-four hours? Was it so that when this impossible demand was made upon her, it would be in his name and she would find it impossible to refuse?

She said, "What's the use? The Council will not let me go with you. They will not have an Auroran taken away on a Settler's vessel."

"My lady, you have been here on Aurora for twenty decades, so you think the Auroran-born consider you an Auroran. It's not so. To them, you are a Solarian still. They'll let you go."

"They won't," said Gladia, her heart pounding and the skin of her upper arms turning to gooseflesh. He was right. She thought of Amadiro, who would surely think of her as nothing but a Solarian. Nevertheless, she repeated, "They won't," trying to reassure herself.

"They will," retorted D.G. "Didn't someone from your Council come to you to ask you to see me?"

She said defiantly, "He asked me only to report on this conversation we have had. And I will do so."

"If they want you to spy on me here in your own home, my lady, they will find it even more useful to have you spy on me on Solaria." He waited for a response and when there was none, he said with a trace of weariness,

"My lady, if you refuse, I won't force you because I won't have to. *They* will force you. But I don't want that. The Ancestor would not want it if he were here. He would want you to come with me out of gratitude to him and for no other reason. —My lady, the Ancestor labored on your behalf under conditions of extreme difficulty. Won't you labor on behalf of his memory?"

Gladia's heart sank. She knew she could not resist that. She said, "I can't go anywhere without robots."

"I wouldn't expect you to." D.G. was grinning again. "Why not take my two namesakes? Do you need more?"

Gladia looked toward Daneel, but he was standing motionless. She looked toward Giskard—the same. And then it seemed to her that, for just a moment, his head moved—very slightly—up and down.

She had to trust him.

She said, "Well, then, I'll come with you. These two robots are all I will need."

PART TWO
SOLARIA

Chapter 5

The Abandoned World

14.

FOR THE FIFTH TIME in her life, Gladia found herself on a spaceship. She did not remember, offhand, exactly how long ago it had been that she and Santirix had gone together to the world of Euterpe because its rain forests were widely recognized as incomparable, especially under the romantic glow of its bright satellite, Gemstone.

The rain forest had, indeed, been lush and green, with the trees carefully planted in rank and file and the animal life thoughtfully selected so as to provide color and delight, while avoiding venomous or other unpleasant creatures.

The satellite, fully 150 kilometers in diameter, was close enough to Euterpe to shine like a brilliant dot of sparkling light. It was so close to the planet that one could see it sweep west to east across the sky, outstripping the planet's slower rotational motion. It brightened as it rose toward zenith and dimmed as it dropped toward the horizon again. One watched it with fascination the first night, with less the second, and with a vague discontent the third—assuming the sky was clear on those nights, which it usually wasn't.

The native Euterpans, she noted, never looked at it, though they praised it loudly to the tourists, of course.

On the whole, Gladia had enjoyed the trip well enough, but what she remembered most keenly was the joy of her return to Aurora and her decision not to travel again except under dire need. (Come to think of it, it had to be at least eight decades ago.)

For a while, she had lived with the uneasy fear that her husband would insist on another trip, but he never mentioned one. It might well be, she sometimes thought at that time, that he had come to the same decision she had and feared she might be the one to want to travel.

It didn't make them unusual to avoid trips. Aurorans generally—Spacers generally, for that matter—tended to be stay-at-homes. Their worlds, their establishments, were too comfortable. After all, what pleasure could be greater than that of being taken care of by your own robots, robots who knew your every signal, and, for that matter, knew your ways and desires even without being told.

She stirred uneasily. Was that what D.G. had meant when he spoke of the decadence of a roboticized society?

But now she was back again in space, after all that time. And on an Earth ship, too.

She hadn't seen much of it, but the little she had glimpsed made her terribly uneasy. It seemed to be nothing but straight lines, sharp angles, and smooth surfaces. Everything that wasn't *stark* had been eliminated, apparently. It was as though nothing must exist but functionality. Even though she didn't know what was exactly functional about any particular object on the ship, she felt it to be all that was required, that nothing was to be allowed to interfere with taking the shortest distance between two points.

On everything Auroran (on everything Spacer, one might almost say, though Aurora was the most advanced in that respect), everything existed in layers. Functionality was at the bottom—one could not entirely rid one's self of that, except in what was pure ornament—but overlying that there was always something to satisfy the eyes and the senses, generally; and overlying *that*, something to satisfy the spirit.

How much better that was! —Or did it represent such an exuberance of human creativity that Spacers could no longer live with the unadorned Universe—and was that bad? Was the future to belong to these from-here-to-there geometrizers? Or was it just that the Settlers had not yet learned the sweetnesses of life?

But then, if life had so many sweetnesses to it, why had she found so few for herself?

She had nothing really to do on board this ship but to ponder and reponder such questions. This D.G., this Elijah-descended barbarian, had put it into her head with his calm assumption that the Spacer worlds were dying, even though he could see all about him even during the shortest stay on Aurora (surely, he would have to) that it was deeply embedded in wealth and security.

She had tried to escape her own thoughts by staring at the holofilms she had been supplied with and watching, with moderate curiosity, the images flickering and capering on the projection surface, as the adventure story (all were adventure stories) hastened from event to event with little time left for conversation and none for thought—or enjoyment, either. Very like their furniture.

D.G. stepped in when she was in the middle of one of the films, but had stopped really paying attention. She was not caught by surprise. Her robots, who guarded her doorway, signaled his coming in ample time and would not have allowed him to enter if she were not in a position to receive him. Daneel entered with him.

D.G. said, "How are you doing?" Then, as her hand touched a contact and the images faded, shriveled, and were gone, he said, "You don't have to turn it off. I'll watch it with you."

"That's not necessary," she said. "I've had enough."

"Are you comfortable?"

"Not entirely. I am—isolated."

"Sorry! But then, I was isolated on Aurora. They would allow none of my men to come with me."

"Are you having your revenge?"

"Not at all. For one thing, I allowed you two robots of your choice to accompany you. For another, it is not I but my crew who enforce this. They don't like either Spacers or robots. —But why do you mind? Doesn't this isolation lessen your fear of infection?"

Gladia's eyes were haughty, but her voice sounded weary. "I wonder if I haven't grown too old to fear infection. In many ways, I think I have lived long enough. Then, too, I have my gloves, my nose filters, and—if necessary —my mask. And besides, I doubt that you will trouble to touch me."

"Nor will anyone else," said D.G. with a sudden edge of grimness to his voice, as his hand wandered to the object at the right side of his hip.

Her eyes followed the motion. "What is that?" she asked.

D.G. smiled and his beard seemed to glitter in the light. There were occasional reddish hairs among the brown. "A weapon," he said and drew it. He held it by a molded hilt that bulged above his hand as though the force of his grip were squeezing it upward. In front, facing Gladia, a thin cylinder stretched some fifteen centimeters forward. There was no opening visible.

"Does that kill people?" Gladia extended her hand toward it.

D.G. moved it quickly away. "Never reach for someone's weapon, my lady. That is worse than bad manners, for any Settler is trained to react violently to such a move and you may be hurt."

Gladia, eyes wide, withdrew her hand and placed both behind her back. She said, "Don't threaten harm. Daneel has no sense of humor in that respect. On Aurora, no one is barbarous enough to carry weapons."

"Well," said D.G., unmoved by the adjective, "we don't have robots to protect us. —And this is not a killing device. It is, in some ways, worse. It emits a kind of vibration that stimulates those nerve endings responsible for the sensation of pain. It hurts a good deal worse than anything you can imagine. No one would willingly endure it twice and someone carrying this weapon rarely has to use it. We call it a neuronic whip."

Gladia frowned. "Disgusting! We have our robots, but they never hurt anyone except in unavoidable emergency—and then minimally."

D.G. shrugged. "That sounds very civilized, but a bit of pain—a bit of killing, even—is better than the decay of spirit brought about by robots. Besides, a neuronic whip is not intended to kill and your people have weapons on their spaceships that can bring about wholesale death and destruction."

"That's because we've fought wars early in our history, when our Earth heritage was still strong, but we've learned better."

"You used those weapons on Earth even after you supposedly learned better."

"That's—" she began and closed her mouth as though to bite off what she was about to say next.

D.G. nodded. "I know. You were about to say, 'That's different.' Think of that, my lady, if you should catch yourself wondering why my crew doesn't like Spacers. Or why I don't. —But you are going to be useful to me, my lady, and I won't let my emotions get in the way."

"How am I going to be useful to you?"

"You are a Solarian."

"You keep saying that. More than twenty decades have passed. I don't know what Solaria is like now. I know nothing about it. What was Baleyworld like twenty decades ago?"

"It didn't exist twenty decades ago, but Solaria did and I shall gamble that you will remember *something* useful."

He stood up, bowed his head briefly in a gesture of politeness that was almost mocking, and was gone.

15.

GLADIA MAINTAINED a thoughtful and troubled silence for a while and then she said, "He wasn't at all polite, was he?"

Daneel said, "Madam Gladia, the Settler is clearly under tension. He is heading toward a world on which two ships like his have been destroyed and their crews killed. He is going into great danger, as is his crew."

"You always defend any human being, Daneel," said Gladia resentfully. "The danger exists for me, too, and I am not facing it voluntarily, but that does not force *me* into rudeness."

Daneel said nothing.

Gladia said, "Well, maybe it does. I *have* been a little rude, haven't I?"

"I don't think the Settler minded," said Daneel. "Might I suggest, madam, that you prepare yourself for bed. It is quite late."

"Very well. I'll prepare myself for bed, but I don't think I feel relaxed enough to sleep, Daneel."

"Friend Giskard assures me you will, madam, and he is usually right about such things."

And she did sleep.

16.

DANEEL AND GISKARD stood in the darkness of Gladia's cabin.

Giskard said, "She will sleep soundly, friend Daneel, and she needs the rest. She faces a dangerous trip."

"It seemed to me, friend Giskard," said Daneel, "that you influenced her to agree to go. I presume you had a reason."

"Friend Daneel, we know so little about the nature of the crisis that is now facing the Galaxy that we cannot safely refuse any action that might increase our knowledge. We must know what is taking place on Solaria and the only way we can do so is to go there—and the only way we can go is for us to arrange for Madam Gladia to go. As for influencing her, that required scarcely a touch. Despite her loud statements to the contrary, she was eager to go. There was an overwhelming desire within her to see Solaria. It was a pain within her that would not cease until she went."

"Since you say so, it is so, yet I find it puzzling. Had she not frequently made it plain that her life on Solaria was unhappy, that she had completely adopted Aurora and never wished to go back to her original home?"

"Yes, that was there, too. It was quite plainly in her mind. Both emotions, both feelings, existed together and simultaneously. I have observed something of this sort in human minds frequently; two opposite emotions simultaneously present."

"Such a condition does not seem logical, friend Giskard."

"I agree and I can only conclude that human beings are not, at all times or in all respects, logical. That must be one reason that it is so difficult to work out the Laws governing human behavior. —In Madam Gladia's case, I have now and then been aware of this longing for Solaria. Ordinarily, it was well hidden, obscured by the far more intense antipathy she also felt for the world. When the news arrived that Solaria had been abandoned by its people, however, her feelings changed."

"Why so? What had the abandonment to do with the youthful experiences that led Madam Gladia to her antipathy? Or, having held in restraint her longing for the world during the decades when it was a working society, why should she lose that restraint once it became an abandoned planet and newly long for a world which must now be something utterly strange to her."

"I cannot explain, friend Daneel, since the more knowledge I gather of the human mind, the more despair I feel at being unable to understand it. It is not an unalloyed advantage to see into that mind and I often envy you the simplicity of behavior control that results from your inability to see below the surface."

Daneel persisted. "Have you guessed an explanation, friend Giskard?"

"I suppose she feels a sorrow for the empty planet. She deserted it twenty decades ago—"

"She was driven out."

"It seems to her, now, to have been a desertion and I imagine she plays with the painful thought that she had set an example; that if she had not left, no one else would have and the planet would still be populated and happy. Since I cannot read her thoughts, I am only groping backward, perhaps inaccurately, from her emotions."

"But she could not have set an example, friend Giskard. Since it is twenty decades since she left, there can be no verifiable causal connection between the much earlier event and the much later one."

"I agree, but human beings sometimes find a kind of pleasure in nursing painful emotions, in blaming themselves without reason or even against reason. —In any case, Madam Gladia felt so sharply the longing to return that I felt it was necessary to release the inhibitory effect that kept her from agreeing to go. It required the merest touch. Yet though I feel it necessary for her to go, since that means she will take us there, I have the uneasy feeling that the disadvantages might, just possibly, be greater than the advantages."

"In what way, friend Giskard?"

"Since the Council was eager to have Madam Gladia accompany the Settler, it may have been for the purpose of having Madam Gladia absent from Aurora during a crucial period when the defeat of Earth and its Settler worlds is being prepared."

Daneel seemed to be considering that statement. At least it was only after a distinct pause that he said, "What purpose would be served, in your opinion, in having Madam Gladia absent?"

"I cannot decide that, friend Daneel. I want your opinion."

"I have not considered this matter."

"Consider it now!" If Giskard had been human, the remark would have been an order.

There was an even longer pause and then Daneel said, "Friend Giskard, until the moment that Dr. Mandamus appeared in Madam Gladia's establishment, she had never shown any concern about international affairs. She was a friend of Dr. Fastolfe and of Elijah Baley, but this friendship was one of personal affection and did not have an ideological basis. Both of them, moreover, are now gone from us. She has an antipathy toward Dr. Amadiro and that is returned, but this is also a personal matter. The antipathy is two centuries old and neither has done anything material about it but have merely each remained stubbornly antipathetic. There can be no reason for Dr. Amadiro—who is now the dominant influence in the Council—to fear Madam Gladia or to go to the trouble of removing her."

Giskard said, "You overlook the fact that in removing Madam Gladia, he also removes you and me. He would, perhaps, feel quite certain Madam Gladia would not leave without us, so can it be us he considers dangerous?"

"In the course of our existence, friend Giskard, we have never, in any way, given any appearance of having endangered Dr. Amadiro. What cause has he to fear us? He does not know of your abilities or of how you have made use of them. Why, then, should he take the trouble to remove us, temporarily, from Aurora?"

"Temporarily, friend Daneel? Why do you assume it is a temporary removal he plans? He knows, it may be, more than the Settler does of the trouble on Solaria and knows, also, that the Settler and his crew will be surely destroyed—and Madam Gladia and you and I with them. Perhaps the destruction of the Settler's ship is his main aim, but he would consider the end of Dr. Fastolfe's friend and Dr. Fastolfe's robots to be an added bonus."

Daneel said, "Surely he would not risk war with the Settler worlds, for that may well come if the Settler's ship is destroyed and the minute pleasure of having us destroyed, when added in, would not make the risk worthwhile."

"Is it not possible, friend Daneel, that war is exactly what Dr. Amadiro has in mind; that it involves no risk in his estimation, so that getting rid of us at the same time adds to his pleasure without increasing a risk that does not exist?"

Daneel said calmly, "Friend Giskard, that is not reasonable. In any war fought under present conditions, the Settlers would win. They are better suited, psychologically, to the rigors of war. They are more scattered and can, therefore, more successfully carry on hit-and-run tactics. They have comparatively little to lose in their relatively primitive worlds, while the Spacers have much to lose in their comfortable, highly organized ones. If the Settlers were willing to offer to exchange destruction of one of their worlds for one of the Spacers', the Spacers would have to surrender at once."

"But would such a war be fought 'under present conditions'? What if the Spacers had a new weapon that could be used to defeat the Settlers quickly? Might that not be the very crisis we are now facing?"

"In that case, friend Giskard, the victory could be better and more effectively gained in a surprise attack. Why go to the trouble of instigating a war, which the Settlers might begin by a surprise raid on Spacer worlds that would do considerable damage?"

"Perhaps the Spacers need to test the weapon and the destruction of a series of ships on Solaria represents the testing."

"The Spacers would have been most uningenious if they could not have found a method of testing that would not give away the new weapon's existence."

It was now Giskard's turn to consider. "Very well, then, friend Daneel, how would you explain this trip we are on? How would you explain the Council's willingness—even eagerness—to have us accompany the Settler? The Settler said they would order Gladia to go and, in effect, they did."

"I have not considered the matter, friend Giskard."

"Then consider it now." Again it had the flavor of an order.

Daneel said, "I will do so."

There was silence, one that grew protracted, but Giskard by no word or sign showed any impatience as he waited.

Finally, Daneel said—slowly, as though he were feeling his way along strange avenues of thought—"I do not think that Baleyworld—or any of the Settler worlds—has a clear right to appropriate robotic property on Solaria. Even though the Solarians have themselves left or have, perhaps, died out, Solaria remains a Spacer world, even if an unoccupied one. Certainly, the remaining forty-nine Spacer worlds would reason so. Most of all, Aurora would reason so—if it felt in command of the situation."

Giskard considered that. "Are you now saying, friend Daneel, that the destruction of the two Settler ships was the Spacer way of enforcing their proprietorship of Solaria?"

Daneel said, "No, that would not be the way if Aurora, the leading Spacer power, felt in command of the situation. Aurora would then simply have announced that Solaria, empty or not, was off-limits to Settler vessels and would have threatened reprisals against the home worlds if any Settler vessel entered the Solarian planetary system. And they would have established a cordon of ships and sensory stations about that planetary system. There was no such warning, no such action, friend Giskard. Why, then, destroy ships that might have been kept away from the world quite easily in the first place?"

"But the ships *were* destroyed, friend Daneel. Will you make use of the basic illogicality of the human mind as an explanation?"

"Not unless I have to. Let us for the moment take that destruction simply as given. Now consider the consequence— The captain of a single Settler vessel approaches Aurora, demands permission to discuss the situation with the Council, insists on taking an Auroran citizen with him to investigate events on Solaria, and the Council gives in to everything. If destroying the ships without prior warning is too strong an action for Aurora, giving in to the Settler captain so cravenly is far too weak an action. Far from seeking a war, Aurora, in giving in, seems to be willing to do anything at all to ward off the possiblity of war."

"Yes," said Giskard, "I see that this is a possible way of interpreting events. But what follows?"

"It seems to me," said Daneel, "that the Spacer worlds are not yet so weak that they must behave with such servility—and, even if they were, the pride of centuries of overlordship would keep them from doing so. It must be something other than weakness that is driving them. I have pointed out that they cannot be deliberately instigating a war, so it is much more likely that they are playing for time."

"To what end, friend Daneel?"

"They want to destroy the Settlers, but they are not yet prepared. They let this Settler have what he wants, to avoid a war until they are ready to fight one on their own terms. I am only surprised that they did not offer to send an Auroran warship with him. If this analysis is correct—and I think it is—Aurora cannot possibly have had anything to do with the incidents on Solaria. They would not indulge in pinpricks that could only serve to alert the Settlers before they are ready with something devastating."

"Then how account for these pinpricks, as you call them, friend Daneel?"

"We will find out perhaps when we land on Solaria. It may be that Aurora is as curious as we are and the Settlers are and that that is another reason why they have cooperated with the captain, even to the point of allowing Madam Gladia to accompany him."

It was now Giskard's turn to remain silent. Finally he said, "And what is this mysterious devastation that they plan?"

"Earlier, we spoke of a crisis arising from the Spacer plan to defeat Earth, but we used Earth in its general sense, implying the Earthpeople together with their descendents on the Settler worlds. However, if we seriously suspect the preparation of a devastating blow that will allow the Spacers to defeat their enemies at a stroke, we can perhaps refine our view. Thus, they cannot be planning a blow at a Settler world. Individually, the Settler worlds are dispensable and the remaining Settler worlds will promptly strike back. Nor can they be planning a blow at several or at all the Settler worlds. There are too many of them; they are too diffusely spread. It is not likely that all the strikes will succeed and those Settler worlds that survive will, in fury and despair, bring devastation upon the Spacer worlds."

"You reason, then, friend Daneel, that it will be a blow at Earth itself."

"Yes, friend Giskard. Earth contains the vast majority of the short-lived human beings; it is the perennial source of emigrants to the Settler worlds and is the chief raw material for the founding of new ones; it is the revered homeland of all the Settlers. If Earth were somehow destroyed, the Settler movement might never recover."

"But would not the Settler worlds then retaliate as strongly and as forcefully as they would if one of themselves were destroyed? That would seem to me to be inevitable."

"And to me, friend Giskard. Therefore, it seems to me that unless the

Spacer worlds have gone insane, the blow would have to be a subtle one; one for which the Spacer worlds would seem to bear no responsibility."

"Why not such a subtle blow against the Settler worlds, which hold most of the actual war potential of the Earthpeople?"

"Either because the Spacers feel the blow against Earth would be more psychologically devastating or because the nature of the blow is such that it would work only against Earth and not against the Settler worlds. I suspect the latter, since Earth is a unique world and has a society that is not like that of any other world—Settler or, for that matter, Spacer."

"To summarize, then, friend Daneel, you come to the conclusion that the Spacers are planning a subtle blow against Earth that will destroy it without evidence of themselves as the cause, and one that would not work against any other world, and that they are not yet ready to launch that blow."

"Yes, friend Giskard, but they may soon be ready—and once they are ready, they will have to strike immediately. Any delay will increase the chance of some leak that will give them away."

"To deduce all this, friend Daneel, from the small indications we have is most praiseworthy. Now tell me the nature of the blow. What is it, precisely, that the Spacers plan?"

"I have come this far, friend Giskard, across very shaky ground, without being certain that my reasoning is entirely sound. But even if we suppose it is, I can go no further. I fear I do not know and cannot imagine what the nature of the blow might be."

Giskard said, "But we cannot take appropriate measures to counteract the blow and resolve the crisis until we know what its nature will be. If we must wait until the blow reveals itself by its results, it will then be too late to do anything."

Daneel said, "If any Spacer knows the nature of the forthcoming event, it would be Amadiro. Could you not force Amadiro to announce it publicly and thus alert the Settlers and make it unusable?"

"I could not do that, friend Daneel, without virtually destroying his mind. I doubt that I could hold it together long enough to allow him to make the announcement. I could not do such a thing."

"Perhaps, then," said Daneel, "we may console ourselves with the thought that my reasoning is wrong and that no blow against Earth is being prepared."

"No," said Giskard. "It is my feeling that you are right and that we must simply wait—helplessly."

17.

GLADIA WAITED, with an almost painful anticipation, for the conclusion of the final Jump. They would then be close enough to Solaria to make out its sun as a disk.

It would just be a disk, of course, a featureless circle of light, subdued to the point where it could be watched unblinkingly after that light had passed through the appropriate filter.

Its appearance would not be unique. All the stars that carried, among their planets, a habitable world in the human sense had a long list of property requirements that ended by making them all resemble one another. They were all single stars—all not much larger or much smaller than the sun that shone on Earth—none too active, or too old, or too quiet, or too young, or too hot, or too cool, or too offbeat in chemical composition. All had sunspots and flares and prominences and all looked just about the same to the eye. It took careful spectroheliography to work out the details that made each star unique.

Nevertheless, when Gladia found herself staring at a circle of light that was absolutely nothing more than a circle of light to her, she found her eyes welling with tears. She had never given the sun a thought when she had lived on Solaria; it was just the eternal source of light and heat, rising and falling in a steady rhythm. When she had left Solaria, she had watched that sun disappear behind her with nothing but a feeling of thankfulness. She had no memory of it that she valued.

—Yet she was weeping silently. She was ashamed of herself for being so affected for no reason that she could explain, but that didn't stop the weeping.

She made a stronger effort when the signal light gleamed. It had to be D.G. at the door; no one else would approach her cabin.

Daneel said, "Is he to enter, madam? You seem emotionally moved."

"Yes, I'm emotionally moved, Daneel, but let him in. I imagine it won't come as a surprise to him."

Yet it did. At least, he entered with a smile on his bearded face—and that smile disappeared almost at once. He stepped back and said in a low voice, "I will return later."

"Stay!" said Gladia harshly. "This is nothing. A silly reaction of the moment." She sniffed and dabbed angrily at her eyes. "Why are you here?"

"I wanted to discuss Solaria with you. If we succeed with a microadjustment, we'll land tomorrow. If you're not quite up to a discussion now—"

"I am *quite* up to it. In fact, I have a question of you. Why is it we took three Jumps to get here? One Jump would have been sufficient. One was sufficient when I was taken from Solaria to Aurora twenty decades ago. Surely the technique of space travel has not retrogressed since."

D.G.'s grin returned. "Evasive action. If an Auroran ship was following us, I wanted to—confuse it, shall we say?"

"Why should one follow us?"

"Just a thought, my lady. The Council was a little overeager to help, I thought. They suggested that an Auroran ship join me in my expedition to Solaria."

"Well, it might have helped, mightn't it?"

"Perhaps—if I were quite certain that Aurora wasn't behind all this. I told the Council quite plainly that I would do without—or, rather"—he pointed his finger at Gladia—"just with you. Yet might not the Council send a ship to accompany me even against my wish—out of pure kindness of heart, let us say? Well, I still don't want one; I expect enough trouble without having to look nervously over my shoulder at every moment. So I made myself hard to follow. —How much do you know about Solaria, my lady?"

"Haven't I told you often enough? Nothing! Twenty decades have passed."

"Now, madam, I'm talking about the psychology of the Solarians. That can't have changed in merely twenty decades. —Tell me why they have abandoned their planet."

"The story, as I've heard it," said Gladia calmly, "is that their population has been steadily declining. A combination of premature deaths and very few births is apparently responsible."

"Does that sound reasonable to you?"

"Of course it does. Births have always been few." Her face twisted in memory. "Solarian custom does not make impregnation easy, either naturally, artificially, or ectogenetically."

"You never had children, madam?"

"Not on Solaria."

"And the premature death?"

"I can only guess. I suppose it arose out of a feeling of failure. Solaria was clearly not working out, even though the Solarians had placed a great deal of emotional fervor into their world's having the ideal society—not only one that was better than Earth had ever had, but more nearly perfect than that of any other Spacer world."

"Are you saying that Solaria was dying of the collective broken heart of its people?"

"If you want to put it in that ridiculous way," said Gladia, displeased.

D.G. shrugged. "It seems to be what you're saying. But would they really leave? Where would they go? How would they live?"

"I don't know."

"But, Madam Gladia, it is well known that Solarians are accustomed to enormous tracts of land, serviced by many thousands of robots, so that each Solarian is left in almost complete isolation. If they abandon Solaria, where can they go to find a society that would humor them in this fashion? Have they, in fact, gone to any of the other Spacer worlds?"

"Not as far as I know. But then, I'm not in their confidence."

"Can they have found a new world for themselves? If so, it would be a raw one and require much in the way of terraforming. Would they be ready for that?"

Gladia shook her head. "I don't know."

"Perhaps they haven't really left."

"Solaria, I understand, gives every evidence of being empty."

"What evidence is that?"

"All interplanetary communication has ceased. All radiation from the planet, except that consistent with robot work or clearly due to natural causes has ceased."

"How do you know that?"

"That is the report on the Auroran news."

"Ah! The report! Could it be that someone is lying?"

"What would be the purpose of such a lie?" Gladia stiffened at the suggestion.

"So that our ships would be lured to the world and destroyed."

"That's ridiculous, D.G." Her voice grew sharper. "What would the Spacers gain by destroying two trading vessels through so elaborate a subterfuge?"

"Something has destroyed two Settler vessels on a supposedly empty planet. How do you explain that?"

"I can't. I presume we are going to Solaria in order to find an explanation."

D.G. regarded her gravely. "Would you be able to guide me to the section of the world that was yours when you lived on Solaria?"

"My estate?" She returned his stare, astonished.

"Wouldn't you like to see it again?"

Gladia's heart skipped a beat. "Yes, I would, but why my place?"

"The two ships that were destroyed landed in widely different spots on the planet and yet each was destroyed fairly quickly. Though every spot may be deadly, it seems to me that yours might be less so than others."

"Why?"

"Because there we might receive help from the robots. You would know them, wouldn't you? They do last more than twenty decades, I suppose. Daneel and Giskard have. And those that were there when you lived on your estate would still remember you, wouldn't they? They would treat you as their mistress and recognize the duty they owed you even beyond that which they would owe to ordinary human beings."

Gladia said, "There were ten thousand robots on my estate. I knew perhaps three dozen by sight. Most of the rest I never saw and they may not have ever seen me. Agricultural robots are not very advanced, you know, nor are forestry robots or mining robots. The household robots would still remember me—if they have not been sold or transferred since I left. Then, too, accidents happen and some robots *don't* last twenty decades. —Besides, whatever you may think of robot memory, human memory is fallible and I might remember none of them."

"Even so," said D.G., "can you direct me to your estate?"

"By latitude and longitude? No."

"I have charts of Solaria. Would that help?"

"Perhaps approximately. It's in the south-central portion of the northern continent of Heliona."

"And once we're approximately there, can you make use of landmarks for greater precision—if we skim the Solarian surface?"

"By seacoasts and rivers, you mean?"

"Yes."

"I *think* I can."

"Good! And meanwhile, see if you can remember the names and appearances of any of your robots. It may prove the difference between living and dying."

18.

D. G. BALEY SEEMED a different person with his officers. The broad smile was not evident, nor the easy indifference to danger. He sat, poring over the charts, with a look of intense concentration on his face.

He said, "*If* the woman is correct, we've got the estate pinned down within narrow limits—and if we move into the flying mode, we should get it exactly before too long."

"Wasteful of energy, Captain," muttered Jamin Oser, who was second-in-command. He was tall and, like D.G., well bearded. The beard was russet-colored, as were his eyebrows, which arched over bright blue eyes. He looked rather old, but one got the impression that this was due to experience rather than years.

"Can't help it," said D.G. "If we had the antigravity that the technos keep promising us just this side of eternity, it would be different."

He stared at the chart again and said, "She says it would be along this river about sixty kilometers upstream from where it runs into this larger one. *If* she is correct."

"You keep doubting it," said Chandrus Nadirhaba, whose insigne showed him to be Navigator and responsible for bringing the ship down in the correct spot—or, in any case, the indicated spot. His dark skin and neat mustache accentuated the handsome strength of his face.

"She's recalling a situation over a time gap of twenty decades," said D.G. "What details would you remember of a site you haven't seen for just three decades? She's not a robot. She may have forgotten."

"Then what was the point of bringing her?" muttered Oser. "And the other one and the robot? It unsettles the crew and I don't exactly like it, either."

D.G. looked up, eyebrows bunching together. He said in a low voice, "It doesn't matter on this ship what you don't like or what the crew doesn't like, mister. I have the responsibility and I make the decisions. We're all liable to be dead within six hours of landing unless that woman can save us."

Nadirhaba said coolly, "If we die, we die. We wouldn't be Traders if we didn't know that sudden death was the other side of big profits. And for this mission, we're all volunteers. Just the same, it doesn't hurt to know where the death's coming from, Captain. If you've figured it out, does it have to be a secret?"

"No, it doesn't. The Solarians are supposed to have left, but suppose a couple of hundred stayed quietly behind just to watch the store, so to speak."

"And what can they do to an armed ship, Captain? Do they have a secret weapon?"

"Not so secret," said D.G. "Solaria is littered with robots. That's the whole reason Settler ships landed on the world in the first place. Each remaining Solarian might have a million robots at his disposal. An enormous army."

Eban Kalaya was in charge of communications. So far he had said nothing, aware as he was of his junior status, which seemed further marked by the fact that he was the only one of the four officers present without facial hair of any kind. Now he ventured a remark. "Robots," he said, "cannot injure human beings."

"So we are told," said D.G. dryly, "but what do *we* know about robots? What we do know is that two ships have been destroyed and about a hundred human beings—good Settlers all—have been killed on widely separated parts of a world littered with robots. How could it have been done except by robots? We don't know what kind of orders a Solarian might give robots or by what tricks the so-called First Law of Robotics might be circumvented.

"So we," he went on, "have to do a little circumventing of our own. As best as we can tell from the reports reaching us from the other ships before they were destroyed, all the men on board ship debarked on landing. It was an empty world after all and they wanted to stretch their legs, breathe fresh air, *and* look over the robots they had come to get. Their ships were unprotected and they themselves unready when the attack came.

"That won't happen this time. I'm getting off, but the rest of you are going to stay on board the ship or in its near vicinity."

Nadirhaba's dark eyes glared disapproval. "Why you, Captain? If you need someone to act as bait, anyone else can be spared more easily than you can be."

"I appreciate the thought, Navigator," said D.G., "but I will not be alone. Coming with me will be the Spacer woman and her companions. She is the one who is essential. She may know some of the robots; at any rate, some may know her. I am hoping that though the robots may have been ordered to attack us, they won't attack her."

"You mean they'll remember Ol' Missy and fall to their knees," said Nadirhaba dryly.

"If you want to put it that way. That's why I brought her and that's why we've landed on her estate. And I've got to be with her because I'm the one who knows her—somewhat—and I've got to see that she behaves. Once we have survived by using her as a shield and in that way have learned exactly what we're facing, we can proceed on our own. We won't need her any more."

Oser said, "And then what do we do with her? Jettison her into space?"

D.G. roared, "We take her back to Aurora!"

Oser said, "I'm bound to tell you, Captain, that the crew would consider that a wasteful and unnecessary trip. They will feel that we can simply leave her on this blasted world. It's where she comes from, after all."

"Yes," said D.G. "That will be the day, won't it, when I take orders from the crew."

"I'm sure you won't," said Oser, "but the crew has its opinions and an unhappy crew makes for a dangerous voyage."

Chapter 6
The Crew

19.

GLADIA STOOD ON THE SOIL of Solaria. She smelled the vegetation—not quite the odors of Aurora—and at once she crossed the gap of twenty decades.

Nothing, she knew, could bring back associations in the way that odors could. Not sights, not sounds.

Just that faint, unique smell brought back childhood—the freedom of running about, with a dozen robots watching her carefully—the excitement of seeing other children sometimes, coming to a halt, staring shyly, approaching one another a half-step at a time, reaching out to touch, and then a robot saying, "Enough, Miss Gladia," and being led away—looking over the shoulder at the other child, with whom there was another set of attendant robots in charge.

She remembered the day that she was told that only by holovision would she see other human beings thereafter. Viewing, she was told—not seeing. The robots said "seeing" as though it were a word they must not say, so that they had to whisper it. She could see *them,* but they were not human.

It was not so bad at first. The images she could talk to were three-dimensional, free-moving. They could talk, run, turn cartwheels if they wished—but they could not be felt. And then she was told that she could actually see someone whom she had often viewed and whom she had liked. He was a grown man, quite a bit older than she was, though he looked quite young, as one did on Solaria. She would have permission to continue to see him—if she wished—whenever necessary.

She wished. She remembered how it was—*exactly* how it was on that first day. She was tongue-tied and so was he. They circled each other, afraid to touch. —But it was marriage.

Of course it was. And then they met again—seeing, not viewing, *because* it was marriage. They would finally touch each other. They were supposed to.

It was the most exciting day of her life—until it took place.

Fiercely, Gladia stopped her thoughts. Of what use to go on? She so warm and eager; he so cold and withdrawn. He continued to be cold. When he came to see her, at fixed intervals, for the rites that might (or might not) succeed in impregnating her, it was with such clear revulsion that she was soon longing for him to forget. But he was a man of duty and he never forgot.

Then came the time, years of dragging unhappiness later, when she found him dead, his skull crushed, and herself as the only possible suspect. Elijah Baley had saved her then and she had been taken away from Solaria and sent to Aurora.

Now she was back, smelling Solaria.

Nothing else was familiar. The house in the distance bore no resemblance to anything she remembered even faintly. In twenty decades it had been modified, torn down, rebuilt. She could not even gain any sense of familiarity with the ground itself.

She found herself reaching backward to touch the Settler ship that had brought her to this world that smelled like home but was home in no other way—just to touch something that was familiar by comparison.

Daneel, who stood next to her in the shadow of the ship, said, "Do you see the robots, Madam Gladia?"

There were a group of them, a hundred yards away, amid the trees of an orchard, watching solemnly, motionlessly, shining in the sun with the grayish well-polished metal finish Gladia remembered Solarian robots to have.

She said, "I do, Daneel."

"Is there anything familiar about them, madam?"

"Not at all. They seem to be new models. I can't remember them and I'm sure they can't remember me. If D.G. was expecting anything hopeful to come of my supposed familiarity with the robots on my estate, he will have to be disappointed."

Giskard said, "They do not seem to be doing anything, madam."

Gladia said, "That is understandable. We're intruders and they've come to observe us and to report on us in accordance with what must be standing orders. They have no one now to report to, however, and can merely silently observe. Without further orders, I presume they will do no more than that, but they won't cease doing so, either."

Daneel said, "It might be well, Madam Gladia, if we retired to our quarters on board ship. The captain is, I believe, supervising the construction of defenses and is not ready to go exploring yet. I suspect he will not approve your having left your quarters without his specific permission."

Gladia said haughtily, "I'm not going to delay stepping out onto the surface of my own world just to suit his whim."

"I understand, but members of the crew are engaged in the vicinity and I believe that some note your presence here."

"And are approaching," said Giskard. "If you would avoid infection—"

"I'm prepared," said Gladia. "Nose plugs and gloves."

Gladia did not understand the nature of the structures being put up on the flat ground about the ship. For the most part, the crewmen, absorbed in the construction, had not seen Gladia and her two companions, standing as they were in the shadows. (It was the warm season on this portion of Solaria, which had a tendency to grow warmer—and on other occasions, colder—than Aurora did, since the Solarian day was nearly six hours longer than the Auroran day.)

The crewmen approaching were five in number and one of them, the tallest and largest, pointed in the direction of Gladia. The other four looked, remained standing for a while as though merely curious, and then, at a gesture from the first, approached again, changing their angle slightly so as to head directly for the Auroran three.

Gladia watched them silently and with her eyebrows raised in contempt. Daneel and Giskard waited impassively.

Giskard said in a low voice to Daneel, "I do not know where the captain is. I cannot distinguish him from the crowd of crewmen in whose midst he must be."

"Shall we retire?" said Daneel aloud.

"That would be disgraceful," said Gladia. "This is *my* world."

She held her ground and the five crewmen came closer in leisurely fashion.

They had been working, doing hard physical labor (Like robots, thought Gladia with disdain) and they were sweating. Gladia became aware of the odor that reeked from them. That would have served to force her away more than threats would, but she held her ground even so. The nose plugs, she was sure, mitigated the effect of the smell.

The large crewman approached more closely than the others. His skin was bronzed. His bare arms glistened with moisture and with shining musculature. He might be thirty (as nearly as Gladia could judge the age of these short-lived beings) and if he were washed and properly dressed, he might prove quite presentable.

He said, "So you are the Spacer lady from Aurora that we've been carrying on our ship?" He spoke rather slowly, obviously trying to attain an aristocratic tinge to his Galactic. He failed, of course, and he spoke like a Settler—even more crudely than D.G. did.

Gladia said, establishing her territorial rights, "I am from Solaria, Settler," and stopped in confused embarrassment. She had spent so much time thinking of Solaria just now that twenty decades had dropped away and she had spoken with a thick Solarian accent. There was the broad "a" in Solaria and the rough "r," while the "I" sounded horribly like "Oi."

She said again, in a much lower, less commanding voice, but one in which the accent of Aurora University—the standard for Galactic speech through all the Spacer worlds—rang clear, "I am from Solaria, Settler."

The Settler laughed and turned to the others. "She speaks la-di-da, but she had to try. Right, mates?"

The others laughed, too, and one cried out, "Get her to talk some more, Niss. Maybe we can all learn to talk like Spacer birdies." And he placed one hand on his hip in as dainty a manner as he could manage, while holding the other hand out limply.

Niss said, still smiling, "Shut up, all of you." There was instant silence.

He turned to Gladia again, "I'm Berto Niss, First-Class Shipper. And your name, little woman?"

Gladia did not venture to speak again.

Niss said, "I'm being polite, little woman. I'm speaking gentlemanly. Spacer-like. I know you're old enough to be my great-grandmother. How old are you, little woman?"

"Four hundred," shouted one of the crewmen from behind Niss, "but she doesn't look it!"

"She doesn't look one hundred," said another.

"She looks suitable for a little ding-donging," said a third, "and hasn't had any for a long time, I guess. Ask her if she'd want some, Niss. Be polite and ask if we can take turns."

Gladia flushed angrily and Daneel said, "First-Class Shipper Niss, your companions are offending Madam Gladia. Would you retire?"

Niss turned to look at Daneel, whom, till now, he had totally ignored. The smile vanished from his face and he said, "Look, you. This little lady is off-limits. The captain said so. We won't bother her. Just a little harmless talk. That thing there is a robot. We won't bother with him and he can't hurt us. We know the Three Laws of Robotics. We order him to stay away from us, see. But *you* are a Spacer and the captain has give us no orders about you. So you"—he pointed a finger—"stay out of this and don't interfere or you'll get your pretty skin all bruised up and then you might cry."

Daneel said nothing.

Niss nodded his head. "Good. I like to see someone smart enough not to start anything he can't finish."

He turned to Gladia, "Now, little Spacer woman, we will leave you alone because the captain doesn't want you bothered. If one of the men here made a crude remark, that's only natural. Just shake hands and let's be friends—Spacer, Settler, what's the difference?"

He thrust out his hand toward Gladia, who shrank away in horror. Daneel's hand moved outward in a flick that was almost too fast to see and caught Niss's wrist, "First-Class Shipper Niss," he said quietly, "do not attempt to touch the lady."

Niss looked down at his hand and at the fingers that enclosed his wrist firmly. He said in a low and menacing growl, "You have till the count of three to let go."

Daneel's hand fell away. He said, "I must do as you say for I do not wish to harm you, but I must protect the lady—and if she doesn't wish to be touched, as I believe she doesn't, I may be forced into a position where I must cause you pain. Please accept my assurance that I will do all I can to minimize that."

One of the crewmen shouted joyously, "Give it to him, Niss. He's a talker."

Niss said, "Look, Spacer, twice I told you to keep out and you touched me once. Now I tell you a third time and that's it. Make a move, say a word, and I take you apart. This little woman is going to shake hands, that's all, friendly-like. Then we all go. Fair enough?"

Gladia said in a low choking voice. "I won't be touched by him. Do what is necessary."

Daneel said, "Sir, with all due respect, the lady does not wish to be touched. I must ask you—all of you—to leave."

Niss smiled and one large arm moved as though to brush Daneel to one side—and to do it hard.

Daneel's left arm flickered and once again Niss was held by the wrist. "Please go, sir," said Daneel.

Niss's teeth continued to show, but he was no longer smiling. Violently, he brought his arm up. Daneel's enclosing hand moved up for a short distance, slowed, and came to a halt. His face showed no strain. His hand moved down, dragging Niss's arm with it, and then, with a rapid twist, he bent Niss's arm behind the Settler's broad back and held it there.

Niss, who found himself unexpectedly with his back to Daneel, brought his other arm up and over his head, groping for Daneel's neck. His other wrist was seized and pulled down farther than it could easily go and Niss grunted in clear misery.

The other four crewmen, who had been watching in eager anticipation, remained in place now, motionless, silent, mouths open.

Niss, staring at them, grunted, "Help me!"

Daneel said, "They will not help you, sir, for the captain's punishment will be all the worse if they try. I must ask you now to assure me that you will no longer trouble Madam Gladia and that you will leave quietly, all of you. Otherwise, I very much regret, First-Class Shipper, that I must pull your arms out of their sockets."

As he said that, he tightened his grip on either wrist and Niss emitted a muffled grunt.

"My apologies, sir," said Daneel, "but I am under the strictest orders. May I have your assurance?"

Niss kicked backward with sudden viciousness, but well before his heavy boot could make contact, Daneel had faded to one side and pulled him off-balance. He went facedown heavily.

"May I have your assurance, sir?" said Daneel, now pulling gently at the two wrists so that the crewman's arms lifted slightly up from the back.

Niss howled and said, half-incoherent, "I give in. Let go."

Daneel let go at once and stepped back. Slowly and painfully, Niss rolled over, moving his arms slowly and rotating his wrists with a twisted grimace.

Then, when his right arm moved near the holster he wore, he snatched clumsily at his sidearm.

Daneel's foot came down on his hand and pinned it to the ground. "Don't do that, sir, or I may be forced to break one or more of the small bones in your hand." He bent down and extracted Niss's blaster from its holster. "Now stand up."

"Well, Mr. Niss," came another voice. "Do as you are told and stand up."

D.G. Baley was standing at their side, beard bristling, face slightly flushed, but his voice was dangerously calm.

"You four," he said, "hand me your sidearms, one at a time. Come on. Move a little faster. One—two—three—four. Now continue to stand there at attention. Sir"—this to Daneel—"give me that sidearm you are holding. Good. Five. And now, Mr. Niss, at attention." And he placed the blasters on the ground beside him.

Niss stiffened to attention, eyes bloodshot, face contorted, in obvious pain.

"Would someone," said D.G., "please say what has been going on?"

"Captain," said Daneel quickly, "Mr. Niss and I have had a playful altercation. No harm has been done."

"Mr. Niss, however, looks somewhat harmed," said D.G.

"No permanent harm, Captain," said Daneel.

"I see. Well, we'll get back to this later. —Madam"—he turned on his heel to address Gladia—"I don't recall that I gave you permission to emerge from the ship. You will go back to your cabin with your two companions at once. I am captain here and this is not Aurora. Do as I say!"

Daneel placed an apologetic hand on Gladia's elbow. Her chin lifted, but she turned and went up the gangplank and into the ship, Daneel at her side, Giskard following.

D.G. then turned to the crewmen. "You five," he said, his voice never lifting from its flat calm, "come with me. We'll get to the bottom of this— or of you." And he gestured to a petty officer to pick up the sidearms and take them away.

20.

D.G. STARED AT the five grimly. He was in his own quarters, the only portion of the ship that had a semblance of size to it and the beginnings of an appearance of luxury.

He said, pointing to each in turn, "Now, this is the way we'll work it. *You* tell me exactly what happened, word for word, motion for motion. When you're finished, *you* tell me anything that was wrong or left out. Then *you* the same, and then *you*, and then I'll get to you, Niss. I expect that you were all out of order, that you all did something unusually stupid that earned you all, but especially Niss, considerable humiliation. If, in your story, it would appear that you did nothing wrong and suffered no humiliation, then I'll know you're lying, especially as the Spacer woman will surely tell me what happened—and I intend to believe every word she says. A lie will make matters worse for you than anything you've actually done. Now," he barked, *"start!"*

The first crewman stumbled hastily through the story, and then the second, somewhat correcting, somewhat expanding, then the third and the fourth. D.G. listened, stony-faced, to the recital, then motioned Berto Niss to one side.

He spoke to the other four, "And while Niss was getting his face rightly mashed into the dirt by the Spacer, what were you four doing? Watching? Scared to move? All four of you? Against one man?"

One of the men broke the thickening silence to say, "It all happened so quick, Captain. We were just getting set to move in and then it was all over."

"And what were you getting ready to do in case you did manage to get to move someday?"

"Well, we were going to pull the Spacer foreigner off our mate."

"Do you think you could have?"

This time no one offered to make a sound.

D.G. leaned toward them. "Now, here's the situation. You had no business interfering with the foreigners, so you're fined one week's pay each. And now let's get something straight. If you tell what has happened to anyone else—in the crew or out, now or ever, whether drunk or sober—you'll be broken, every one of you, to apprentice shipper. It doesn't matter which one of you talks, you'll all four be broken, so keep an eye on each other. Now get to your assigned tasks and if you cross me at any time during this voyage, if you as much as hiccup against regulations, you'll be in the brig."

The four left, mournful, hangdog, tight-lipped. Niss remained, a bruise developing on his face, his arms clearly in discomfort.

D.G. regarded him with a threatening quiet, while Niss stared to the left, to the right, at his feet, everywhere but at the face of the captain. It was only when Niss's eyes, running out of evasion, caught the glare of the captain that D.G. said, "Well, you look very handsome, now that you have tangled with a sissy Spacer half your size. Next time you better hide when one of them shows up."

"Yes, Captain," said Niss miserably.

"Did you or did you not, Niss, hear me in my briefing, before we left Aurora, say that the Spacer woman and her companions were on no account to be disturbed or spoken to?"

"Captain, I wanted only a polite howdydo. We was curious for a closer look. No harm meant."

"You meant no harm? You asked how old she was. Was that your business?"

"Just curious. Wanted to know."

"One of you made a sexual suggestion."

"Not me, Captain."

"Someone else? Did you apologize for it?"

"To a Spacer?" Niss sounded horrified.

"Certainly. You were going against my orders."

"I meant no harm," said Niss doggedly.

"You meant no harm to the man?"

"He put his hand on me, Captain."

"I know he did. Why?"

"Because he was ordering me around."

"And you wouldn't stand for it?"

"Would you, Captain?"

"All right, then. You didn't stand for it. You fell down for it. Right on your face. How did that happen?"

"I don't rightly know, Captain. He was fast. Like the camera was sped up. And he had a grip like iron."

D.G. said, "So he did. What did you expect, you idiot? He *is* iron."

"Captain?"

"Niss, is it possible you don't know the story of Elijah Baley?"

Niss rubbed his ear in embarrassment. "I know he's your great-something-thing-grandfather, Captain."

"Yes, everyone knows that from my name. Have you ever viewed his life story?"

"I'm not a viewing man, Captain. Not on history." He shrugged and, as he did so, winced and made as though to rub his shoulder, then decided he didn't quite dare do so.

"Did you ever hear of R. Daneel Olivaw?"

Niss squeezed his brows together. "He was Elijah Baley's friend."

"Yes, he was. You do know something then. Do you know what the 'R' stands for in R. Daneel Olivaw?"

"It stands for 'Robot,' right? He was a robot friend. There was robots on Earth in them days."

"There were, Niss, and still are. But Daneel wasn't just a robot. He was a

Spacer robot who looked like a Spacer man. Think about it, Niss. Guess
who the Spacer man you picked a fight with really was."

Niss's eyes widened, his face reddened dully. "You mean that Spacer was
a ro—"

"That was R. Daneel Olivaw."

"But, Captain, that was two hundred years ago."

"Yes and the Spacer woman was a particular friend of my Ancestor Elijah. She's been alive for two hundred and thirty-three years, in case you still
want to know, and do you think a robot can't do as well as that? You were
trying to fight a robot, you great fool."

"Why didn't it say so?" Niss said with great indignation.

"Why should it? Did you ask? See here, Niss. You heard what I told the
others about telling this to anyone. It goes for you, too, but much more so.
They are only crewmen, but I had my eye on you for crew leader. *Had* my
eye on you. If you're going to be in charge of the crew, you've got to have
brains and not just muscle. So now it's going to be harder for you because
you're going to have to prove you have brains against my firm opinion that
you don't."

"Captain, I—"

"Don't talk. Listen. If this story gets out, the other four will be apprentice shippers, but you will be *nothing.* You will never go on shipboard again.
No ship will take you, I promise you that. Not as crew, not as passenger. Ask
yourself what kind of money you can make on Baleyworld—and doing
what? That's if you talk about this, or if you cross the Spacer woman in any
way, or even just look at her for more than half a second at a time, or at her
two robots. And you are going to have to see to it that no one else among
the crew is in the least offensive. You're responsible. —And you're fined two
weeks' pay."

"But, Captain," said Niss weakly, "the others—"

"I expected less from the others, Niss, so I fined them less. Get out of
here."

21.

D.G. PLAYED IDLY with the photocube that always stood on his desk. Each
time he turned it, it blackened, then cleared when stood upon one of its
sides as its base. When it cleared, the smiling three-dimensional image of a
woman's head could be seen.

Crew rumor was that each of the six sides lead to the appearance of a different woman. The rumor was quite correct.

Jamin Oser watched the flashing appearance and disappearance of images totally without interest. Now that the ship was secured—or as secured as it could be against attack of any expected variety—it was time to think of the next step.

D.G., however, was approaching the matter obliquely—or, perhaps, not approaching it at all. He said, "It was the woman's fault, of course."

Oser shrugged and passed his hand over his beard, as though he were reassuring himself that he, at least, was not a woman. Unlike D.G., Oser had his upper lip luxuriantly covered as well.

D.G. said, "Apparently, being on the planet of her birth removed any thought of discretion. She left the ship, even though I had asked her not to."

"You might have *ordered* her not to."

"I don't know that that would have helped. She's a spoiled aristocrat, used to having her own way and to ordering her robots about. Besides, I plan to use her and I want her cooperation, not her pouting. And again— she was the Ancestor's friend."

"And still alive," said Oser, shaking his head. "It makes the skin crawl. An old, old woman."

"I know, but she looks quite young. Still attractive. And nose in the air. Wouldn't retire when the crewmen approached, wouldn't shake hands with one of them. —Well, it's over."

"Still, Captain, was it the right thing to tell Niss he had tackled a robot?"

"Had to! Had to, Oser. If he thought he'd been beaten and humiliated before four of his mates by an effeminate Spacer half his size, he'd be useless to us forever. It would have broken him completely. And we don't want anything to happen that will start the rumor that Spacers—that *human* Spacers—are supermen. That's why I had to order them so strenuously not to talk about it. Niss will ride herd on all of them—and if it *does* get out, it will also get out that the Spacer was a robot. —But I suppose there was a good side to the whole thing."

"Where, Captain?" asked Oser.

"It got me to thinking about robots. How much do we know about them? How much do *you* know?"

Oser shrugged. "Captain, it's not something I think about much."

"Or something anyone else thinks about, either. At least, any Settler. We know that the Spacers have robots, depend on them, go nowhere without them, can't do a thing without them, are parasites on them, and we're sure they're fading away because of them. We know that Earth once had robots forced on them by the Spacers and that they are gradually disappearing from Earth and are not found at all in Earth Cities, only in the countryside. We know that the Settler worlds don't and won't have them anywhere—town or country. So Settlers never meet them on their own worlds and hardly ever on Earth." (His voice had a curious inflection each time he said "Earth," as though one could hear the capital, as though one could hear the words "home" and "mother" whispered behind it.) "What else do we know?"

Oser said, "There's the Three Laws of Robotics."

"Right," D.G. pushed the photocube to one side and leaned forward. "Especially the First Law. 'A robot may not injure a human being or, through inaction, allow a human being to come to harm.' Yes? Well, don't rely on it. It doesn't mean a thing. We all feel ourselves to be absolutely safe from robots because of that and that's fine if it gives us confidence, but not if it gives us *false* confidence. R. Daneel injured Niss and it didn't bother the robot at all, First Law or no First Law."

"He was defending—"

"Exactly. What if you must balance injuries? What if it was a case of either hurt Niss or allow your Spacer owner to come to harm? Naturally, she comes first."

"It makes sense."

"Of course it does. And here we are on a planet of robots, a couple of hundred million of them. What orders do they have? How do they balance the conflict between different harms? How can we be sure that none of them will touch us? Something on this planet has destroyed two ships already."

Oser said uneasily, "This R. Daneel is an unusual robot, looks more like a man than we do. It may be we can't generalize from him. That other robot, what's his name—"

"Giskard. It's easy to remember. My name is Daneel Giskard."

"I think of you as captain, Captain. Anyway, that R. Giskard just stood there and didn't do a thing. He looks like a robot and he acts like one. We've got lots of robots out there on Solaria watching us right now and they're not doing a thing, either. Just watching."

"And if there are some special robots that *can* harm us?"

"I think we're prepared for them."

"*Now* we are. That's why the incident with Daneel and Niss was a good thing. We've been thinking that we can only be in trouble if some of the Solarians are still here. They don't have to be. They can be gone. It may be that the robots—or at least some specially designed robots—can be dangerous. And if Lady Gladia can mobilize her robots in this place—it used to be her estate—and make them defend her and us, too, we may well be able to neutralize anything they've left behind."

"Can she do that?" said Oser.

"We're going to see," said D.G.

22.

"THANK YOU, DANEEL," Gladia said, "You did well." Her face seemed pinched together, however. Her lips were thin and bloodless, her cheeks pale. Then, in a lower voice, "I wish I had not come."

Giskard said, "It is a useless wish, Madam Gladia. Friend Daneel and I will remain outside the cabin to make sure you are not further disturbed."

The corridor was empty and remained so, but Daneel and Giskard managed to speak in sound-wave intensities below the human threshold, exchanging thoughts in their brief and condensed way.

Giskard said, "Madam Gladia made an injudicious decision in refusing to retire. That is clear."

"I presume, friend Giskard," said Daneel, "that there was no possibility of maneuvering her into changing that decision."

"It was far too firm, friend Daneel, and taken too quickly. The same was true of the intention of Niss, the Settler. Both his curiosity concerning Madam Gladia and his contempt and animosity toward you were too strong to manage without serious mental harm. The other four I could handle. It was quite possible to keep them from intervening. Their astonishment at your ability to handle Niss froze them naturally and I had only to strengthen that slightly."

"That was fortunate, friend Giskard. Had those four joined Mr. Niss, I would have been faced with the difficult choice of forcing Madam Gladia into a humiliating retreat or of badly damaging one or two of the Settlers to frighten off the rest. I think I would have had to choose the former alternative but it, too, would have caused me grave discomfort."

"You are well, friend Daneel?"

"Quite well. My damage to Mr. Niss was minimal."

"Physically, friend Daneel, it was. Within his mind, however, there was great humiliation, which was to him much worse than the physical damage.

Since I could sense that, I could not have done what you did so easily. And yet, friend Daneel—"

"Yes, friend Giskard?"

"I am disturbed over the future. On Aurora, through all the decades of my existence, I have been able to work slowly, to wait for opportunities of touching minds gently, without doing harm; of strengthening what is already there, of weakening what is already attenuated, of pushing gently in the direction of existing impulse. Now, however, we are coming to a time of crisis in which emotions will run high, decisions will be taken quickly, and events will race past us. If I am to do any good at all, I will have to act quickly, too, and the Three Laws of Robotics prevent me from doing so. It takes time to weigh the subtleties of comparative physical *and* mental harm. Had I been alone with Madam Gladia at the time of the Settlers' approach, I do not see what course I could have taken that I would not have recognized as entailing serious damage to Madam Gladia, to one or more of the Settlers, to myself—or possibly to all who were involved."

Daneel said, "What is there to do, friend Giskard?"

"Since it is impossible to modify the Three Laws, friend Daneel, once again we must come to the conclusion that there is nothing we can do but await failure."

Chapter 7

The Overseer

23.

IT WAS MORNING on Solaria, morning on the estate—*her* estate. Off in the distance was the establishment that might have been *her* establishment. Somehow twenty decades dropped away and Aurora seemed to her to be a far-off dream that had never happened.

She turned to D.G., who was tightening the belt about his thin outer garment, a belt from which two sidearms hung. On his left hip was the neuronic whip; on his right, something shorter and bulkier that she guessed was a blaster.

"Are we going to the house?" she asked.

"Eventually," said D.G. with a certain absence of mind. He was inspecting each sidearm in turn, holding one of them to his ear as though he were listening for a faint buzz that would tell him it was alive.

"Just the four of us?" She automatically turned her eyes to each of the others: D.G., Daneel—

She said to Daneel, "Where is Giskard, Daneel?"

Daneel said, "It seemed to him, Madam Gladia, that it would be wise to act as an advance guard. As a robot, he might not be noticeable among other robots—and if there should be anything wrong, he could warn us. In any case, he is more expendable than either yourself or the captain."

"Good robotic thinking," said D.G. grimly. "It's just as well. Come, we're moving forward now."

"Just the three of us?" said Gladia, a touch plaintively. "To be honest, I lack Giskard's robotic ability to accept expendability."

D.G. said, "We're all expendable, Lady Gladia. Two ships have been destroyed, every member of each crew indiscriminately brought to an end. There's no safety in numbers here."

"You're not making me feel any better, D.G."

"Then I'll try. The earlier ships were not prepared. Our ship is. And I'm prepared, too." He slapped his two hands to his hips. "And you've got a robot with you who has showed himself to be an efficient protector. What's more, you yourself are our best weapon. You know how to order robots to do what you want them to do and that may well be crucial. You are the only one with us who can do that and the earlier ships had no one at all of your caliber. Come, then—"

They moved forward. Gladia said, after a while, "We're not walking toward the house."

"No, not yet. First, we're walking toward a group of robots. You see them, I hope."

"Yes, I do, but they're not doing anything."

"No, they're not. There were many more robots present when we first landed. Most of them have gone, but these remain. Why?"

"If we ask them, they'll tell us."

"*You* will ask them, Lady Gladia."

"They'll answer you, D.G., as readily as they'll answer me. We're equally human."

D.G. stopped short and the other two stopped with him. He turned to Gladia and said, smiling, "My dear Lady Gladia, *equally* human? A Spacer and a Settler? Whatever has come over you?"

"We are equally human to a robot," she said waspishly. "And please don't play games. I did not play the game of Spacer and Earthman with your Ancestor."

D.G.'s smile vanished. "That's true. My apologies, my lady. I shall try to control my sense of the sardonic for, after all, on this world we are allies."

He said, a moment later, "Now, madam, what I want you to do is to find out what orders the robots have been given—if any; if there are any robots that might, by some chance, know you; if there are any human beings on the estate or on the world; or anything else it occurs to you to ask. They shouldn't be dangerous; they're robots and you're human; they can't hurt you. To be sure," he added, remembering, "your Daneel rather manhandled Niss, but that was under conditions that don't apply here. And Daneel may go with you."

Respectfully, Daneel said, "I would in any case accompany Lady Gladia, Captain. That is my function."

"Giskard's function, too, I imagine," said D.G., "and yet he's wandered off."

"For a purpose, Captain, that he discussed with me and that we agreed was an essential way of protecting Lady Gladia."

"Very well. You two move forward. I'll cover you both." He drew the weapon on his right hip. "If I call out 'Drop,' the two of you fall down instantly. This thing doesn't play favorites."

"Please don't use it as anything but a last resort, D.G.," said Gladia. "There would scarcely be an occasion to against robots. —Come, Daneel!"

Off she went, stepping forward rapidly and firmly toward the group of about a dozen robots that were standing just in front of a line of low bushes with the morning sun reflecting in glints here and there from their burnished exteriors.

24.

THE ROBOTS DID NOT retreat, nor did they advance. They remained calmly in place. Gladia counted them. Eleven in plain sight. There might be others, possibly, that were unseen.

They were designed Solaria-fashion. Very polished. Very smooth. No illusion of clothing and not much realism. They were almost like mathematical abstractions of the human body, with no two of them quite alike.

She had the feeling that they were by no means as flexible or complex as Auroran robots but were more single-mindedly adapted to specific tasks.

She stopped at least four meters from the line of robots and Daneel (she sensed) stopped as soon as she did and remained less than a meter behind. He was close enough to interfere at once in case of need, but was far enough back to make it clear that she was the dominant spokesperson of the pair. The robots before her, she was certain, viewed Daneel as a human being, but she also knew that Daneel was too conscious of himself as a robot to presume upon the misconception of other robots.

Gladia said, "Which one of you will speak with me?"

There was a brief period of silence, as though an unspoken conference were taking place. Then one robot took a step forward. "Madam, I will speak."

"Do you have a name?"

"No, madam. I have only a serial number."

"How long have you been operational?"

"I have been operational twenty-nine years, madam."

"Has anyone else in this group been operational for longer?"

"No, madam. It is why I, rather than another, am speaking."

"How many robots are employed on this estate?"

"I do not have that figure, madam."

"Roughly."

"Perhaps ten thousand, madam."

"Have any been operational for longer than twenty decades?"

"The agricultural robots include some who may, madam."

"And the household robots?"

"They have not been operational long, madam. The masters prefer new-model robots."

Gladia nodded, turned to Daneel, and said, "That makes sense. It was so in my day, too."

She turned back to the robot. "To whom does this estate belong?"

"It is the Zoberlon Estate, madam."

"How long has it belonged to the Zoberlon family?"

"Longer, madam, than I have been operational. I do not know how much longer, but the information can be obtained."

"To whom did it belong before the Zoberlons took possession?"

"I do not know, madam, but the information can be obtained."

"Have you ever heard of the Delmarre family?"

"No, madam."

Gladia turned to Daneel and said, rather ruefully, "I'm trying to lead the robot, little by little, as Elijah might once have done, but I don't think I know how to do it properly."

"On the contrary, Lady Gladia," said Daneel gravely, "it seems to me you have established much. It is not likely that any robot on this estate, except perhaps for a few of the agriculturals, would have any memory of you. Would you have encountered any of the agriculturals in your time?"

Gladia shook her head. "Never! I don't recall seeing any of them even in the distance."

"It is clear, then, that you are not known on this estate."

"Exactly. And poor D.G. has brought us along for nothing. If he expected any good of me, he has failed."

"To know the truth is always useful, madam. Not to be known is, in this case, less useful than to be known, but not to know whether one is known or not would be less useful still. Are there not, perhaps, other points on which you might elicit information?"

"Yes, let's see—" For a few seconds, she was lost in thought, then she said softly, "It's odd. When I speak to these robots, I speak with a pronounced Solarian accent. Yet I do not speak so to you."

Daneel said, "It is not surprising, Lady Gladia. The robots speak with such an accent, for they are Solarian. That brings back the days of your youth and you speak, automatically, as you spoke then. You are at once yourself, however, when you turn to me because I am a part of your present world."

A slow smile appeared on Gladia's face and she said, "You reason more and more like a human being, Daneel."

She turned back to the robots and was keenly aware of the peacefulness of the surroundings. The sky was an almost unmarked blue, except for a thin line of clouds on the western horizon (indicating that it might turn cloudy in the afternoon). There was the sound of rustling leaves in a light wind, the whirring of insects, a lonely birdcall. No sound of human beings. There might be many robots about, but they worked silently. There weren't the exuberant sounds of human beings that she had grown accustomed to (painfully, at first) on Aurora.

But now back on Solaria, she found the peace wonderful. It had not been all bad on Solaria. She had to admit it.

She said to the robot quickly, with a note of compulsion edging her voice, "Where are your masters?"

It was useless, however, to try to hurry or alarm a robot or to catch it off-guard. It said, without any sign of perturbation, "They are gone, madam."

"Where have they gone?"

"I do not know, madam. I was not told."

"Which of you knows?"

There was a complete silence.

Gladia said, "Is there any robot on the estate who would know?"

The robot said, "I do not know of any, madam."

"Did the masters take robots with them?"

"Yes, madam."

"Yet they didn't take you. Why do you remain behind?"

"To do our work, madam."

"Yet you stand here and do nothing. Is that work?"

"We guard the estate from those from outside, madam."

"Such as we?"

"Yes, madam."

"But here we are and yet you still do nothing. Why is that?"

"We observe, madam. We have no further orders."

"Have you reported your observations?"

"Yes, madam."

"To whom?"

"To the overseer, madam."

"Where is the overseer?"

"In the mansion, madam."

"Ah." Gladia turned and walked briskly back to D.G.

Daneel followed.

"Well?" said D.G. He was holding both weapons at the ready, but put them back in their holsters as they returned.

Gladia shook her head. "Nothing. No robot knows me. No robot, I'm sure, knows where the Solarians have gone. *But* they report to an overseer."

"An overseer?"

"On Aurora and the other Spacer worlds, the overseer on large estates with numerous robots is some human whose profession it is to organize and direct groups of working robots in the fields, mines, and industrial establishments."

"Then there *are* Solarians left behind."

Gladia shook her head. "Solaria is an exception. The ratio of robots to human beings has always been so high that it has not been the custom to assign a man or woman to oversee the robots. That job has been done by another robot, one that is specially programmed."

"Then there is a robot in that mansion"—D.G. nodded with his head—"who is more advanced than these and who might profitably be questioned."

"Perhaps, but I am not certain it is safe to attempt to go into the mansion."

D.G. said sardonically, "It is only another robot."

"The mansion may be booby-trapped."

"This field may be booby-trapped."

Gladia said, "It would be better to send one of the robots to the mansion to tell the overseer that human beings wish to speak to him."

D.G. said, "That will not be necessary. That job has apparently been done already. The overseer is emerging and is neither a robot nor a 'him.' What I see is a human female."

Gladia looked up in astonishment. Advancing rapidly toward them was a tall, well-formed, and exceedingly attractive woman. Even at a distance, there was no doubt whatever as to her sex.

25.

D.G. SMILED BROADLY. He seemed to be straightening himself a bit, squaring his shoulders, throwing them back. One hand went lightly to his beard, as though to make sure it was sleek and smooth.

Gladia looked at him with disfavor. She said, "That is *not* a Solarian woman."

"How can you tell?" said D.G.

"No Solarian woman would allow herself to be seen so freely by other human beings. *Seen,* not viewed."

"I know the distinction, my lady. Yet you allow me to see you."

"I have lived over twenty decades on Aurora. Even so I have enough Solarian left in me still not to appear to others like *that.*"

"She has a great deal to display, madam. I would say she is taller than I am and as beautiful as a sunset."

The overseer had stopped twenty meters short of their position and the robots had moved aside so that none of them remained between the woman on one side and the three from the ship on the other.

D.G. said, "Customs can change in twenty decades."

"Not something as basic as the Solarian dislike of human contact," said Gladia sharply. "Not in two hundred decades." She had slipped into her Solarian twang again.

"I think you underestimate social plasticity. Still, Solarian or not, I presume she's a Spacer—and if there are other Spacers like that, I'm all for peaceful coexistence."

Gladia's look of disapproval deepened. "Well, do you intend to stand and gaze in that fashion for the next hour or two? Don't you want me to question the woman?"

D.G. started and turned to look at Gladia with distinct annoyance. "You question the robots, as you've done. *I* question the human beings."

"Especially the females, I suppose."

"I wouldn't like to boast, but—"

"It is a subject on which I have never known a man who didn't."

Daneel interposed, "I do not think the woman will wait longer. If you wish to retain the initiative, Captain, approach her now. I will follow, as I did with Madam Gladia."

"I scarcely need the protection," said D.G. brusquely.

"You are a human being and I must not, through inaction, allow harm to come to you."

D.G. walked forward briskly, Daneel following. Gladia, reluctant to remain behind alone, advanced a bit tentatively.

The overseer watched quietly. She wore a smooth white robe that reached down to mid-thigh and was belted at the waist. It showed a deep and inviting cleavage and her nipples were clearly visible against the thin material of the robe. There was no indication that she was wearing anything else but a pair of shoes.

When D.G. stopped, a meter of space separated them. Her skin, he could see, was flawless, her cheekbones were high, her eyes wide-set and somewhat slanted, her expression serene.

"Madam," said D.G., speaking as close an approximation to Auroran Patrician as he could manage, "have I the pleasure of speaking to the overseer of this estate?"

The woman listened for a moment and then said, in an accent so thickly Solarian as to seem almost comic when coming from her perfectly shaped mouth, "You are not a human being."

She then flashed into action so quickly that Gladia, still some ten meters off, could not see in detail what had happened. She saw only a blur of motion and then D.G. lying on his back motionless and the woman standing there with his weapons, one in each hand.

26.

WHAT STUPEFIED Gladia most in that one dizzying moment was that Daneel had not moved in either prevention or reprisal.

But even as the thought struck her, it was out of date, for Daneel had already caught the woman's left wrist and twisted it, saying, "Drop those weapons at once," in a harsh peremptory voice she had never heard him use before. It was inconceivable that he should so address a human being.

The woman said, just as harshly in her higher register, "You are not a human being." Her right arm came up and she fired the weapon it held. For a moment, a faint glow flickered over Daneel's body and Gladia, unable to make a sound in her state of shock, felt her sight dim. She had never in her life fainted, but this seemed a prelude.

Daneel did not dissolve, nor was there an explosive report. Daneel, Gladia realized, had prudently seized the arm that held the blaster. The other held the neuronic whip and it was that which had been discharged in full—and at close range—upon Daneel. Had he been human, the massive stimulation of his sensory nerves might well have killed him or left him permanently disabled. Yet he was, after all, however human in appearance, a robot and his equivalent of a nervous system did not react to the whip.

Daneel seized the other arm now, forcing it up. He said again, "Drop those weapons or I will tear each arm from its socket."

"Will you?" said the woman. Her arms contracted and, for a moment, Daneel was lifted off the ground. Daneel's legs swung backward, then forward, pendulumlike, using the points where the arms joined as a pivot. His feet struck the woman with force and both fell heavily to the ground.

Gladia, without putting the thought into words, realized that although the woman looked as human as Daneel did, she was just as nonhuman. A sense of instant outrage flooded Gladia, who was suddenly Solarian to the core—outrage that a robot should use force on a human being. Granted that she might somehow have recognized Daneel for what he was, but how *dare* she strike D.G.

Gladia was running forward, screaming. It never occurred to her to fear a robot simply because it had knocked down a strong man with a blow and was battling an even stronger robot to a draw.

"How dare you?" she screamed in a Solarian accent so thick that it grated on her own ear—but how else does one speak to a Solarian robot? "How dare you, *girl?* Stop all resistance *immediately!*"

The woman's muscles seemed to relax totally and simultaneously, as though an electric current had suddenly been shut off. Her beautiful eyes looked at Gladia without enough humanity to seem startled. She said in an indistinct, hesitating voice, "My regrets, madam."

Daneel was on his feet, staring down watchfully at the woman who lay on the grass. D.G., suppressing a groan, was struggling upright.

Daneel bent for the weapons, but Gladia waved him away furiously.

"Give me those weapons, *girl,*" she said.

The woman said, "Yes, madam."

Gladia snatched at them, chose the blaster swiftly, and handed it to Daneel. "Destroy her when that seems best, Daneel. That's an order." She handed the neuronic whip to D.G. and said, "This is useless here, except against me—and yourself. Are you all right?"

"No, I'm *not* all right," muttered D.G., rubbing one hip. "Do you mean she's a *robot?*"

"Would a *woman* have thrown you like that?"

"Not any whom I have ever met before. I *said* there might be special robots on Solaria who were programmed to be dangerous."

"Of course," said Gladia unkindly, "but when you saw something that looked like your idea of a beautiful woman, you forgot."

"Yes, it is easy to be wise after the fact."

Gladia sniffed and turned again to the robot, "What is your name, girl?"

"I am called Landaree, madam."

"Get up, Landaree."

Landaree rose much as Daneel had—as though she were on springs. Her struggle with Daneel seemed to have left her totally unharmed.

Gladia said, "Why, against the First Law, have you attacked these human beings?"

"Madam," said Landaree firmly, "these are not human beings."

"And do you say that *I* am not a human being?"

"No, madam, you are a human being."

"Then, as a human being, I am defining these two men as human beings. —Do you hear me?"

"Madam," said Landaree a little more softly, "these are not human beings."

"They are indeed human beings because I tell you they are. You are forbidden to attack them or harm them in any way."

Landaree stood mute.

"Do you understand what I have said?" Gladia's voice grew more Solarian still as she reached for greater intensity.

"Madam," said Landaree, "these are not human beings."

Daneel said to Gladia softly, "Madam, she has been given orders of such firmness that you cannot easily countervail them."

"We'll see about that," said Gladia, breathing quickly.

Landaree looked about. The group of robots, during the few minutes of conflict, had come closer to Gladia and her two companions. In the background were two robots who, Gladia decided, were not members of the original group and they were carrying between them, with some difficulty, a large and very massive device of some sort. Landaree gestured to them and they moved forward a bit more quickly.

Gladia cried out, "Robots, stop!"

They stopped.

Landaree said, "Madam, I am fulfilling my duties. I am following my instructions."

Gladia said, "Your duty, girl, is to obey my orders!"

Landaree said, "I cannot be ordered to disobey my instructions!"

Gladia said, "Daneel, blast her!"

Afterward, Gladia was able to reason out what had happened. Daneel's reaction time was much faster than a human being's would have been and he knew that he was facing a robot against which the Three Laws did not inhibit violence. However, she looked so human that even the precise knowledge that she was a robot did not totally overcome his inhibition. He followed the order more slowly than he should have.

Landaree, whose definition of "human being" was clearly not the one Daneel used, was not inhibited by his appearance and she struck the more quickly. She had her grip on the blaster and again the two struggled.

D.G. turned his neuronic whip butt-first and came in at a half-run to strike. He hit her head squarely, but it had no effect on the robot and her leg sent him flailing backward.

Gladia said, "Robot! Stop!" Her clenched hands were raised.

Landaree shouted in a stentorian contralto, "All of you! Join me! The two apparent males are not human beings. Destroy them without harming the female in any way."

If Daneel could be inhibited by a human appearance, the same was true in considerably greater intensity for the simple Solarian robots, who inched forward slowly and intermittently.

"Stop!" shrieked Gladia. The robots stopped, but the order had no effect on Landaree.

Daneel held fast to the blaster, but was bending backward under the force of Landaree's apparently greater strength.

Gladia, in distraction, looked about as though hoping to find *some* weapon somewhere.

D.G. was attempting to manipulate his radio transmitter. He said, grunting, "It's been damaged. I think I fell on it."

"What do we do?"

"We have to make it back to the ship. Quickly."

Gladia said, "Then run. I can't abandon Daneel." She faced the battling robots, crying out wildly, "Landaree, stop! Landaree, stop!"

"I must not stop, madam," said Landaree. "My instructions are precise."

Daneel's fingers were forced open and Landaree had the blaster again.

Gladia threw herself before Daneel. "You must not harm this human being."

"Madam," said Landaree, her blaster pointed at Gladia, unwavering. "You are standing in front of something that looks like a human being but is not a human being. My instructions are to destroy such on sight." Then, in a louder voice, "You two porters—to the ship."

The two robots, carrying the massive device between them, renewed their forward movement.

"Robots, stop!" screamed Gladia and the forward motion stopped. The robots trembled in place, as though attempting to move forward and yet not quite able to do so.

Gladia said, "You cannot destroy my human friend Daneel without destroying me—and you yourself admit that I am a human being and therefore must not be harmed."

Daneel said in a low voice, "My lady, you must not draw harm upon yourself in an effort to protect me."

Landaree said, "This is useless, madam. I can remove you easily from your present position and then destroy the nonhuman being behind you. Since that may harm you, I ask you, with all respect, to move from your present position voluntarily."

"You must, my lady," said Daneel.

"No, Daneel. I'll stay here. In the time it will take her to move me, you run!"

"I cannot run faster than the beam of a blaster—and if I try to run, she will shoot through you rather than not at all. Her instructions are probably that firm. I regret, my lady, that this will cause you unhappiness."

And Daneel lifted the struggling Gladia and tossed her lightly to one side.

Landaree's finger tightened on the contact, but never completed the pressure. She remained motionless.

Gladia, who had staggered to a sitting position, got to her feet. Cautiously, D.G., who had remained in place during the last exchanges, approached Landaree. Daneel quite calmly reached out and took the blaster from her unresisting fingers.

"I believe," said Daneel, "that this robot is permanently deactivated."

He pushed her gently and she fell over in one piece, with her limbs, torso, and head in the relative positions they occupied when she was standing. Her arm was still bent, her hand was holding an invisible blaster, and her finger was pressing on an invisible contact.

Through the trees to one side of the grassy field on which the drama had played itself out Giskard was approaching, his robotic face showing no signs of curiosity, though his words might have.

"What has taken place in my absence?" he asked.

27.

THE WALK BACK to the ship was rather anticlimactic. Now that the frenzy of fear and action was over, Gladia felt hot and cross. D.G. limped rather painfully and they progressed slowly, partly because of the limp and partly because the two Solarian robots were still carrying their massive instrument, plodding along under its weight.

D.G. looked over his shoulder at them. "They obey my orders now that that overseer is out of action."

Gladia said through her teeth, "Why didn't you run at the end and get help? Why did you remain helplessly watching?"

"Well," said D.G., with an attempt at the kind of lightness he would have showed easily were he feeling better, "with you refusing to leave Daneel, I rather hesitated to play the coward by comparison."

"You fool! I was safe. She would not have harmed *me.*"

Daneel said, "Madam, it distresses me to contradict you, but I think she would have done so as her urge to destroy me grew stronger."

Gloria turned on him hotly. "And that was a smart thing *you* did, pushing me out of the way. Did you *want* to be destroyed?"

"Rather than see you harmed, madam, yes. My failure to stop the robot through inhibitions set up by her human appearance demonstrated, in any case, an unsatisfactory limit to my usefulness to you."

"Even so," said Gladia, "she would have hesitated to shoot me, since I am human, for a perceptible period of time and you could have had the blaster in your own possession by that time."

"I couldn't gamble your life, madam, on anything as uncertain as her hesitation," said Daneel.

"And *you,*" said Gladia, showing no signs of having heard Daneel and turning to D.G. again, "shouldn't have brought the blaster in the first place."

D.G. said, frowning, "Madam, I am making allowances for the fact that we have all been very close to death. The robots do not mind that and I have grown somehow accustomed to danger. To you, however, this was an unpleasant novelty and you are being childish as a result. I forgive you—a little. But please listen. There was no way I could have known the blaster would be taken from me so easily. Had I not brought the weapon, the overseer could have killed me with her bare hands as quickly and as effectively as she could have by blaster. Nor was there any point in my running, to answer an earlier complaint of yours. I could not outrun a blaster. Now please continue if you must still get it out of your system, but I do not intend to reason with you any further."

Gladia looked from D.G. to Daneel and back and said in a low voice, "I suppose I *am* being unreasonable. Very well, no more hindsights."

They had reached the ship. Crew members poured out at the sight of them. Gladia noticed they were armed.

D.G. beckoned to his second-in-command. "Oser, I presume you see that object the two robots are carrying?"

"Yes, sir."

"Well, have them carry it on board. Have it put in the security room and kept there. The security room is then to be locked and kept locked." He turned away for a moment, then turned back. "And Oser, as soon as that is done, we will prepare to take off again."

Oser said, "Captain, shall we keep the robots as well?"

"No. They are too simple in design to be worth much and, under the circumstances, taking them would create undesirable consequences. The device they are carrying is much more valuable than they are."

Giskard watched the device being slowly and very carefully maneuvered into the ship. He said, "Captain, I am guessing that that is a dangerous object."

"I'm under that impression, too," said D.G. "I suspect that the ship would have been destroyed soon after we were."

"That thing?" said Gladia. "What is it?"

"I can't be certain, but I *believe* it is a nuclear intensifier. I've seen experimental models on Baleyworld and this looks like a big brother."

"What is a nuclear intensifier?"

"As the name implies, Lady Gladia, it's a device that intensifies nuclear fusion."

"How does it do that?"

D.G. shrugged. "I'm not a physicist, my lady. A stream of W particles is involved and they mediate the weak interaction. That's all I know about it."

"What does that do?" asked Gladia.

"Well, suppose the ship has its power supply as it has right now, for instance. There are small numbers of protons, derived from our hydrogen fuel supply, that are ultrahot and fusing to produce power. Additional hydrogen is constantly being heated to produce free protons, which, when hot enough, also fuse to maintain that power. If the stream of W particles from the nuclear intensifier strikes the fusing protons, these fuse more quickly and deliver more heat. That heat produces protons and sets them to fusing more quickly than they should be and their fusion produces still more heat, which intensifies the vicious cycle. In a tiny fraction of a second, enough of the fuel fuses to form a tiny thermonuclear bomb and the entire ship and everything upon it is vaporized."

Gladia looked awed. "Why doesn't everything ignite? Why doesn't the whole planet blow up?"

"I don't suppose there's danger of that, madam. The protons have to be ultrahot and fusing. Cold protons are so unapt to fuse that even when the tendency is intensified to the full extent of such a device, that still is not enough to allow fusion. At least, that's what I gathered from a lecture I once attended. And nothing but hydrogen is affected, as far as I know. Even in the case of ultrahot protons, the heat produced does not increase without measure. The temperature cools with distance from the intensifier beam, so that only a limited amount of fusion can be forced. Enough to destroy the ship, of course, but there's no question of blowing up the hydrogen-rich oceans, for instance, even if part of the ocean were ultraheated— and certainly not if it were cold."

"But if the machine gets turned on accidentally in the storage room—"

"I don't think it can get turned on." D.G. opened his hand and in it rested a two-centimeter cube of polished metal. "From what little I know of such things, this is an activator and the nuclear intensifier can do nothing without it."

"Are you sure?"

"Not entirely, but we'll just have to chance it, since I must get that thing back to Baleyworld. Now let's get on board."

Gladia and her two robots moved up the gangplank and into the ship. D.G. followed and spoke briefly to some of his officers.

He then said to Gladia, his weariness beginning to show, "It will take us a couple of hours to place all our gear on board and be ready for takeoff and every moment increases the danger."

"Danger?"

"You don't suppose that fearful woman robot is the only one of its kind that may exist on Solaria, do you? Or that the nuclear intensifier we have captured is the only one of its kind? I suppose it will take time for other humanoid robots and other nuclear intensifiers to be brought to this spot— perhaps considerable time—but we must give them as little as possible. And in the meantime, madam, let us go to your room and conduct some necessary business."

"What necessary business would that be, Captain?"

"Well," said D.G., motioning them forward, "in view of the fact that I may have been victimized by treason, I think I will conduct a rather informal court-martial."

28.

D.G. SAID, after seating himself with an audible groan, "What I really want is a hot shower, a rubdown, a good meal, and a chance to sleep, but that will all have to wait till we're off the planet. It will have to wait in your case, too, madam. Some things will not wait, however. —My question is this. Where were you, Giskard, while the rest of us were faced with considerable danger?"

Giskard said, "Captain, it did not seem to me that if robots alone were left on the planet, they would represent any danger. Moreover, Daneel remained with you."

Daneel said, "Captain, I agreed that Giskard would reconnoiter and that I would remain with Madam Gladia and with you."

"You two agreed, did you?" said D.G. "Was anyone else consulted?"

"No, Captain," said Giskard.

"If you were certain that the robots were harmless, Giskard, how did you account for the fact that two ships were destroyed?"

"It seemed to me, Captain, that there must remain human beings on the planet, but that they would do their best not to be seen by you. I wanted to know where they were and what they were doing. I was in search of them, covering the ground as rapidly as I could. I questioned the robots I met."

"Did you find any human beings?"

"No, Captain."

"Did you examine the house out of which the overseer emerged?"

"No, Captain, but I was certain there were no human beings within it. I still am."

"It contained the overseer."

"Yes, Captain, but the overseer was a robot."

"A dangerous robot."

"To my regret, Captain, I did not realize that."

"You feel regret, do you?"

"It is an expression I choose to describe the effect on my positronic circuits. It is a rough analogy to the term as human beings seem to use it, Captain."

"How is it you didn't realize a robot might be dangerous?"

"By the Three Laws of Robotics—"

Gladia interrupted, "Stop this, Captain. Giskard only knows what he is programmed to know. No robot is dangerous to human beings, unless there is a deadly quarrel between human beings and the robot must attempt to stop it. In such a quarrel, Daneel and Giskard would undoubtedly have defended us with as little harm to others as possible."

"Is that so?" D.G. put two fingers to the bridge of his nose and pinched. "Daneel *did* defend us. We were fighting robots, not human beings, so he had no problem in deciding whom to defend and to what extent. Yet he showed astonishing lack of success, considering that the Three Laws do not prevent him from doing harm to robots. Giskard remained out of it, returning at the precise moment when it was over. Is it possible that there is a bond of sympathy among robots? Is it possible that robots, when defending human beings against robots, somehow feel what Giskard calls 'regret' at having to do so and perhaps fail—or absent themselves—"

"No!" exploded Gladia forcefully.

"No?" said D.G. "Well, I don't pretend to be an expert roboticist. Are you, Lady Gladia?"

"I am not a roboticist of any sort," said Gladia, "but I have lived with robots all my life. What you suggest is ridiculous. Daneel was quite prepared to give his life for me and Giskard would have done the same."

"Would any robot have done so?"

"Of course."

"And yet this overseer, this Landaree, was quite ready to attack me and destroy me. Let us grant that, in some mysterious way, she detected that Daneel, despite appearances, was as much a robot as she herself was—despite appearances—and that she had no inhibitions when it came to harming him. How is it, though, that she attacked me when I am unquestionably a human being? She hesitated at you, admitting you were human, but not me. How could a robot discriminate between the two of us? Was she perhaps not really a robot?"

"She was a robot," said Gladia. "Of course she was. But—the truth is, I don't know why she acted as she did. I have never before heard of such a thing. I can only suppose that the Solarians, having learned how to construct humanoid robots, designed them without the protection of the Three Laws, though I would have sworn that the Solarians—of all Spacers—would have been the last to do so. Solarians are so outnumbered by their own robots as to be utterly dependent on them—to a far greater extent than any other Spacers are—and for that reason they fear them more. Subservience and even a bit of stupidity were built into all Solarian robots. The Three Laws were stronger on Solaria than anywhere else, not weaker. Yet I can think of no other way of explaining Landaree than to suppose that the First Law was—"

Daneel said, "Excuse me, Madam Gladia, for interrupting. May I have your permission to attempt an explanation of the overseer's behavior?"

D.G. said sardonically, "It comes to that, I suppose. Only a robot can explain a robot."

"Sir," said Daneel, "unless we understand the overseer, we might not be able to take effective measures in the future against the Solarian danger. I believe I have a way of accounting for her behavior."

"Go ahead," said D.G.

"The overseer," said Daneel, "did not take instant measures against us. She stood and watched us for a while, apparently uncertain as to how to proceed. When you, Captain, approached and addressed her, she announced that you were not human and attacked you instantly. When I intervened and cried out that she was a robot, she announced that I was not human and attacked me at once, too. When Lady Gladia came forward, however, shouting at her, the overseer recognized her as human and, for a while, allowed herself to be dominated."

"Yes, I remember all that, Daneel. But what does it mean?"

"It seems to me, Captain, that it is possible to alter a robot's behavior fundamentally without ever touching the Three Laws, provided, for instance, that you alter the definition of a human being. A human being, after all, is only what it is defined to be."

"Is that so? What do *you* consider a human being to be?"

Daneel was not concerned with the presence or absence of sarcasm. He said, "I was constructed with a detailed description of the appearance and behavior of human beings, Captain. Anything that fits that description is a human being to me. Thus, you have the appearance and the behavior, while the overseer had the appearance but not the behavior.

"To the overseer, on the other hand, the key property of a human being was speech, Captain. The Solarian accent is a distinctive one and to the overseer something that looked like a human being was defined as a human being only if it spoke like a Solarian. Apparently, anything that looked like a human being but did not speak with a Solarian accent was to be destroyed without hesitation, as was any ship carrying such beings."

D.G. said thoughtfully, "You may be right."

"You have a Settler accent, Captain, as distinctive in its way as the

Solarian accent is, but the two are widely different. As soon as you spoke, you defined yourself as nonhuman to the overseer, who announced that and attacked."

"And you speak with an Auroran accent and were likewise attacked."

"Yes, Captain, but Lady Gladia spoke with an authentic Solarian accent and so she was recognized as human."

D.G. considered the matter silently for a while, then said, "That's a dangerous arrangement, even for those who would make use of it. If a Solarian, for any reason, at any time addressed such a robot in a way that the robot did not consider an authentic Solarian accent, that Solarian would be attacked at once. If I were a Solarian, I would be afraid to approach such a robot. My very effort to speak pure Solarian might very likely throw me off and get me killed."

"I agree, Captain," said Daneel, "and I would imagine that that is why those who manufacture robots do not ordinarily limit the definition of a human being, but leave it as broad as possible. The Solarians, however, have left the planet. One might suppose that the fact that overseer robots have this dangerous programming is the best indication that the Solarians have really left and are not here to encounter the danger. The Solarians, it appears, are at this moment concerned only that no one who is not a Solarian be allowed to set foot on the planet."

"Not even other Spacers?"

"I would expect, Captain, that it would be difficult to define a human being in such a way as to include the dozens of different Spacer accents and yet exclude the scores of different Settler accents. Keying the definition to the distinctive Solarian accent alone would be difficult enough."

D.G. said, "You are very intelligent, Daneel. I disapprove of robots, of course, not in themselves but as an unsettling influence on society. And yet, with a robot such as yourself at my side, as you were once at the Ancestor's—"

Gladia interrupted. "I'm afraid not, D.G. Daneel will never be a gift, nor will he ever be sold, nor can he be easily taken by force."

D.G. lifted his hand in a smiling negative. "I was merely dreaming, Lady Gladia. I assure you that the laws of Baleyworld would make my possession of a robot unthinkable."

Giskard said suddenly, "May I have your permission, Captain, to add a few words?"

D.G. said, "Ah, the robot who managed to avoid the action and who returned when all was safely over."

"I regret that matters appear to be as you have stated. May I have your permission, Captain, to add a few words, notwithstanding?"

"Well, go on."

"It would seem, Captain, that your decision to bring the Lady Gladia with you on this expedition has worked out very well. Had she been absent and had you ventured on your exploratory mission with only members of the ship's crew as companions, you would all have been quickly killed and the ship destroyed. It was only Lady Gladia's ability to speak like a Solarian and her courage in facing the overseer that changed the outcome."

"Not so," said D.G., "for we would all have been destroyed, possibly even Lady Gladia, but for the fortuitous event that the overseer spontaneously inactivated."

"It was not fortuitous, Captain," said Giskard, "and it is extremely unlikely that any robot will inactivate spontaneously. There has to be a reason for inactivation and I can suggest one possibility. Lady Gladia ordered the robot to stop on several occasions, as friend Daneel has told me, but the instructions under which the overseer worked were more forceful.

"Nevertheless, Lady Gladia's actions served to blunt the overseer's resolution, Captain. The fact that Lady Gladia was an undoubted human being, even by the overseer's definition, and that she was acting in such a way as to make it necessary, perhaps, for the overseer to harm her—or even kill her—blunted it even farther. Thus, at the crucial moment, the two contrary requirements—having to destroy nonhuman beings and having to refrain from harming human beings—balanced and the robot froze, unable to do anything. Its circuits burned out."

Gladia's brows drew together in a puzzled frown. "But—" she began and then subsided.

Giskard went on, "It strikes me that it might be well for you to inform the crew of this. It might well ease their distrust of Lady Gladia if you stress what her initiative and courage have meant to every man in the crew, since it has kept them alive. It might also give them an excellent opinion of your own foresight in insisting on having her on board on this occasion, perhaps even against the advice of your own officers."

D.G. let loose a great shout of laughter. "Lady Gladia, I see now why you will not be separated from these robots. They are not only as intelligent as human beings, they are every bit as devious. I congratulate you on your having them. —And now, if you don't mind, I must hurry the crew. I don't want to stay on Solaria for one moment more than necessary. And I promise you that you won't be disturbed for hours. I know you can use freshening and rest as much as I can."

After he was gone, Gladia remained for a while in deep thought, then turned to Giskard and said in Auroran Common, a patter version of Galactic Standard that was widespread on Aurora and difficult for any non-Auroran to understand, "Giskard, what is all this nonsense about the burning out of circuits?"

"My lady," said Giskard, "I advanced it only as a possibility and nothing more. I thought it well to emphasize your role in putting an end to the overseer."

"But how could you think he would believe that a robot could burn out that easily?"

"He knows very little about robots, madam. He may traffic in them, but he is from a world that doesn't make use of them."

"Yet I know a great deal about them and so do you. The overseer showed no signs whatever of balancing circuits; no stuttering, no trembling, no behavior difficulty of any kind. It just—stopped."

Giskard said, "Madam, since we do not know the precise specifications to which the overseer was designed, we may have to be content with ignorance as to the rationale behind the freeze."

Gladia shook her head. "Just the same, it's puzzling."

PART THREE
BALEYWORLD

Chapter 8

The Settler World

29.

D.G.'s SHIP WAS in space again, surrounded by the everlasting changelessness of the endless vacuum.

It had not come too soon for Gladia, who had but imperfectly suppressed the tension that arose from the possibility that a second overseer—with a second intensifier—might arrive without warning. The fact that it would be a quick death if it happened, an unexperienced death, was not quite satisfying. The tension had spoiled what would have otherwise been a luxuriant shower, along with various other forms of renewal of comfort.

It was not till after actual takeoff, after the coming of the soft, distant buzz of the protonic jets, that she could compose herself to sleep. Odd, she thought as consciousness began to slip away, that space should feel safer than the world of her youth, that she should leave Solaria with even greater relief the second time than she had the first.

But Solaria was no longer the world of her youth. It was a world without humanity, guarded over by distorted parodies of humanity; humanoid robots that made a mockery of the gentle Daneel and the thought-filled Giskard.

She slept at last—and while she slept, Daneel and Giskard, standing guard, could once more speak to each other.

Daneel said, "Friend Giskard, I am quite certain that it was you who destroyed the overseer."

"There was clearly no choice, friend Daneel. It was purely an accident that I arrived in time, for my senses were entirely occupied with searching out human beings and I found none. Nor would I have grasped the significance of events if it were not for Lady Gladia's rage and despair. It was that which I sensed at a distance and which caused me to race to the scene—barely in time. In that respect, Lady Gladia *did* save the situation, at least as far as the captain's existence and yours were concerned. I would still have saved the ship, I believe, even if I had arrived too late to save you." He paused a moment and added, "I would have found it most unsatisfactory, friend Daneel, to arrive too late to save you."

Daneel said, with a grave and formal tone of voice, "I thank you, friend Giskard. I am pleased that you were not inhibited by the human appearance of the overseer. That had slowed my reactions, as my appearance had slowed hers."

"Friend Daneel, her physical appearance meant nothing to me because I was aware of the pattern of her thoughts. That pattern was so limited and so entirely different from the full range of human patterns that there was no need for me to make any effort to identify her in a positive manner. The negative identification as nonhuman was so clear I acted at once. I was not aware of my action, in fact, until after it had taken place."

"I had thought this, friend Giskard, but I wished confirmation lest I misunderstand. May I assume, then, that you feel no discomfort over having killed what was, in appearance, a human being?"

"None, since it was a robot."

"It seems to me that, had I succeeded in destroying her, I would have suffered some obstruction to the free positronic flow, no matter how thoroughly I understood her to be a robot."

"The humanoid appearance, friend Daneel, cannot be fought off when that is all one can directly judge by. Seeing is so much more immediate than deducing. It was only because I could observe her mental structure and concentrate on that, that I could ignore her physical structure."

"How do you suppose the overseer would have felt if she had destroyed us, judging from her mental structure?"

"She was given exceedingly firm instructions and there was no doubt in her circuits that you and the captain were nonhuman by her definition."

"But she might have destroyed Madam Gladia as well."

"Of that we cannot be certain, friend Daneel."

"Had she done so, friend Giskard, would she have survived? Have you any way of telling?"

Giskard was silent for a considerable period. "I had insufficient time to study the mental pattern. I cannot say what her reaction might have been had she killed Madam Gladia."

"If I imagine myself in the place of the overseer"—Daneel's voice trembled and grew slightly lower in pitch—"it seems to me that I might kill a human being in order to save the life of another human being, whom, there might be some reason to think, it was more necessary to save. The action would, however, be difficult and damaging. To kill a human being merely in order to destroy something I considered nonhuman would be inconceivable."

"She merely threatened. She did not carry through the threat."

"Might she have, friend Giskard?"

"How can we say, since we don't know the nature of her instructions?"

"Could the instructions have so completely negated the First Law?"

Giskard said, "Your whole purpose in this discussion, I see, has been to raise this question. I advise you to go no further."

Daneel said stubbornly, "I will put it in the conditional, friend Giskard. Surely what may not be expressed as fact can be advanced as fantasy. *If* instructions could be hedged about with definitions and conditions, *if* the instructions could be made sufficiently detailed in a sufficiently forceful manner, *might* it be possible to kill a human being for a purpose less overwhelming than the saving of the life of another human being?"

Giskard said tonelessly, "I do not know, but I suspect that this might be possible."

"But, then, *if* your suspicion should be correct, that would imply that it was possible to neutralize the First Law under specialized conditions. The First Law, *in that case*, and, therefore, certainly the other Laws *might* be modified into almost nonexistence. The Laws, even the First Law, might not be an absolute then, but might be whatever those who design robots defined it to be."

Giskard said, "It is enough, friend Daneel. Go no further."

Daneel said, "There is one more step, friend Giskard. Partner Elijah would have taken that additional step."

"He was a human being. He could."

"I must try. *If* the Laws of Robotics—even the First Law—are not absolutes and *if* human beings can modify them, might it not be that *perhaps*, under proper conditions, we ourselves might mod—"

He stopped.

Giskard said faintly, "Go no further."

Daneel said, a slight hum obscuring his voice, "I go no further."

There was a silence for a long time. It was with difficulty that the positronic circuitry in each ceased undergoing discords.

Finally, Daneel said, "Another thought arises. The overseer was dangerous not ony because of the set of her instructions but because of her appearance. It inhibited me and probably the captain and could mislead and deceive human beings generally, as I deceived, without meaning to, First-Class Shipper Niss. He clearly was not aware, at first, that I was a robot."

"And what follows from that, friend Daneel?"

"On Aurora, a number of humanoid robots were constructed at the Robotics Institute, under the leadership of Dr. Amadiro, after the designs of Dr. Fastolfe had been obtained."

"This is well known."

"What happened to those humanoid robots?"

"The project failed."

In his turn, Daneel said, "This is well known. But it does not answer the question. What happened to those humanoid robots?"

"One can assume they were destroyed."

"Such an assumption need not necessarily be correct. Were they, in actual fact, destroyed?"

"That would have been the sensible thing to do. What else with a failure?"

"How do we know the humanoid robots were a failure, except in that they were removed from sight?"

"Isn't that sufficient, if they were removed from sight and destroyed?"

"I did not say 'and destroyed,' friend Giskard. That is more than we know. We know only that they were removed from sight."

"Why should that be so, unless they were failures?"

"And if they were *not* failures, might there be no reason for their being removed from sight?"

"I can think of none, friend Daneel."

"Think again, friend Giskard. Remember, we are talking now of humanoid robots who, we now think, might from the mere fact of their humanoid nature be dangerous. It has seemed to us in our previous discussion that there was a plan on foot on Aurora to defeat the Settlers—drastically, surely, and at a blow. We decided that these plans must be centered on the planet Earth. Am I correct so far?"

"Yes, friend Daneel."

"Then might it not be that Dr. Amadiro is at the focus and center of this plan? His antipathy to Earth has been made plain these twenty decades. And if Dr. Amadiro has constructed a number of humanoid robots, where might these have been sent if they have disappeared from view? Remember that if Solarian roboticists can distort the Three Laws, Auroran roboticists can do the same."

"Are you suggesting, friend Daneel, that the humanoid robots have been sent to Earth?"

"Exactly. There to deceive the Earthpeople through their human appearance and to make possible whatever it is that Dr. Amadiro intends as his blow against Earth."

"You have no evidence for this."

"Yet it is possible. Consider for yourself the steps of the argument."

"If that were so, we would have to go to Earth. We would have to be there and somehow prevent the disaster."

"Yes, that is so."

"But we cannot go unless Lady Gladia goes and that is not likely."

"If you can influence the captain to take this ship to Earth, Madam Gladia would have no choice but to go as well."

Giskard said, "I cannot without harming him. He is firmly set on going to his own planet of Baleyworld. We must maneuver his trip to Earth—if we can—after he has done whatever he plans in Baleyworld."

"Afterward may be too late."

"I cannot help that. I must not harm a human being."

"If it is too late— Friend Giskard, consider what that would mean."

"I cannot consider what that would mean. I know only that I cannot harm a human being."

"Then the First Law is not enough and we must—"

He could go no farther and both robots lapsed into helpless silence.

30.

BALEYWORLD CAME slowly into sharper view as the ship approached it. Gladia watched it intently in her cabin's viewer; it was the first time she had ever seen a Settler world.

She had protested this leg of the journey when she had first been made aware of it by D.G., but he shrugged it off with a small laugh. "What would you have, my lady? I must lug this weapon of your people"—he emphasized "your" slightly—"to my people. And I must report to them, too."

Gladia said coldly, "Your permission to take me along to Solaria was granted you by the Auroran Council on the condition that you bring me back."

"Actually that is not so, my lady. There may have been some informal understanding to that effect, but there is nothing in writing. No formal agreement."

"An informal understanding would bind *me*—or any civilized individual, D.G."

"I'm sure of that, Madam Gladia, but we Traders live by money and by written signatures on legal documents. I would never, under any circumstances, violate a written contract or refuse to do that for which I have accepted payment."

Gladia's chin turned upward. "Is that a hint that I must pay you in order to be taken home?"

"Madam!"

"Come, come, D.G. Don't waste mock indignation on me. If I am to be kept prisoner on your planet, say so and tell me why. Let me know exactly where I stand."

"You are not my prisoner and will not be. In fact, I will honor this unwritten understanding. I *will* take you home—eventually. First, however, I must go to Baleyworld and you must come with me."

"Why must I come with you?"

"The people of my world will want to see you. You are the heroine of Solaria. You saved us. You can't deprive them of a chance of shouting themselves hoarse for you. Besides, you were the good friend of the Ancestor."

"What do they know—or think they know—of that?" Gladia said sharply.

D.G. grinned. "Nothing to your discredit, I assure you. You are a legend and legends are larger than life—though I admit it would be easy for a legend to be larger than you, my lady—and a good deal nobler. Ordinarily, I wouldn't want you on the world because you couldn't live up to the legend. You're not tall enough, beautiful enough, majestic enough. *But* when the story of Solaria comes out, you will suddenly meet all requirements. In fact, they may not want to let you go. You must remember we are talking of Baleyworld, the planet on which the story of the Ancestor is taken more seriously than on any other—and you are part of the story."

"You are not to use that as an excuse to keep me in prison."

"I promise you I won't. And I promise I will get you home—when I can —when I can."

Gladia did not remain as indignant somehow as she felt she had every right to be. She did want to see what a Settler world was like and, after all, this was Elijah Baley's peculiar world. His son had founded it. He himself had spent his last decades here. On Baleyworld, there would be remnants of him—the name of the planet, his descendants, his legend.

So she watched the planet—and thought of Elijah.

31.

THE WATCHING BROUGHT her little and she felt disappointed. There was not much to be seen through the cloud layer that covered the planet. From her relatively small experience as a space traveler it seemed to her that the cloud layer was denser than usual for inhabited planets. They would be landing within hours, now, and—

The signal light flashed and Gladia scrambled to push the HOLD button in answer. A few moments more and she pushed the ENTER button.

D.G. came in, smiling. "Inconvenient moment, my lady?"

"Not really," said Gladia. "Simply a matter of putting on my gloves and inserting my nose plugs. I suppose I should wear them all the time, but both grow tiresome and, for some reason, I grow less concerned about infection."

"Familiarity breeds contempt, my lady."

"Let's not call it contempt," said Gladia, who found herself smiling.

"Thank you," said D.G. "We'll be landing soon, madam, and I have brought you a coverall, carefully sterilized and placed inside this plastic bag so that it has since been untouched by Settler hands. It's simple to put on. You'll have no trouble and you'll find it covers everything but the nose and eyes."

"Just for me, D.G.?"

"No, no, my lady. We all wear such things when outdoors at this season of the year. It is winter in our capital city at the present time and it is cold. We live on a rather cold world—heavy cloud cover, much precipitation, often snow."

"Even in the tropical regions?"

"No, there it tends to be hot and dry. The population clusters in the cooler regions, however. We rather like it. It's bracing and stimulating. The seas, which were seeded with Earth species of life, are fertile, so that fish and other creatures have multiplied abundantly. There's no food shortage, consequently, even though land agriculture is limited and we'll never be the breadbasket of the Galaxy. —The summers are short but quite hot and the beaches are then well populated, although you might find them uninteresting since we have a strong nudity taboo."

"It seems like peculiar weather."

"A matter of land-sea distribution, a planetary orbit that is a bit more eccentric than most, and a few other things. Frankly, I don't bother with it." He shrugged. "It's not my field of interest."

"You're a Trader. I imagine you're not on the planet often."

"True, but I'm not a Trader in order to escape. I like it here. And yet perhaps I would like it less if I were here more. If we look at it that way, Baleyworld's harsh conditions serve an important purpose. They encourage trading. Baleyworld produces men who scour the seas for food and there's a certain similarity between sailing the seas and sailing through space. I would say fully a third of all the Traders plying the space lanes are Baleypeople."

"You seem in a semimanic state, D.G.," said Gladia.

"Do I? I think of myself right now as being in a good humor. I have reason to be. So have you."

"Oh?"

"It's obvious, isn't it? We got off Solaria alive. We know exactly what the Solarian danger is. We've gained control of an unusual weapon that should interest our military. And you will be the heroine of Baleyworld. The world officials already know the outline of events and are eager to greet you. For that matter, you're the heroine of this ship. Almost every man on board volunteered to bring you this coverall. They are all anxious to get close and bathe in your aura, so to speak."

"Quite a change," said Gladia dryly.

"Absolutely. Niss—the crewman whom your Daneel chastised—"

"I remember well, D.G."

"He is anxious to apologize to you. And bring his four mates so that they, too, might apologize. And to kick, in your presence, the one of them who made an improper suggestion. He is not a bad person, my lady."

"I am certain he isn't. Assure him he is forgiven and the incident forgotten. And if you'll arrange matters, I will—will shake hands with him and perhaps some of the others before debarking. But you mustn't let them crowd about me."

"I understand, but I can't gurantee there won't be a certain amount of crowding in Baleytown—that's the capital city of Baleyworld. There's no way of stopping various government officials from trying to gain political advantage by being seen with you, while grinning away and bowing."

"Jehoshaphat! As your Ancestor would say."

"Don't say that once we land, madam. It's an expression reserved for him. It is considered bad taste for anyone else to say it. —There'll be speeches and cheering and all kinds of meaningless formalities. I'm sorry, my lady."

She said thoughtfully, "I could do without it, but I suppose there's no way of stopping it."

"No way, my lady."

"How long will it continue?"

"Till they get tired. Several days, perhaps, but there'll be a certain variety to it."

"And how long do we stay on the planet?"

"Till *I* get tired. I'm sorry, my lady, but I have much to do—places to go —friends to see—"

"Women to make love to."

"Alas for human frailty," said D.G., grinning broadly.

"You're doing everything but slobber."

"A weakness. I can't bring myself to slobber."

Gladia smiled. "You're not totally committed to sanity, are you?"

"I never claimed to be. But, leaving that aside, I also have to consider such dull matters as the fact that my officers and crew would want to see *their* families and friends, catch up on their sleep, and have a little planet-side fun. —And if you want to consider the feelings of inanimate objects, the ship will have to be repaired, refurbished, refreshed, and refueled. Little things like that."

"How long will all those little things take?"

"It could be months. Who knows?"

"And what do I do meanwhile?"

"You could see our world, broaden your horizons."

"But your world is not exactly the playground of the Galaxy."

"Too true, but we'll try to keep you interested." He looked at his watch. "One more warning, madam. Do not refer to your age."

"What cause would I have to do that?"

"It might show up in some casual reference. You'll be expected to say a few words and you might say, for instance, 'In all my more than twenty-three decades of life, I have never been so glad to see anyone as I am to see the people of Baleyworld.' If you're tempted to say anything like that initial clause, resist it."

"I will. I have no intention of indulging in hyperbole in any case. —But, as a matter of idle curiosity, why not?"

"Simply because it is better for them not to know your age."

"But they *do* know my age, don't they? They know I was your Ancestor's friend and they know how long ago he lived. Or are they under the impression"—she looked at him narrowly—"that I'm a distant descendant of *the* Gladia?"

"No, no, they know who you are and how old you are, but they know it only with their heads"—he tapped his forehead—"and few people have working heads, as you may have noticed."

"Yes, I have. Even on Aurora."

"That's good. I wouldn't want the Settlers to be special in this respect. Well, then, you have the appearance of"—he paused judiciously—"forty, maybe forty-five, and they'll accept you as that in their guts, which is where the average person's real thinking mechanism is located. *If* you don't rub it in about your real age."

"Does it really make a difference?"

"Does it? Look, the average Settler really doesn't want robots. He has no liking for robots, no desire for robots. There we are satisfied to differ from the Spacers. Long life is different. Forty decades is considerably more than ten."

"Few of us actually reach the forty-decade mark."

"And few of us actually reach the ten-decade mark. We teach the advantage of short life—quality versus quantity, evolutionary speed, ever-changing world—but nothing really makes people happy about living ten decades when they imagine they could live forty, so past a point the propaganda produces a backlash and it's best to keep quiet about it. They don't often see Spacers, as you can imagine, and so they don't have occasion to grind their teeth over the fact that Spacers look young and vigorous even when they are twice as old as the oldest Settler who ever lived. They'll see that in *you* and if they think about it, it will unsettle them."

Gladia said bitterly, "Would you like to have me make a speech and tell them exactly what forty decades means? Shall I tell them for how many years one outlives the springtime of hope, to say nothing of friends and acquaintances. Shall I tell them of the meaninglessness of children and family; of the endless comings and goings of one husband after another, of the misty blurring of the informal matings between and alongside; of the coming of the time when you've seen all you want to see, and heard all you want to hear, and find it impossible to think a new thought, of how you forget what excitement and discovery are all about, and learn each year how much more intense boredom can become?"

"Baleypeople wouldn't believe that. I don't think I do. Is that the way all Spacers feel or are you making it up?"

"I only know for certain how I myself feel, but I've watched others dim as they aged; I've watched their dispositions sour, and their ambitions narrow, and their indifferences broaden."

D.G.'s lips pressed together and he looked somber. "Is the suicide rate high among Spacers? I've never heard that it is."

"It's virtually zero."

"But that doesn't fit what you're saying."

"Consider! We're surrounded by robots who are dedicated to keeping us alive. There's no way we can kill ourselves when our sharp-eyed and active robots are forever about us. I doubt that any of us would even think of trying. I wouldn't dream of it myself, if only because I can't bear the thought of what it would mean to all my household robots and, even more so, to Daneel and Giskard."

"They're not really alive, you know. They don't have feelings."

Gladia shook her head. "You say that only because you've never lived with them. —In any case, I think you overestimate the longing for prolonged life among your people. *You* know my age, *you* look at my appearance, yet it doesn't bother you."

"Because I'm convinced that the Spacer worlds must dwindle and die, that it is the Settler worlds that are the hope of humanity's future, and that it is our short-lived characteristic that ensures it. Listening to what you've just said, assuming it is all true, makes me the more certain."

"Don't be too sure. You may develop your own insuperable problems—if you haven't already."

"That is undoubtedly possible, my lady, but for now I must leave you. The ship is coasting in for a landing and I must stare intelligently at the computer that controls it or no one will believe that I am the captain."

He left and she remained in gloomy abstraction for a while, her fingers plucking at the plastic that enclosed the coverall.

She had come to a sense of equilibrium on Aurora, a way of allowing life to pass quietly. Meal by meal, day by day, season by season, it had been passing and the quiet had insulated her, almost, from the tedious waiting for the only adventure that remained, the final one of death.

And now she had been to Solaria and had awakened the memories of a childhood that had long passed on a world that had long passed, so that the quiet had been shattered—perhaps forever—and so that she now lay uncovered and bare to the horror of continuing life.

What could substitute for the vanished quiet?

She caught Giskard's dimly glowing eyes upon her and she said, "Help me on with this, Giskard."

32.

IT WAS COLD. The sky was gray with clouds and the air glittered with a very light snowfall. Patches of powdery snow were swirling in the fresh breeze and off beyond the landing field Gladia could see distant heaps of snow.

There were crowds of people gathered here and there, held off by barriers from approaching too closely. They were all wearing coveralls of different types and colors and they all seemed to balloon outward, turning humanity into a crowd of shapeless objects with eyes. Some were wearing visors that glittered transparently over their faces.

Gladia pressed her mittened hand to her face. Except for her nose, she felt warm enough. The coverall did more than insulate; it seemed to exude warmth of its own.

She looked behind her. Daneel and Giskard were within reach, each in a coverall.

She had protested that at first. "They don't need coveralls. They're not sensitive to cold."

"I'm sure they're not," D.G. had said, "but you say you won't go anywhere without them and we can't very well have Daneel sitting there exposed to the cold. It would seem against nature. Nor do we wish to arouse hostility by making it too clear you have robots."

"They must know I've got robots with me and Giskard's face will give him away—even in a coverall."

"They might know," said D.G., "but the chances are they won't think about it if they're not forced to—so let's not force it."

Now D.G. was motioning her into a ground-car that had a transparent roof and sides. "They'll want to see you as we travel, my lady," he said, smiling.

Gladia seated herself at one side and D.G. followed on the other. "I'm co-hero," he said.

"Do you value that?"

"Oh, yes. It means a bonus for my crew and a possible promotion for me. I don't scorn that."

Daneel and Giskard entered, too, and sat down in seats that faced the two human beings. Daneel faced Gladia; Giskard faced D.G.

There was a ground-car before them, without transparency, and a line of about a dozen behind them. There was the sound of cheering and a forest of arm-waving from the assembled crowd. D.G. smiled and lifted an arm in response and motioned to Gladia to do the same. She waved in a perfunctory manner. It was warm inside the car and her nose had lost its numbness.

She said, "There's a rather unpleasant glitter to these windows. Can that be removed?"

"Undoubtedly, but it won't be," said D.G. "That's as unobtrusive a force field as we can set up. Those are enthusiastic people out there and they've been searched, but someone *may* have managed to conceal a weapon and we don't want you hurt."

"You mean someone might try to kill me?"

(Daneel's eyes were calmly scanning the crowd to one side of the car; Giskard's scanned the other side.)

"Very unlikely, my lady, but you're a Spacer and Settlers don't like Spacers. A few might hate them with such a surpassing hatred as to see only the Spacerness in you. —But don't worry. Even if someone were to try—which is, as I say, unlikely—they won't succeed."

The line of cars began to move, all together and very smoothly.

Gladia half-rose in astonishment. There was no one in front of the partition that closed them off. "Who's driving?" she asked.

"The cars are thoroughly computerized," said D.G. "I take it that Spacer cars are not?"

"We have robots to drive them."

D.G. continued waving and Gladia followed his lead automatically. "We don't," he said.

"But a computer is essentially the same as a robot."

"A computer is not humanoid and it does not obtrude itself on one's notice. Whatever the technological similarities might be, they are worlds apart psychologically."

Gladia watched the countryside and found it oppressively barren. Even allowing for winter, there was something desolate in the scattering of leafless bushes and in the sparsely distributed trees, whose stunted and dispirited appearance emphasized the death that seemed to grip everything.

D.G., noting her depression and correlating it with her darting glances here and there, said, "It doesn't look like much now, my lady. In the summer, though, it's not bad. There are grassy plains, orchards, grain fields—"

"Forests?"

"Not wilderness forests. We're still a growing world. It's still being

molded. We've only had a little over a century and a half, really. The first
step was to cultivate home plots for the initial Settlers, using imported seed.
Then we placed fish and invertebrates of all kinds in the ocean, doing our
best to establish a self-supporting ecology. That is a fairly easy procedure—
if the ocean chemistry is suitable. If it isn't, then the planet is not habitable
without extensive chemical modification and that has never been tried in
actuality, though there are all sorts of plans for such procedures. —Finally,
we try to make the land flourish, which is always difficult, always slow."

"Have all the Settler worlds followed that path?"

"Are following. None are really finished. Baleyworld is the oldest and
we're not finished. Given another couple of centuries, the Settler worlds
will be rich and full of life—land as well as sea—though by that time there
will be many still-newer worlds that will be working their way through
various preliminary stages. I'm sure the Spacer worlds went through the
same procedure."

"Many centuries ago—and less strenuously , I think. We had robots to
help."

"We'll manage," said D.G. briefly.

"And what about the native life—the plants and animals that evolved on
this world before human beings arrived?"

D.G. shrugged. "Insignificant. Small, feeble things. The scientists are, of
course, interested, so the indigenous life still exists in special aquaria, botan-
ical gardens, zoos. There are out-of-the-way bodies of water and considerable stretches of land area that have not yet been converted. Some indigenous life still lives out there in the wild."

"But these stretches of wilderness will eventually all be converted."

"We hope so."

"Don't you feel that the planet really belongs to these insignificant,
small, feeble things?"

"No. I'm not that sentimental. The planet and the whole Universe belongs to intelligence. The Spacers agree with that. Where is the indigenous
life of Solaria? Or of Aurora?"

The line of cars, which had been progressing tortuously from the space-
port, now came to a flat, paved area on which several low, domed buildings
were evident.

"Capital Plaza," said D.G. in a low voice. "This is the official heartbeat
of the planet. Government offices are located here, the Planetary Congress
meets here, the Executive Mansion is found here, and so on."

"I'm sorry, D.G., but this is not very impressive. These are small and uninteresting buildings."

D.G. smiled. "You see only an occasional top, my lady. The buildings themselves are located underground—all interconnected. It's a single complex, really, and is still growing. It's a self-contained city, you know. It, along with the surrounding residential areas, makes up Baleytown."

"Do you plan to have everything underground eventually? The whole city? The whole world?"

"Most of us look forward to an underground world, yes."

"They have underground Cities on Earth, I understand."

"Indeed they do, my lady. The so-called Caves of Steel."

"You imitate that here, then?"

"It's not simple imitation. We add our own ideas and— We're coming to a halt, my lady, and any moment we'll be asked to step out. I'd cling to the coverall openings if I were you. The whistling wind on the Plaza in winter is legendary."

Gladia did so, fumbling rather as she tried to put the edges of the openings together. "It's not simple imitation, you say."

"No. We design our underground with the weather in mind. Since our weather is, on the whole, harsher than Earth's, some modification in architecture is required. Properly built, almost no energy is required to keep the complex warm in winter and cool in summer. In a way, indeed, we keep warm in winter, in part, with the stored warmth of the previous summer and cool in summer with the coolness of the previous winter."

"What about ventilation?"

"That uses up some of the savings, but not all. It works, my lady, and someday we will match Earth's structures. That, of course, is the ultimate ambition—to make Baleyworld a reflection of Earth."

"I never knew that Earth was so admirable as to make imitation desirable," said Gladia lightly.

D.G. turned his eyes on her sharply. "Make no jokes of that sort, my lady, while you are with Settlers—not even with me. Earth is no joking matter."

Gladia said, "I'm sorry, D.G. I meant no disrespect."

"You didn't know. But *now* you know. Come, let's get out."

The side door of the car slid open noiselessly and D.G. turned in his seat and stepped out. He then held out one hand to help Gladia and said, "You'll be addressing the Planetary Congress, you know, and every government official who can squeeze in will do so."

Gladia, who had stretched out her hand to seize D.G.'s and who already felt—painfully—the cold wind on her face, shrank back suddenly. "I must make an address? I hadn't been told that."

D.G. looked surprised. "I rather thought you would take something of the sort for granted."

"Well, I didn't. And I can't make an address. I've never done such a thing."

"You must. It's nothing terrible. It's just a matter of saying a few words after some long and boring speeches of welcome."

"But what can I possibly say?"

"Nothing fancy, I assure you. Just peace and love and blah— Give them half a minute's worth. I'll scrawl out something for you if you wish."

And Gladia stepped out of the car and her robots followed her. Her mind was in a whirl.

Chapter 9

The Speech

33.

As THEY WALKED into the building, they removed their coveralls and handed them to attendants. Daneel and Giskard removed theirs, too, and the attendants cast sharp glances at the latter, approaching him gingerly.

Gladia adjusted her nose plugs nervously. She had never before been in the presence of large crowds of short-lived human beings—short-lived in part, she knew (or had always been told), because they carried in their bodies chronic infections and hordes of parasites.

She whispered, "Will I get back my own coverall?"

"You will wear no one else's," said D.G. "They will be kept safe and radiation-sterilized."

Gladia looked about cautiously. Somehow she felt that even optical contact might be dangerous.

"Who are those people?" She indicated several people who wore brightly colored clothing and were obviously armed.

"Security guards, madam," said D.G.

"Even here? In a government building?"

"Absolutely. And when we're on the platform, there will be a force-field curtain dividing us from the audience."

"Don't you trust your own legislature?"

D.G. half-smiled. "Not entirely. This is a raw world still and we go our own ways. We haven't had all the edges knocked off and we don't have robots watching over us. Then, too, we've got militant minority parties; we've got our war hawks."

"What are war hawks?"

Most of the Baleyworlders had their coveralls removed now and were helping themselves to drinks. There was a buzz of conversation in the air and many people stared at Gladia, but no one came over to speak to her. Indeed, it was clear to Gladia that there was a circle of avoidance about her.

D.G. noticed her glance from side to side and interpreted it correctly. "They've been told," he said, "that you would appreciate a little elbow room. I think they understand your fear of infection."

"They don't find it insulting, I hope."

"They may, but you've got something that is clearly a robot with you and most Baleyworlders don't want *that* kind of infection. The war hawks, particularly."

"You haven't told me what they are."

"I will if there's time. You and I and others on the platform will have to move in a little while. —Most Settlers think that, in time, the Galaxy will be theirs, that the Spacers cannot and will not compete successfully in the race for expansion. We also know it will take time. We won't see it. Our children probably won't. It may take a thousand years, for all we know. The war hawks don't want to wait. They want it settled now."

"They want *war?*"

"They don't say that, precisely. And they don't call themselves war hawks. That's what we sensible people call them. They call themselves Earth Supremacists. After all, it's hard to argue with people who announce they are in favor of Earth being supreme. We all favor that, but most of us don't necessarily expect it to happen tomorrow and are not ferociously upset that it won't."

"And these war hawks may attack me? Physically?"

D.G. gestured for her to move forward. "I think we'll have to get moving, madam. They're getting us into line. —No, I don't think you'll really be attacked, but it's always best to be cautious."

Gladia held back as D.G. indicated her place in line.

"Not without Daneel and Giskard, D.G. I'm still not going anywhere without them. Not even onto the platform. Not after what you just told me about the war hawks."

"You're asking a lot, my lady."

"On the contrary, D.G. I'm not asking for anything. Take me home right now—with my robots."

Gladia watched tensely as D.G. approached a small group of officials. He made a half-bow, arms in downward-pointing diagonals. It was what Gladia suspected to be a Baleyworlder gesture of respect.

She did not hear what D.G. was saying, but a painful and quite involuntary fantasy passed through her mind. If there was any attempt to separate her from her robots against her will, Daneel and Giskard would surely do what they could to prevent it. They would move too quickly and precisely to really hurt anyone—but the security guards would use their weapons at once.

She would have to prevent that at all costs—pretend she was separating from Daneel and Giskard voluntarily and ask them to wait behind for her. How could she do that? She had never been entirely without robots in her life. How could she feel safe without them? And yet what other way out of the dilemma offered itself?

D.G. returned. "Your status as heroine, my lady, is a useful bargaining chip. And, of course, I am a persuasive fellow. Your robots may go with you. They will sit on the platform behind you, but there will be no spotlight upon them. And, for the sake of the Ancestor, my lady, don't call attention to them. Don't even look at them."

Gladia sighed with relief. "You're a good fellow, D.G.," she said shakily. "Thank you."

She took her place near the head of the line, D.G. at her left, Daneel and Giskard behind her, and behind them a long tail of officials of both sexes.

A woman Settler, carrying a staff that seemed to be a symbol of office, having surveyed the line carefully, nodded, moved forward to the head of the line, then walked on. Everyone followed.

Gladia became aware of music in simple and rather repetitive march rhythm up ahead and wondered if she were supposed to march in some choreographed fashion. (Customs vary infinitely and irrationally from world to world, she told herself.)

Looking out of the corner of her eye, she noticed D.G. ambling forward in an indifferent way. He was almost slouching. She pursed her lips disapprovingly and walked rhythmically, head erect, spine stiff. In the absence of direction, she was going to march the way *she* wanted to.

They came out upon a stage and, as they did so, chairs rose smoothly from recesses in the floor. The line split up, but D.G. caught her sleeve lightly and she accompanied him. The two robots followed her.

She stood in front of the seat that D.G. quietly pointed to. The music grew loud, but the light was not quite as bright as it had been. And then, after what seemed an almost interminable wait, she felt D.G.'s touch pressing lightly downward. She sat and so did they all.

She was aware of the faint shimmer of the force-field curtain and beyond that an audience of several thousand. Every seat was filled in an amphitheater that sloped steeply upward. All were dressed in dull colors, browns and blacks, both sexes alike (as nearly as she could tell them apart). The security guards in the aisles stood out in their green and crimson uniforms. No doubt it lent them instant recognition. (Though, Gladia thought, it must make them instant targets as well.)

She turned to D.G. and said in a low voice, "You people have an enormous legislature."

D.G. shrugged slightly. "I think everyone in the governmental apparatus is here, with mates and guests. A tribute to your popularity, my lady."

She cast a glance over the audience from right to left and back and tried at the extreme of the arc to catch sight, out of the corner of her eye, of either Daneel or Giskard—just to be sure they were there. And then she thought, rebelliously, that nothing would happen because of a quick glance and deliberately turned her head. They were there. She also caught D.G. rolling his eyes upward in exasperation.

She started suddenly as a spotlight fell upon one of the persons on the stage, while the rest of the room dimmed further into shadowy insubstantiality.

The spotlighted figure rose and began to speak. His voice was not terribly loud, but Gladia could hear a very faint reverberation bouncing back from the far walls. It must penetrate every cranny of the large hall, she thought. Was it some form of amplification by a device so unobtrusive that she did not see it or was there a particularly clever acoustical shape to the hall? She did not know, but she encouraged her puzzled speculation to continue, for it relieved her, for a while, of the necessity of having to listen to what was being said.

At one point she heard a soft call of "Quackenbush" from some undetermined point in the audience. But for the perfect acoustics (if that was what it was), it would probably have gone unheard.

The word meant nothing to her, but from the soft, brief titter of laughter that swept the audience, she suspected it was a vulgarism. The sound quenched itself almost at once and Gladia rather admired the depth of the silence that followed.

Perhaps if the room were so perfectly acoustic that every sound could he heard, the audience *had* to be silent or the noise and confusion would be intolerable. Then, once the custom of silence was established and audience noise became a taboo, anything but silence would become unthinkable.

—Except where the impulse to mutter "Quackenbush" became irresistable, she supposed.

Gladia realized that her thinking was growing muddy and her eyes were closing. She sat upright with a small jerk. The people of the planet were trying to honor her and if she fell asleep during the proceedings, that would surely be an intolerable insult. She tried to keep herself awake by listening, but that seemed to make her sleepier. She bit the inside of her cheeks instead and breathed deeply.

Three officials spoke, one after the other, with semimerciful semibrevity, and then Gladia jolted wide awake (Had she been actually dozing despite all her efforts—with thousands of pairs of eyes on her?) as the spotlight fell just to her left and D.G. rose to speak, standing in front of his chair.

He seemed completely at ease, with his thumbs hooked in his belt.

"Men and women of Baleyworld," he began. "Officials, lawgivers, honored leaders, and fellow planetfolk, you have heard something of what happened on Solaria. You know that we were completely successful. You know that Lady Gladia of Aurora contributed to that success. It is time now to present some of the details to you and to all my fellow planetfolk who are watching on hypervision."

He proceeded to describe the events in modified form and Gladia found herself dryly amused at the nature of the modifications. He passed over his own discomfiture at the hands of a humanoid robot lightly. Giskard was never mentioned; Daneel's role was minimized; and Gladia's heavily emphasized. The incident became a duel between two women—Gladia and Landaree—and it was the courage and sense of authority of Gladia that had won out.

Finally, D.G. said, "And now Lady Gladia, Solarian by birth, Auroran by citizenship, but Baleyworlder by deed—" (There was strong applause at the last, the loudest Gladia had yet heard, for the earlier speakers had been but tepidly received.)

D.G. raised his hands for silence and it came at once. He then concluded, "—will now address you."

Gladia found the spotlight on herself and turned to D.G. in sudden panic. There was applause in her ears and D.G., too, was clapping his hands. Under the cover of the applause, he leaned toward her and whispered, "You love them all, you want peace, and since you're not a legislator, you're unused to long speeches of small content. Say that, then sit down."

She looked at him uncomprehendingly, far too nervous to have heard what he said.

She rose and found herself staring at endless tiers of people.

34.

GLADIA FELT VERY SMALL (not for the first time in her life, to be sure) as she faced the stage. The men on the stage were all taller than she was and so were the other three women. She felt that even though they were all sitting and she was standing, they still towered over her. As for the audience, which was waiting now in almost menacing silence, those who composed it were, she felt quite certain, one and all larger than her in every dimension.

She took a deep breath and said, "Friends—" but it came out in a thin, breathless whistle. She cleared her throat (in what seemed a thunderous rasp) and tried again.

"Friends!" This time there was a certain normality to the sound. "You are all descended from Earthpeople, every one of you. *I* am descended from Earthpeople. There are no human beings anywhere on all the inhabited worlds—whether Spacer worlds, Settler worlds, or Earth itself—that are not either Earthpeople by birth or Earthpeople by descent. All other differences fade to nothing in the face of that enormous fact."

Her eyes flickered leftward to look at D.G. and she found that he was smiling very slightly and that one eyelid trembled as though it were about to wink.

She went on. "That should be our guide in every thought and act. I thank you all for thinking of me as a fellow human being and for welcoming me among you without regard to any other classification in which you might have been tempted to place me. Because of that, and in the hope that the day will soon come when sixteen billion human beings, living in love and peace, will consider themselves as just that and nothing more—or less—I think of you not merely as friends but as kinsmen and kinswomen."

There was an outbreak of applause that thundered in upon her and Gladia half-closed her eyes in relief. She remained standing to let it continue and bathe her in its welcome indication that she had spoken well and —what was more—enough. When it began to fade, she smiled, bowed to right and left, and began to sit down.

And then a voice came out of the audience. "Why don't you speak in Solarian?"

She froze halfway to her seat and looked, in shock, at D.G.

He shook his head slightly and mouthed soundlessly: "Ignore it." He gestured as unobtrusively as possible that she seat herself.

She stared at him for a second or two, then realized what an ungainly sight she must present, with her posterior protruding in the unfinished process of seating herself. She straightened at once and flashed a smile at the audience as she turned her head slowly from side to side. For the first time she became aware of objects in the rear whose glistening lenses focused upon her.

Of course! D.G. had mentioned that the proceedings were being watched via hyperwave. Yet it scarcely seemed to matter now. She had spoken and had been applauded and she was facing the audience she could see, erect and without nervousness. What could the unseen addition matter?

She said, still smiling, "I consider that a friendly question. You want me to show you my accomplishments. How many want me to speak as a Solarian might? Don't hesitate. Raise your right hands."

A few right arms went up.

Gladia said, "The humanoid robot on Solaria heard me speak Solarian. That was what defeated it in the end. Come—let me see everyone who would like a demonstration."

More right arms went up and, in a moment, the audience became a sea of upraised arms. Gladia felt a hand tweaking at her pants leg and, with a rapid movement, she brushed it away.

"Very well. You may lower your arms now, kinsmen and kinswomen. Understand that what I speak now is Galactic Standard, which is your language, too. I, however, am speaking it as an Auroran would and I know you all understand me even though the way I pronounce my words may well strike you as amusing and my choice of words may on occasion puzzle you a bit. You'll notice that my way of speaking has notes to it and goes up and down—almost as though I were singing my words. This always sounds ridiculous to anyone not an Auroran, even to other Spacers.

"On the other hand, if I slip into the Solarian way of speaking as I am now doing, you will notice at once that the notes stop and that it becomes throaty with 'r's' that just about neverrr let go—especially if therrre is no 'rrrrr' anywherrrre on the vocal panoramarrrrrr."

There was a burst of laughter from the audience and Gladia confronted it with a serious expression on her face. Finally, she held up her arms and made a cutting movement downward and outward and the laughter stopped.

"However," she said, "I will probably never go to Solaria again, so I will have no occasion to use the Solarian dialect any further. And the good Captain Baley"—she turned and made a half-bow in his direction, noting that there was a distinct outbreak of perspiration on his brow—"informs me there is no telling when I'll be going back to Aurora, so I may have to drop the Auroran dialect as well. My only choice, then, will be to speak the Baleyworld dialect, which I shall at once begin to practice."

She hooked the fingers of each hand into an invisible belt, stretched her chest outward, pulled her chin downward, put on D.G.'s unself-conscious grin, and said, in a gravelly attempt at baritone, "Men and women of Baleyworld, officials, lawgivers, honored leaders, and fellow planetfolk—and that should include everyone, except, perhaps, dishonored leaders—" She did her best to include the glottal stops and the flat "a's" and carefully pronounced the "h" of "honored" and "dishonored" in what was almost a gasp.

The laughter was still louder this time and more prolonged and Gladia allowed herself to smile and to wait calmly while it went on and on. After all, she was persuading them to laugh at themselves.

And when things were quiet again, she said simply, in an unexaggerated version of the Auroran dialect, "Every dialect is amusing—or peculiar—to those who are not accustomed to it and it tends to mark off human beings into separate—and frequently mutually unfriendly—groups. Dialects, however, are only languages of the tongue. Instead of those, you and I and every other human being on every inhabited world should listen to the language of the heart—and there are no dialects to that. That language—if we will only listen—rings out the same in all of us."

That was it. She was ready to sit down again, but another question sounded. It was a woman's voice this time.

"How old are you?"

Now D.G. forced a low growl between his teeth. "Sit *down*, madam! Ignore the question."

Gladia turned to face D.G. He had half-risen. The others on the stage, as nearly as she could see them in the dimness outside the spotlight, were tensely leaning toward her.

She turned back to the audience and cried out ringingly, "The people here on the stage want me to sit down. How many of you out there want me to sit down? —I find you are silent. —How many want me to stand here and answer the question honestly?"

There was sharp applause and cries of "Answer! Answer!"

Gladia said, "The voice of the people! I'm sorry, D.G. and all the rest of you, but I am commanded to speak."

She looked up at the spotlight, squinting, and shouted, "I don't know who controls the lights, but light the auditorium and turn off the spotlight. I don't care what it does to the hyperwave cameras. Just make sure the sound is going out accurately. No one will care if I look dim, as long as they can hear me. Right?"

"Right!" came the multivoiced answer. Then "Lights! Lights!"

Someone on the stage signaled in a distraught manner and the audience was bathed in light.

"Much better," said Gladia. "Now I can see you all, my kinspeople. I would like, particularly, to see the woman who asked the question, the one who wants to know my age. I would like to speak to her directly. Don't be backward or shy. If you have the courage to ask the question, you should have the courage to ask it openly."

She waited and finally a woman rose in the middle distance. Her dark hair was pulled back tightly, the color of her skin was a light brown, and her clothing, worn tightly to emphasize a slim figure, was in shades of darker brown.

She said, just a bit stridently, "I'm not afraid to stand up. And I'm not afraid to ask the question again. How old are you?"

Gladia faced her calmly and found herself even welcoming the confrontation. (How was this possible? Throughout her first three decades, she had been carefully trained to find the real presence of even one human being intolerable. Now look at her—facing thousands without a tremble. She was vaguely astonished and entirely pleased.)

Gladia said, "Please remain standing, madam, and let us talk together. How shall we measure age? In elapsed years since birth?"

The woman said with composure, "My name is Sindra Lambid. I'm a member of the legislature and therefore one of Captain Baley's 'lawgivers' and 'honored leaders.' I hope 'honored,' at any rate." (There was a ripple of laughter as the audience seemed to grow increasingly good-natured.) "To answer your question, I think that the number of Galactic Standard Years that have elapsed since birth is the usual definition of a person's age. Thus, I am fifty-four years old. How old are you? How about just giving us a figure?"

"I will do so. Since my birth, two hundred and thirty-three Galactic Standard Years have come and gone, so that I am over twenty-three decades old—or a little more than four times as old as you are." Gladia held herself straight and she knew that her small, slim figure and the dim light made her look extraordinarily childlike at that moment.

There was a confused babble from the audience and something of a groan from her left. A quick glance in that direction showed her that D.G. had his hand to his forehead.

Gladia said, "But that is an entirely passive way of measuring time lapse. It is a measure of quantity that takes no account of quality. My life has been spent quietly, one might say dully. I have drifted through a set routine, shielded from all untoward events by a smoothly functioning social system that left no room for either change or experimentation and by my robots, who stood between me and misadventure of any kind.

"Only twice in my life have I experienced the breath of excitement and both times tragedy was involved. When I was thirty-three, younger in years than many of you who are now listening to me, there was a time—not a long one—during which a murder accusation hung over me. Two years later, there was another period of time—not long—during which I was involved in another murder. On both those occasions, Plainclothesman Elijah Baley was at my side. I believe most of you—or perhaps all of you—are familiar with the story as given in the account written by Elijah Baley's son.

"I should now add a third occasion for, this last month, I have faced a great deal of excitement, reaching its climax with my being required to stand up before you all, something which is entirely different from anything I have ever done in all my long life. And I must admit it is only your own good nature and kind acceptance of me that makes it possible.

"Consider, each of you, the contrast of all this with your own lives. You are pioneers and you live on a pioneer world. This world has been growing all your lives and will continue to grow. This world is anything but settled down and each day is—and must be—an adventure. The very climate is an adventure. You have first cold, then heat, then cold again. It is a climate rich in wind and storms and sudden change. At no time can you sit back and let time pass drowsily in a world that changes gently or not at all.

"Many Baleyworlders are Traders or can choose to be Traders and can then spend half their time scouring the space lanes. And if ever this world grows tame, many of its inhabitants can choose to transfer their sphere of activities to another less-developed world or join an expedition that will find a suitable world that has not yet felt the step of human beings and take their share in shaping it and seeding it and making it fit for human occupancy.

"Measure the length of life by events and deeds, accomplishments and exictements, and I am a child, younger than any of you. The large number of my years has served merely to bore and weary me; the smaller number of yours to enrich and excite you. —So tell me again, Madam Lambid, how old are you?"

Lambid smiled. "Fifty-four *good* years, Madam Gladia."

She sat down and again the applause welled up and continued. Under cover of that, D.G. said hoarsely, "Lady Gladia, who taught you how to handle an audience like this?"

"No one," she whispered back. "I never tried before."

"But quit while you're ahead. The person now getting to his feet is our leading war hawk. There's no need to face him. Say you are tired and sit down. We will tackle Old Man Bistervan ourselves."

"But I'm not tired," said Gladia. "I'm enjoying myself."

The man now facing her from her extreme right but rather near the stage was a tall, vigorous man with shaggy white eyebrows hanging over his eyes. His thinning hair was also white and his garments were a somber black, relieved by a white stripe running down each sleeve and trouser leg, as though setting sharp limits to his body.

His voice was deep and musical. "My name," he said, "is Tomas Bistervan and I'm known to many as the Old Man, largely, I think, because they wish I were and that I would not delay too long in dying. I do not know how to address you because you do not seem to have a family name and because I do not know you well enough to use your given name. To be honest, I do not wish to know you that well.

"Apparently, you helped save a Baleyworld ship on your world against the booby traps and weapons set up by your people and we are thanking you for that. In return, you have delivered some pious nonsense about friendship and kinship. Pure hypocrisy!

"When have your people felt kin to us? When have the Spacers felt any relationship to Earth and its people? Certainly, you Spacers are descended from Earthmen. We don't forget that. Nor do we forget that *you* have forgotten it. For well over twenty decades, the Spacers controlled the Galaxy and treated Earthpeople as though they were hateful, short-lived, diseased animals. Now that we are growing strong, you hold out the hand of friendship, but that hand has a glove on it, as your hands do. You try to remember not to turn up your nose at us, but the nose, even if not turned up, has plugs in it. Well? Am I correct?"

Gladia held up her hands. "It may be," she said, "that the audience here in this room—and, even more so, the audience outside the room that sees me via hyperwave—is not aware that I am wearing gloves. They are not obtrusive, but they are there. I do not deny that. And I have nose plugs that filter out dust and microorganisms without too much interference with breathing. And I am careful to spray my throat periodically. And I wash perhaps a bit more than the requirements of cleanliness alone make necessary. I deny none of it.

"But this is the result of my shortcomings, not yours. My immune system is not strong. My life has been too comfortable and I have been exposed to too little. That was not my deliberate choice, but I must pay the penalty for it. If any of you were in my unfortunate position, what would you do? In particular, Mr. Bistervan, what would *you* do?"

Bistervan said grimly, "I would do as you do and I would consider it a sign of weakness, a sign that I was unfit and unadjusted to life and that I therefore ought to make way for those who are strong. Woman, don't speak of kinship to us. You are no kin of mine. You are of those who persecuted and tried to destroy us when you were strong and who come whining to us when you are weak."

There was a stir in the audience—and by no means a friendly one—but Bistervan held his ground firmly.

Gladia said softly, "Do you remember the evil we did when we were strong?"

Bistervan said, "Don't fear that we will forget. It is in our minds every day."

"Good! Because now you know what to avoid. You have learned that when the strong oppress the weak, that is wrong. Therefore, when the table turns and when you are strong and we are weak, you will not be oppressive."

"Ah, yes. I have heard the argument. When you were strong, you never heard of morality, but now that you are weak, you preach it earnestly."

"In your case, though, when you were weak, you knew all about morality and were appalled by the behavior of the strong—and now that you are strong, you forget morality. Surely it is better that the immoral learn morality through adversity than that the moral forget morality in prosperity."

"We will give what we received," said Bistervan, holding up his clenched fist.

"You should give what you would have liked to receive," said Gladia, holding out her arms, as though embracing. "Since everyone can think of some past injustice to avenge, what you are saying, my friend, is that it is right for the strong to oppress the weak. And when you say that, you justify the Spacers of the past and should therefore have no complaint of the present. What I say is that oppression was wrong when we practiced it in the past and that it will be equally wrong when you practice it in the future. We cannot change the past, unfortunately, but we can still decide on what the future shall be."

Gladia paused. When Bistervan did not answer immediately, she called out, "How many want a new Galaxy, not the bad old Galaxy endlessly repeated?"

The applause began, but Bistervan threw his arms up and shouted in stentorian fashion, "Wait! Wait! Don't be fools! Stop!"

There was a slow quieting and Bistervan said, "Do you suppose this woman believes what she's saying? Do you suppose the Spacers intend us any good whatever? They still think they are strong, and they still despise us, and they intend to destroy us—if we don't destroy them first. This woman comes here and, like fools, we greet her and make much of her. Well, put her words to the test. Let any of you apply for permission to visit a Spacer world and see if you can. Or if you have a world behind you and can use threats, as Captain Baley did, so that you are allowed to land on the world, how will you be treated? Ask the captain if he was treated like kin.

"This woman is a hypocrite, in spite of all her words—no, because of them. They are the spoken advertisements of her hypocrisy. She moans and whines about her inadequate immune system and says that she must protect herself against the danger of infection. Of course, she doesn't do this because she thinks we are foul and diseased. That thought, I suppose, never occurs to her.

"She whines of her passive life, protected from mischance and misfortune by a too-settled society and a too-solicitous crowd of robots. How she must hate that.

"But what endangers her here? What mischance does she feel will befall her on our planet? Yet she has brought two robots with her. In this hall, we meet in order to honor her and make much of her, yet she brought her two robots even here. They are there on the platform with her. Now that the room is generally lit, you can see them. One is an imitation human being and its name is R. Daneel Olivaw. Another is a shameless robot, openly metallic in structure, and its name is R. Giskard Reventlov. Greet them, my fellow Baleyworlders. *They* are this woman's kinfolk."

"Checkmate!" groaned D.G. in a whisper.

"Not yet," said Gladia.

There were craning necks in the audience, as if a sudden itch had affected them all, and the word "Robots" ran across the length and breadth of the hall in thousands of intakes of breath.

"You can see them without trouble," Gladia's voice rang out. "Daneel, Giskard, stand up."

The two robots rose at once behind her.

"Step to either side of me," she said, "so that my body does not block the view. —Not that my body is large enough to do much blocking, in any case.

"Now let me make a few things clear to all of you. These two robots did not come with me in order to service me. Yes, they help run my establishment on Aurora, along with fifty-one other robots, and I do no work for myself that I wish a robot to do for me. That is the custom on the world on which I live.

"Robots vary in complexity, ability, and intelligence and these two rate very high in those respects. Daneel, in particular, is, in my opinion, the robot, of all robots, whose intelligence most nearly approximates the human in those areas where comparison is possible.

"I have brought *only* Daneel and Giskard with me, but they perform no great services for me. If you are interested, I dress myself, bathe myself, use my own utensils when I eat, and walk without being carried.

"Do I use them for personal protection? No. They protect me, yes, but they equally well protect anyone else who needs protection. On Solaria, just recently, Daneel did what he could to protect Captain Baley and was ready to give up his existence to protect me. Without him, the ship could not have been saved.

"And I certainly need no protection on this platform. After all, there is a force field stretched across the stage that is ample protection. It is not there at my request, but it is there and it supplies all the protection I need.

"Then why are my robots here with me?

"Those of you who know the story of Elijah Baley, who freed Earth of its Spacer overlords, who initiated the new policy of settlement, and whose son led the first human being to Baleyworld—why else is it called that?—know that well before he knew me, Elijah Baley worked with Daneel. He worked with him on Earth, on Solaria, and on Aurora—on each of his great cases. To Daneel, Elijah Baley was always 'Partner Elijah.' I don't know if that fact appears in his biography, but you may safely take my word for it. And although Elijah Baley, as an Earthman, began with a strong distrust of

Daneel, a friendship between them developed. When Elijah Baley was dying, here on this planet over sixteen decades ago, when it was just a cluster of prefabricated houses surrounded by garden patches, it was not his son who was with him in his last moment. Nor was it I." (For a treacherous moment, she thought her voice would not hold steady.) "He sent for Daneel and he held on to life until Daneel arrived.

"Yes, this is Daneel's second visit to this planet. I was with him, but I remained in orbit." (Steady!) "It was Daneel alone who made planetfall, Daneel who received his last words. —Well, does this mean nothing to you?"

Her voice rose a notch as she shook her fists in the air. "Must I tell you this? Don't you already know it? Here is the robot that Elijah Baley loved. Yes, loved. I wanted to see Elijah before he died, to say good-bye to him; but he wanted Daneel—and this is Daneel. This is the very one.

"And this other is Giskard, who knew Elijah only on Aurora, but who managed to save Elijah's life there.

"Without these two robots, Elijah Baley would not have achieved his goal. The Spacer worlds would still be supreme, the Settler worlds would not exist, and none of you would be here. I know that. You know that. I wonder if Mr. Tomas Bistervan knows that?

"Daneel and Giskard are honored names on this world. They are used commonly by the descendants of Elijah Baley at his request. I have arrived on a ship the captain of which is named Daneel Giskard Baley. How many, I wonder, among the people I face now—in person and via hyperwave— bear the name of Daneel or Giskard? Well, these robots behind me are the robots those names commemorate. And are they to be denounced by Tomas Bistervan?"

The growing murmur among the audience was becoming loud and Gladia lifted her arms imploringly. "One moment. One moment. Let me finish. I have not told you why I brought these two robots."

There was immediate silence.

"These two robots," Gladia said, "have never forgotten Elijah Baley, any more than I have forgotten him. The passing decades have not in the least dimmed those memories. When I was ready to step on to Captain Baley's ship, when I knew that I might visit Baleyworld, how could I refuse to take Daneel and Giskard with me? They wanted to see the planet that Elijah Baley had made possible, the planet on which he passed his old age and on which he died.

"Yes, they are robots, but they are intelligent robots who served Elijah

Baley faithfully and well. It is not enough to have respect for all human beings; one must have respect for all intelligent beings. So I brought them here." Then, in a final outcry that demanded a response, *"Did I do wrong?"*

She received her response. A gigantic cry of *"No!"* resounded throughout the hall and everyone was on his or her feet, clapping, stamping, roaring, screaming—on . . . and on . . . and on.

Gladia watched, smiling, and, as the noise continued endlessly, became aware of two things. First, she was wet with perspiration. Second, she was happier than she had ever been in her life.

It was as though all her life she had waited for this moment—the moment when she, having been brought up in isolation, could finally learn, after twenty-three decades, that she could face crowds, and move them, and bend them to her will.

She listened to the unwearying, noisy response—on . . . and on . . . and on . . .

35.

IT WAS A CONSIDERABLE time later—how long she had no way of telling—that Gladia finally came to herself.

There had first been unending noise, the solid wedge of security people herding her through the crowd, the plunge into endless tunnels that seemed to sink deeper and deeper into the ground.

She lost contact with D.G. early and was not sure that Daneel and Giskard were safely with her. She wanted to ask for them, but only faceless people surrounded her. She thought distantly that the robots had to be with her, for they would resist separation and she would hear the tumult if an attempt were made.

When she finally reached a room, the two robots were there with her. She didn't know precisely where she was, but the room was fairly large and clean. It was poor stuff compared to her home on Aurora, but compared to the shipboard cabin it was quite luxurious.

"You will be safe here, madam," said the last of the guards as he left. "If you need anything, just let us know." He indicated a device on a small table next to the bed.

She stared at it, but by the time she turned back to ask what it was and how it worked, he was gone.

Oh, well, she thought, I'll get by.

"Giskard," she said wearily, "find out which of those doors leads to the bathroom and find out how the shower works. What I *must* have now is a shower."

She sat down gingerly, aware that she was damp and unwilling to saturate the chair with her perspiration. She was beginning to ache with the unnatural rigidity of her position when Giskard emerged.

"Madam, the shower is running," he said, "and the temperature is adjusted. There is a solid material which I believe is soap and a primitive sort of toweling material, along with various other articles that may be useful."

"Thank you, Giskard," said Gladia, quite aware that despite her grandiloquence on the manner in which robots such as Giskard did not perform menial service, that is precisely what she had required him to do. But circumstances alter cases—

If she had never needed a shower, it seemed to her, as badly as now, she had also never enjoyed one as much. She remained in it much longer than she had to and when it was over it didn't even occur to her to wonder if the towels had been in any way irradiated to sterility until after she had dried herself—and by that time it was too late.

She rummaged about among the material Giskard had laid out for her—powder, deodorant, comb, toothpaste, hair dryer—but she could not locate anything that would serve as a toothbrush. She finally gave up and used her finger, which she found most unsatisfactory. There was no hairbrush and that too was unsatisfactory. She scrubbed the comb with soap before using it, but cringed away from it just the same. She found a garment that looked as though it were suitable for wearing to bed. It smelled clean, but it hung far too loosely, she decided.

Daneel said quietly, "Madam, the captain wishes to know if he may see you."

"I suppose so," said Gladia, still rummaging for alternate nightwear. "Let him in."

D.G. looked tired and even haggard, but when she turned to greet him, he smiled wearily at her and said, "It is hard to believe that you are over twenty-three decades old."

"What? In this thing?"

"That helps. It's semitransparent. —Or didn't you know?"

She looked down at the nightgown uncertainly, then said, "Good, if it amuses you, but I have been alive, just the same, for two and a third centuries."

"No one would guess it to look at you. You must have been very beautiful in your youth."

"I have never been told so, D.G. Quiet charm, I always believed, was the most I could aspire to. —In any case, how do I use that instrument?"

"The call box? Just touch the patch on the right side and someone will ask if you can be served and you can carry on from there."

"Good. I will need a toothbrush, a hairbrush, and clothing."

"The toothbrush and hairbrush I will see that you get. As for clothing, that has been thought of. You have a clothes bag hanging in your closet. You'll find it contains the best in Baleyworld fashion, which may not appeal to you, of course. And I won't guarantee they'll fit you. Most Baleyworld women are taller than you and certainly wider and thicker. —But it doesn't matter. I think you'll remain in seclusion for quite a while."

"Why?"

"Well, my lady. It seems you delivered a speech this past evening and, as I recall, you would not sit down, though I suggested you do that more than once."

"It seemed quite successful to me, D.G."

"It was. It was a howling success." D.G. smiled broadly and scratched the right side of his beard as though considering the word very carefully. "However, success has its penalties too. Right now, I should say you are the most famous person on Baleyworld and every Baleyworlder wants to see you and touch you. If we take you out anywhere, it will mean an instant riot. At least, until things cool down. We can't be sure how long that will take.

"Then, too, you had even the war hawks yelling for you, but in the cold light of tomorrow, when the hypnotism and hysteria dies down, they're going to be furious. If Old Man Bistervan didn't actually consider killing you outright after your talk, then by tomorrow he will certainly have it as the ambition of his life to murder you by slow torture. And there are people of his party who might conceivably try to oblige the Old Man in this small whim of his.

"That's why you're here, my lady. That's why this room, this floor, this entire hotel is being watched by I don't know how many platoons of security people, among whom, I hope, are no cryptowar hawks. And because I have been so closely associated with you in this hero-and-heroine game, I'm penned up here, too, and can't get out."

"Oh," said Gladia blankly. "I'm sorry about that. You can't see your family, then."

D.G. shrugged. "Traders don't really have much in the way of family."

"Your woman friend, then."

"She'll survive. —Probably better than I will." He cast his eyes on Gladia speculatively.

Gladia said evenly, "Don't even *think* it, Captain."

D.G.'s eyebrows rose. "There's no way I can be prevented from thinking it, but I won't *do* anything, madam."

Gladia said, "How long do you think I will stay here? Seriously."

"It depends on the Directory."

"The Directory?"

"Our five-fold executive board, madam. Five people"—he held up his hand with the fingers spread apart—"each serving five years in staggered fashion, with one replacement each year, plus special elections in case of death or disability. This supplies continuity and reduces the danger of one-person rule. It also means that every decision must be argued out and that takes time, sometimes more time than we can afford."

"I should think," said Gladia, "that if one of the five were a determined and forceful individual—"

"That he could impose his views on the others. Things like that have happened at times, but these times are not one of those times—if you know what I mean. The Senior Director is Genovus Pandaral. There's nothing evil about him, but he's indecisive—and sometimes that's the same thing. I talked him into allowing your robots on the stage with you and that turned out to be a bad idea. Score one against both of us."

"But why was it a bad idea? The people were *pleased.*"

"*Too* pleased, my lady. We wanted you to be our pet Spacer heroine and help keep public opinion cool so that we wouldn't launch a premature war. You were very good on longevity; you had them cheering short life. But then you had them cheering robots and we don't want that. For that matter, we're not so keen on the public cheering the notion of kinship with the Spacers."

"You don't want premature war, but you don't want premature peace, either. Is that it?"

"Very well put, madam."

"But, then, what do you want?"

"We want the Galaxy, the *whole* Galaxy. We want to settle and populate every habitable planet in it and establish nothing less than a Galactic Empire. And we don't want the Spacers to interfere. They can remain on their own worlds and live in peace as they please, but they must not interfere."

"But then you'll be penning them up on their fifty worlds, as we penned up Earthpeople on Earth for so many years. The same old injustice. You're as bad as Bistervan."

"The situations are different. Earthpeople were penned up in defiance of their expansive potential. You Spacers have no such potential. You took the path of longevity and robots and the potential vanished. You don't even have fifty worlds any longer. Solaria has been abandoned. The others will go, too, in time. The Settlers have no interest in pushing the Spacers along the path to extinction, but why should we interfere with their voluntary choice to do so? Your speech tended to interfere with that."

"I'm glad. What did you think I would say?"

"I told you. Peace and love and sit down. You could have finished in about one minute."

Gladia said angrily, "I can't believe you expected anything so foolish of me. What did you take me for?"

"For what you took yourself for—someone frightened to death of speaking. How did we know that you were a madwoman who could, in half an hour, persuade the Baleyworlders to howl in favor of what for lifetimes we have been persuading them to howl against? But talk will get us nowhere" —he rose heavily to his feet—"I want a shower, too, and I had better get a night's sleep—if I can. See you tomorrow."

"But when do we find out what the Directors will decide to do with me?"

"When *they* find out, which may not be soon. Good night, madam."

36.

"I HAVE MADE A DISCOVERY," said Giskard, his voice carrying no shade of emotion. "I have made it because, for the first time in my existence, I faced thousands of human beings. Had I done this two centuries ago, I would have made the discovery then. Had I never faced so many at once, then I would never have made the discovery at all.

"Consider, then, how many vital points I might easily grasp, but never have and never will, simply because the proper conditions for it will never come my way. I remain ignorant except where circumstance helps me and I cannot count on circumstance."

Daneel said, "I did not think, friend Giskard, that Lady Gladia, with her long-sustained way of life, could face thousands with equanimity. I did not think she would be able to speak at all. When it turned out that she could, I assumed you had adjusted her and that you had discovered that it could be done without harming her. Was that your discovery?"

. Giskard said, "Friend Daneel, actually all I dared do was loosen a very few strands of inhibition, only enough to allow her to speak a few words, so that she might be heard."

"But she did far more than that."

"After this microscopic adjustment, I turned to the multiplicity of minds I faced in the audience. I had never experienced so many, any more than Lady Gladia had, and I was as taken aback as she was. I found, at first, that I could do nothing in the vast mental interlockingness that beat in upon me. I felt helpless.

"And then I noted small friendlinesses, curiosities, interests—I cannot describe them in words—with a color of sympathy for Lady Gladia about them. I played with what I could find that had this color of sympathy, tightening and thickening them just slightly. I wanted some small response in Lady Gladia's favor that might encourage her, that might make it unnecessary for me to be tempted to tamper further with Lady Gladia's mind. That was all I did. I do not know how many threads of the proper color I handled. Not many."

Daneel said, "And what then, friend Giskard?"

"I found, friend Daneel, that I had begun something that was autocatalytic. Each thread I strengthened, strengthened a nearby thread of the same kind and the two together strengthened several others nearby. I had to do nothing further. Small stirs, small sounds, and small glances that seemed to approve of what Lady Gladia said encouraged still others.

"Then I found something stranger yet. All these little indications of approval, which I could detect only because the minds were open to me, Lady Gladia must have also detected in some manner, for further inhibitions in her mind fell without my touching them. She began to speak faster, more confidently, and the audience responded better than ever—without my doing anything. And in the end, there was hysteria, a storm, a tempest of mental thunder and lightning so intense that I had to close my mind to it or it would have overloaded my circuits.

"Never, in all my existence, had I encountered anything like that and yet it started with no more modification introduced by me in all that crowd than I have, in the past, introduced among a mere handful of people. I suspect, in fact, that the effect spread beyond the audience sensible to my mind—to the greater audience reached via hyperwave."

Daneel said, "I do not see how this can be, friend Giskard."

"Nor I, friend Daneel. I am not human. I do not directly experience the possession of a human mind with all its complexities and contradictions, so

I do not grasp the mechanisms by which they respond. But, apparently, crowds are more easily managed than individuals. It seems paradoxical. Much weight takes more effort to move than little weight. Much energy takes more effort to counter than little energy. Much distance takes longer to traverse than little distance. Why, then, should many people be easier to sway than few? You think like a human being, friend Daneel. Can you explain?"

Daneel said, "You yourself, friend Giskard, said that it was an autocatalytic effect, a matter of contagion. A single spark of flame may end by burning down a forest."

Giskard paused and seemed deep in thought. Then he said, "It is not reason that is contagious but emotion. Madam Gladia chose arguments she felt would move her audience's feelings. She did not attempt to reason with them. It may be, then, that the larger the crowd, the more easily they are swayed by emotion rather than by reason.

"Since emotions are few and reasons are many, the behavior of a crowd can be more easily predicted than the behavior of one person can. And that, in turn, means that if laws are to be developed that enable the current of history to be predicted, then one must deal with large populations, the larger the better. That might itself be the First Law of Psychohistory, the key to the study of Humanics. Yet—"

"Yes?"

"It strikes me that it has taken me so long to understand this only because I am not a human being. A human being would, perhaps, instinctively understand his own mind well enough to know how to handle others like himself. Madam Gladia, with no experience at all in addressing huge crowds, carried off the matter expertly. How much better off we would be if we had someone like Elijah Baley with us. —Friend Daneel, are you not thinking of him?"

Daneel said, "Can you see his image in my mind? That is surprising, friend Giskard."

"I do not see him, friend Daneel. I cannot receive your thoughts. But I can sense emotions and mood—and your mind has a texture which, by past experience, I know to be associated with Elijah Baley."

"Madam Gladia made mention of the fact that I was the last to see Partner Elijah alive, so I listen again, in memory, to that moment. I think again of what he said."

"Why, friend Daneel?"

"I search for the meaning. I feel it was important."

"How could what he said have meaning beyond the import of the words? Had there been hidden meaning, Elijah Baley would have expressed it."

"Perhaps," said Daneel slowly, "Partner Elijah did not himself understand the significance of what he was saying."

Chapter 10

After the Speech

37.

MEMORY!

It lay in Daneel's mind like a closed book of infinite detail, always available for his use. Some passages were called upon frequently for their information, but only a very few were called upon merely because Daneel wished to feel their texture. Those very few were, for the most part, those that contained Elijah Baley.

Many decades ago, Daneel had come to Baleyworld while Elijah Baley was still alive. Madam Gladia had come with him, but after they entered into orbit about Baleyworld, Bentley Baley soared upward in his small ship to meet them and was brought aboard. By then, he was a rather gnarled man of middle age.

He looked at Gladia with faintly hostile eyes and said, "You cannot see him, madam."

And Gladia, who had been weeping, said, "Why not?"

"He does not wish it, madam, and I must respect his wishes."

"I cannot believe that, Mr. Baley."

"I have a handwritten note and I have a voice recording, madam. I do not know if you can recognize his handwriting or his voice, but you have my word of honor these are his and that no untoward influence was used upon him to produce them."

She went into her own cabin to read and listen alone. Then she emerged —with an air of defeat about her—but she managed to say firmly, "Daneel, you are to go down alone to see him. It is his wish. But you are to report to me everything that is done and said."

"Yes, madam," Daneel said.

Daneel went down in Bentley's ship and Bentley said to him, "Robots are not allowed on this world, Daneel, but an exception is being made in your case because it is my father's wish and because he is highly revered here. I have no personal animus against you, you understand, but your presence here must be an entirely limited one. You will be taken directly to my father. When he is done with you, you will be taken back into orbit at once. Do you understand?"

"I understand, sir. How is your father?"

"He is dying," Bentley said with perhaps conscious brutality.

"I understand that, too," said Daneel, his voice quivering noticeably, not out of ordinary emotion but because the consciousness of the death of a human being, however unavoidable, disordered his positronic brain paths. "I mean, how much longer before he must die?"

"He should have died some time ago. He is tied to life because he refuses to go until he sees you."

They landed. It was a large world, but the inhabited portion—if this were all—was small and shabby. It was a cloudy day and it had rained recently. The wide, straight streets were empty, as though what population existed there was in no mood to assemble in order to stare at a robot.

The ground-car took them through the emptiness and brought them to a house somewhat larger and more impressive than most. Together they entered. At an inner door, Bentley halted.

"My father is in there," he said sadly. "You are to go in alone. He will not have me there with you. Go in. You might not recognize him."

Daneel went into the gloom of the room. His eyes adjusted rapidly and he was aware of a body covered by a sheet inside a transparent cocoon that was made visible only by its faint glitter. The light within the room brightened a bit and Daneel could then see the face clearly.

Bentley had been right. Daneel saw nothing of his old partner in it. It was gaunt and bony. The eyes were closed and it seemed to Daneel that what he saw was a dead body. He had never seen a dead human being and when this thought struck him, he staggered and it seemed to him that his legs would not hold him up.

But the old man's eyes opened and Daneel recovered his equilibrium, though he continued to feel an unaccustomed weakness just the same.

The eyes looked at him and a small, faint smile curved the pale, cracked lips.

"Daneel. My old friend Daneel." There was the faint timbre of Elijah

Baley's remembered voice in that whispered sound. An arm emerged slowly from under the sheet and it seemed to Daneel that he recognized Elijah after all.

"Partner Elijah," he said softly.

"Thank you—thank you for coming."

"It was important for me to come, Partner Elijah."

"I was afraid they might not allow it. They—the others—even my son—think of you as a robot."

"I *am* a robot."

"Not to me, Daneel. You haven't changed, have you? I don't see you clearly, but it seems to me you are exactly the same as I remember. When did I last see you? Twenty-nine years ago?"

"Yes—and in all that time, Partner Elijah, I have not changed, so you see, I *am* a robot."

"I have changed, though, and a great deal. I should not have let you see me like this, but I was too weak to resist my desire to see you once again." Baley's voice seemed to have grown a bit stronger, as though it had been fortified by the sight of Daneel.

"I am pleased to see you, Partner Elijah, however you have changed."

"And Lady Gladia? How is she?"

"She is well. She came with me."

"She is not—" A touch of painful alarm came into his voice as he tried to look about.

"She is not on this world, but is still in orbit. It was explained to her that you did not wish to see her—and she understood."

"That is wrong. I *do* wish to see her, but I have been able to withstand *that* temptation. She has not changed, has she?"

"She still has the appearance she had when you last saw her."

"Good. —But I couldn't let her see me like this. I could not have *this* be her last memory of me. With you, it is different."

"That is because I am a robot, Partner Elijah."

"Stop insisting on that," said the dying man peevishly. "You could not mean more to me, Daneel, if you were a man."

He lay silently in his bed for a while, then he said, "All these years, I have never hypervised, never written to her. I could not allow myself to interfere with her life. —Is Gladia still married to Gremionis?"

"Yes, sir."

"And happy?"

"I cannot judge that. She does not behave in a fashion that might be interpreted as unhappy."

"Children?"

"The permitted two."

"She has not been angry that I have not communicated?"

"It is my belief she understood your motives."

"Does she ever—mention me?"

"Almost never, but it is Giskard's opinion that she often thinks of you."

"How is Giskard?"

"He functions properly—in the manner that you know."

"You know, then—of his abilities."

"He has told me, Partner Elijah."

Again Baley lay there silently. Then he stirred and said, "Daneel, I wanted you here out of a selfish desire to see you, to see for myself that you haven't changed, that there is a breath of the great days of my life still existing, that you remember me and will continue to remember me. —But I also want to tell you something.

"I will be dead soon, Daneel, and I knew the word would reach you. Even if you weren't here, even if you were on Aurora, the word would come to you. My death will be Galactic news." His chest heaved in a weak and silent laugh. "Who would have thought it once?"

He said, "Gladia would hear of it as well, of course, but Gladia knows I must die and she will accept the fact, however sadly. I feared the effect on you, however, since you are—as you insist and I deny—a robot. For old times' sake you may feel it is incumbent upon you to keep me from dying and the fact that you cannot do so may perhaps have a permanently deleterious effect on you. Let me, then, argue with you about that."

Baley's voice was growing weaker. Though Daneel sat motionless, his face was in the unusual condition of reflecting emotion. It was set in an expression of concern and sorrow. Baley's eyes were closed and he could not see that.

"My death, Daneel," he said, "is not important. No individual death among human beings is important. Someone who dies leaves his work behind and that does *not* entirely die. It never entirely dies as long as humanity exists. —Do you understand what I'm saying?"

Daneel said, "Yes, Partner Elijah."

"The work of each individual contributes to a totality and so becomes an undying part of the totality. That totality of human lives—past and present and to come—forms a tapestry that has been in existence now for many tens of thousands of years and has been growing more elaborate and, on the whole, more beautiful in all that time. Even the Spacers are an offshoot of the tapestry and they, too, add to the elaborateness and beauty of the pattern. An individual life is one thread in the tapestry and what is one thread compared to the whole?

"Daneel, keep your mind fixed firmly on the tapestry and do not let the trailing off of a single thread affect you. There are so many other threads, each valuable, each contributing—"

Baley stopped speaking, but Daneel waited patiently.

Baley's eyes opened and, looking at Daneel, he frowned slightly.

"You are still here? It is time for you to go. I have told you what I meant to tell you."

"I do not wish to go, Partner Elijah."

"You must. I cannot hold off death any longer. I am tired—desperately tired. I want to die. It is time."

"May I not wait while you live?"

"I don't wish it. If I die while you watch, it may affect you badly despite all my words. Go now. That is an—order. I will allow you to be a robot if you wish but, in that case, you must follow my orders. You cannot save my life by anything you can do, so there is nothing to come ahead of Second Law. Go!"

Baley's finger pointed feebly and he said, "Good-bye, friend Daneel."

Daneel turned slowly, following Baley's orders with unprecedented difficulty. "Good-bye, Partner—" He paused and then said, with a faint hoarseness, "Good-bye, friend Elijah."

Bentley confronted Daneel in the next room. "Is he still alive?"

"He was alive when I left."

Bentley went in and came out almost at once. "He isn't now. He saw you and then—let go."

Daneel found he had to lean against the wall. It was some time before he could stand upright.

Bentley, eyes averted, waited and then together they returned to the small ship and moved back up into orbit where Gladia waited.

And she, too, asked if Elijah Baley was still alive and when they told her gently that he was not, she turned away, dry-eyed, and went into her own cabin to weep.

37a.

DANEEL CONTINUED his thought as though the sharp memory of Baley's death in all its details had not momentarily intervened. "And yet I may understand something more of what Partner Elijah was saying now in the light of Madam Gladia's speech."

"In what way?"

"I am not yet sure. It is very difficult to think in the direction I am trying to think."

"I will wait for as long as is necessary," said Giskard.

38.

GENOVUS PANDARAL was tall and not, as yet, very old for all his thick shock of white hair which, together with his fluffy white sideburns, gave him a look of dignity and distinction. His general air of looking like a leader had helped his advancement through the ranks, but as he himself knew very well, his appearance was much stronger than his inner fiber.

Once he had been elected to the Directory, he had gotten over the initial elation rather rapidly. He was in beyond his depth and, each year, as he was automatically pushed up a notch, he knew that more clearly. Now he was Senior Director.

Of all the times to be Senior Director!

In the old days, the task of ruling had been nothing. In the time of Nephi Morler, eight decades before, the same Morler who was always being held up to the schoolchildren as the greatest of all Directors, it had been nothing. What had Baleyworld been then? A small world, a trickle of farms, a handful of towns clustered along natural lines of communication. The total population had been no more than five million and its most important exports had been raw wool and some titanium.

The Spacers had ignored them completely under the more or less benign influence of Han Fastolfe of Aurora and life was simple. People could always make trips back to Earth—if they wanted a breath of culture or the feel of technology—and there was a steady flow of Earthpeople arriving as immigrants. Earth's mighty population was inexhaustible.

Why shouldn't Morler have been a great Director, then? He had had nothing to do.

And, in the future, ruling would again be simple. As the Spacers continued to degenerate (every schoolchild was told that they would, that they must drown in the contradictions of their society—though Pandaral wondered, sometimes, whether this was really certain) and as the Settlers continued to increase in numbers and strength, the time would soon come when life would be again secure. The Settlers would live in peace and develop their own technology to the utmost.

As Baleyworld filled, it would assume the proportion and ways of another Earth, as would all the worlds, while new ones would spring up here and there in ever greater numbers, finally making up the great Galactic Empire to come. And surely Baleyworld, as the oldest and most populous of the Settler worlds, would always have a prime place in that Empire, under the benign and perpetual rule of Mother Earth.

But it was not in the past that Pandaral was Senior Director. Nor was it in the future. It was now.

Han Fastolfe was dead now, but Kelden Amadiro was alive. Amadiro had held out against Earth being allowed to send out Settlers twenty decades ago and he was still alive now to make trouble. The Spacers were still too strong to be disregarded; the Settlers were still not quite strong enough to move forward with confidence. Somehow the Settlers had to hold off the Spacers till the balance had shifted sufficiently.

And the task of keeping the Spacers quiet and the Settlers at once resolute and yet sensible fell more upon Pandaral's shoulders than on anyone else's—and it was a task he neither liked nor wanted.

Now it was morning, a cold, gray morning with more snow coming—though *that* was no surprise—and he made his way through the hotel alone. He wanted no retinue.

The security guards, out in force, snapped to attention as he passed and he acknowledged them wearily. He spoke to the captain of the guard when the latter advanced to meet him. "Any trouble, Captain?"

"None, Director. All is quiet."

Pandaral nodded. "In which room has Baley been put? —Ah. —And the Spacer woman and her robots are under strict guard? —Good."

He passed on. On the whole, D.G. had behaved well. Solaria, abandoned, could be used by Traders as an almost endless supply of robots and as a source of large profits—though profits were not to be taken as the natural equivalent of world security, Pandaral thought morosely. But Solaria, booby-trapped, had best be left alone. It was not worth a war. D.G. had done well to leave at once.

And to take the nuclear intensifier with him. So far, such devices were so overwhelmingly massive that they could be used only in huge and expensive installations designed to destroy invading ships—and even these had never gotten beyond the planning stage. Too expensive. Smaller and cheaper versions were absolutely necessary, so D.G. was right in feeling that bringing home a Solarian intensifier was more important than all the robots on that world put together. That intensifier should help the scientists of Baleyworld enormously.

And yet if one Spacer world had a portable intensifier, why not others? Why not Aurora? If those weapons grew small enough to place on warships, a Spacer fleet could wipe out any number of Settler ships without trouble. How far toward that development were they? And how fast could Baleyworld progress in the same direction with the help of the intensifier D.G. had brought back?

He signaled at D.G.'s hotel room door, then entered without quite waiting for a response and sat down without quite waiting for an invitation. There were *some* useful perquisites that went along with being Senior Director.

D.G. looked out of the bathroom and said through the towel with which he was giving his hair a first dry, "I would have liked to greet your Directorial Excellence in a properly imposing manner, but you catch me at a disadvantage, since I am in the extremely undignified predicament of having just emerged from my shower."

"Oh, shut up," said Pandaral pettishly.

Ordinarily, he enjoyed D.G.'s irrepressible breeziness, but not now. In some ways, he never really understood D.G. at all. D.G. was a Baley, a lineal descendant of the great Elijah and the Founder, Bentley. That made D.G. a natural for a Director's post, especially since he had the kind of bonhomie that endeared him to the public. Yet he chose to be a Trader, which was a difficult life—and a dangerous one. It might make you rich, but it was much more likely to kill you or—what was worse—prematurely age you.

What's more, D.G.'s life as a Trader took him away from Baleyworld for months at a time and Pandaral preferred his advice to those of most of his department heads. One couldn't always tell when D.G. was serious, but, allowing for that, he was worth listening to.

Pandaral said heavily, "I don't think that that woman's speech was the best thing that could have happened to us."

D.G., mostly dressed, shrugged his shoulders. "Who could have foretold it?"

"You might have. You must have looked up her background—if you had made up your mind to carry her off."

"I *did* look up her background, Director. She spent over three decades on Solaria. It was Solaria that formed her and she lived there entirely with robots. She saw human beings only by holographic images, except for her husband—and he didn't visit her often. She had a difficult adjustment to make when she came to Aurora and even there she lived mostly with robots. At no time in twenty-three decades would she have faced as many as twenty people all together, let alone four thousand. I assumed she wouldn't be able to speak more than a few words—if that. I had no way of knowing she was a rabble-rouser."

"You might have stopped her, once you found out she was. You were sitting right next to her."

"Did you want a riot? The people were enjoying her. You were there. You know they were. If I had forced her down, they would have mobbed the stage. After all, Director, *you* didn't try to stop her."

Pandaral cleared his throat. "I had that in mind, actually, but each time I looked back, I'd catch the eye of her robot—the one who looks like a robot."

"Giskard. Yes, but what of it? He wouldn't harm you."

"I know. Still, he made me nervous and it put me off somehow."

"Well, never mind, Director," said D.G. He was fully clothed now and he shoved the breakfast tray toward the other. "The coffee is still warm. Help yourself to the buns and jams if you want any. —It will pass. I don't think the public will really overflow with love for the Spacers and spoil our policy. It might even serve a purpose. If the Spacers hear of it, it might strengthen the Fastolfe party. Fastolfe may be dead, but his party isn't—not altogether—and we need to encourage their policy of moderation."

"What I'm thinking of," said Pandaral, "is the All-Settler Congress that's coming up in five months. I'm going to have to listen to any number of sarcastic references to Baleyworld appeasement and to Baleyworlders being Spacer-lovers. —I tell you," he added gloomily, "the smaller the world, the more war hawkish it is."

"Then tell them that," said D.G. "Be very statesmanlike in public, but when you get them to one side, look them right in the eye—unofficially—and say that there's freedom of expression on Baleyworld and we intend to keep it that way. Tell them Baleyworld has the interests of Earth at heart, but that if any world wishes to prove its greater devotion to Earth by declaring war on the Spacers, Baleyworld will watch with interest but nothing more. That would shut them up."

"Oh, no," said Pandaral with alarm. "A remark like that would leak out. It would create an impossible stink."

D.G. said, "You're right, which is a pity. But *think* it and don't let those bigmouthed small brains get to you."

Pandaral sighed. "I suppose we'll manage, but last night upset our plans to end on a high note. That's what I really regret."

"What high note?"

Pandaral said, "When you left Aurora for Solaria, two Auroran warships went to Solaria as well. Did you know that?"

"No, but it was something I expected," said D.G. indifferently. "It was for that reason I took the trouble of going to Solaria by way of an evasive path."

"One of the Auroran ships landed on Solaria, thousands of kilometers away from you—so it didn't seem to be making any effort to keep tabs on you—and the second remained in orbit."

"Sensible. It's what I would have done if I had had a second ship at my disposal."

"The Auroran ship that landed was destroyed in a matter of hours. The ship in orbit reported the fact and was ordered to return. —A Trader monitoring station picked up the report and it was sent to us."

"Was the report uncoded?"

"Of course not, but it was in one of the codes we've broken."

D.G. nodded his head thoughtfully, then said, "Very interesting. I take it they didn't have anyone who could speak Solarian."

"Obviously," said Pandaral weightily. "Unless someone can find where the Solarians went, this woman of yours is the only available Solarian in the Galaxy."

"And they let me have her, didn't they? Tough on the Aurorans."

"At any rate, I was going to announce the destruction of the Auroran ship last night. In a matter-of-fact way—no gloating. Just the same, it would have excited every Settler in the Galaxy. I mean, we got away and the Aurorans didn't."

"We had a Solarian," said D.G. dryly. "The Aurorans didn't."

"Very well. It would make you and the woman look good, too. —But it all came to nothing. After what the woman did, anything else would have come as anticlimax, even the news of the destruction of an Auroran warship."

D.G. said, "To say nothing of the fact that once everyone has finished applauding kinship and love, it would go against the grain—for the next half hour anyway—to applaud the death of a couple of hundred of the Auroran kin."

"I suppose so. So that's an enormous psychological blow that we've lost."

D.G. was frowning. "Forget that, Director. You can always work the propaganda at some other, more appropriate time. The important thing is what it all means. —An Auroran ship was blown up. That means they weren't expecting a nuclear intensifier to be used. The other ship was ordered away and that may mean it wasn't equipped with a defense against it —and maybe they don't even have a defense. I should judge from this that the portable intensifier—or semiportable one, anyway—is a Solarian development specifically and not a Spacer development generally. That's good news for us—if it's true. For the moment, let's not worry about propaganda brownie points but concentrate on squeezing every bit of information we can out of that intensifier. We want to be ahead of the Spacers in this—if possible."

Pandaral munched away at a bun and said, "Maybe you're right. But in that case, how do we fit in the other bit of news?"

D.G. said, "What other bit of news? Director, are you going to give me the information I need to make intelligent conversation or do you intend to toss them into the air one by one and make me jump for them?"

"Don't get huffy, D.G. There's no point in talking with you if I can't be informal. Do you know what it's like at a Directory meeting? Do you want my job? You can have it, you know."

"No, thank you, I don't want it. What I want is your bit of news."

"We have a message from Aurora. An actual message. They actually deigned to communicate directly with us instead of sending it by way of Earth."

"We might consider it an important message, then—to them. What do they want?"

"They want the Solarian woman back again."

"Obviously, then, they know our ship got away from Solaria and has come to Baleyworld. They have their monitoring stations, too, and eavesdrop on our communications as we eavesdrop on theirs."

"Absolutely," said Pandaral with considerable irritation. "They break our codes as fast as we break theirs. My own feeling is we ought to come to an agreement that we both send messages in the clear. Neither of us would be worse off."

"Did they say why they want the woman?"

"Of course not. Spacers don't give reasons; they give orders."

"Have they found out exactly what it was that the woman accomplished on Solaria? Since she's the only person who speaks authentic Solarian, do they want her to clear the planet of its overseers?"

"I don't see how they could have found out, D.G. We only announced her role last night. The message from Aurora was received well before that. —But it doesn't matter why they want her. The question is: What do we do? If we don't return her, we may have a crisis with Aurora that I don't want. If we do return her, it will look bad to the Baleyworlders and Old Man Bistervan will have a field day pointing out that we're crawling to the Spacers."

They stared at each other, then D.G. said slowly, "We'll have to return her. After all, she's a Spacer and an Auroran citizen. We can't keep her against Aurora's will or we'll put at risk every Trader who ventures into Spacer territory on business. But *I'll* take her back, Director, and you can put the blame on me. Say that the conditions of my taking her to Solaria were that I would return her to Aurora, which is true, actually, even if not a matter of written formality, and that I am a man of ethics and felt I had to keep my agreement. —And it may turn out to our advantage."

"In what way?"

"I'll have to work it out. But if it's to be done, Director, my ship will have to be refitted at planetary expense. And my men will need healthy bonuses. —Come, Director, they're giving up their leave."

39.

CONSIDERING THAT he had not intended to be in his ship again for at least three additional months, D.G. seemed in genial spirits.

And considering that Gladia had larger and more luxurious quarters than she had before, she seemed rather depressed.

"Why all this?" she asked.

"Looking a gift horse in the mouth?" asked D.G.

"I'm just asking. Why?"

"For one thing, my lady, you're a class-A heroine and when the ship was refurbished, this place was rather tarted up for you."

"Tarted up?"

"Just an expression. Fancied up, if you prefer."

"This space wasn't just created. Who lost out?"

"Actually, it was the crew's lounge, but they insisted, you know. You're their darling, too. In fact, Niss—you remember Niss?"

"Certainly."

"He wants you to take him on in place of Daneel. He says Daneel doesn't enjoy the job and keeps apologizing to his victims. Niss says he will destroy anyone who gives you the least trouble, will take pleasure in it, and will never apologize."

Gladia smiled. "Tell him I will keep his offer in mind and tell him I would enjoy shaking his hand if that can be arranged. I didn't get a chance to do so before we landed on Baleyworld."

"You'll wear your gloves, I hope, when you shake hands."

"Of course, but I wonder if that's entirely necessary. I haven't as much as sniffled since I left Aurora. The injections I've been getting have probably strengthened my immune system beautifully." She looked about again. "You even have wall niches for Daneel and Giskard. That's quite thoughtful of you, D.G."

"Madam," said D.G., "we work hard to please and we're delighted that you're pleased."

"Oddly enough"—Gladia sounded as though she were actually puzzled by what she was about to say—"I'm not entirely pleased. I'm not sure I want to leave your world."

"No? Cold—snow—dreary—primitive—endlessly cheering crowds everywhere. What can possibly attract you here?"

Gladia reddened. "It's not the cheering crowds."

"I'll pretend to believe you, madam."

"It's *not*. It's something altogether different. I—I have never done anything. I've amused myself in various trivial ways, I've engaged in force-field coloring and robot exodesign. I've made love and been a wife and mother and—and—in none of these things have I ever been an individual of any account. If I had suddenly disappeared from existence or if I had never been born, it wouldn't have affected anyone or anything—except, perhaps, one or two close personal friends. Now it's different."

"Yes?" There was the faintest touch of mockery in D.G.'s voice.

Gladia said, "Yes! I can influence people. I can choose a cause and make it my own. I *have* chosen a cause. I want to prevent war. I want the Universe populated by Spacer and Settler alike. I want each group to keep their own peculiarities, yet freely accept the others', too. I want to work so hard at this that after I am gone, history will have changed because of me and people will say, 'Things would not be as satisfactory as they are had it not been for her.' "

She turned to D.G., her face glowing. "Do you know what a difference it makes, after two and one-third centuries of being nobody, to have a chance of being *somebody;* to find that a life you thought of as empty turns out to contain something after all, something wonderful; to be happy long, long after you had given up any hope of being happy?"

"You don't have to be on Baleyworld, my lady, to have all that." Somehow D.G. seemed a little abashed.

"I won't have it on Aurora. I am only a Solarian immigrant on Aurora. On a Settler world, I'm a Spacer—something unusual."

"Yet on a number of occasions—and quite forcefully—you have stated you wanted to return to Aurora."

"Some time ago, yes—but I'm not saying it now, D.G. I don't really want it now."

"Which would influence us a great deal, except that Aurora wants *you.* They've told us so."

Gladia was clearly astonished. "They *want* me?"

"An official message from Aurora's Chairman of the Council tells us they do," said D.G. lightly. "We would enjoy keeping you, but the Directors have decided that keeping you is not worth an interstellar crisis. I'm not sure I agree with them, but they outrank me."

Gladia frowned. "Why should they want me? I've been on Aurora for over twenty decades and at no time have they ever seemed to want me. —Wait! Do you suppose they see me now as the only way of stopping the overseers on Solaria?"

"That thought had occurred to me, my lady."

"I won't do it. I held off that one overseer by a hair and I may never be able to repeat what I did then. I know I won't. —Besides, why need they land on the planet? They can destroy the overseers from a distance, now that they know what they are."

"Actually," said D.G., "the message demanding your return was sent out long before they could possibly have known of your conflict with the overseer. They must want you for something else."

"Oh." She looked taken aback. Then, catching fire again, "I don't care what else. I don't want to return. I have my work out here and I mean to continue it."

D.G. rose. "I am glad to hear you say so, Madam Gladia. I was hoping you would feel like that. I promise you I will do my best to take you with me when we leave Aurora. Right now, though, I *must* go to Aurora and you *must* go with me."

40.

GLADIA WATCHED BALEYWORLD, as it receded, with emotions quite different from those with which she had watched it approach. It was precisely the cold, gray, miserable world now that it had seemed at the start, but there was a warmth and life to the people. They were real, solid.

Solaria, Aurora, the other Spacer worlds that she had visited or had viewed on hypervision, all seemed filled with people who were insubstantial —gaseous.

That was the word. Gaseous.

No matter how few the human beings who lived upon a Spacer world, they spread out to fill the planet in the same way that molecules of gas spread out to fill a container. It was as if Spacers repelled each other.

And they did, she thought gloomily. Spacers had always repelled her. She had been brought up to such repulsion on Solaria, but even on Aurora, when she was experimenting madly with sex just at first, the least enjoyable aspect of it was the closeness it made necessary.

Except—except with Elijah. —But he was not a Spacer.

Baleyworld was not like that. Probably all the Settler worlds were not. Settlers clung together, leaving large tracts desolate about them as the price of the clinging—empty, that is, until population increase filled it. A Settler world was a world of people clusters, of pebbles and boulders, not gas.

Why was this? Robots, perhaps! They lessened the dependence of people upon people. They filled the interstices between. They were the insulation that diminished the natural attraction people had for each other, so that the whole system fell apart into isolates.

It had to be. Nowhere were there more robots than on Solaria and the insulating effect there had been so enormous that the separate gas molecules that were human beings became so totally inert that they almost never interrelated at all. (Where had the Solarians gone, she wondered again, and how were they living?)

And long life had something to do with it, too. How could one make an emotional attachment that wouldn't turn slowly sour as the multidecades passed—or, if one died, how could another bear the loss for multidecades? One learned, then, not to make emotional attachments but to stand off, to insulate one's self.

On the other hand, human beings, if short-lived, could not so easily outlive fascination with life. As the generations passed by rapidly, the ball of fascination bounced from hand to hand without ever touching the ground.

How recently she had told D.G. that there was no more to do or know, that she had experienced and thought everything, that she had to live on in utter boredom. —And she hadn't known or even dreamed, as she spoke, of crowds of people, one upon another; of speaking to many as they melted into a continuous sea of heads; of hearing their response, not in words but in wordless sounds; of melting together with them, feeling their feelings, becoming one large organism.

It was not merely that she had never experienced such a thing before, it was that she had never dreamed anything like that *might* be experienced. How much more did she know nothing of despite her long life? What more existed for the experiencing that she was incapable of fantasying?

Daneel said gently, "Madam Gladia, I believe the captain is signaling for entrance."

Gladia started. "Let him enter, then."

D.G. entered, eyebrows raised. "I am relieved. I thought perhaps you were not at home."

Gladia smiled. "In a way, I wasn't. I was lost in thought. It happens to me sometimes."

"You are fortunate," said D.G. "My thoughts are never large enough to be lost in. Are you reconciled to visiting Aurora, madam?"

"No, I'm not. And among the thoughts in which I was lost was one to the effect that I still do not have any idea why you must go to Aurora. It can't be only to return me. Any spaceworthy cargo tug could have done the job."

"May I sit down, madam?"

"Yes, of course. That goes without saying, Captain. I wish you'd stop treating me as aristocracy. It becomes wearing. And if it's an ironic indication that I'm a Spacer, then it's worse than wearing. In fact, I'd almost rather you called me Gladia."

"You seem to be anxious to disown your Spacer identity, Gladia," said D.G. as he seated himself and crossed his legs.

"I would rather forget nonessential distinctions."

"Nonessential? Not while you live five times as long as I do."

"Oddly enough, I have been thinking of that as a rather annoying disadvantage for Spacers. —How long before we reach Aurora?"

"No evasive action this time. A few days to get far enough from our sun to be able to make a Jump through hyperspace that will take us to within a few days of Aurora—and that's it."

"And why must *you* go to Aurora, D.G.?"

"I might say it was simply politeness, but in actual fact, I would like an opportunity to explain to your Chairman—or even to one of his subordinates—exactly what happened on Solaria."

"Don't they know what happened?"

"In essentials, they do. They were kind enough to tap our communications, as we would have done theirs if the situation had been reversed. Still, they may not have drawn the proper conclusions. I would like to correct them—if that is so."

"What are the proper conclusions, D.G.?"

"As you know, the overseers on Solaria were geared to respond to a person as human only if he or she spoke with a Solarian accent, as you did. That means that not only were Settlers not considered human, but non-Solarian Spacers were not considered human, either. To be precise, Aurorans would not be considered human beings if they had landed on Solaria."

Gladia's eyes widened. "That's unbelievable. The Solarians wouldn't arrange to have the overseers treat Aurorans as they treated you."

"Wouldn't they? They have already destroyed an Auroran ship. Did you know that?"

"An Auroran ship! No, I didn't know that."

"I assure you they did. It landed about the time we did. We got away, but they didn't. We had you, you see, and they didn't. The conclusion is—or should be—that Aurora cannot automatically treat other Spacer worlds as allies. In an emergency, it will be each Spacer world for itself."

Gladia shook her head violently. "It would be unsafe to generalize from a single instance. The Solarians would have found it difficult to have the overseers react favorably to fifty accents and unfavorably to scores of others. It was easier to pin them to a single accent. That's all. They gambled that no other Spacers would try to land on their world and they lost."

"Yes, I'm sure that is how the Auroran leadership will argue, since people generally find it much easier to make a pleasant deduction than an unpleasant one. What I want to do is to make certain they see the possibility of the unpleasant one—and that this makes them uncomfortable indeed. Forgive my self-love, but I can't trust anyone to do it as well as I can and therefore I think that I, rather than anyone else, should go to Aurora."

Gladia felt uncomfortably torn. She did not want to be a Spacer; she wanted to be a human being and forget what she had just called "nonessential distinctions." And yet when D.G. spoke with obvious satisfaction of forcing Aurora into a humiliating position, she found herself still somehow a Spacer.

She said in annoyance, "I presume the Settler worlds are at odds among themselves, too. Is it not each Settler world for itself?"

D.G. shook his head. "It may seem to you that this must be so and I wouldn't be surprised if each individual Settler world had the impulse at times to put its own interest over the good of the whole, but we have something you Spacers lack."

"And what is that. A greater nobility?"

"Of course not. We're no more noble than Spacers are. What we've got is the Earth. It's our world. Every Settler visits Earth as often as he can. Every Settler knows that there is a world, a large, advanced world, with an incredibly rich history and cultural variety and ecological complexity that is his or hers and to which he or she belongs. The Settler worlds might quarrel with each other, but the quarrel cannot possibly result in violence or in a permanent breach of relations, for the Earth government is automatically called in to mediate all problems and its decision is sufficient and unquestioned."

"Those are our three advantages, Gladia: the lack of robots, something that allows us to build new worlds with our own hands; the rapid succession of generations, which makes for constant change; and, most of all, the Earth, which gives us our central core."

Gladia said urgently, "But the Spacers—" and she stopped.

D.G. smiled and said with an edge of bitterness, "Were you going to say that the Spacers are also descended from Earthpeople and that it is their planet, too? Factually true, but psychologically false. The Spacers have done their best to deny their heritage. They don't consider themselves Earthmen once-removed—or any-number-removed. If I were a mystic, I would say that by cutting themselves away from their roots, the Spacers cannot survive long. Of course, I'm not a mystic so I don't put it that way—but they cannot survive long, just the same. I believe that."

Then, after a short pause, he added, with a somewhat troubled kindness, as though he realized that in his exultation he was striking a sensitive spot within her, "But please think of yourself as a human being, Gladia, rather than as a Spacer, and I will think of myself as a human being, rather than as a Settler. Humanity *will* survive, whether it will be in the form of Settlers or Spacers or both. I believe it will be in the form of Settlers only, but I may be wrong."

"No," said Gladia, trying to be unemotional. "I think you're right—

unless somehow people learn to stop making the Spacer/Settler distinction. It is my goal—to help people do that."

"However," said D.G., glancing at the dim time strip that circled the wall, "I delay your dinner. May I eat with you?"

"Certainly," said Gladia.

D.G. rose to his feet. "Then I'll go get it. I'd send Daneel or Giskard, but I don't ever want to get into the habit of ordering robots about. Besides, however much the crew adores you, I don't think their adoration extends to your robots."

Gladia did not actually enjoy the meal when D.G. brought it. She did not seem to grow accustomed to the lack of subtlety in its flavors that might be the heritage of Earth cooking of yeast for mass consumption, but then, neither was it particularly repulsive. She ate stolidly.

D.G., noting her lack of enthusiasm, said, "The food doesn't upset you, I hope?"

She shook her head. "No. Apparently, I'm acclimated. I had some unpleasant episodes when I first got on the ship, but nothing really severe."

"I'm glad of that, but, Gladia—"

"Yes?"

"Can you suggest no reason why the Auroran government should want you back so urgently? It can't be your handling of the overseer and it can't be your speech. The request was sent out well before they could have known of either."

"In that case, D.G.," Gladia said sadly, "they can't possibly want me for anything. They never have."

"But there must be something. As I told you, the message arrived in the name of the Chairman of the Council of Aurora."

"This particular Chairman at this particular time is thought to be rather a figurehead."

"Oh? Who stands behind him? Kelden Amadiro?"

"Exactly. You know of him, then."

"Oh, yes," said D.G. grimly, "the center of anti-Earth fanaticism. The man who was politically smashed by Dr. Fastolfe twenty decades ago survives to threaten us again. There's an example of the dead hand of longevity."

"But there's the puzzle, too." Gladia said. "Amadiro is a vengeful man. He knows that it was Elijah Baley who was the cause of that defeat you speak of and Amadiro believes I shared responsibility. His dislike—*extreme* dislike—extends to me. If the Chairman wants me, that can only be because Amadiro wants me—and why should Amadiro want me? He would rather get rid of me. That's probably why he sent me along with you to Solaria. Surely he expected your ship would be destroyed—and me along with it. And that would not have pained him at all."

"No uncontrollable tears, eh?" said D.G. thoughtfully. "But surely that's not what you were told. No one said to you, 'Go with this mad Trader because it would give us pleasure to have you killed.' "

"No. They said that you wanted my help badly and that it was politic to cooperate with the Settler worlds at the moment and that it would do Aurora a great deal of good if I would report back to them on all that occurred on Solaria once I returned."

"Yes, they would say so. They might even have meant it to some extent. Then, when—against all their expectations—our ship got off safely while an Auroran ship was destroyed, they might well have wanted a firsthand account of what happened. Therefore, when I took you to Baleyworld instead of back to Aurora, they would scream for your return. That might possibly be it. By now, of course, they know the story, so they might no longer want you. Though"—he was talking to himself rather than to Gladia—"what they know is what they picked up from Baleyworld hypervision and they may not choose to accept that at face value. And yet—"

"And yet what, D.G.?"

"Somehow instinct tells me that their message could not have been sparked only by their desire to have you report. The forcefulness of the demand, it seems to me, went beyond that."

"There's nothing else they can want. *Nothing,*" said Gladia.

"I wonder," said D.G.

41.

"I WONDER AS WELL," said Daneel from his wall niche that night.

"You wonder concerning what, friend Daneel?" asked Giskard.

"I wonder concerning the true significance of the message from Aurora demanding Lady Gladia. To me, as to the captain, a desire for a report seems a not altogether sufficient motivation."

"Have you an alternate suggestion?"

"I have a thought, friend Giskard."

"May I know it, friend Daneel?"

"It has occurred to me that, in demanding the return of Madam Gladia, the Auroran Council may expect to see more than they ask for—and it may not be Madam Gladia they want."

"What is there more than Madam Gladia that they will get?"

"Friend Giskard, is it conceivable that Lady Gladia will return without you and me?"

"No, but of what use to the Auroran Council would you and I be?"

"I, friend Giskard, would be of no use to them. You, however, are unique, for you can sense minds directly."

"That is true, friend Daneel, but they do not know this."

"Since our leaving, is it not possible that they have somehow discovered the fact and have come to regret bitterly having allowed you to leave Aurora?"

Giskard did not hesitate perceptibly. "No, it is not possible, friend Daneel. How would they have found out?"

Daneel said carefully, "I have reasoned in this fashion. You have, on your long-ago visit to Earth with Dr. Fastolfe, managed to adjust a few Earth robots so as to allow them a very limited mental capacity, merely enough to enable them to continue your work of influencing officials on Earth to look with courage and favor on the process of Settlement. So, at least, you once told me. There are, therefore, robots on Earth that are capable of mind-adjusting.

"Then, too, as we have come recently to suspect, the Robotics Institute of Aurora has sent humanoid robots to Earth. We do not know their precise purpose in doing so, but the least that can be expected of such robots is that they observe events there on Earth and report on them.

"Even if the Auroran robots cannot sense minds, they can send back reports to the effect that this or that official has suddenly changed his attitude toward Settlement and, perhaps, in the time since we have left Aurora, it has dawned on someone in power in Aurora—on Dr. Amadiro himself perhaps—that this can only be explained by the existence of mind-adjusting robots on Earth. It may be, then, that the establishment of mind-adjusting can be traced back to either Dr. Fastolfe or yourself.

"This might, in turn, make clear to Auroran officials the meaning of certain other events, which might be traced back to you rather than to Dr. Fastolfe. As a result, they would want you back desperately, yet not be able to ask for you directly, for that would give away the fact of their new knowledge. So they ask for Lady Gladia—a natural request—knowing that if she is brought back, you will be, too."

Giskard was silent for a full minute, then he said, "It is interestingly reasoned, friend Daneel, but it does not hold together. Those robots whom I designed for the task of encouraging Settlement completed their job more than eighteen decades ago and have been inactive since, at least as far as mind-adjustment is concerned. What's more, the Earth removed robots from their Cities and confined them to the unpopulated non-City areas quite a considerable time ago.

"This means that the humanoid robots who were, we speculate, sent to Earth, would, even so, not have had occasion to meet my mind-adjusting robots or be aware of any mind-adjustment either, considering that the robots are no longer engaged in that. It is impossible, therefore, for my special ability to have been uncovered in the manner you suggest."

Daneel said, "Is there no other way of discovery, friend Giskard?"

"None," said Giskard firmly.

"And yet—I wonder," said Daneel.

PART FOUR
AURORA

Chapter 11

The Old Leader

42.

KELDEN AMADIRO WAS NOT immune from the human plague of memory. He was, in fact, more subject to it than most. In his case, moreover, the tenacity of memory had, as its accompaniment, a content unusual for the intensity of its deep and prolonged rage and frustration.

All had been going so well for him twenty decades before. He was the founding head of the Robotics Institute (he was *still* the founding head) and for one flashing and triumphant moment it had seemed to him that he could not fail to achieve total control of the Council, smashing his great enemy, Han Fastolfe, and leaving him in helpless opposition.

If he had—if he only had—

(How he tried not to think of it and how his memory presented him with it, over and over again, as though it could never get enough of grief and despair.)

If he had won out, Earth would have remained isolated and alone and he would have seen to it that Earth declined, decayed, and finally faded into dissolution. Why not? The short-lived people of a diseased, overcrowded world were better off dead—a hundred times better off dead than living the life they had forced themselves to lead.

And the Spacer worlds, calm and secure, would then have expanded further. Fastolfe had always complained that the Spacers were too long-lived and too comfortable on their robotic cushions to be pioneers, but Amadiro would have proved him wrong.

Yet Fastolfe had won out. At the moment of certain defeat, he had somehow, unbelievably, incredibly, reached into empty space, so to speak, and found victory in his grasp—plucked from nowhere.

It was that Earthman, of course, Elijah Baley—

But Amadiro's otherwise uncomfortable memory always balked at the Earthman and turned away. He could not picture that face, hear that voice, remember that deed. The name was enough. Twenty centuries had not sufficed to dim the hatred he felt in the slightest—or to soften the pain he felt by an iota.

And with Fastolfe in charge of policy, the miserable Earthmen had fled their corrupting planet and established themselves on world after world. The whirlwind of Earth's progress dazed the Spacer worlds and forced them into frozen paralysis.

How many times had Amadiro addressed the Council and pointed out that the Galaxy was slipping from Spacer fingers, that Aurora was watching blankly while world after world was being occupied by submen, that each year apathy was taking firmer hold of the Spacer spirit?

"Rouse yourself," he had called out. "Rouse yourself. See their numbers grow. See the Settler worlds multiply. What is it you wait for? To have them at your throats?"

And always Fastolfe would answer in that soothing lullaby of a voice of his and the Aurorans and the other Spacers (always following Aurora's lead, when Aurora chose not to lead) would settle back and return to their slumber.

The obvious did not seem to touch them. The facts, the figures, the indisputable worsening of affairs from decade to decade left them unmoved. How was it possible to shout the truth at them so steadily, to have every prediction he made come to pass, and yet to have to watch a steady majority following Fastolfe like sheep?

How was it possible that Fastolfe himself could watch everything he said prove to be sheer folly and yet never swerve from his policies? It was not even that he stubbornly insisted on being wrong, it was that he simply never seemed to notice he was wrong.

If Amadiro were the kind of man who doted on fantasy, he would surely imagine that some kind of spell, some kind of apathetic enchantment, had fallen upon the Spacer worlds. He would imagine that somewhere someone possessed the magic power of lulling otherwise active brains and blinding to the truth otherwise sharp eyes.

To add the final exquisite agony, people pitied Fastolfe for having died in frustration. In frustration, they said, because the Spacers would not seize new worlds of their own.

It was Fastolfe's own policies that kept them from doing so! What right had he to feel frustration over that? What would he do if he had, like Amadiro, always seen and spoken the truth and been unable to force the Spacers—enough Spacers—to listen to him.

How many times had he thought that it would be better for the Galaxy to be empty than under the domination of the submen? If he had some magic power to destroy the Earth—Elijah Baley's world—with a nod of his head, how eagerly he would.

Yet to find refuge in such fantasy could only be a sign of his total despair. It was the other side of his recurrent, futile wish to give up and welcome death—if his robots would allow it.

And then the time came when the power to destroy Earth was given him —even forced upon him against his will. That time was some three-fourths of a decade before, when he had first met Levular Mandamus.

43.

MEMORY! Three-fourths of a decade before—

Amadiro looked up and noted that Maloon Cicis had entered the office. He had undoubtedly signaled and he had the right to enter if the signal were not acknowledged.

Amadiro sighed and put down his small computer. Cicis had been his right-hand man ever since the Institute had been established. He was getting old in his service. Nothing drastically noticeable, just a general air of mild decay. His nose seemed to be a bit more asymmetrical than it once had been.

He rubbed his own somewhat bulbous nose and wondered how badly the flavor of mild decay was enveloping him. He had once been 1.95 meters tall, a good height even by Spacer standards. Surely he stood as straight now as he always had and yet when he had actually measured his height recently, he could not manage to make it more than 1.93 meters. Was he beginning to stoop, to shrivel, to settle?

He put away these dour thoughts that were themselves a surer sign of aging than mere measurements and said, "What is it, Maloon?"

Cicis had a new personal robot dogging his steps—very modernistic and with glossy trim. That was a sign of aging, too. If one can't keep one's body young, one can always buy a new young robot. Amadiro was determined never to rouse smiles among the truly young by falling prey to that particular delusion—especially since Fastolfe, who was eight decades older than Amadiro, had never done so.

Cicis said, "It's this Mandamus fellow again, Chief."

"Mandamus?"

"The one who keeps wanting to see you."

Amadiro thought a while. "You mean the idiot who's a descendant of the Solarian woman?"

"Yes, Chief."

"Well, I don't want to see him. Haven't you made that clear to him yet, Maloon?"

"Abundantly clear. He asks that I hand you a note and he says you will then see him."

Amadiro said slowly, "I don't think so, Maloon. What does the note say?"

"I don't understand it, Chief. It isn't Galactic."

"In that case, why should I understand it any more than you do?"

"I don't know, but he asked me to give it to you. If you care to look at it, Chief, and say the word, I will go back and get rid of him one more time."

"Well, then, let me see it," said Amadiro, shaking his head. He glanced at it with distaste.

It read: *"Ceterum censeo, delenda est Carthago."*

Amadiro read the message, glared up at Maloon, then turned his eyes back to the message. Finally, he said, "You must have looked at this, since you know it isn't Galactic. Did you ask him what it meant?"

"Yes, I did, Chief. He said it was Latin, but that left me no wiser. He said you would understand. He is a very determined man and said he would sit there all day waiting till you read this."

"What does he look like?"

"Thin. Serious. Probably humorless. Tall, but not quite as tall as you. Intense, deep-set eyes, thin lips."

"How old is he?"

"From the texture of his skin, I should say four decades or so. He is very young."

"In that case, we must make allowances for youth. Send him in."

Cicis looked surprised. "You will see him?"

"I have just said so, haven't I? Send him in."

44.

THE YOUNG MAN ENTERED the room in what was almost a march step. He stood there stiffly in front of the desk and said, "I thank you, sir, for agreeing to see me. May I have your permission to have my robots join me?"

Amadiro raised his eyebrows. "I would be pleased to see them. Would you permit me to keep mine with me?"

It had been many years since he had heard anyone mouth the old robot formula. It was one of those good old customs that sank into abeyance as the notion of formal politeness decayed and as it came to be taken more and more for granted that one's personal robots were part of one's self.

"Yes, sir," said Mandamus and two robots entered. They did not do so, Amadiro noted, till permission had been given. They were new robots, clearly efficient, and showed all the signs of good workmanship.

"Your own design, Mr. Mandamus?" There was always some extra value in robots that were designed by their owners.

"Indeed, sir."

"Then you are a roboticist?"

"Yes, sir. I have my degree from the University of Eos."

"Working under—"

Mandamus said smoothly, "Not under Dr. Fastolfe, sir. Under Dr. Maskellnik."

"Ah, but you are not a member of the Institute."

"I have applied for entrance, sir."

"I see." Amadiro adjusted the papers on his desk and then said quickly, without looking up, "Where did you learn Latin?"

"I do not know Latin well enough to speak it or read it, but I know enough about it to know that quotation and where to find it."

"That in itself is remarkable. How does that come about?"

"I cannot devote every moment of my time to robotics, so I have my side interests. One of them is planetology, with particular reference to Earth. That led me to Earth's history and culture."

"That is not a popular study among Spacers."

"No, sir, and that is too bad. One should always know one's enemies—as you do, sir."

"As I do?"

"Yes, sir. I believe you are acquainted with many aspects of Earth and are more learned in that respect than I am, for you have studied the subject longer."

"How do you know that?"

"I have tried to learn as much about you as I can, sir."

"Because I am another one of your enemies?"

"No, sir, but because I want to make you an ally."

"Make me an ally? You plan to make use of me, then? Does it strike you that you are being a little impertinent?"

"No, sir, for I am sure you will want to be an ally of mine."

Amadiro stared at him. "Nevertheless, it strikes *me* that you are being rather more than a little impertinent. —Tell me, do you understand this quotation you have found for me?"

"Yes, sir."

"Then translate it into Standard Galactic."

"It says, 'In my opinion, Carthage must be destroyed.' "

"And what does that mean, in *your* opinion?"

"The speaker was Marcus Porcius Cato, a senator of the Roman Republic, a political unit of ancient Earth. It had defeated its chief rival, Carthage, but had not destroyed it. Cato held that Rome could not be secure until Carthage was entirely destroyed—and eventually, sir, it was."

"But what is Carthage to us, young man?"

"There are such things as analogies."

"Which means?"

"That the Spacer worlds, too, have a chief rival that, in my opinion, must be destroyed."

"Name the enemy."

"The planet Earth, sir."

Amadiro drummed his fingers very softly upon the desk before him. "And you want me to be your ally in such a project. You assume I will be happy and eager to be one. —Tell me, Dr. Mandamus, when have I ever said in any of my numerous speeches and writings on the subject that Earth must be destroyed?"

Mandamus's thin lips tightened and his nostrils flared. "I am not here," he said, "in an attempt to trap you into something that can be used against you. I have not been sent here by Dr. Fastolfe or any of his party. Nor am *I* of his party. Nor do I attempt to say what is in your mind. I tell you only what is in *my* mind. In my opinion, Earth must be destroyed."

"And how do you propose to destroy Earth? Do you suggest that we drop nuclear bombs on it until the blasts and radiation and dust clouds destroy the planet? Because, if so, how do you propose to keep avenging Settler ships from doing the same to Aurora and to as many of the other Spacer worlds as they can reach? Earth might have been blasted with impunity as recently as fifteen decades ago. It can't be now."

Mandamus looked revolted. "I have nothing like that in mind, Dr. Amadiro. I would not unnecessarily destroy human beings, even if they are Earthpeople. There is a way, however, in which Earth can be destroyed without necessarily killing its people wholesale—and there will be no retaliation."

"You are a dreamer," said Amadiro, "or perhaps not quite sane."

"Let me explain."

"No, young man. I have little time and because your quotation, which I understood perfectly well, piqued my curiosity, I have already allowed myself to spend too much of it on you."

Mandamus stood up. "I understand, Dr. Amadiro, and I beg your pardon for taking up more of your time than you could afford. Think of what I have said, however, and if you should become curious, why not call upon me when you have more time to devote to me than you now have. Do not wait too long, however, for if I must, I will turn in other directions, for destroy Earth I will. I am frank with you, you see."

The young man attempted a smile that stretched his thin cheeks without producing much of an effect on his face otherwise. He said, "Good-bye—and thank you again," turned, and left.

Amadiro looked after him for a while thoughtfully, then touched a contact on the side of his desk.

"Maloon," he said when Cicis entered, "I want that young man watched around the clock and I want to know everyone he speaks to. Everyone. I want them all identified and I want them all questioned. Those whom I indicate are to be brought to me. —But, Maloon, everything must be done quietly and with an attitude of sweet and friendly persuasion. I am not yet master here, as you know."

But he would be eventually. Fastolfe was thirty-six decades old and clearly failing and Amadiro was eight decades younger.

45.

AMADIRO RECEIVED his reports for nine days.

Mandamus talked to his robots, occasionally to colleagues at the university, and even more occasionally to individuals at the establishments neighboring his. His conversations were utterly trivial and, long before the nine days had passed, Amadiro had decided he could not outwait the young man. Mandamus was only at the beginning of a long life and might have thirty decades ahead of him; Amadiro had only eight to ten at the very most.

And Amadiro, thinking of what the young man had said, felt, with increasing restlessness, that he could not take the chance that a way of destroying Earth might exist and that he might be ignoring it. Could he allow the destruction to take place after his death, so that he would not witness it? Or, almost as bad, have it take place during his lifetime, but with someone else's mind in command, someone else's fingers on the contact?

No, he had to see it, witness it, and *do* it; else why had he endured his long frustration? Mandamus might be a fool or a madman, but, in that case, Amadiro had to know for certain that he was a fool or a madman.

Having reached that point in his thinking, Amadiro called Mandamus to his office.

Amadiro realized that in so doing, he was humiliating himself, but the humiliation was the price he had to pay to make certain that there wasn't the slightest chance of Earth being destroyed without him. It was a price he was willing to pay.

He steeled himself even for the possibility that Mandamus would enter his presence, smirking and contemptuously triumphant. He would have to endure that, too. After the endurance, of course, if the young man's suggestion proved foolish, he would see him punished to the full extent that a civilized society would permit, but otherwise—

He was pleased, then, when Mandamus entered his office with an attitude of reasonable humility and thanked him, in all apparent sincerity, for a second interview. It seemed to Amadiro he would have to be gracious in his turn.

"Dr. Mandamus," he said, "In sending you away without listening to your plan, I was guilty of discourtesy. Tell me, then, what you have in mind and I will listen until it is quite clear to me—as I suspect it will be—that your plan is, perhaps, more the result of enthusiasm than of cold reason. At that time, I will dismiss you again, but without contempt on my part, and I hope that you will respond without anger on your part."

Mandamus said, "I could not be angry at having been accorded a fair and patient hearing, Dr. Amadiro, but what if what I say makes sense to you and offers hope?"

"In that case," said Amadiro slowly, "it would be conceivable that we two could work together."

"That would be wonderful, sir. Together we could accomplish more than we could separately. But would there be something more tangible than the privilege of working together? Would there be a reward?"

Amadiro looked displeased. "I would be grateful, of course, but all I am is a Councilman and the head of the Robotics Institute. There would be a limit to what I could do for you."

"I understand that, Dr. Amadiro. But within those limits could I not have something on account? Now?" He looked at Amadiro steadily.

Amadiro frowned at finding himself gazing into a pair of keen and unblinkingly determined eyes. No humility there!

Amadiro said coldly, "What do you have in mind?"

"Nothing you can't give me, Dr. Amadiro. Make me a member of the Institute."

"If you qualify—"

"No fear. I qualify."

"We can't leave that decision to the candidate. We have to—"

"Come, Dr. Amadiro, this is no way to begin a relationship. Since you've had me under observation every moment since I left you last, I can't believe you haven't studied my record thoroughly. As a result, you must *know* I qualify. If, for any reason, you felt I did *not* qualify, you would have no hope whatever that I would be ingenious enough to work out a plan for the destruction of our particular Carthage and I wouldn't be back here at your call."

For an instant, Amadiro felt a fire blaze within him. For that instant, he felt that even Earth's destruction was not worth enduring this hectoring attitude from a child. But only for that instant. Then his sense of due proportion was back and he could even tell himself that a person so young, yet so bold and so icily sure of himself, was the kind of man he needed. Besides, he *had* studied Mandamus's record and there was no question that he qualified for the Institute.

Amadiro said evenly (at some cost to his blood pressure), "You are right. You qualify."

"Then enroll me. I'm sure you have the necessary forms in your computer. You have but to enter my name, my school, my year of graduation, and whatever other statistical trivia you require and then sign your own name."

Without a word in reply, Amadiro turned to his computer. He entered the necessary information, retrieved the form, signed it, and handed it to Mandamus. "It is dated today. You are a fellow of the Institute."

Mandamus studied the paper, then handed it to one of his robots, who placed it in a small portfolio which he then placed under his arm.

"Thank you," said Mandamus, "it is most kind of you and I hope I will never fail you or cause you to regret this kind estimate you have given me of my abilities. That, however, leaves one more thing."

"Indeed? What?"

"Might we discuss the nature of the final reward—in case of success only, of course. Total success."

"Might we not leave that, more logically, to the point where total success is achieved or is reasonably close to being achieved?"

"As a matter of rationality, yes. But I am a creature of dreams as well as of reason. I would like to dream a little."

"Well," said Amadiro, "what is it you would like to dream?"

"It seems to me, Dr. Amadiro, that Dr. Fastolfe is now by no means well. He has lived long and cannot stave off death for many more years."

"And if so?"

"Once he dies, your party will become more aggressive and the more lukewarm members of Fastolfe's party will find it expedient to change allegiance, perhaps. The next election, without Fastolfe, will surely be yours."

"It is possible. And if so?"

"You will become the de facto leader of the Council and the guide of Aurora's foreign policy which would, in fact, mean the foreign policy of the Spacer worlds in general. And if my plans flourish, your direction will be so successful that the Council will scarcely fail to elect you Chairman at their earliest opportunity."

"Your dreams soar, young man. And if all you foresee were to come true, what then?"

"You would scarcely have time to run Aurora and the Robotics Institute, too. So I ask that when you finally decide to resign from your present position as the head of the Institute, you be prepared to support me as your successor to the post. You could scarcely expect to have your personal choice rejected."

Amadiro said, "There is such a thing as qualification for the post."

"I will qualify."

"Let us wait and see."

"I am willing to wait and see, but you will find that well before complete success is ours, you will wish to grant this request of mine. Please grow accustomed to the idea, therefore."

"All this before I hear a word," murmured Amadiro. "Well, you are a member of the Institute and I will strive to grow accustomed to your personal dream, but now let us have an end to preliminaries and tell me how you intend to destroy Earth."

Almost automatically, Amadiro made the sign that indicated to his robots that they were not to remember any part of the conversation. And Mandamus, with a small smile, did the same for his.

"Let us start, then," said Mandamus.

But before he could speak further, Amadiro moved to the attack.

"Are you sure you're not pro-Earth?"

Mandamus looked startled. "I am coming to you with a proposal to *destroy* Earth."

"And yet you are a descendant of the Solarian woman—in the fifth generation, I understand."

"Yes, sir, it is on public record. What of that?"

"The Solarian woman is—and has been for a long time—a close associate —friend—protegée—of Fastolfe. I wonder you do not sympathize with his pro-Earth views, therefore."

"Because of my ancestry?" Mandamus seemed honestly astonished. For a moment, what might have been a flash of annoyance or even anger seemed to tighten his nostrils, but that vanished and he said quietly, "An equally longtime close associate—friend—protegée—of your own is Dr. Vasilia Fastolfe, who is Dr. Fastolfe's daughter. She is a descendant in the first generation. I wonder she does not sympathize with his views."

"I have in the past also wondered," said Amadiro, "but she doesn't sympathize with them and, in her case, I have ceased wondering."

"You may cease wondering in my case, too, sir. I am a Spacer and I want to see the Spacers in control of the Galaxy."

"Very well, then. Go on with the description of your plan."

Mandamus said, "I will, but—if you don't mind—from the beginning.

"Dr. Amadiro, astronomers agree that there are millions of Earthlike planets in our Galaxy, planets on which human beings can live after necessary adjustments to the environment but without any need for geological terraforming. Their atmospheres are breathable, an ocean of water is present, the land and climate is suitable, life exists. Indeed, the atmospheres would not contain free oxygen without the presence of ocean plankton at the very least.

"The land is often barren, but once it and the ocean undergo biological terraforming—that is, once they are seeded with Earth life—such life flourishes and the planet can then be settled. Hundreds of such planets have been recorded and studied and about half of them are already occupied by Settlers.

"And yet not one habitable planet of all those which have been discovered to date has the enormous variety and excess of life that Earth has. Not one has anything larger or more complex than a small array of wormlike or insectlike invertebrates or, in the plant world, anything more advanced than some fernlike shrubbery. No question of intelligence, of anything even approaching intelligence."

Amadiro listened to the stiff sentences and thought: He's speaking by rote. He's memorized all this. —He stirred and said, "I am not a planetologist, Dr. Mandamus, but I ask you to believe that you are telling me nothing I don't already know."

"As I said, Dr. Amadiro, I am starting from the beginning. —Astronomers are increasingly of the belief that we have a fair sample of the habitable planets of the Galaxy and that all—or almost all—are markedly different from Earth. For some reason, Earth is a surprisingly unusual planet and evolution has proceeded on it at a radically rapid pace and in a radically abnormal manner."

Amadiro said, "The usual argument is that if there were another intelligent species in the Galaxy that was as advanced as we are, it would have become aware of our expansion by now and have made themselves known to us—one way or another."

Mandamus said, "Yes, sir. In fact, if there were another intelligent species in the Galaxy that was more advanced than we are, we would not have had a chance to expand in the first place. That we are the only species in the Galaxy capable of traveling in hyperspace would seem certain, then. That we are the only species in the Galaxy that is intelligent is perhaps not quite certain, but there is a very good chance that we are."

Amadiro was now listening with a weary half-smile. The young man was being didactic, like a man stamping out the rhythm of his monomania in a dull beat. It was one of the marks of the crank and the mild hope Amadiro had had that Mandamus might actually have something that would turn the tide of history was beginning to fade.

He said, "You continue to tell me the known, Dr. Mandamus. Everyone knows Earth seems unique and that we are probably the only intelligent species in the Galaxy."

"But no one seems to ask the simple question: 'Why?' The Earthpeople and the Settlers don't ask it. They accept it. They have a mystic attitude toward Earth and consider it a holy world, so that its unusual nature is taken as a matter of course. As for the Spacers, we don't ask it. We ignore it. We do our best not to think of Earth at all, since if we do, we are liable to go further and think of ourselves as having descended from Earthpeople."

Amadiro said, "I see no virtue in the question. We need not seek for complex answers to the 'Why?'. Random processes play an important role in evolution and, to some extent, in all things. If there are millions of habitable worlds, evolution may proceed on each of them at a different rate. On most, the rate will have some intermediate value; on some the rate will be distinctly slow, on others distinctly fast; on perhaps one it would proceed exceedingly slow and on another exceedingly fast. Earth happens to be the one on which it proceeded exceedingly fast and we are here because of that. Now if we ask 'Why?', the natural—and sufficient—answer is 'Chance.' "

Amadiro waited for the other to betray the crank by exploding in rage at a preeminently logical statement, presented in an amused way, that served to shatter his thesis completely. Mandamus, however, merely stared at him for a few moments out of his deep-set eyes and then said quietly, "No."

Mandamus let that stand for perhaps two beats and then said, "It takes more than a lucky chance or two to speed evolution a thousandfold. On every planet but Earth, the speed of evolution is closely related to the flux of cosmic radiation in which that planet is bathed. That speed is not the result of chance at all but the result of cosmic radiation producing mutations at a slow rate. On Earth, something produces many more mutations than are produced on other habitable planets and that has nothing to do with cosmic rays, for they do not strike Earth in any remarkable profusion. Perhaps you see a little more clearly, now, why the 'Why?' could be important."

"Well, then, Dr. Mandamus, since I am still listening, with rather more patience than I would have expected myself to possess, answer the question you so insistently raise. Or do you merely have the question and no answer?"

"I have an answer," said Mandamus, "and it depends upon the fact that Earth is unique in a second way."

Amadiro said, "Let me anticipate. You are referring to its large satellite. Surely, Dr. Mandamus, you are not advancing this as a discovery of yours."

"Not at all," said Mandamus stiffly, "but consider that large satellites seem to be common. Our planetary system has five, Earth's has seven and so on. All the known large satellites but one, however, circle gas giants.

Only Earth's satellite, the moon, circles a planet not much larger than itself."

"Dare I use the word 'chance' again, Dr. Mandamus?"

"In this case, it may be chance, but the moon remains unique."

"Even so. What possible connection can the satellite have with Earth's profusion of life?"

"That may not be obvious and a connection may be unlikely—but it is far more unlikely that two such unusual examples of uniqueness in a single planet can have no connection at all. I have found such a connection."

"Indeed?" said Amadiro alertly. Now ought to come unmistakable evidence of crackpotism. He looked casually at the time strip on the wall. There really wasn't much more time he could possibly spend on this, for all that his curiosity continued to be aroused.

"The moon," said Mandamus, "is slowly receding from Earth, due to its tidal effect on the Earth. Earth's large tides are a unique consequence of the existence of this large satellite. Earth's sun produces tides, too, but to only a third of the extent of the moon's tides—just as our sun produces small tides on Aurora.

"Since the moon recedes because of its tidal action, it was far closer to Earth during the early history of its planetary system. The closer the moon to the Earth, the higher the tides on Earth. These tides had two important effects on Earth. It flexed the Earth's crust continually as the Earth rotated and it slowed the Earth's rotation, both through that flexing and through the friction of the ocean's water tides on shallow sea bottoms—so that rotational energy was converted to heat.

"The Earth, therefore, has a thinner crust than any other habitable planet we know of and it is the only habitable planet that displays volcanic action and that has a lively system of plate tectonics."

Amadiro said, "But even all this can have nothing to do with Earth's profusion of life. I think you must either get to the point, Dr. Mandamus, or leave."

"Please bear with me, Dr. Amadiro, for just a little while longer. It is important to understand the point once we get to it. I have made a careful computer simulation of the chemical development of Earth's crust, allowing for the effect of tidal action and plate tectonics, something that no one has ever done before in as meticulous and elaborate a way as I have managed to do—if I may praise myself."

"Oh, by all means," murmured Amadiro.

"And it turns out, quite clearly—I will show you all the necessary data at any time you wish—that uranium and thorium collect in Earth's crust and upper mantle in concentrations of up to a thousand times as high as in any other habitable world. Moreover, they collect unevenly, so that scattered over the Earth are occasional pockets where uranium and thorium are even more concentrated."

"And, I take it, dangerously high in radioactivity?"

"No, Dr. Amadiro. Uranium and thorium are very weakly radioactive and even where they are relatively concentrated, they are not very concentrated in an absolute sense. —All this, I repeat, is because of the presence of a large moon."

"I assume, then, that the radioactivity, even if not intense enough to be dangerous to life, does suffice to increase the mutation rate. Is that it, Dr. Mandamus?"

"That is it. There would be more rapid extinctions now and then, but also more rapid development of new species—resulting in an enormous variety and profusion of life-forms. And, eventually, on Earth alone, this would have reached the point of developing an intelligent species and a civilization."

Amadiro nodded. The young man was not a crank. He might be wrong, but he was not a crank. And he might be right, too.

Amadiro was not a planetologist, so he would have to check books on the subject to see whether Mandamus had perhaps discovered only the already-known, as so many enthusiasts did. There was, however, a more important point that he had to check at once.

He said in a soft voice, "You've spoken of the possible destruction of Earth. Is there some connection between that and Earth's unique properties?"

"One can take advantage of unique properties in a unique manner," said Mandamus just as softly.

"In this particular case—in what way?"

"Before discussing the method, Dr. Amadiro, I must explain that, in one respect, the question as to whether destruction is physically possible depends on you."

"On me?"

"Yes," said Mandamus firmly. "On you. Why, otherwise, should I come to you with this long story if not to persuade you that I know what I'm talking about, so that you would be willing to cooperate with me in a manner that will be essential to my success?"

Amadiro drew a long breath. "And if I refused, would anyone else serve your purpose?"

"It might be possible for me to turn to others if you refuse. *Do* you refuse?"

"Perhaps not, but I am wondering how essential I am to you."

"The answer is, not quite as essential as I am to you. You *must* cooperate with me."

"Must?"

"I would like you to—if you prefer it phrased in that fashion. But if you wish Aurora and the Spacers to triumph, now and forever, over Earth and the Settlers, then you *must* cooperate with me, whether you like the phrase or not."

Amadiro said, "Tell me what it is, exactly, that I *must* do."

"Begin by telling me if it is not true that the Institute has, in the past, designed and constructed humanoid robots."

"Yes, we did. Fifty of them all together. That was between fifteen and twenty decades ago."

"That long ago? And what happened to them?"

"They failed," said Amadiro indifferently.

Mandamus sat back in his chair with a horrified expression on his face. "They were destroyed?"

Amadiro's eyebrows shot upward. "Destroyed? No one destroys expensive robots. They are in storage. The power units are removed and a special long-lived microfusion battery is in each to keep the positronic paths minimally alive."

"Then they can be brought back to full action?"

"I am sure they can."

Mandamus's right hand beat out a tightly controlled rhythm against the arm of the chair. He said grimly, "Then we can win!"

Chapter 12

The Plan and the Daughter

46.

IT HAD BEEN A LONG TIME since Amadiro had thought of the humanoid robots. It was a painful thought and he had, with some difficulty, trained himself to keep his mind away from that topic. And now Mandamus had unexpectedly brought it up.

The humanoid robot had been Fastolfe's great trump card in those long-gone days when Amadiro had been within a millimeter of taking the game, trump card and all. Fastolfe had designed and built two humanoid robots (of which one still existed) and no one else could build any. The entire membership of the Robotics Institute, working together, could not build them.

All that Amadiro had salvaged out of his great defeat had been that trump card. Fastolfe had been forced to make public the nature of the humanoid design.

That meant humanoid robots could be built and *were* built and—behold—they were not wanted. The Aurorans would not have them in their society.

Amadiro's mouth twisted in the remnant of remembered chagrin. The tale of the Solarian woman had somehow come to be known—the fact that she had had the use of Jander, one of Fastolfe's two humanoid robots, and that the use had been sexual. Aurorans had no objection to such a situation in theory. When they stopped to think of it, however, Auroran women simply did not enjoy the thought of having to compete with robot women. Nor did Auroran men wish to compete with robot men.

The Institute had labored mightily to explain that the humanoid robots were not intended for Aurora itself, but were meant to serve as the initial wave of pioneers who would seed and adjust new habitable planets for Aurorans to occupy later, after they had been terraformed.

That, too, was rejected, as suspicion and objection fed on itself. Someone had called the humanoids "the entering wedge." The expression spread and the Institute was forced to give up.

Stubbornly, Amadiro had insisted on mothballing those which existed for possible future use—a use that had never yet materialized.

Why had there been this objection to the humanoids? Amadiro felt a faint return of the irritation that had all but poisoned his life those many decades ago. Fastolfe himself, though reluctant, had agreed to back the project and, to do him justice, had done so, though without quite the eloquence he devoted to those matters to which his heart was truly given. —But it had not helped.

And yet—and yet—if Mandamus now really had some project in mind that would work and would require the robots—

Amadiro had no great fondness for mystical cries of: "It was better so. It was meant to be." Yet it was only with an effort that he kept himself from thinking this, as the elevator took them down to a spot well below ground level—the only place in Aurora that might be similar, in a tiny way, to Earth's fabled Caves of Steel.

Mandamus stepped out of the elevator at Amadiro's gesture and found himself in a dim corridor. It was chilly and there was a soft ventilating wind. He shivered slightly. Amadiro joined him. But a single robot followed each.

"Few people come here," Amadiro said matter-of-factly.

"How far underground are we?" asked Mandamus.

"About fifteen meters. There are a number of levels. It is on this one that the humanoid robots are stored."

Amadiro stopped a moment, as though in thought, then turned firmly to the left. "This way!"

"No directing signs?"

"As I said, few people come here. Those who do know where they should go to find what they need."

As he said that, they came to a door that looked solid and formidable in the dim light. On either side stood a robot. They were not humanoid.

Mandamus regarded them critically and said, "These are simple models."

"Very simple. You wouldn't expect us to waste anything elaborate on the task of guarding a door." Amadiro raised his voice, but kept it impassive. "I am Kelden Amadiro."

The eyes of both robots glowed briefly. They turned outward, away from the door, which opened noiselessly, rising upward.

Amadiro directed the other through and, as he passed the robots, said calmly, "Leave it open and adjust the lighting to personal need."

Mandamus said, "I don't suppose just anyone could enter here."

"Certainly not. Those robots recognize my appearance and voiceprint and require both before opening the door." Half to himself, he added, "No need for locks or keys or combinations anywhere on the Spacer worlds. The robots guard us faithfully and always."

"I had sometimes thought," said Mandamus broodingly, "that if an Auroran were to borrow one of those blasters that Settlers seem to carry with them wherever they go, there would be no locked doors for him. He could destroy robots in an instant, then go wherever he wished, do whatever he wanted."

Amadiro darted a fiery glance at the other. "But what Spacer would dream of using such weapons on a Spacer world? We live our lives without weapons and without violence. Don't you understand that *that* is why I have devoted my life to the defeat and destruction of Earth and its poisoned brood. —Yes, we had violence once, but that was long ago, when the Spacer worlds were first established and we had not yet rid ourselves of the poison of the Earth from which we came, and before we had learned the value of robotic security.

"Aren't peace and security worth fighting for? Worlds without violence! Worlds in which reason rules! Was it right for us to hand over scores of habitable worlds to short-lived barbarians who, as you say, carry blasters about with them everywhere?"

"And yet," murmured Mandamus, "are you ready to use violence to destroy Earth?"

"Violence briefly—and for a purpose—is the price we probably will have to pay for putting an end to violence forever."

"I am Spacer enough," said Mandamus, "to want even that violence minimized."

They had now entered a large and cavernous room and, as they entered, walls and ceiling came to life with diffuse and unglaring light.

"Well, is this what you want, Dr. Mandamus?" asked Amadiro.

Mandamus looked about, stunned. Finally, he managed to say, "Incredible!"

They stood there, a solid regiment of human beings, with a little more life to them than so many statues might have showed, but with far less life than sleeping human beings would have displayed.

"They're standing," muttered Mandamus.

"They take up less room that way. Obviously."

"But they've been standing about fifteen decades. They *can't* still be in working order. Surely their joints are frozen, their organs broken down."

Amadiro shrugged. "Perhaps. Still, if the joints have deteriorated—and that isn't out of the question, I suppose—those can be replaced—if necessary. It would depend on whether there would be reason to do so."

"There would be reason," said Mandamus. He looked from head to head. They were staring in slightly different directions and that gave them a somewhat unsettling appearance, as though they were on the point of breaking ranks.

Mandamus said, "Each has an individual appearance and they differ in height, build, and so on."

"Yes. Does that surprise you? We were planning to have these, along with others we might have built, be the pioneers in the development of new worlds. To have them do so properly, we wanted them to be as human as possible, which meant making them as individual as Aurorans are. Doesn't that seem sensible to you?"

"Absolutely. I'm glad this is so. I've read all I can about the two proto-humaniforms that Fastolfe himself built—Daneel Olivaw and Jander Panell. I've seen holographs of them and they seemed identical."

"Yes," said Amadiro impatiently. "Not only identical, but each virtually a caricature of one's conception of the ideal Spacer. That was Fastolfe's romanticism. I'm sure that he would have built a race of interchangeable humanoid robots, with both sexes possessing such ethereal good looks—or what he considered to be that—as to make them completely inhuman. Fastolfe may be a brilliant roboticist, but he is an incredibly stupid man."

Amadiro shook his head. To have been beaten by such an incredibly stupid man, he thought—and then he thrust the thought away. He had not been beaten by Fastolfe, but by that infernal Earthman. Lost in thought, he did not hear Mandamus's next question.

"Pardon me," he said with an edge of irritation.

"I said, 'Did you design these, Dr. Amadiro?' "

"No, by an odd coincidence—and one that strikes me as possessing a peculiar irony—these were designed by Fastolfe's daughter Vasilia. She's as brilliant as he is and much more intelligent—which may be one reason why they never got along."

"As I have heard the story concerning them—" began Mandamus.

Amadiro waved him into silence. "I have heard the story, too, but it doesn't matter. It's enough that she does her work very well and that there is no danger that she will ever find herself in sympathy with someone who, despite the accident that he is her biological father, is—and must remain—forever alien and hateful to her. She even calls herself Vasilia Aliena, you know."

"Yes, I know. Do you have the brain patterns of these humanoid robots on record?"

"Certainly."

"For *each* of these?"

"Of course."

"And can they be made available to me?"

"If there's a reason for it."

"There will be," said Mandamus firmly. "Since these robots were designed for pioneering activities, may I assume they are equipped to explore a world and deal with primitive conditions?"

"That should be self-evident."

"That's perfect—but there may have to be some modifications. Do you suppose that Vasilia Fast—Aliena would be able to help me with that—if necessary? Obviously, she would be best-acquainted with the brain patterns."

"Obviously. Still, I don't know whether she would be willing to help you. I do know that it is physically impossible for her to do so at the moment, since she is not on Aurora."

Mandamus looked surprised and displeased. "Where is she, then, Dr. Amadiro?"

Amadiro said, "You have seen these humaniforms and I do not wish to expose myself to these rather dismal surroundings. You have kept me waiting long enough and you must not complain if I keep you waiting now. If you have any further questions, let us deal with them in my office."

47.

ONCE IN THE OFFICE, Amadiro delayed things a while longer. "Wait here for me," he said rather peremptorily and left.

Mandamus waited stiffly, sorting out his thoughts, wondering when Amadiro would return—or if he would. Was he to be arrested or simply ejected? Had Amadiro grown tired of waiting for the point?

Mandamus refused to believe that. He had gained a shrewd idea of Amadiro's desperate desire for evening an old score. It seemed evident that Amadiro wouldn't get tired of listening as long as there seemed the slightest chance that Mandamus would make revenge possible.

As he looked idly about Amadiro's office, Mandamus found himself wondering whether there might be any information that might be of help to him in the computerized files almost immediately at hand. It would be useful not to have to depend directly on Amadiro for everything.

The thought was a useless one. Mandamus did not know the entry code for the files and, even if he did, there were several of Amadiro's personal robots standing in their niches and they would stop him if he took a single step toward anything that was labeled in their minds as sensitive. Even his own robots would.

Amadiro was right. Robots were so useful and efficient—and incorruptible—as guards that the very concept of anything criminal, illegal, or simply underhanded did not occur to anyone. The tendency just atrophied—at least as against other Spacers.

He wondered how Settlers could manage without robots. Mandamus tried to imagine human personalities clashing, with no robotic bumpers to cushion the interaction, no robotic presence to give them a decent sense of security and to enforce—without their being consciously aware of it most of the time—a proper mode of morality.

It would be impossible for Settlers to be anything but barbarians under the circumstance and the Galaxy could not be left to them. Amadiro was right in that respect and had always been right, while Fastolfe was fantastically wrong.

Mandamus nodded, as though he had once again persuaded himself as to the correctness of what he was planning. He sighed and wished it were not necessary, then prepared to go over, once again, the line of reasoning that proved to him that it *was* necessary, when Amadiro strode in.

Amadiro was still an impressive figure, even though he was within a year of his twenty-eighth decade-day. He was very much what a Spacer ought to look like, except for the unfortunate shapelessness of his nose.

Amadiro said, "I'm sorry to have kept you waiting, but there was business I had to attend to. I am the head of this Institute and that entails responsibilities."

Mandamus said, "Could you tell me where Dr. Vasilia Aliena is? I will then describe my project to you without delay."

"Vasilia is on tour. She's visiting each of the Spacer worlds to find out where they stand on robot research. She appears to think that, since the Robot Institute was founded to coordinate individual research on Aurora, interplanetary coordination would advance the cause even farther. A good idea, actually."

Mandamus laughed, shortly and without humor. "They won't tell her anything. I doubt any Spacer world wants to hand Aurora a more enormous lead than she already has."

"Don't be too sure. The Settler situation has disturbed us all."

"Do you know where she is now?"

"We have her itinerary."

"Get her back, Dr. Amadiro."

Amadiro frowned. "I doubt I can do that easily. I believe she wants to be away from Aurora until her father dies."

"Why?" asked Mandamus in surprise.

Amadiro shrugged. "I don't know. I don't care. —But what I do know is that your time has run out. Do you understand? Get to the point or leave." He pointed to the door grimly and Mandamus felt that the other's patience would stretch no farther.

Mandamus said, "Very well. There is yet a third way in which Earth is unique—"

He talked easily and with due economy, as though he were going through an exposition that he had frequently rehearsed and polished for the very purpose of presenting it to Amadiro. And Amadiro found himself increasingly absorbed.

This was it! Amadiro first felt a huge sense of relief. He had been correct to gamble on the young man's not being a crackpot. He was entirely sane.

Then came triumph. It would surely work. Of course, the young man's view, as it was expounded, veered a bit from the path Amadiro felt it ought to follow, but that could be taken care of eventually. Modifications were always possible.

And when Mandamus was done, Amadiro said in a voice he strove to hold steady, "We won't need Vasilia. There is appropriate expertise at the Institute to allow us to begin at once. Dr. Mandamus"—a note of formal respect entered Amadiro's voice—"let this thing work out as planned—and I cannot help but think it will—and you will be the head of the Institute when I am Chairman of the Council."

Mandamus smiled narrowly and briefly, while Amadiro sat back in his chair and, just as briefly, allowed himself to look into the future with satisfaction and confidence, something he had not been able to do for twenty long and weary decades.

How long would it take? Decades? One decade? Part of a decade?

Not long. Not long. It must be hastened by all means so that he could live to see that old decision overturned and himself lord of Aurora—and therefore of the Spacer worlds—and therefore (with Earth and the Settler worlds doomed) even lord of the Galaxy before he died.

48.

WHEN DR. HAN FASTOLFE died, seven years after Amadiro and Mandamus met and began their project, the hyperwave carried the news with explosive force to every corner of the occupied worlds. It merited the greatest attention everywhere.

In the Spacer worlds it was important because Fastolfe had been the most powerful man on Aurora and, therefore, in the Galaxy for over twenty decades. In the Settler worlds and on Earth, it was important because Fastolfe had been a friend—insofar as a Spacer could be a friend—and the question now was whether Spacer policy would change and, if so, how.

The news came also to Vasilia Aliena and it was complicated by the bitterness that had tinged her relationship with her biological father almost from the beginning.

She had schooled herself to feel nothing when he died, yet she had not wanted to be on the same world that he was on at the time the event took place. She did not want the questions that would be leveled at her anywhere, but most frequently and insistently on Aurora.

The parent-child relationship among the Spacers was a weak and indifferent one at best. With long lives, that was a matter of course. Nor would anyone have been interested in Vasilia in that respect, but for the fact that Fastolfe was so continually prominent a party leader and Vasilia almost as prominent a partisan on the other side.

It was poisonous. She had gone to the trouble of making Vasilia Aliena her legal name and of using it on all documents, in all interviews, in all dealings of any kind—and yet she knew for a fact that most people thought of her as Vasilia Fastolfe. It was as though *nothing* could wipe out that thoroughly meaningless relationship, so that she was reduced to having to be content with being addressed by her first name only. It was, at least, an uncommon name.

And that, too, seemed to emphasize her mirror-image relationship with the Solarian woman who, for thoroughly independent reasons, had denied her first husband as Vasilia had denied her father. The Solarian woman, too, could not live with the early surnames fastened upon her and ended with a first name only—Gladia.

Vasilia and Gladia, misfits, deniers— They even resembled each other.

Vasilia stole a look at the mirror hanging in her spaceship cabin. She had not seen Gladia in many decades, but she was sure that the resemblance remained. They were both small and slim. Both were blond and their faces were somewhat alike.

But it was Vasilia who always lost and Gladia who always won. When Vasilia had left her father and had struck him from her life, he had found Gladia instead—and she was the pliant and passive daughter he wanted, the daughter that Vasilia could never be.

Nevertheless, it embittered Vasilia. She herself was a roboticist, as competent and as skillful, at last, as ever Fastolfe had been, while Gladia was merely an artist, who amused herself with force-field coloring and with the illusions of robotic clothing. How could Fastolfe have been satisfied to lose the one and gain, in her place, nothing more than the other?

And when that policeman from Earth, Elijah Baley, had come to Aurora, he had bullied Vasilia into revealing far more of her thoughts and feelings than she had ever granted anyone else. He was, however, softness itself to Gladia and had helped her—and her protector, Fastolfe—win out against all the odds, though to this day Vasilia had not been able to understand clearly how that had happened.

It was Gladia who had been at Fastolfe's bedside during the final illness, who had held his hand to the end, and who had heard his last words. Why Vasilia should resent that, she didn't know, for she herself would, under no circumstances, have acknowledged the old man's existence to the extent of visiting him to witness his passage into nonexistence in an absolute, rather than a subjective sense—and yet she raged against Gladia's presence.

It's the way I feel, she told herself defiantly, and I owe no one an explanation.

And she had lost Giskard. Giskard had been *her* robot, Vasilia's own robot when she had been a young girl, the robot granted her by a then seemingly fond father. It was Giskard through whom she had learned robotics and from whom she had felt the first genuine affection. She had not, as a child, speculated on the Three Laws or dealt with the philosophy of positronic automatism. Giskard had *seemed* affectionate, he had *acted* as though he were affectionate, and that was enough for a child. She had never found such affection in any human being—certainly not her father.

To this day, she had yet to be weak enough to play the foolish love game with anyone. Her bitterness over her loss of Giskard had taught her that any initial gain was not worth the final deprivation.

When she had left home, disowning her father, he would not let Giskard go with her, even though she herself had improved Giskard immeasurably in the course of her careful reprogramming of him. And when her father had died, he had left Giskard to the Solarian woman. He had also left her Daneel, but Vasilia cared nothing for that pale imitation of a man. She wanted Giskard, who was her own.

Vasilia was on her way back to Solaria now. Her tour was quite done. In fact, as far as usefulness was concerned, it had been essentially over months ago. But she had remained on Hesperos for a needed rest, as she had explained in her official notice to the Institute.

Now, however, Fastolfe was dead and she could return. And while she could not undo the past entirely, she could undo part of it. Giskard must be hers again.

She was determined on that.

49.

AMADIRO WAS QUITE ambivalent in his response to Vasilia's return. She had not come back until old Fastolfe (he could say the name to himself quite easily now that he was dead) was a month in his urn. That flattered his opinion of his own understanding. After all, he had told Mandamus her motive had been that of remaining away from Aurora till her father died.

Then, too, Vasilia was comfortably transparent. She lacked the exasperating quality of Mandamus, his new favorite, who always seemed to have yet another unexpressed thought tucked away no matter how thoroughly he seemed to have discharged the contents of his mind.

On the other hand, she was irritatingly hard to control, the least likely to go quietly along the path he indicated. Leave it to her to probe the other-world Spacers to the bone during the years she had spent away from Aurora —but then leave it also to her to interpret it all in dark and riddling words.

So he greeted her with an enthusiasm that was somewhere between feigned and unfeigned.

"Vasilia, I'm so happy to have you back. The Institute flies on one wing when you're gone."

Vasilia laughed. "Come, Kelden"—she alone had no hesitation or inhibition in using his given name, though she was two and a half decades younger than he—"that one remaining wing is yours and how long has it been now since you ceased being perfectly certain that your one wing was sufficient?"

"Since you decided to stretch out your absence to years. Do you find Aurora much changed in the interval?"

"Not a bit—which ought perhaps to be a concern of ours. Changelessness is decay."

"A paradox. There is no decay without a change for the worse."

"Changelessness is a change for the worse, Kelden, in comparison to the surrounding Settler worlds. They change rapidly, extending their control into more numerous worlds and over each individual world more thoroughly. They increase their strength and power and self-assurance, while we sit here dreaming and find our unchanging might diminishing steadily in comparison."

"Beautiful, Vasilia! I think you memorized that carefully on your flight here. However, there has been a change in the political situation on Aurora."

"You mean my biological father is dead."

Amadiro spread his arms with a little bow of his head. "As you say. He was largely responsible for our paralysis and he is gone, so I imagine there will now be change, though it may not necessarily be visible change."

"You keep secrets from me, do you?"

"Would I do that?"

"Certainly. That false smile of yours gives you away every time."

"Then I must learn to be grave with you. —Come, I have your report. Tell me what is not included in it."

"All is included in it—almost. Each Spacer world states vehemently that it is disturbed by growing Settler arrogance. Each is firmly determined to resist the Settlers to the end, enthusiastically following the Auroran lead with vigor and death-defying gallantry."

"Follow our lead, yes. And if we don't lead?"

"Then they'll wait and try to mask their relief that we are not leading. Otherwise— Well, each one is engaged in technological advance and each one is reluctant to reveal what it is, exactly, that it is doing. Each is working independently and is not even unified within its own globe. There is not a single research team anywhere on any of the Spacer worlds that resembles our own Robotics Institute. Each world consists of individual researchers, each of whom diligently guards his own data from all the rest."

Amadiro was almost complacent as he said, "I would not expect them to have advanced as far as we have."

"Too bad they haven't," replied Vasilia tartly. "With all the Spacer worlds a jumble of individuals, progress is too slow. The Settler worlds meet regularly at conventions, have their institutes—and though they lag well behind us, they *will* catch up. —Still, I've managed to uncover a few technological advances being worked on by the Spacer worlds and I have them all listed in my report. They are all working on the nuclear intensifier, for instance, but I don't believe that such a device has passed beyond the laboratory demonstration level on a single world. Something that would be practical on shipboard is not yet here."

"I hope you are right in that, Vasilia. The nuclear intensifier is a weapon our fleets could use, for it would finish the Settlers at once. However, I think, on the whole, it would be better if Aurora had the weapon ahead of our Spacer brothers. —But you said that all was included in your report— *almost.* I heard that 'almost.' What is not included, then?"

"Solaria!"

"Ah, the youngest and most peculiar of the Spacer worlds."

"I got almost nothing directly out of them. They viewed me with absolute hostility as, I believe, they would have viewed any non-Solarian, whether Spacer or Settler. And when I say 'viewed,' I mean that in their sense. I remained nearly a year on the world, a considerably longer time than I spent on any other world, and in all those months I never *saw* a single Solarian face-to-face. In every case, I *viewed* him—or her—by hyperwave hologram. I could never deal with anything tangible—images only. The world was comfortable, incredibly luxurious, in fact, and for a nature lover, totally unspoiled, but how I missed *seeing.*"

"Well, viewing is a Solarian custom. We all know that, Vasilia. Live and let live."

"Humph," said Vasilia. "Your tolerance may be misplaced. Are your robots in the nonrepeat mode?"

"Yes, they are. And I assure you we are not being eavesdropped upon."

"I hope not, Kelden. —I am under the distinct impression that the Solarians are closer to developing a miniaturized nuclear intensifier than any other world—than we are. They may be close to making one that's portable and that's possessed of a power consumption small enough to make it practical for space vessels."

Amadiro frowned deeply. "How do they manage that?"

"I cannot say. You don't suppose they showed me blueprints, do you? My impressions are so inchoate I dared not put them in the report, but from small things I heard here—or observed there—I think they are making important progress. This is something we should think about carefully."

"We will. —Is there anything else you would like to tell me?"

"Yes—and also not in the report. Solaria has been working toward humanoid robots for many decades and I think they have achieved *that* goal. No other Spacer world—outside of ourselves, of course—has even attempted the matter. When I asked, on each world, what they were doing with respect to humanoid robots, the reaction was uniform. They found the very concept unpleasant and horrifying. I suspect they all noticed our failure and took it to heart."

"But not Solaria? Why not?"

"For one thing, they have always lived in the most extremely robotized society in the Galaxy. They're surrounded by robots—ten thousand per individual. The world is saturated with them. If you were to wander through it aimlessly, searching for humans, you would find nothing. So why should the few Solarians, living in such a world, be upset by the thought of a few more robots just because they're humaniform? Then, too, that pseudo-human wretch that Fastolfe designed and built and that still exists—"

"Daneel," said Amadiro.

"Yes, that one. He—*it* was on Solaria twenty decades ago and the Solarians treated it as human. They have never recovered from that. Even if they had no use for humaniforms, they were humiliated at having been deceived. It was an unforgettable demonstration that Aurora was far ahead of them in that one facet of robotics, at any rate. The Solarians take inordinate pride in being the most advanced roboticists in the Galaxy and, ever since, individual Solarians have been working on humaniforms—if for no other reason than to wipe out that disgrace. If they had had greater numbers or an institute that could coordinate their work, they would undoubtedly have come up with some long ago. As it is, I think they have them now."

"You don't really know, do you? This is just suspicion based on scraps of data here and there."

"Exactly right, but it's a fairly strong suspicion and it merits further investigation. —And a third point. I could swear they were working on telepathic communication. There was some equipment that I was incautiously allowed to see. And once when I had one of their roboticists on view, the hyperwave screen showed a blackboard with a positronic pattern matrix that was like nothing I ever remember seeing, yet it seemed to me that pattern might fit a telepathic program."

"I suspect, Vasilia, that this item is woven of even airier gossamer than the bit about the humanoid robots."

A look of mild embarrassment crossed Vasilia's face. "I must admit you're probably right there."

"In fact, Vasilia, it sounds like mere fantasy. If the pattern matrix you saw was like nothing you remember ever having seen before, how could you think it would fit anything?"

Vasilia hesitated. "To tell you the truth, I've been wondering about that myself. Yet when I saw the pattern, the word 'telepathy' occurred to me at once."

"Even though telepathy is impossible, even in theory."

"It is *thought* to be impossible, even in theory. That is not quite the same thing."

"No one has ever been able to make any progress toward it."

"Yes, but why should I have looked at that pattern and thought 'telepathy'?"

"Ah, well, Vasilia, there may be a personal psychoquirk there that is useless to try to analyze. I'd forget it. —Anything else?"

"One more thing—and the most puzzling of all. I gathered the impression, Kelden, from one little indication or another, that the Solarians are planning to leave their planet."

"Why?"

"I don't know. Their population, small as it is, is declining further. Perhaps they want to make a new start elsewhere before they die out altogether."

"What kind of new start? Where would they go?"

Vasilia shook her head. "I have told you all I know."

Amadiro said slowly, "Well, then, I will take all this into account. Four things: nuclear intensifier, humanoid robots, telepathic robots, and abandoning the planet. Frankly, I have no faith in any of the four, but I'll persuade the Council to authorize talks with the Solarian regent. —And now, Vasilia, I believe you could use a rest, so why not take a few weeks off and grow accustomed to the Auroran sun and fine weather before getting back to work?"

"That is kind of you, Kelden," said Vasilia, remaining firmly seated, "but there remain two items I must bring up."

Involuntarily, Amadiro's eyes sought the time strip. "This won't take up very much time, will it, Vasilia?"

"However much time it takes, Kelden, is what it will take up."

"What is it you want, then?"

"To begin with, who is this young know-it-all who seems to think he is running the Institute, this what's-his-name, Mandamus?"

"You've met him, have you?" said Amadiro, his smile masking a certain uneasiness. "You see, things *do* change on Aurora."

"Certainly not for the better in this case," said Vasilia grimly. "Who *is* he?"

"He is exactly what you have described—a know-it-all. He is a brilliant young man, bright enough in robotics, but just as knowledgeable in general physics, in chemistry, in planetology—"

"And how old is this monster of erudition?"

"Not quite five decades."

"And what will this child be when he grows up?"

"Wise as well as brilliant, perhaps."

"Don't pretend to mistake my meaning, Kelden. Are you thinking of grooming him as the next head of the Institute?"

"I intend to live for a good many decades yet."

"That is no answer."

"It is the only answer I have."

Vasilia shifted in her seat restlessly and her robot, standing behind her, sent his eyes from side to side as though preparing to ward off an attack—pushed into that mode of behavior, perhaps, by Vasilia's uneasiness.

Vasilia said, "Kelden, I am to be the next head. That is settled. You have told me so."

"I have, but in actual fact, Vasilia, once I die, the Board of Directors will make the choice. Even if I leave behind me a directive as to who the next head will be, the Board can reverse me. That much is clear in the terms of incorporation that founded the Institute."

"You just write your directive, Kelden, and I will take care of the Board of Directors."

And Amadiro, the space between his eyebrows furrowing, said, "This is not something I will discuss any further at this moment. What is the other item you want to bring up? Please make it brief."

She stared at him in silent anger for a moment, then said, seeming to bite off the word, "Giskard!"

"The robot?"

"Of course the robot. Do you know any other Giskard that I am likely to be talking about?"

"Well, what of him?"

"He is *mine.*"

Amadiro looked surprised. "He is—or was—the legal property of Fastolfe."

"Giskard was mine when I was a child."

"Fastolfe lent him to you and eventually took him back. There was no formal transfer of ownership, was there?"

"Morally, he was mine. But in any case, Fastolfe owns him no longer. He is dead."

"He made a will, too. And if I remember correctly, by that will, two robots—Giskard and Daneel—are now the property of the Solarian woman."

"But I don't want them to be. I am Fastolfe's daughter—"

"Oh?"

Vasilia flushed. "I have a claim to Giskard. Why should a stranger—an alien—have him?"

"For one thing, because Fastolfe willed it so. And she's an Auroran citizen."

"Who says so? To every Auroran she is 'the Solarian woman.' "

Amadiro brought his fist down on the arm of his chair in a sudden spilling over of fury. "Vasilia, what is it you wish of me? I have no liking for the Solarian woman. I have, in fact, a profound dislike of her and, if there were a way, I would"—he looked briefly at the robots, as though unwilling to unsettle them—"get her off the planet. But I can't upset the will. Even if there were a legal way to do so—and there isn't—it wouldn't be wise to do it. Fastolfe is dead."

"Precisely the reason Giskard should be mine now."

Amadiro ignored her. "And the coalition he headed is falling apart. It was held together in the last few decades only by his personal charisma. Now what I would like to do is to pick up fragments of that coalition and add it to my own following. In that way, I may put a group together that would be strong enough to dominate the Council and win control in the coming elections."

"With you becoming the next Chairman?"

"Why not? Aurora could do worse, for it would give me a chance to reverse our longtime policy of built-in disaster before it is too late. The trouble is that I don't have Fastolfe's personal popularity. I don't have his gift of exuding saintliness as a cover for stupidity. Consequently, if I seem to be triumphing in an unfair and petty way over a dead man, it will not look good. No one must say that, having been defeated by Fastolfe while he was alive, I overturned his will out of trivial spite after he was dead. I won't have anything as ridiculous as that standing in the way of the great life-and-death decisions Aurora must make. Do you understand me? You'll have to do without Giskard!"

Vasilia arose, body stiff, eyes narrow. "We'll see about that."

"We have already seen. This meeting is over and if you have any ambitions to be the head of the Institute, I don't ever want to see you threatening me about anything. So if you're going to make a threat now, of any kind at all, I advise you to reconsider."

"I make no threats," said Vasilia, every ounce of body language contradicting her words—and she left with a sweep, beckoning her robot, unnecessarily, to follow.

50.

THE EMERGENCY—or rather, the series of emergencies—began some months later when Maloon Cicis entered Amadiro's office for the usual morning conference.

Ordinarily, Amadiro looked forward to that. Cicis was always a restful interlude in the course of the busy day. He was the one senior member of the Institute who had no ambitions and who was not calculating against the day of Amadiro's death or retirement. Cicis was, in fact, the perfect subordinate. He was happy to be of service and delighted to be in Amadiro's confidence.

For this reason, Amadiro had been disturbed, in the last year or so, at the flavor of decay, the slight concavity of the chest, the touch of stiffness in the walk of his perfect subordinate. Could Cicis be getting old? Surely he was only a few decades older than Amadiro.

It struck Amadiro most unpleasantly that perhaps along with the gradual degeneration of so many facets of Spacer life, the life expectancy was falling. He meant to look up the statistics, but kept forgetting to do so—or was unconsciously afraid of doing so.

On this occasion, though, the appearance of age in Cicis was drowned in violent emotion. His face was red (pointing up the graying of his bronze hair) and he appeared virtually exploding with astonishment.

Amadiro did not have to inquire as to the news. Cicis delivered it as though it was something he could not contain.

When he finished exploding, Amadiro said, stupefied, "All radio-wave emissions ceased? All?"

"*All*, Chief. They must all be dead—or gone. No inhabited world can avoid emitting *some* electromagnetic radiation at our level of—"

Amadiro waved him silent. One of Vasilia's points—the fourth, as he recalled—had been that the Solarians were preparing to leave their world. It had been a nonsensical suggestion; all four had been more or less nonsensical. He had said he would keep it in mind and, of course, he hadn't. Now, apparently, that had proved to be a mistake.

What had made it seem nonsensical when Vasilia had advanced the notion still made it seem nonsensical. He asked the question now that he had asked then, even though he expected no answer. (What answer could there be?) "Where in Space could they go, Maloon?"

"There's no word on that, Chief."

"Well, then, *when* did they go?"

"There's no word on that, either. We got the news this morning. The trouble is the radiational intensity is so low on Solaria, anyway. It's very sparsely inhabited and its robots are well-shielded. The intensity is an order of magnitude lower than that of any other Spacer world; two orders lower than ours."

"So one day someone noticed that what was very small had actually declined to zero, but no one actually caught it as it was declining. *Who* noticed it?"

"A Nexonian ship, Chief."

"How?"

"The ship was being forced into orbit about Solaria's sun in order to carry through emergency repairs. They hyperwaved for permission and got no answer. They had no choice but to disregard that, continue into orbit, and carry through their repairs. They were not interfered with in any way in that time. It was not till after they had left that, in checking through their records, they found that not only had they gotten no answer, but that they had gotten no radiational signal of any kind. There's no way of telling exactly when radiation had ceased. The last recorded receipt of any message from Solaria was over two months ago."

"And the other three points she made?" Amadiro muttered.

"Pardon me, Chief?"

"Nothing. Nothing," said Amadiro, but he frowned heavily and was lost in thought.

Chapter 13

The Telepathic Robot

51.

MANDAMUS WAS NOT AWARE of developments on Solaria when he returned some months later from an extended third trip to Earth.

On his first trip, six years before, Amadiro had managed, with some difficulty, to have him sent as an accredited emissary from Aurora to discuss some trifling matter of an overstepping into Spacer territory by Trader vessels. He had endured the ceremony and bureaucratic ennui and it quickly became clear that as such an emissary his mobility was limited. That didn't matter, for he learned what he had come to learn.

He had returned with the news. "I doubt, Dr. Amadiro, that there will be any problem at all. There is no way, no possible way, in which the Earth officials can control either entry or exit. Every year many millions of Settlers visit Earth from any of dozens of worlds and every year as many millions of visiting Settlers leave for home again. Every Settler seems to feel that life is not complete unless he or she periodically breathes the air of Earth and treads its crowded underground spaces. It's a search for roots, I imagine. They don't seem to feel the absolute nightmare that existence on Earth is."

"I know about it, Mandamus," said Amadiro wearily.

"Only *intellectually*, sir. You can't truly understand it until you experience it. Once you do, you'll find that none of your 'knowing' will prepare you in the least for the reality. Why anyone should want to go back, once gone—"

"Our ancestors certainly didn't want to go back, once they had left the planet."

"No," said Mandamus, "but interstellar flight was not then as advanced as it is now. It used to take months then and the hyperspatial Jump was a tricky thing. Now it takes merely days and the Jumps are routine and never go wrong. *If* it were as easy to return to Earth in our ancestors' time as it is now, I wonder if we would have broken away as we did."

"Let's not philosophize, Mandamus. Proceed to the point."

"Certainly. In addition to the coming and going of endless streams of Settlers, millions of Earthmen each year head out as emigrants to one or another of the Settler worlds. Some return almost at once, having failed to adapt. Others make new homes but come back particularly frequently to visit. There's no way of keeping track of exits and entrances and Earth doesn't even try. To attempt to set up systematic methods for identifying and keeping track of visitors might stem the flow and Earth is very aware that each visitor brings money with him. The tourist trade—if we want to call it that—is currently Earth's most profitable industry."

"You are saying, I suppose, that we can get the humanoid robots into Earth without trouble."

"With no trouble at all. There's no question in my mind as to that. Now that we have them properly programmed, we can send them to Earth in half a dozen batches with forged papers. We can't do anything about their robotic respect and awe of human beings, but that may not give them away. It will be interpreted as the usual Settler respect and awe for the ancestral planet. —But, then, I strongly suspect we don't have to drop them into one of the City airports. The vast spaces between Cities are virtually untenanted except by primitive work-robots and the incoming ships would go unnoticed—or at least disregarded."

"Too risky, I think," said Amadiro.

51a.

Two BATCHES OF humanoid robots were sent to Earth and these mingled with the Earthpeople of the City before finding their way outward into the blank areas between and communicating with Aurora on shielded hyperbeam.

Mandamus said (he had thought about it deeply and had hesitated long), "I will have to go again, sir. I can't be positive they've found the right spot."

"Are you sure *you* know the right spot, Mandamus?" asked Amadiro sardonically.

"I have delved into Earth's ancient history thoroughly, sir. I know I can find it."

"I don't think I can persuade the Council to send a warship with you."

"No, I wouldn't want that. It would be worse than useless. I want a one-person vessel, with just enough power to get there and back."

And in that way, Mandamus made his second visit to Earth, dropping down into a region outside one of the smaller Cities. With mingled relief and satisfaction, he found several of the robots in the right place and remained with them to view their work, to give a few orders in connection with that work, and to make some fine adjustments in their programming.

And then, under the uninterested glance of a few primitive Earth-formed agricultural robots, Mandamus made for the nearby City.

It was a calculated risk and Mandamus, no fearless hero, could feel his heart thudding uncomfortably within his chest. But it went well. There was some surprise shown by the gate warden when a human being presented himself at the gate, showing all signs of having spent a considerable time in the open.

Mandamus had papers identifying him as a Settler, however, and the warden shrugged. Settlers didn't mind the open and it was far from unheard of for them to take small excursions through the fields and woods that lay about the unimpressive upper layers of a City that jutted above the ground.

The warden gave but a cursory glance at his papers and no one else asked for them at all. Mandamus's off-Earth accent (as weakly Auroran as he could make it) was accepted without comment and, as nearly as he could tell, no one wondered whether he might be a Spacer. But, then, why should they? The days when the Spacers held a permanent outpost on Earth was two centuries in the past and official emissaries from the Spacer worlds were few and—of late—growing steadily fewer. The provincial Earthpeople might not even remember that Spacers existed.

Mandamus was a little concerned that the thin, transparent gloves he always wore might be noted or that his nose plugs would be remarked upon, but neither event took place. No restrictions were placed on his travels around the City or to other Cities. He had enough money for that and money spoke loudly on Earth (and, to tell the truth, even on Spacer worlds).

He grew accustomed to having no robot dog his heels and when he met with some of Aurora's own humanoid robots in this City or that, he had to explain to them quite firmly that *they* must not dog his heels. He listened to their reports, gave them any instructions they seemed to require, and made arrangements for further robot shipments out-of-City. Eventually, he found his way back to his ship and left.

He was not challenged on his way out, any more than he had been on his way in.

"Actually," he said thoughtfully to Amadiro, "these Earthpeople are not really barbarians."

"Aren't they, though?"

"In their own world, they behave in quite a human fashion. In fact, there is something winning in their friendliness."

"Are you beginning to regret the task you're engaged in?"

"It does give me a grisly feeling as I wander among them thinking that they don't know what is going to happen to them. I can't make myself *enjoy* what I'm doing."

"Of course you can, Mandamus. Think of the fact that once the job is done, you will be sure of a post as the head of the Institute before very much time has elapsed. That will sweeten the job for you."

And Amadiro kept a close eye on Mandamus thereafter.

51b.

ON MANDAMUS'S THIRD TRIP, much of his earlier uneasiness had worn off and he could carry himself almost as though he were an Earthman. The project was proceeding slowly but dead center along the projected line of progress.

He had experienced no health problems on his earlier visits, but on this third one—no doubt due to his overconfidence—he must have exposed himself to something or other. At least, for a time he had an alarming drippiness of the nose, accompanied by a cough.

A visit to one of the City dispensaries resulted in a gamma globulin injection that relieved the condition at once, but he found the dispensary more frightening than the illness. Everyone there, he knew, was likely to be ill with something contagious or to be in close contact with those who were ill.

But now, at last, he was back in the quiet orderliness of Aurora and incredibly thankful to be so. He was listening to Amadiro's account of the Solarian crisis.

"Have you heard nothing of it at all?" demanded Amadiro.

Mandamus shook his head. "Nothing, sir. Earth is an incredibly provincial world. Eight hundred Cities with a total of eight billion people—all interested in nothing but the eight hundred Cities with a total of eight billion people. You would think that Settlers existed only to visit Earth and that Spacers did not exist at all. Indeed, the news reports in any one City deal about ninety percent of the time with that City alone. Earth is an enclosed, claustrophilic world, mentally as well as physically."

"And yet you say they are not barbarian."

"Claustrophilia isn't necessarily barbarism. In their own terms, they are civilized."

"In their own terms! —But never mind. The problem at the moment is Solaria. Not one of the Spacer worlds will move. The principle of noninterference is paramount and they insist that Solaria's internal problems are for Solaria alone. Our own Chairman is as inert as any other, even though Fastolfe is dead and his palsied hand no longer rests on us all. I can do nothing by myself—until such time as *I* am Chairman."

Mandamus said, "How can they suppose Solaria to have internal problems that may not be interfered with when the Solarians are gone?"

Amadiro said sardonically, "How is it you see the folly of it at once and they don't? —They say there is no hard evidence that the Solarians are totally gone and as long as they—or even some of them—might be on the world, there is no right for any other Spacer world to intrude uninvited."

"How do they explain the absence of radiational activity?"

"They say that the Solarians may have moved underground or that they may have developed a technological advance of some sort that obviates radiation leakage. They also say that the Solarians were not seen to leave and that they have absolutely nowhere to go to. Of course, they were not seen leaving because no one was watching."

Mandamus said, "How do they argue that the Solarians have nowhere to go to? There are many empty worlds."

"The argument is that the Solarians cannot live without their incredible crowds of robots and they can't take those robots with them. If they came here, for instance, how many robots do you suppose we could allot to them —if any?"

"And what is your argument against that?"

"I haven't any. Still, whether they are gone or not, the situation is strange and puzzling and it is incredible that no one will move to investigate it. I've warned everyone, just as strenuously as I can, that inertia and apathy will be the end of us; that as soon as the Settler worlds become aware of the fact that Solaria was—or might be—empty, *they* would have no hesitation in investigating the matter. Those swarmers have a mindless curiosity that I wish we had some share in. They will, without thinking twice, risk their lives if some profit lures them on."

"What profit in this case, Dr. Amadiro?"

"If the Solarians are gone, they have, perforce, left almost all their robots behind. They are—or were—particularly ingenious roboticists and the Settlers, for all their hatred of robots, will not hesitate to appropriate them and ship them to us for good Space credits. In fact, they have announced this.

"Two Settler ships have already landed on Solaria. We have sent a protest over this, but they will surely disregard the protest and, just as surely, we will do nothing further. Quite the contrary. Some of the Spacer worlds are sending out quiet queries as to the nature of the robots that might be salvaged and what their prices would be."

"Perhaps just as well," said Mandamus quietly.

"Just as well that we're behaving exactly as the Settler propagandists say we will? That we act as though we *are* degenerating and turning into soft pulps of decadence?"

"Why repeat their buzz words, sir? That fact is that we are quiet and civilized and have not yet been touched where it hurts. If we were, we would fight back strongly enough and, I'm sure, smash them. We still far outstrip them technologically."

"But the damage to ourselves will not be exactly pleasurable."

"Which means that we must not be too ready to go to war. If Solaria is deserted and the Settlers wish to plunder it, perhaps we ought to let them. After all, I predict that we will be all set to make our move within months."

A rather hungry and ferocious look came over Amadiro's face. "Months?"

"I'm sure of it. So the first thing we must do is to avoid being provoked. We will ruin everything if we move toward a conflict there is no need to fight and undergo damage—even if we win—that we don't need to suffer. After all, in a little while, we are going to win totally, without fighting and without damage. —Poor Earth!"

"If you're going to be sorry for them," said Amadiro with spurious lightness, "perhaps you'll do nothing to them."

"On the contrary," said Mandamus coolly. "It's precisely because I fully intend to do something to them—and know that it will be done—that I am sorry for them. You will be Chairman!"

"And you will be the head of the Institute."

"A small post in comparison to yours."

"And after I die?" said Amadiro in half a snarl.

"I do not look that far ahead."

"I am quite—" began Amadiro, but was interrupted by the steady buzz of the message unit. Without looking and quite automatically, Amadiro placed his hand at the EXIT slot. He looked at the thin strip of paper that emerged and a slow smile appeared on his lips.

"The two Settler ships that landed on Solaria—" he said.

"Yes, sir?" asked Mandamus, frowning.

"Destroyed! Both destroyed!"

"How?"

"In an explosive blaze of radiation, easily detected from space. You see what it means? The Solarians have not left after all and the weakest of our worlds can easily handle Settler ships. It is a bloody nose for the Settlers and not something they'll forget. —Here, Mandamus, read for yourself."

Mandamus pushed the paper aside. "But that doesn't necessarily mean that the Solarians are still on the planet. They may merely have booby-trapped it somehow."

"What is the difference? Personal attack or booby-trap, the ships were destroyed."

"This time they were caught by surprise. What about next time, when they are prepared? And what if they consider the event a deliberate Spacer attack?"

"We will reply that the Solarians were merely defending themselves against a deliberate Settler invasion."

"But, sir, are you suggesting a battle of words? What if the Settlers don't bother talking, but consider the destruction of their ships an act of war and retaliate at once?"

"Why should they?"

"Because they are as insane as we can be once pride is hurt; more so, since they have a greater background of violence."

"They will be beaten."

"You yourself admit they will inflict unacceptable damage upon us, even if they are beaten."

"What would you have me do? Aurora did not destroy those ships."

"Persuade the Chairman to make it quite plain that Aurora had nothing to do with it, that none of the Spacer worlds had anything to do with it, that the blame for the action rests on Solaria alone."

"And abandon Solaria? That would be a cowardly act."

Mandamus blazed into excitement. "Dr. Amadiro, have you never heard of anything called a strategic retreat? Persuade the Spacer worlds to back off for only a little while on some plausible pretext. It is only a matter of some months till our plan on Earth comes to fruition. It may be hard for everyone else to back off and be apologetic to the Spacers, for they don't know what is coming—but we do. In fact, you and I, with our special knowledge, can look upon this event as a gift from what used to be called the gods. Let the Settlers remain preoccupied with Solaria while their destruction is prepared—all unobserved by them—on Earth. —Or would you prefer us to be ruined on the very brink of final victory?"

Amadiro found himself flinching before the direct glare of the other's deep-set eyes.

52.

AMADIRO HAD NEVER had a worse time than during the period following the destruction of the Settler ships. The Chairman, fortunately, could be persuaded to follow a policy of what Amadiro termed "masterful yielding." The phrase caught the Chairman's imagination, even though it was an oxymoron. Besides, the Chairman was good at masterful yielding.

The rest of the Council was harder to handle. The exasperated Amadiro exhausted himself in picturing the horrors of war and the necessity of choosing the proper moment to strike—and not the improper one—if war there must be. He invented novel plausibilities for why the moment was not yet and used them in discussions with the leaders of the other Spacer Worlds. Aurora's natural hegemony had to be exercised to the utmost to get them to yield.

But when Captain D. G. Baley arrived with his ship and his demand, Amadiro felt he could do no more. It was too much.

"It is altogether impossible," said Amadiro. "Are we to allow him to land on Aurora with his beard, his ridiculous clothing, his incomprehensible accent? Am I expected to ask the Council to agree to hand over a Spacer woman to him? It would be an act absolutely unprecedented in our history. A Spacer woman!"

Mandamus said dryly, "You have always referred to that particular Spacer woman as 'the Solarian woman.' "

"She is 'the Solarian woman' to us, but she will be considered a Spacer woman once a Settler is involved. If his ship lands on Solaria, as he suggests it will, it may be destroyed as the others were, together with him and the woman. I may then be accused by my enemies, with some color of justification, of murder—and my political career may not survive that."

Mandamus said, "Think, instead, of the fact that we have labored nearly seven years in order to arrange the final destruction of Earth and that we are now only a few months from the completion of the project. Shall we risk war now and, at a stroke, ruin everything we've done when we are so close to final victory?"

Amadiro shook his head. "It isn't as though I have a choice in the matter, my friend. The Council wouldn't follow me if I try to argue them into surrendering the woman to a Settler. And the mere fact that I have suggested it will be used against me. My political career will be shaken and we may then have a war in addition. Besides, the thought of a Spacer woman dying in service to a Settler is unbearable."

"One would suppose you were fond of the Solarian woman."

"You know I am not. With all my heart I wish she had died twenty decades ago, but not this way, not on a Settler ship. —But I should remember that she is an ancestress of yours in the fifth generation."

Mandamus looked a bit more dour than he usually did. "Of what consequence is that to me? I am a Spacer individual, conscious of myself and of my society. I am not an ancestor-worshiping member of a tribal conglomerate."

For a moment, Mandamus fell silent and his thin face took on a look of intense concentration. "Dr. Amadiro," he said, "could you not explain to the Council that this ancestress of mine is being taken, not as a Spacer hostage but only because her unique knowledge of Solaria, where she spent her childhood and youth, could make her an essential part of the exploration and that this exploration might even be helpful to us, as well as to the Settlers? After all, in truth, wouldn't it be desirable for us to know what those miserable Solarians are up to? The woman will presumably bring back a report of the events—if she survives."

Amadiro thrust out his lower lip. "That might work if the woman went on board voluntarily, if she made it clear that she understood the importance of the work and wished to perform her patriotic duty. To put her on board ship by force, though, is unthinkable."

"Well, then, suppose I were to see this ancestress of mine and try to persuade her to get on the ship willingly; and suppose, also, that you speak to this Settler captain by hyperwave and tell them he can land on Aurora and have the woman *if* he can persuade her to go with him willingly—or, at least, *say* that she'll go with him willingly, whether she does or not."

"I suppose we can't lose by making the effort, but I don't see how we can win."

Yet to Amadiro's surprise, they did win. He had listened with astonishment as Mandamus told him the details.

"I brought up the matter of the humanoid robots," Mandamus said, "and it's clear she knew nothing about them, from which I deduced Fastolfe had known nothing about them. It has been one of those things that nagged at me. Then I talked a great deal about my ancestry in such a way as to force her to talk of that Earthman Elijah Baley."

"What about him?" said Amadiro harshly.

"Nothing, except that she talked about him and remembered. This Settler who wants her is a descendant of Baley and I thought it might influence her to consider the Settler's request more favorably than she might otherwise have done."

In any case, it had worked and for a few days Amadiro felt a relief from the almost continuous pressure that had plagued him from the start of the Solarian crisis.

But only for a very few days.

53.

ONE POINT THAT WORKED to Amadiro's advantage at this time was that he had not seen Vasilia, thus far, during the Solarian crisis.

It would certainly not have been an appropriate time to see her. He did not wish to be annoyed by her petty concern over a robot she claimed as her own—with total disregard for the legalities of the situation—at a time when a true crisis exercised his every nerve and thought. Nor did he wish to expose himself to the kind of quarrel that might easily arise between her and Mandamus over the question of which was eventually to preside over the Robotics Institute.

In any case, he had about come to the decision that Mandamus ought to be his successor. Throughout the Solarian crisis, he had kept his eye fixed on what was important. Even when Amadiro himself had felt shaken, Mandamus had remained icily calm. It was Mandamus who thought it conceivable that the Solarian woman might accompany the Settler captain voluntarily and it was he who maneuvered her into doing so.

And if his plan for the destruction of Earth worked itself out as it should —as it must—then Amadiro could see Mandamus succeeding as Council Chairman eventually. It would even be just, thought Amadiro, in a rare burst of selflessness.

On this particular evening, in consequence, he did not so much as expend a thought upon Vasilia. He left the Institute with a small squad of robots seeing him safely to his ground-car. That ground-car, driven by one robot and with two more in the backseat with him, passed quietly through a twilit and chilly rain and brought him to his establishment, where two more robots ushered him indoors. And all this time he did not think of Vasilia.

To find her sitting in his living room, then, in front of his hyperwave set, watching an intricate robot ballet, with several of Amadiro's robots in their niches and two of her own robots behind her chair, struck him at first not so much with the anger of violated privacy, as with pure surprise.

It took some time for him to control his breathing well enough to be able to speak and then his anger arose and he said harshly, "What are you doing here? How did you get in?"

Vasilia was calm enough. Amadiro's appearance was, after all, entirely expected. "What I'm doing here," she said, "is waiting to see you. Getting in was not difficult. Your robots know my appearance very well and they know my standing at the Institute. Why shouldn't they allow me to enter if I assure them I have an appointment with you?"

"Which you haven't. You have violated my privacy."

"Not really. There's a limit to how much trust you can squeeze out of someone else's robots. Look at them. They have never once taken their eyes from me. If I had wanted to disturb your belongings, look through your papers, take advantage of your absence in any way, I assure you I could not have. My two robots are no match against them."

"Do you know," said Amadiro bitterly, "that you have acted in a thoroughly un-Spacer fashion. You are despicable and I will not forget this."

Vasilia seemed to blanch slightly at the adjectives. She said in a low, hard voice, "I hope you don't forget it, Kelden, for I've done what I've done for *you*—and if I reacted as I should to your foul mouth, I would leave now and let you continue for the rest of your life to be the defeated man you have been for the past twenty decades."

"I will not remain a defeated man—whatever you do."

Vasilia said, "You sound as though you believe that, but, you see, you do not know what I know. I must tell you that without my intervention you will remain defeated. I don't care what scheme you have in mind. I don't care what this thin-lipped, acid-faced Mandamus has cooked up for you—"

"Why do you mention him?" said Amadiro quickly.

"Because I wish to," said Vasilia with a touch of contempt. "Whatever he has done or thinks he is doing—and don't be frightened, for I haven't any idea what that might be—it won't work. I may not know anything else about it, but I do know it won't work."

"You're babbling idiocies," said Amadiro.

"You had better listen to these idiocies, Kelden, if you don't want everything to fall into ruin. Not just you, but possibly the Spacer worlds, one and all. Still, you may not want to listen to me. It's your choice. Which, then, is it to be?"

"Why should I listen to you? What possible reason is there for me to listen to you?"

"For one thing, I told you the Solarians were preparing to leave their world. If you had listened to me then, you would not have been caught so by surprise when they did."

"The Solarian crisis will yet turn to our advantage."

"No, it will not," said Vasilia. "You may think it will, but it won't. It will destroy you—no matter what you are doing to meet the emergency—unless you are willing to let me have my say."

Amadiro's lips were white and were trembling slightly. The two centuries of defeat Vasilia had mentioned had had a lasting effect upon him and the Solarian crisis had not helped, so he lacked the inner strength to order his robots to see her out, as he should have. He said sullenly, "Well, then, put it in brief."

"You would not believe what I have to say if I did, so let me do it my own way. You can stop me at any time, but then you will destroy the Spacer worlds. Of course, they will last my time and it won't be I who will go down in history—*Settler* history, by the way—as the greatest failure on record. Shall I speak?"

Amadiro folded into a chair. "Speak, then, and when you are through— leave."

"I intend to, Kelden, unless, of course, you ask me—*very* politely—to stay and help you. Shall I start?"

Amadiro said nothing and Vasilia began, "I told you that during my stay on Solaria I became aware of some very peculiar positronic pathway patterns they had designed, pathways that struck me—very forcefully—as representing attempts at producing telepathic robots. Now, why should I have thought that?"

Amadiro said bitterly, "I cannot tell what pathological drives may power your thinking."

Vasilia brushed that aside with a grimace. "Thank you, Kelden. —I've spent some months thinking about that, since I was acute enough to think the matter involved not pathology but some subliminal memory. My mind went back to my childhood when Fastolfe, whom I then considered my father, in one of his generous moods—he would experiment now and then with generous moods, you understand—gave me a robot of my own."

"Giskard again?" muttered Amadiro with impatience.

"Yes, Giskard. Giskard, always. I was in my teenage years and I already had the instinct of a roboticist or, I should say, I was born with the instinct. I had as yet very little mathematics, but I had a grasp of patterns. With the passing of scores of decades, my knowledge of mathematics steadily improved, but I don't think I have advanced very far in my feeling for patterns. My father would say, 'Little Vas'—he also experimented in loving diminutives to see how that would affect me—'you have a genius for patterns.' I think I did—"

Amadiro said, "Spare me. I'll concede your genius. Meanwhile, I have not yet had my dinner, do you know that?"

"Well," said Vasilia sharply, "order your dinner and invite me to join you."

Amadiro, frowning, raised his arm perfunctorily and made a quick sign. The quiet motion of robots at work made itself evident at once.

Vasilia said, "I would play with pathway patterns for Giskard. I would come to Fastolfe—my father, as I then thought of him—and I would show him a pattern. He might shake his head and laugh and say, 'If you add that to poor Giskard's brain, he will no longer be able to talk and he will be in a great deal of pain.' I remember asking if Giskard could really feel pain and my father said, 'We don't know what he would *feel*, but he would *act* as we would act if we were in a great deal of pain, so we might as well say he would feel pain.'

"Or else I would take one of my patterns to him and he would smile indulgently and say, 'Well, that won't hurt him, Little Vas, and it might be interesting to try.'

"And I would. Sometimes I would take it out again and sometimes I would leave it. I was not simply fiddling with Giskard for the sadistic joy of it, as I imagine I might have been tempted to do if I were someone other than myself. The fact is, I was very fond of Giskard and I had no desire to harm him. When it seemed to me that one of my improvements—I always thought of them as improvements—made Giskard speak more freely or react more quickly or more interestingly—and seemed to do no harm—I would let it stay.

"And then one day—"

A robot standing at Amadiro's elbow would not have dared to interrupt a guest unless a true emergency existed, but Amadiro had no difficulty in understanding the significance of the waiting. He said, "Is dinner ready?"

"Yes, sir," said the robot.

Amadiro gestured rather impatiently in Vasilia's direction. "You are invited to have dinner with me."

They walked into Amadiro's dining room, which Vasilia had never entered before. Amadiro was, after all, a private person and was notorious for his neglect of the social amenities. He had been told more than once that he would succeed better in politics if he entertained in his home and he had always smiled politely and said, "Too high a price."

It was perhaps because of his failure to entertain, thought Vasilia, that there was no sign of originality or creativity in the furnishings. Nothing could be plainer than the table, the dishes, and the cutlery. As for the walls, they were merely flat-colored vertical planes. Put together, it rather dampened one's appetite, she thought.

The soup they began with—a clear bouillon—was as plain as the furniture and Vasilia began to dispose of it without enthusiasm.

Amadiro said, "My dear Vasilia, you see I am being patient. I have no objection to having you write your autobiography if you wish. But is it really your plan to recite several chapters of it to me? If it is, I must tell you bluntly that I'm not really interested."

Vasilia said, "You will become extremely interested in just a little while. Still, if you're really enamored of failure and want to continue to achieve nothing you wish to achieve, simply say so. I will then eat in silence and leave. Is that what you wish?"

Amadiro sighed. "Well, go on, Vasilia."

Vasilia said, "And then one day I came up with a pattern more elaborate, more pleasant, and more enticing than I had ever seen before or, in all truth, than I have ever seen since. I would have loved to show it to my father, but he was away at some meeting or other on one of the other worlds.

"I didn't know when he'd be back and I put aside my pattern, but each day I would look at it with more interest and more fascination. Finally, I could wait no longer. I simply could not. It seemed so beautiful that I thought it ludicrous to suppose it could do harm. I was only an infant in my second decade and had not yet completely outgrown irresponsibility, so I modified Giskard's brain by incorporating the pattern into it.

"And it did no harm. That was immediately obvious. He responded to me with perfect ease and—it seemed to me—was far quicker in understanding and much more intelligent than he had been. I found him far more fascinating and lovable than before.

"I was delighted and yet I was nervous, too. What I had done—modifying Giskard without clearing it with Fastolfe—was strictly against the rules Fastolfe had set for me and I knew that well. Yet clearly, I was not going to undo what I had done. When I had modified Giskard's brain, I excused it to myself by saying that it would only be for a little while and that I would then neutralize the modification. Once the modification had been made, however, it became quite clear to me that I would *not* neutralize it. I was simply *not* going to do that. In fact, I never modified Giskard again, for fear of disturbing what I had just done.

"Nor did I ever tell Fastolfe what I had done. I destroyed all record of the marvelous pattern I had devised and Fastolfe never found out that Giskard had been modified without his knowledge. Never!

"And then we went our separate ways, Fastolfe and I, and Fastolfe would not give up Giskard. I screamed that he was mine and that I loved him, but Fastolfe's kindly benevolence, of which he made such a parade all his life—that business of loving all things, great and small—was never allowed to stand in the way of his own desires. I received other robots I cared nothing for, but he kept Giskard for himself.

"And when he died, he left Giskard to the Solarian woman—a last bitter slap at me."

Amadiro had only managed to get halfway through the salmon mousse. "If all this is intended to advance your case of having Giskard's ownership transferred from the Solarian woman to yourself, it won't help. I have already explained to you why I cannot set aside Fastolfe's will."

"There's something more to it than that, Kelden," said Vasilia. "A great deal more. Infinitely more. Do you want me to stop now?"

Amadiro stretched his lips into a rueful grin. "Having listened to so much of this, I will play the madman and listen to more."

"You would play the madman if you did not, for I now come to the point. —I have never stopped thinking of Giskard and of the cruelty and injustice of my having been deprived of him, but somehow I never thought of that pattern with which I had modified him with no one's knowledge but my own. I am quite certain I could not have reproduced that pattern if I had tried and from what I can now remember it was like nothing else I have ever seen in robotics until—until I saw, briefly, something like that pattern during my stay on Solaria.

"The Solarian pattern seemed familiar to me, but I didn't know why. It took some weeks of intense thought before I dredged out of some well-hidden part of my unconscious mind the slippery thought of that pattern I had dreamed out of nothing twenty-five decades ago.

"Even though I can't remember my pattern exactly, I know that the Solarian pattern was a whiff of it and no more. It was just the barest suggestion of something I had captured in miraculously complex symmetry. But I looked at the Solarian pattern with the experience I had gained in twenty-five decades of deep immersion in robotics theory and it suggested telepathy to me. If that simple, scarcely interesting pattern suggested it, what must my original have meant—the thing I invented as a child and have never recaptured since?"

Amadiro said, "You keep saying that you're coming to the point, Vasilia. Would I be completely unreasonable if I asked you to stop moaning and reminiscing and simply set out that point in a simple, declarative sentence?"

Vasilia said, "Gladly. What I am telling you, Kelden, is that, without my ever knowing it, I converted Giskard into a telepathic robot and that he has been one ever since."

54.

AMADIRO LOOKED AT Vasilia for a long time and, because the story seemed to have come to an end, he returned to the salmon mousse and ate some of it thoughtfully.

He then said, "Impossible! Do you take me for an idiot?"

"I take you for a failure," said Vasilia. "I don't say Giskard can read conversations in minds, that he can transmit and receive words or ideas. Perhaps that *is* impossible, even in theory. But I am quite certain he can detect emotions and the general set of mental activity and perhaps can even modify it."

Amadiro shook his head violently. "Impossible!"

"Impossible? Think a while. Twenty decades ago, you had almost achieved your aims. Fastolfe was at your mercy, Chairman Horder was your ally. What happened? Why did everything go wrong?"

"The Earthman—" Amadiro began, choking at the memory.

"The Earthman," Vasilia mimicked. "The Earthman. Or was it the Solarian woman? It was neither! Neither! It was Giskard, who was there all the time. Sensing. Adjusting."

"Why should he be interested? He is a robot."

"A robot loyal to his master, to Fastolfe. By the First Law, he had to see to it that Fastolfe came to no harm and, being telepathic, he could not interpret that as signifying physical harm only. He knew that if Fastolfe could not have his way, could not encourage the settlement of the habitable worlds of the Galaxy, he would undergo profound disappointment—and that would be 'harm' in Giskard's telepathic Universe. He could not let that happen and he intervened to keep it from happening."

"No, no, no," said Amadiro in disgust. "You want that to be so, out of some wild, romantic longing, but that doesn't make it so. I remember too well what happened. It was the Earthman. It needs no telepathic robot to explain the events."

"And what has happened since, Kelden?" demanded Vasilia. "In twenty decades, have you ever managed to win out over Fastolfe? With all the facts in your favor, with the obvious bankruptcy of Fastolfe's policy, have you ever been able to dispose of a majority in the Council? Have you ever been able to sway the Chairman to the point where you could possess real power?

"How do you explain that, Kelden? In all those twenty decades, the Earthman has not been on Aurora. He has been dead for over sixteen decades, his miserably short life running out in eight decades or so. Yet you continue to fail—you have an unbroken record of failure. Even now that Fastolfe is dead, have you managed to profit completely from the broken pieces of his coalition or do you find that success still seems to elude you?

"What is it that remains? The Earthman is gone. Fastolfe is gone. It is Giskard who has worked against you all this time—and Giskard remains. He is as loyal now to the Solarian woman as he was to Fastolfe and the Solarian woman has no cause to love you, I think."

Amadiro's face twisted into a mask of anger and frustration. "It's not so. None of this is so. You're imagining things."

Vasilia remained quite cool. "No, I'm not. I'm explaining things. I've explained things you haven't been able to explain. Or have you an alternate explanation? —And I can give you the cure. Transfer ownership of Giskard from the Solarian woman to me and, quite suddenly, events will begin to twist themselves to your benefit."

"No," said Amadiro. "They are moving to my benefit already."

"You may think so, but they won't, as long as Giskard is working against you. No matter how close you come to winning, no matter how sure of victory you become, it will all melt away as long as you don't have Giskard on your side. That happened twenty decades ago; it will happen now."

Amadiro's face suddenly cleared. He said, "Well, come to think of it, though I don't have Giskard and neither do you, it doesn't matter, for I can show you that Giskard is not telepathic. If Giskard were telepathic, as you say, if he had the ability to order affairs to his own liking or to the liking of the human being who is his owner, then why would he have allowed the Solarian woman to be taken to what will probably be her death?"

"Her death? What are you talking about, Kelden?"

"Are you aware, Vasilia, that two Settler ships have been destroyed on Solaria? Or have you been doing nothing lately but dreaming of patterns and of the brave days of childhood when you were modifying your pet robot?"

"Sarcasm doesn't become you, Kelden. I have heard about the Settler ships on the news. What of them?"

"A third Settler ship is going out to investigate. It may be destroyed, too."

"Possibly. On the other hand, it would take precautions."

"It did. It demanded and received the Solarian woman, feeling that she knows the planet well enough to enable them to avoid destruction."

Vasilia said, "That's scarcely likely, since she hasn't been there in twenty decades."

"Right! The chances are, then, that she'll die with them. It would mean nothing to me personally. I would be delighted to have her dead and, I think, so would you. And, putting that to one side, it would give us good grounds for complaint to the Settler worlds and it would make it difficult for them to argue that the destruction of the ships is a deliberate action on the part of Aurora. Would we destroy one of our own? —Now the question is, Vasilia, why would Giskard, if he had the powers you claim he has—and the loyalties—allow the Solarian woman to volunteer to be taken to what is very likely to be her death?"

Vasilia was taken aback. "Did she go of her own free will?"

"Absolutely. She was perfectly willing. It would have been politically impossible to force her to do so against her will."

"But I don't understand—"

"There is nothing to understand except that Giskard is merely a robot."

For a moment, Vasilia froze in her seat, one hand to her chin. Then she said slowly, "They don't allow robots on Settler worlds or on Settler ships. That means she went alone. Without robots."

"Well, no, of course not. They had to accept personal robots if they expected to get her willingly. They took along that man-mimic robot

Daneel and the other was"—he paused and brought out the word with a hiss—"Giskard. Who else? So this miracle robot of your fantasy goes to his destruction as well. He could no more—"

His voice faded away. Vasilia was on her feet, eyes blazing, face suffused with color.

"You mean *Giskard* went? He's off this world and on a Settler ship? Kelden, you may have ruined us all!"

55.

NEITHER FINISHED THE MEAL.

Vasilia walked hastily out of the dining room and disappeared into the Personal. Amadiro, struggling to remain coldly logical, shouted to her through the closed door, perfectly aware that it damaged his dignity to do so.

He called out, "It's all the stronger an indication that Giskard is no more than a robot. Why should he be willing to go to Solaria to face destruction with his owner?"

Eventually, the sound of running water and splashing ceased and Vasilia emerged with her face freshly washed and almost frozen in its grip on calmness.

She said, "You really don't understand, do you? You amaze me, Kelden. Think it through. Giskard can never be in danger, as long as he can influence human minds, can he? Nor can the Solarian woman, as long as Giskard devotes himself to her. The Settler who carried off the Solarian woman must have found out, on interviewing her, that she had not been on Solaria in twenty decades, so he can't really have continued to believe, after that, that she could do him much good. With her he took Giskard, but he didn't know that Giskard could do him good, either— Or could he have known that?"

She thought a while and then said slowly, "No, there is no way he could have known it. If, in more than twenty decades, no one has penetrated the fact that Giskard has mental abilities, then Giskard is clearly interested in having no one guess it—and if that is so, then no one can possibly have guessed it."

Amadiro said spitefully, *"You* claim to have worked it out."

Vasilia said, "I had special knowledge, Kelden, and even so it was not till now that I saw the obvious—and then only because of the hint on Solaria.

Giskard must have darkened my mind in that respect, too, or I would have seen it long ago. I wonder if Fastolfe knew—"

"How much easier," said Amadiro restlessly, "to accept the simple fact that Giskard is simply a robot."

"You will walk the easy road to ruin, Kelden, but I don't think I will let you do that, no matter how much you want to. —What it amounts to is that the Settler came for the Solarian woman and took her along, even though he discovered she would be of little—if any—use to him. And the Solarian woman volunteered to go, even though she must dread being on a Settler ship along with diseased barbarians—and even though her destruction on Solaria must have seemed to her a very likely consequence.

"It seems to me, then, that this is all the work of Giskard, who forced the Settler to continue to demand the Solarian woman against reason and forced the Solarian woman to accede to the request against reason."

Amadiro said, "But why? May I ask that simple question? Why?"

"I suppose, Kelden, that Giskard felt it was important to get away from Aurora. —Could he have guessed that I was on the point of learning his secret? If so, he may well have been uncertain of his present ability to tamper with me. I am, after all, a skilled roboticist. Besides, he would remember that he was once mine and a robot does not easily ignore the demands of loyalty. The only way, perhaps, that he felt he could keep the Solarian woman secure was to move himself away from my influence."

She looked up at Amadiro and said firmly, "Kelden, we must get him back. We can't let him work at promoting the Settler cause in the safe haven of a Settler world. He did enough damage right here among us. We must get him back and you must make me his legal owner. I can handle him, I assure you, and make him work for us. Remember! I am the *only* one who can handle him."

Amadiro said, "I do not see any reason to worry. In the very likely case that he is a mere robot, he will be destroyed on Solaria and we will be rid of both him and the Solarian woman. In the unlikely case that he is what you say he is, he won't be destroyed on Solaria, but then he will have to return to Aurora. After all, the Solarian woman, though she is not an Auroran by birth, has lived on Aurora far too long to be able to face life among the barbarians—and when she insists on returning to civilization, Giskard will have no alternative but to return with her."

Vasilia said, "After all this, Kelden, you still don't understand Giskard's abilities. If he feels it important to remain away from Aurora, he can easily adjust the Solarian woman's emotions in such a way as to make her stand life on a Settler world, just as he made her willing to board a Settler ship."

"Well, then, if necessary, we can simply escort that Settler ship—with the Solarian woman and with Giskard—back to Aurora."

"How do you propose to do that?"

"It can be done. We are *not* fools here on Aurora, for all that it seems clearly your opinion that you yourself are the only rational person on the planet. The Settler ship is going to Solaria to investigate the destruction of the earlier two ships, but I hope you don't think we intend to depend upon its good offices or even upon those of the Solarian woman. We are sending two of our warships to Solaria and we do not expect that *they* will have trouble. If there are Solarians still on the planet, they may be able to destroy primitive Settler ships, but they won't be able to touch an Auroran vessel of war. If, then, the Settler ship, through some magic on the part of Giskard—"

"Not magic," Vasilia interrupted tartly. "Mental influence."

"If, then, the Settler ship, for whatever reason, should be able to rise from the surface of Solaria, our ships will cut them off and politely ask for the delivery of the Solarian woman and her robots. Failing that, they will insist that the Settler ship accompany our ship to Aurora. There will be no hostility about it. Our ship will merely be escorting an Auroran national to her home world. Once the Solarian woman and her two robots disembark on Aurora, the Settler ship will then be able to proceed at will to its own destination."

Vasilia nodded wearily at this. "It sounds good, Kelden, but do you know what I suspect will happen?"

"What, Vasilia?"

"It is my opinion that the Settler ship will rise from the surface of Solaria, but that our warships won't. Whatever is on Solaria can be countered by Giskard, but, I fear, by nothing else."

"If *that* happens," said Amadiro with a grim smile, "then I'll admit there may be something, after all, to your fantasy. —But it won't happen."

56.

THE NEXT MORNING Vasilia's chief personal robot, delicately designed to appear female, came to Vasilia's bedside. Vasilia stirred and, without opening her eyes, said, "What is it, Nadila?" (There was no need to open her eyes. In many decades, no one had ever approached her bedside but Nadila.)

Nadila said softly, "Madam, you are desired at the Institute by Dr. Amadiro."

Vasilia's eyes flew open. "What time is it?"

"It is 0517, madam."

"Before sunrise?" Vasilia was indignant.

"Yes, madam."

"When does he want me?"

"Now, madam."

"Why?"

"His robots have not informed us, madam, but they say it is important."

Vasilia threw aside the bed sheets. "I will have breakfast first, Nadila, and a shower before that. Inform Amadiro's robots to take visitors' niches and wait. If they urge speed, remind them they are in *my* establishment."

Vasilia, annoyed, did not hasten unduly. If anything, her toilette was more painstaking than usual and her breakfast more leisurely. (She was not ordinarily one to spend much time over either.) The news, which she watched, gave no indication of anything that might explain Amadiro's call.

By the time the ground-car (containing herself and four robots—two of Amadiro's and two of her own) had brought her to the Institute, the sun was making its appearance over the horizon.

Amadiro looked up and said, "You are finally here, then." The walls of his office were still glowing, though their light was no longer needed.

"I'm sorry," said Vasilia stiffly. "I quite realize that sunrise is a terribly late hour at which to begin work."

"No games, Vasilia, please. Very soon I will have to be at the Council chamber. The Chairman has been up longer than I have. —Vasilia, I apologize, quite humbly, for doubting you."

"The Settler ship has lifted off safely, then."

"Yes. And one of *our* ships has been destroyed, as you predicted. —The fact has not been publicized yet, but the news will leak out eventually, of course."

Vasilia's eyes widened. She had predicted this outcome with a bit more in the way of outward confidence than she had felt, but clearly this was not the time to say so. What she did say was "Then you accept the fact that Giskard has extraordinary powers."

Cautiously, Amadiro said, "I don't consider the matter to be mathematically proven, but I'm willing to accept it pending further information.

What I want to know is what we ought to do next. The Council knows nothing of Giskard and I do not propose to tell them."

"I'm glad your thinking is clear to that extent, Kelden."

"But you're the one who understands Giskard and you can best tell what ought to be done. What do I tell the Council, then, and how do I explain the action without giving away the whole truth?"

"It depends. Now that the Settler ship has left Solaria, where is it going? Can we tell? After all, if it is returning now to Aurora, we need do nothing but prepare for its arrival."

"It is not coming to Aurora," said Amadiro emphatically. "You were right there, too, it seems. Giskard—assuming he is running the show—seems determined to stay away. We have intercepted the ship's messages to its own world. Encoded, of course, but there isn't a Settler code we haven't broken—"

"I suspect they've broken ours, too. I wonder why everyone won't agree to send messages in the clear and save a lot of trouble."

Amadiro shrugged it away. "Never mind that. The point is that the Settler ship is going back to its own planet."

"With the Solarian woman and the robots?"

"Of course."

"You're sure of that? They haven't been left on Solaria?"

"We're sure of that," said Amadiro impatiently. "Apparently, the Solarian woman was responsible for their getting off the surface."

"She? In what way?"

"We don't yet know."

Vasilia said, "It had to be Giskard. He made it appear to be the Solarian woman."

"And what do we do now?"

"We must get Giskard back."

"Yes, but I can't very well persuade the Council to risk an interstellar crisis over the return of a robot."

"You don't, Kelden. You ask for the return of the Solarian woman, something we certainly have a right to request. And do you think for one moment she would return without her robots? Or that Giskard will allow the Solarian woman to return without him? Or that the Settler world would want to keep the robots if the Solarian woman returns? Ask for *her*. Firmly. She's an Auroran citizen, lent out for a job on Solaria, which is done, and she must now be returned forthwith. Make it belligerent, as though it were a threat of war."

"We can't risk war, Vasilia."

"You won't risk it. Giskard can't take an action that might lead directly to war. If the Settler leaders resist and become belligerent in their return, Giskard will perforce make the necessary modifications in the attitude of the Settler leaders so as to have the Solarian woman returned peaceably to Aurora. And he himself will, of course, have to return with her."

Amadiro said drearily, "And once he's back, he will alter *us*, I suppose, and we will forget his powers, and disregard him, and he will still be able to follow his own plan whatever it is."

Vasilia leaned her head back and laughed. "Not a chance. I *know* Giskard, you see, and I can handle him. Just bring him back and persuade the Council to disregard Fastolfe's will—it can be done and you can do it—and to assign Giskard to me. He will then be working for us; Aurora will rule the Galaxy; you will spend the remaining decades of your life as Chairman of the Council; and I will succeed you as the head of the Robotics Institute."

"Are you sure it will work out that way?"

"Absolutely. Just send the message and make it strong and I will guarantee all the rest—victory for the Spacers and ourselves, defeat for Earth and the Settlers."

Chapter 14
The Duel

57.

GLADIA WATCHED AURORA'S GLOBE on the screen. Its cloud cover seemed caught in mid-swirl along the thick crescent that was shining in the light of its sun.

"Surely we're not that close," she said.

D.G. smiled. "By no means. We're seeing it through a rather good lens. It's still several days away, counting the spiral approach. If we ever get an antigravitic drive, which the physicists keep dreaming about but seem helpless to bring about, spaceflight will become really simple and fast. As it is, our Jumps can only deliver us safely to a rather goodish distance from a planetary mass."

"It's odd," said Gladia thoughtfully.

"What is, madam?"

"When we went to Solaria, I thought to myself, 'I'm going home,' but when I landed I found that I wasn't home at all. Now we're going to Aurora and I thought to myself, 'Now I'm going home,' and yet—that world down there isn't home, either."

"Where is home, then, madam?"

"I'm beginning to wonder. —But why do you persist in calling me 'madam'?"

D.G. looked surprised. "Do you prefer 'Lady Gladia,' Lady Gladia?"

"That's also mock respect. Do you feel that way about me?"

"Mock respect? Certainly not. But how else does a Settler address a Spacer? I'm trying to be polite and to conform to your customs—to do what makes you feel comfortable."

"But it doesn't make me feel comfortable. Just call me Gladia. I've suggested it before. After all, I call you 'D.G.' "

"And that suits me fine, although in front of my officers and men, I would prefer to have you address me as 'Captain,' and I will call you 'madam.' Discipline must be maintained."

"Yes, of course," said Gladia absently, staring at Aurora again. "I have no home."

She whirled toward D.G., "Is it possible that you might take me to Earth, D.G.?"

"Possible," said D.G., smiling. "You might not want to go—Gladia."

"I think I want to go," said Gladia, "unless I lose my courage."

"Infection does exist," said D.G., "and that's what Spacers fear, isn't it?"

"Too much, perhaps. After all, I knew your Ancestor and wasn't infected. I have been on this ship and have survived. Look, you're near me right now. I was even on your world, with thousands crowding near me. I think I've worked up a certain amount of resistance."

"I must tell you, Gladia, that Earth is a thousand times as crowded as Baleyworld."

"Even so," said Gladia, her voice warming, "I've changed my mind completely—about many things. I've told you there was nothing left to live for after twenty-three decades and it turns out there *is*. What happened to me on Baleyworld—the talk I gave, the way it moved people—was something new, something I'd never imagined. It was like being born all over, starting again at the first decade. It seems to me now that, even if Earth kills me, it would be worth it, for I would die young and trying and fighting death, not old and weary and welcoming it."

"Well!" said D.G., lifting his arms in a mock-heroic gesture, "you sound like a hyperwave historical. Have you ever watched them on Aurora?"

"Of course. They're very popular."

"Are you rehearsing for one, Gladia, or do you really mean what you say?"

Gladia laughed. "I suppose I do sound rather silly, D.G., but the funny thing is that I *do* mean it—if I don't lose my courage."

"In that case, we'll do it. We'll go to Earth. I don't think they'll consider you worth a war, especially if you report fully on events on Solaria, as they want you to, and if you give your word of honor as a Spacer woman—if you do things like that—to return."

"But I won't."

"But you may want to someday. —And now, my lady—I mean, Gladia—

it is always a pleasure to speak with you, but I'm always tempted to spend too much time at it and I am certain I am needed in the control room. If I'm not and they can do without me, then I'd rather they didn't find out."

58.

"Was that your doing, friend Giskard?"

"To what is it that you refer, friend Daneel?"

"Lady Gladia is anxious to go to Earth and even perhaps not to return. That is a desire so antithetical to what a Spacer such as she would want that I cannot help but suspect that you did something to her mind to make her feel so."

Giskard said, "I did not touch her. It is difficult enough to tamper with any human being within the cage of the Three Laws. To tamper with the mind of the particular individual for whose safety one is directly responsible is more difficult still."

"Then why does she wish to go to Earth?"

"Her experiences on Baleyworld have changed her point of view considerably. She has a mission—that of ensuring peace in the Galaxy—and burns to work at it."

"In that case, friend Giskard, would it not be better to do what you can to persuade the captain, in your own fashion, to go to Earth directly?"

"That would create difficulties. The Auroran authorities are so insistent on Lady Gladia being returned to Aurora that it would be better to do so, at least temporarily."

"Yet it could be dangerous to do so," said Daneel.

"Then you still think, friend Daneel, that it is I whom they want to retain because they have learned of my abilities?"

"I see no other reason for their insistence on Lady Gladia's return."

Giskard said, "Thinking like a man has its pitfalls, I see. It becomes possible to suppose difficulties that cannot exist. Even if someone on Aurora were to suspect the existence of my abilities, it is with those abilities that I would remove the suspicion. There is nothing to fear, friend Daneel."

And Daneel said reluctantly, "As you say, friend Giskard."

59.

Gladia looked about thoughtfully, sending off the robots with a careless motion of her hand.

She looked at her hand, as she did so, almost as though she were seeing it for the first time. It had been the hand with which she had shaken the hand of each of the crewmen of the ship before getting into the small tender that took her and D.G. down to Aurora. When she promised to return, they had cheered her and Niss had bawled out, "We won't leave without you, my lady."

The cheering had pleased her enormously. Her robots served her endlessly, loyally, patiently, but they never cheered her.

D.G., watching her curiously, said, "Surely you are at home now, Gladia."

"I am in my establishment," she said in a low voice. "It has been my establishment since Dr. Fastolfe assigned it to me twenty decades ago and yet it feels strange to me."

"It is strange to *me*," said D.G. "I'd feel rather lost staying here alone." He looked about with a half-smile at the ornate furnishings and the elaborately decorated walls.

"You won't be alone, D.G.," said Gladia. "My household robots will be with you and they have full instructions. They will devote themselves to your comfort."

"Will they understand my Settler accent?"

"If they fail to understand, they will ask you to repeat and you must then speak slowly and make gestures. They will prepare food for you, show you how to use the facilities in the guest rooms—and they will also keep a sharp eye on you to make sure that you do not act in an unguestly manner. They will stop you—if necessary—but they will do so without hurting you."

"I trust they won't consider me nonhuman."

"As the overseer did? No, I guarantee you that, D.G., though your beard and accent may confuse them to the point where they will be a second or two slow in reacting."

"And I suppose they'll protect me against intruders?"

"They will, but there won't be any intruders."

"The Council may want to come and get me."

"Then they will send robots and mine will turn them away."

"What if their robots overpower your robots?"

"That can't happen, D.G. An establishment is inviolate."

"Come on, Gladia. Do you mean that nobody has ever—"

"Nobody has ever!" she replied at once. "You just stay here comfortably and my robots will take care of all your needs. If you want to get in touch with your ship, with Baleyworld, even with the Auroran Council, they will know exactly what to do. You won't have to lift a finger."

D.G. sank down into the nearest chair, spread himself out over it, and sighed deeply. "How wise we are to allow no robots on the Settler worlds. Do you know how long it would take to corrupt me into idleness and sloth if I stayed in this kind of society? Five minutes at most. In fact, I'm corrupted already." He yawned and stretched luxuriously. "Would they mind if I sleep?"

"Of course they wouldn't. If you do, the robots will see to it that your surroundings are kept quiet and dark."

Then D.G. straightened suddenly. "What if you don't come back?"

"Why shouldn't I come back?"

"The Council seems to want you rather urgently."

"They can't hold me. I'm a free Auroran citizen and I go where I please."

"There are always emergencies when a government wishes to manufacture one—and in an emergency, rules can always be broken."

"Nonsense. Giskard, am I going to be kept there?"

Giskard said, "Madam Gladia, you will not be kept there. The captain need not be concerned with respect to that."

"There you are, D.G. And your Ancestor, the last time he saw me, told me I was always to trust Giskard."

"Good! Excellent! Just the same, the reason I came down with you, Gladia, was to make sure I get you back. Remember that and tell it to your Dr. Amadiro if you have to. If they try to keep you against your will, they will have to try to keep me as well—and my ship, which is in orbit, is fully capable of reacting to that."

"No, please," said Gladia, disturbed. "Don't think of doing that. Aurora has ships as well and I'm sure yours is under observation."

"There's a difference, though, Gladia. I doubt very much that Aurora would want to go to war over you. Baleyworld, on the other hand, would be quite prepared to."

"Surely not. I wouldn't want them to go to war on my account. And why should they, anyway? Because I was a friend of your Ancestor?"

"Not exactly. I don't think anyone can quite believe that you were that friend. Maybe your great-grandmother, not you. Even *I* don't believe it was you."

"You *know* it was I."

"Intellectually, yes. Emotionally, I find it impossible. That was twenty decades ago."

Gladia shook her head. "You have the short-lived view."

"Maybe we all do, but it doesn't matter. What makes you important to Baleyworld is the speech you gave. You're a heroine and they will decide you must be presented at Earth. Nothing will be allowed to prevent that."

Gladia said, a trifle alarmed, "Presented at Earth? With full ceremony?"

"The fullest."

"Why should that be thought so important as to be worth a war?"

"I'm not sure I can explain that to a Spacer. Earth is a special world. Earth is a—holy world. It's the only real world. It's where human beings came into being and it's the only world in which they evolved and developed and lived against a full background of life. We have trees on Baleyworld and insects—but on Earth they have a wild riot of trees and insects that none of us ever see except on Earth. Our worlds are imitations, pale imitations. They don't exist and can't exist except for the intellectual, cultural, and spiritual strength they draw from Earth."

Gladia said, "This is quite opposed to the opinion of Earth held by Spacers. When we refer to Earth, which we seldom do, it is as a world that is barbarous and in decay."

D.G. flushed. "That is why the Spacer worlds have been growing steadily weaker. As I said before, you are like plants that have pulled themselves loose from their roots, like animals that have cut out their hearts."

Gladia said, "Well, I look forward to seeing Earth for myself, but I will have to go now. Please treat this as your own establishment till I return." She walked briskly toward the door, stopped, then turned. "There are no alcoholic drinks in this establishment or anywhere on Aurora, no tobacco, no alkaloidal stimulants, nothing of any artificial kinds of—of whatever you may be used to."

D.G. grinned sourly. "We Settlers are aware of that. Very puritanical, you people."

"Not puritanical at all," said Gladia, frowning. "Thirty to forty decades of life must be paid for—and that's one of the ways. You don't suppose we do it by magic, do you?"

"Well, I'll make do on healthful fruit juices and sanitized near-coffee—and I'll smell flowers."

"You'll find an ample supply of such things," said Gladia coldly, "and when you get back to your ship, I'm sure you can compensate for any withdrawal symptoms you will now suffer."

"I will suffer only from *your* withdrawal, my lady," said D.G. gravely.

Gladia found herself forced to smile. "You're an incorrigible liar, my captain. I'll be back. —Daneel. —Giskard."

60.

GLADIA SAT STIFFLY in Amadiro's office. In many decades, she had seen Amadiro only in the distance or on a viewing screen—and on such occasions, she had made it a practice to turn away. She remembered him only as Fastolfe's great enemy and now that she found herself, for the first time, in the same room with him—in face-to-face confrontation—she had to freeze her face into expressionlessness, in order not to allow hate to peep through.

Although she and Amadiro were the only palpable human beings in the room, there were at least a dozen high officials—the Chairman himself among them—who were present by way of sealed-beam holovision. Gladia had recognized the Chairman and some of the others, but not all.

It was rather a grisly experience. It seemed so like the viewing that was universal of Solaria and to which she had been so accustomed as a girl—and which she recalled with such distaste.

She made an effort to speak clearly, undramatically, and concisely. When asked a question, she was as brief as was consistent with clarity and as noncommittal as was consistent with courtesy.

The Chairman listened impassively and the others took their cue from him. He was clearly elderly—Chairmen always were, somehow, for it was usually late in life that they attained the position. He had a long face, a still-thick head of hair, and prominent eyebrows. His voice was mellifluous, but in no way friendly.

When Gladia was done, he said, "It is your suggestion, then, that the Solarians had redefined 'human being' in a narrow sense that restricted it to Solarians."

"I do not suggest anything, Mr. Chairman. It is merely that no one has been able to think of another explanation that would account for the events."

"Are you aware, Madam Gladia, that in all the history of robotic science, no robot has ever been designed with a narrowed definition of 'human being'?"

"I am not a roboticist, Mr. Chairman, and I know nothing of the mathematics of positronic pathways. Since you say it has never been done, I, of course, accept that. I cannot say, of my own knowledge, however, whether the fact that it has never been done means that it can never be done in the future."

Her eyes had never looked as wide and innocent as they did now and the Chairman flushed and said, "It is not theoretically impossible to narrow the definition, but it is unthinkable."

Gladia said, with a downcast glance at her hands, which were loosely clasped in her lap, "People can think such peculiar things sometimes."

The Chairman changed the subject and said, "An Auroran ship was destroyed. How do you account for that?"

"I was not present at the site of the incident, Mr. Chairman. I have no idea what happened, so I can't account for it."

"You were on Solaria and you were born on the planet. Given your recent experience and early background, what would you say happened?" The Chairman showed signs of a badly strained patience.

"If I must guess," said Gladia, "I should say that our warship was exploded by the use of a portable nuclear intensifier similar to the one that was almost used on the Settler ship."

"Does it not strike you, however, that the two cases are different. In one, a Settler ship invaded Solaria to confiscate Solarian robots; in the other, an Auroran vessel came to Solaria to help protect a sister planet."

"I can only suppose, Mr. Chairman, that the overseers—the humanoid robots left to guard the planet—were insufficiently well-instructed to know the difference."

The Chairman looked offended. "It is inconceivable that they would not be instructed in the difference between Settlers and fellow Spacers."

"If you say so, Mr. Chairman. Nevertheless, if the only definition of a human being is someone with the physical appearance of a human being, together with the ability to speak in Solarian fashion—as it seemed to us, who were on the spot, that it must be—then Aurorans, who do not speak in Solarian fashion, might not fall under the heading of human beings where the overseers were concerned."

"Then you are saying that the Solarians defined their fellow Spacers as nonhuman and subjected them to destruction."

"I present it merely as a possibility because I can't think of any other way to explain the destruction of an Auroran warship. More experienced people may be able to present alternate explanations, to be sure." Again that innocent, almost blank, look.

The Chairman said, "Are you planning to return to Solaria, Madam Gladia?"

"No, Mr. Chairman, I have no such plan."

"Have you been requested to do so by your Settler friend, in order to clear the planet of its overseers?"

Slowly Gladia shook her head. "I have not been requested to do this. Had I been, I would have refused. Nor did I go to Solaria, to begin with, for any reason but that of fulfilling my duty to Aurora. I was requested to go to Solaria by Dr. Levular Mandamus of the Robotics Institute, working under Dr. Kelden Amadiro. I was requested to go so that, on my return, I might report on events—as I have just done. The request had, to my ears and understanding, the flavor of an order and I took the order"—she glanced briefly in Amadiro's direction—"as coming from Dr. Amadiro himself."

Amadiro made no visible response to that.

The Chairman said, "What are your plans for the future, then?"

Gladia waited a heartbeat or two, then decided she might as well confront the situation boldly.

"It is my intention, Mr. Chairman," said Gladia, speaking very clearly, "to visit Earth."

"Earth? Why should you wish to visit Earth?"

"It may be important, Mr. Chairman, for Auroran authorities to know what is taking place on Earth. Since I have been invited by the Baleyworld authorities to visit Earth and since Captain Baley stands ready to take me there, it would be an opportunity to bring back a report on events—as I have now reported on events taking place on Solaria and on Baleyworld."

Well, then, thought Gladia, will he violate custom and, in effect, imprison her on Aurora? If so, there had to be ways of challenging the decision.

Gladia felt her tension rising and she cast a quick glance in the direction of Daneel, who, of course, seemed totally impassive.

However, the Chairman, looking sour, said, "In that respect, Madam Gladia, you have the right of an Auroran to do as you wish—but it will be on your own responsibility. No one is requesting this of you, as some requested, according to you, your visit to Solaria. For that reason I must warn you that Aurora will not feel bound to help you in case of any misadventure."

"I understand that, sir."

The Chairman said brusquely, "There will be much to discuss on the matter later on, Amadiro. I will be in touch with you."

The images blanked out and Gladia found herself and her robots suddenly alone with Amadiro and his robots.

61.

GLADIA ROSE and said stiffly, carefully refusing to look directly at Amadiro as she did so, "The meeting, I presume, is over, so I will now leave."

"Yes, of course, but I have a question or two, which I hope you don't mind my asking." His tall figure seemed overwhelming as he rose and he smiled and addressed her in all courtesy as though friendliness were long established between them. "Let me escort you, Lady Gladia. So you are going to Earth?"

"Yes. The Chairman raised no objections and an Auroran citizen may freely travel through the Galaxy in time of peace. And pardon me, but my robots—and yours, if necessary—will be sufficient escort."

"As you say, my lady." A robot held the door open for them. "I assume you will take robots with you when you go to Earth."

"There's no question as to that."

"Which robots, madam, if I may ask?"

"These two. The two robots I have with me." Her shoes made a firm clicking sound as she walked rapidly along the corridor, her back to Amadiro, making no effort to see to it that he heard her.

"Is that wise, my lady? They are advanced robots, unusual products of the great Dr. Fastolfe. You will be surrounded by barbarian Earthmen, who may covet them."

"Should they covet them, they nevertheless wouldn't get them."

"Don't underestimate the danger, nor overestimate robotic protection. You will be in one of their Cities, surrounded by tens of millions of these Earthmen, and robots may not harm human beings. Indeed, the more advanced a robot, the more sensitive it is to the nuances of the Three Laws and the less likely it is to take any action that will harm a human being in any way. —Isn't that so, Daneel?"

"Yes, Dr. Amadiro," said Daneel.

"Giskard, I imagine, agrees with you."

"I do," said Giskard.

"You see, my lady? Here on Aurora, in a nonviolent society, your robots can protect you against others. On Earth—mad, decadent, barbarous— there will be no way two robots can protect you or themselves. We would not want you to be deprived. Nor, to place it on a more selfish basis, would we of the Institute and the government care to see advanced robots in the hands of the barbarians. Would it not be better to take robots of a more ordinary type that the Earthpeople would ignore? You can take any number in that case. A dozen if you wish."

Gladia said, "Dr. Amadiro, I took these two robots on a Settler ship and visited a Settler world. No one made a move to appropriate them."

"The Settlers don't use robots and claim to disapprove of them. On Earth itself, they still use robots."

Daneel said, "If I may interpose, Dr. Amadiro— It is my understanding that robots are being phased out on Earth. There are very few in the Cities. Almost all robots on Earth are now used in agricultural or mining operations. For the rest, nonrobotic automation is the norm."

Amadiro looked at Daneel briefly, then said to Gladia, "Your robot is probably right and I suppose there would be no harm in taking Daneel. He could well pass as human, for that matter. Giskard, however, may well be left in your establishment. He might arouse the acquisitive instincts of an acquisitive society—even if it is true that they are trying to free themselves of robots."

Gladia said, "Neither will be left, sir. They will come with me. I am the sole judge of which portions of my property may come with me and which may not."

"Of course." Amadiro smiled in his most amiable fashion. "No one disputes that. —Would you wait here?"

Another door opened, showing a room that was most comfortably furnished. It was without windows, but was illuminated by soft light and suffused with even softer music.

Gladia stopped at the threshold and said sharply, "Why?"

"A member of the Institute wishes to see you and speak to you. It will not take long, but it is necessary. Once that is done, you are free to go. You will not even be plagued by my presence from this moment on. Please." There was a touch of hidden steel in the last word.

Gladia reached out her arms for Daneel and Giskard. "We enter together."

Amadiro laughed genially. "Do you think I'm trying to separate you from your robots? Do you think they would allow that? You have been too long with Settlers, my dear."

Gladia looked at the closed door and said between her teeth, "I dislike that man intensely. And most intensely when he smiles and tries to be soothing."

She stretched, her elbow joints cracking slightly. "In any case, I'm tired.

If someone comes with further questions about Solaria and Baleyworld, they are going to get short answers, I tell you."

She sat down on a couch that gave softly under her weight. She slipped her shoes off and lifted her feet to the couch. She smiled sleepily, took a deep breath as she sank to one side, and, with her head turned away from the room, was instantly and deeply asleep.

62.

"It is well she was naturally sleepy," said Giskard. "I was able to deepen it without any hint of damage to her at all. —I would not want Lady Gladia to hear what is likely to come."

"What is likely to come, friend Giskard?" asked Daneel.

"What is to come is the result, I think, of my being wrong, friend Daneel, and of your being right. I should have taken your excellent mind more seriously."

"It is you, then, they want to keep on Aurora?"

"Yes. And in urgently calling for Lady Gladia's return, they were calling for mine. You heard Dr. Amadiro ask for us to be left behind. At first both of us and then myself alone."

"Might it be that his words have but the surface meaning, that he feels it dangerous to lose an advanced robot to the Earthmen?"

"There was an underlying current of anxiety, friend Daneel, that I judge to be far too strong to match his words."

"Can you tell whether he knows of your special abilities?"

"I cannot tell directly, since I cannot read thoughts themselves. Nevertheless, twice in the course of the interview with the Council members, there was a sudden sharp rise in the level of emotional intensity in Dr. Amadiro's mind. Extraordinarily sharp rises. I cannot describe it in words, but it would be analogous, perhaps, to watching a scene in black and white and having it splash—suddenly and briefly—into intense color."

"When did this happen, friend Giskard?"

"The second time was when Lady Gladia mentioned she would be going to Earth."

"That created no visible stir among the Council members. What were their minds like?"

"I could not tell. They were present through holovision and such images are not accompanied by any mental sensations that I can detect."

"We may conclude, then, that whether the Council is—or is not—disturbed by Lady Gladia's projected trip to Earth, Dr. Amadiro, at least, *is* disturbed."

"It was not simple disturbance. Dr. Amadiro seemed anxious in the highest degree; as we would expect, for instance, if he indeed had a project in hand, as we suspect, for the destruction of Earth and feared its discovery. What is more, at Lady Gladia's mention of this intention of hers, friend Daneel, Dr. Amadiro glanced briefly at me; the only moment in all the session that he did. The flash of emotional intensity coincided with that glance. I think it was the thought of *my* going to Earth that made him anxious. —As we might expect, if he felt that I, with my special powers, would be a particular danger to his plans."

"His actions might also be taken, friend Giskard, as fitting his expressed fear that the Earthmen would try to appropriate you as an advanced robot and that this would be bad for Aurora."

"The chance of that happening, friend Daneel, and the extent of damage that might do the Spacer community is too small to account for his level of anxiety. What harm could I do Aurora if I were in Earth's possession—if I were simply the Giskard I am taken to be?"

"You conclude, then, that Dr. Amadiro knows you are *not* simply the Giskard you are taken to be."

"I am not sure. He may simply suspect it. If he *knew* what I was, would he not make every effort to avoid making his plans in my presence?"

"It may simply be his misfortune that Lady Gladia will not be separated from us. He cannot insist on your not being present, friend Giskard, without giving away his knowledge to you." Daneel paused, then said, "It is a great advantage you have, friend Giskard, being able to weigh the emotional contents of minds. —But you said that Dr. Amadiro's flash of emotion at the trip to Earth was the second. What was the first?"

"The first came with the mention of the nuclear intensifier—and that, too, seems significant. The concept of a nuclear intensifier is well known on Aurora. They don't have a portable device; not one light enough and efficient enough to be practical on shipboard, but it's not something that would break upon him like a thunderbolt. Why, then, so much anxiety?"

"Possibly," said Daneel, "because an intensifier of that sort has something to do with his plans on Earth."

"Possibly."

And it was at this point that the door opened, a person entered, and a voice said, "Well—Giskard!"

63.

GISKARD LOOKED AT the newcomer and said in a calm voice, "Madam Vasilia."

"You remember me, then," said Vasilia, smiling warmly.

"Yes, madam. You are a well-known roboticist and your face is on the hyperwave news now and then."

"Come, Giskard. I do not mean that you recognize me. Anyone can do that. I mean, you *remember* me. You once called me *Miss* Vasilia."

"I remember that, too, madam. It was a long time ago."

Vasilia closed the door behind her and sat down in one of the chairs. She turned her face toward the other robot. "And you are Daneel, of course."

Daneel said, "Yes, madam. To make use of the distinction you have just advanced, I both remember you, for I was with Plainclothesman Elijah Baley once when he interviewed you, and I recognize you, too."

Vasilia said sharply, "You are not to refer to that Earthman again. —I recognize you as well, Daneel. You are as famous as I am in your own way. You are both famous, for you are the greatest creations of the late Dr. Han Fastolfe."

"Of your father, madam," said Giskard.

"You know very well, Giskard, that I attach no importance to that purely genetic relationship. You are not to refer to him in that manner again."

"I will not, madam."

"And this one?" She looked casually at the sleeping figure on the couch. "Since you two are here, I can reasonably assume that the sleeping beauty is the Solarian woman."

Giskard said, "She is Lady Gladia and I am her property. Do you want her awake, madam?"

"We will merely disturb her, Giskard, if you and I talk of old times. Let her sleep."

"Yes, madam."

Vasilia said to Daneel, "Perhaps the discussion that Giskard and I will have will be of no interest to you, either, Daneel. Would you wait outside?"

Daneel said, "I fear I cannot leave, my lady. My task is to guard Lady Gladia."

"I don't think she needs much guarding from me. You'll notice I do not have any of my robots with me, so Giskard alone will be ample protection for your Solarian lady."

Daneel said, "You have no robots in the room, madam, but I saw four robots just outside in the corridor when the door was opened. It will be best if I stay."

"Well, I won't try to override your orders. You can stay. —Giskard!"

"Yes, madam?"

"Do you remember when you were first activated?"

"Yes, madam."

"What do you remember?"

"First light. Then sound. Then a crystallization into the sight of Dr. Fastolfe. I could understand Galactic Standard and I had a certain amount of innate knowledge built into my positronic brain paths. The Three Laws, of course; a large vocabulary, with definitions; robotic duties; social customs. Other things I learned rapidly."

"Do you remember your first owner?"

"As I said, Dr. Fastolfe."

"Think again, Giskard. Wasn't it I?"

Giskard paused, then said, "Madam, I was assigned the task of guarding you in my capacity as a possession of Dr. Han Fastolfe."

"It was a bit more than that, I think. You obeyed only me for ten years. If you obeyed anyone else, including Dr. Fastolfe, it was only incidentally, as a consequence of your robotic duties and only insofar as it fit your prime function of guarding me."

"I was assigned to you, it is true, Lady Vasilia, but Dr. Fastolfe retained ownership. Once you left his establishment, he resumed full control of me as my owner. He remained my owner even when he later assigned me to Lady Gladia. He was my only owner for as long as he lived. Upon his death, by his will, ownership of me was transferred to Lady Gladia and that is how it stands now."

"Not so. I asked you if you remembered when you were first activated and what you remembered. What you were when you were first activated is not what you are now."

"My memory banks, madam, are now incomparably fuller than they were then and I have much in the way of experience that I did not have then."

Vasilia's voice grew sterner. "I am not talking about memory, nor am I talking about experience. I am talking about capacities. I added to your positronic pathways. I adjusted them. I improved them."

"Yes, madam, you did so, with Dr. Fastolfe's help and approval."

"At one time, Giskard, on one occasion, I introduced an improvement— at least, an extension, and *without* Dr. Fastolfe's help and approval. Do you remember that?"

Giskard was silent for a substantial period of time. Then he said, "I remember one occasion on which I did not witness your consulting him. I assumed that you consulted him at a time when I was not a witness."

"If you assumed that, you assumed incorrectly. In fact, since you knew he was off the world at the time, you could not possibly have assumed it. You are being evasive, to use no stronger word."

"No, madam. You might have consulted him by hyperwave. I considered that a possibility."

Vasilia said, "Nevertheless, that addition was entirely mine. The result was that you became a substantially different robot afterward from what you had been before. The robot you have been ever since that change has been *my* design, *my* creation, and you know that well."

Giskard remained silent.

"Now, Giskard, by what right was Dr. Fastolfe your master at the time you were activated?" She waited, then said sharply, "Answer me, Giskard. That is an order!"

Giskard said, "Since he was designer and supervised the construction, I was his property."

"And when I, in effect, redesigned and reconstructed you in a very fundamental way, did you not then become my property?"

Giskard said, "I cannot answer that question. It would require the decision of a law court to argue out the specific case. It would depend, perhaps, on the degree to which I was redesigned and reconstructed."

"Are you aware of the degree to which that took place?"

Giskard was again silent.

"This is childish, Giskard," said Vasilia. "Am I to be required to nudge you after each question? You are not to make me do that. In this case, at any rate, silence is a sure indication of an affirmative. You know what the change was and how fundamental it was and you know that I know what it was. You put the Solarian woman to sleep because you did not want her to learn from me what it was. She doesn't know, does she?"

"She does not, madam," said Giskard.

"And you don't want her to know?"

"I do not, madam," said Giskard.

"Does Daneel know?"

"He does, madam."

Vasilia nodded. "I rather suspected that from his eagerness to stay. —Now, then, listen to me, Giskard. Suppose that a court of law finds out that, before I redesigned you, you were an ordinary robot and that, after I redesigned you, you were a robot who could sense the mind-set of an individual human being and adjust it to his liking. Do you think they could possibly fail to consider it a change great enough to warrant the ownership to have passed into my hands?"

Giskard said, "Madam Vasilia, it would not be possible to let this come before a court of law. Under the circumstances, I would surely be declared the property of the state for obvious reasons. I might even be ordered inactivated."

"Nonsense. Do you take me for a child? With your abilities, you could keep the court from making any such judgment. But that is not the point. I'm not suggesting that we take this to court. I am asking you for your own judgment. Would you not say that I am your rightful owner and have been since I was a very young woman?"

Giskard said, "Madam Gladia considers herself to be my owner and, until the law speaks to the contrary, she must be considered that."

"But *you* know that both she and the law labor under a misapprehension. If you worry about the feelings of your Solarian woman, it would be very easy to adjust her mind-set so that she wouldn't mind your no longer being her property. You can even cause her to feel relieved that I will take you off her hands. I will order you to do so as soon as you can bring yourself to admit what you already know—that I am your owner. How long has Daneel known your nature?"

"For decades, madam."

"You can make *him* forget. For some time now, Dr. Amadiro has known and you can make *him* forget. There will be only you and I who will know."

Daneel said suddenly, "Madam Vasilia, since Giskard does not consider himself your property, he can easily make *you* forget and you will then be perfectly content with matters as they are."

Vasilia turned a cold eye on Daneel. "Can he? But you see, it is not for you to decide who it is that Giskard considers his owner. I know that Giskard knows that *I* am his owner, so that his duty, within the Three Laws, belongs entirely to me. If he must make *someone* forget and can do so without physical harm, it will be necessary for him, in making a choice, to choose anyone but me. He cannot make me forget or tamper with my mind in any way. I thank you, Daneel, for giving me the occasion of making this quite plain."

Daneel said, "But Madam Gladia's emotions are so enwrapped in Giskard that for him to force forgetfulness upon her might harm her."

Vasilia said, "Giskard is the one to decide that. —Giskard, you are mine.

You know you are mine and I order you to induce forgetfulness in this man-aping robot who stands beside you and in the woman who wrongfully treated you as her property. Do it while she is asleep and there will be no harm done to her of any kind."

Daneel said, "Friend Giskard. Lady Gladia is your legal owner. If you induce forgetfulness in Lady Vasilia, it will not harm her."

"But it will," said Vasilia at once. "The Solarian woman will not be harmed, for she need only forget that she is under the impression that she is Giskard's owner. I, on the other hand, also know that Giskard has mental powers. Digging that out will be more complex and Giskard can surely tell by my intense determination to keep that knowledge that he could not help but inflict damage on me in the process of removing it."

Daneel said, "Friend Giskard—"

Vasilia said, in a voice that was diamond-hard, "I order *you*, Robot Daneel Olivaw, to be silent. I am not your owner, but your owner is asleep and does not countermand it, so my order *must* be obeyed."

Daneel fell silent, but his lips trembled as though he were trying to talk despite the order.

Vasilia watched that manifestation with an amused smile on her lips. "You see, Daneel, you cannot talk."

And Daneel said in a hoarse whisper, "I can, madam, I find it difficult, but I can, for I find that something takes precedence over your order, which is governed by only the Second Law."

Vasilia's eyes opened wide and she said sharply, "Silence, I say. Nothing takes precedence over my order but the First Law and I have already shown that Giskard will do least harm—indeed, no harm at all—if he returns to me. He *will* do harm to me, to whom he is least capable of doing harm, if he follows any other course of action." She pointed her finger at Daneel and said again with a soft hiss, "Silence!"

It was a clear effort for Daneel to make any sound at all. The small pump within him that manipulated the air current that produced the sound made a small, humming noise as it labored. Yet, though he spoke in an even lower whisper, he could still be heard.

He said, "Madam Vasilia, there is something that transcends even the First Law."

Giskard said, in a voice equally low, but unforced, "Friend Daneel, you must not say that. Nothing transcends the First Law."

Vasilia, frowning slightly, showed a spark of interest. "Indeed? Daneel, I warn you that if you attempt to progress further in this odd line of argument, you will surely destroy yourself. I have never seen or heard of a robot doing what you are doing and it would be fascinating to watch your self-destruction. Speak on."

With the order given, Daneel's voice returned immediately to normal. "I thank you, Madam Vasilia. —Years ago, I sat at the deathbed of an Earthman to whom you have asked me not to refer. May I now refer to him or do you know who it is that I speak of?"

"You speak of that policeman Baley," said Vasilia tonelessly.

"Yes, madam. He said to me on his deathbed, 'The work of each individual contributes to a totality and so becomes an undying part of the totality. That totality of human lives—past and present and to come—forms a tapestry that has been in existence now for many tens of thousands of years and has been growing more elaborate and, on the whole, more beautiful in all that time. Even the Spacers are an offshoot of the tapestry and they, too, add to the elaborateness and beauty of the pattern. An individual life is one thread in the tapestry and what is one thread compared to the whole? Daneel, keep your mind fixed firmly on the tapestry and do not let the trailing off of a single thread affect you.' "

"Mawkish sentimentality," murmured Vasilia.

Daneel said, "I believe Partner Elijah was attempting to protect me against the fact of his soon-to-come death. It was his own life he spoke of as but a thread in the tapestry; it was his own life that was 'the trailing off of a single thread' that was not to affect me. His words did protect me in that crisis."

"No doubt," said Vasilia, "but get to the point of transcending the First Law, for it is that which will now destroy you."

Daneel said, "For decades I have brooded over Plainclothesman Elijah Baley's statement and it is quite likely I would have understood it at once if the Three Laws had not stood in the way. I have been helped in my search by my friend Giskard, who has long felt the Three Laws to be incomplete. I have been helped also by points Lady Gladia made in a recent speech on a Settler world. What's more, this present crisis, Lady Vasilia, has served to sharpen my thinking. I am certain, now, as to the manner in which the Three Laws are incomplete."

"A robot who is also a roboticist," said Vasilia with a touch of contempt. "How are the Three Laws incomplete, robot?"

Daneel said, "The tapestry of life is more important than a single thread. Apply that not to Partner Elijah alone, but generalize it and—and—and we conclude that humanity as a whole is more important than a single human being."

"You stumble as you say it, robot. You do not believe it."

Daneel said, "There is a law that is greater than the First Law: 'A robot may not injure humanity or, through inaction, allow humanity to come to harm.' I think of it now as the Zeroth Law of Robotics. The First Law should then be stated: 'A robot may not injure a human being or, through inaction, allow a human being to come to harm, unless this would violate the Zeroth Law of Robotics.'"

Vasilia snorted. "And you still stand on your feet, robot?"

"I still stand on my feet, madam."

"Then I will explain something to you, robot, and we will see if you can survive the explanation. —The Three Laws of Robotics involve individual human beings and individual robots. You can point to an individual human being or to an individual robot. But what is your 'humanity' but an abstraction? Can you point to humanity? You can injure or fail to injure a specific human being and understand the injury or lack of injury that has taken place. Can you see an injury to humanity? Can you understand it? Can you point to it?"

Daneel was silent.

Vasilia smiled broadly. "Answer, robot. Can you see an injury to humanity and can you point to it?"

"No, madam, I cannot. But I believe such injury can exist nevertheless and you see that I still stand on my feet."

"Then ask Giskard as to whether he will—or can—obey your Zeroth Law of Robotics."

Daneel's head turned to Giskard. "Friend Giskard?"

Slowly Giskard said, "I cannot accept the Zeroth Law, friend Daneel. You know that I have read widely in human history. In it, I have found great crimes committed by some human beings against each other and the excuse has always been that the crimes were justified by the needs of the tribe, or of the state, or even of humanity. It is precisely because humanity is an abstraction that it can be called upon so freely to justify anything at all and your Zeroth Law is therefore unsuitable."

Daneel said, "But you know, friend Giskard, the fact that a danger to humanity now exists and that it will surely come to fruition if you become the property of Madam Vasilia. That, at least, is not an abstraction."

Giskard said, "The danger to which you refer is not something known, but is merely inferred. We cannot build our actions in defiance of the Three Laws on that."

Daneel paused, then said in a lower voice, "But you hope that your studies of human history will help you develop the Laws governing human behavior, that you will learn to predict and guide human history—or at least make a beginning, so that someone someday will learn to predict and guide it. You even call the technique 'psychohistory.' In this, are you not dealing with the human tapestry? Are you not trying to work with humanity as a generalized whole, rather than with collections of individual human beings?"

"Yes, friend Daneel, but it is thus far no more than a hope and I cannot base my actions upon a mere hope, nor can I modify the Three Laws in accordance with it."

To that, Daneel did not respond.

Vasilia said, "Well, robot, all your attempts have come to nothing and yet you stand on your feet. You are strangely stubborn and a robot such as yourself that can denounce the Three Laws and still remain functional is a clear danger to every and any individual human being. For that reason, I believe you should be dismantled without delay. The case is too dangerous to await the slow majesty of the law, especially since you are, after all, a robot and not the human being you attempt to resemble."

Daneel said, "Surely, my lady, it is not fitting for you to reach such a decision on your own."

"I have reached it nevertheless and if there are legal repercussions hereafter, I shall deal with them."

"You will be depriving Lady Gladia of a second robot—and one to which you make no claim."

"She and Fastolfe, between them, have deprived me of my robot, Giskard, for more than twenty decades and I do not believe this ever distressed either of them for a moment. It will not now distress me to deprive her. She has dozens of other robots and there are many here at the Institute who will faithfully see to her safety until she can return to her own."

Daneel said, "Friend Giskard, if you will wake Lady Gladia, it may be that she may persuade Lady Vasilia—"

Vasilia, looking at Giskard, frowned and said sharply, "*No*, Giskard. Let the woman sleep."

Giskard, who had stirred at Daneel's words, subsided.

Vasilia snapped the finger and thumb of her right hand three times and the door at once opened and four robots filed in. "You were right, Daneel.

There are four robots. They will dismantle you and you are ordered not to resist. Thereafter Giskard and I will deal with all remaining matters."

She looked over her shoulder at the entering robots. "Close the door behind you. Now, quickly and efficiently, dismantle this robot," and she pointed at Daneel.

The robots looked at Daneel and for a few seconds did not move. Vasilia said impatiently, "I've told you he is a robot and you must disregard his human appearance. Daneel, tell them you are a robot."

"I am a robot," said Daneel, "and I will not resist."

Vasilia stepped to one side and the four robots advanced. Daneel's arms remained at his side. He turned to look at the sleeping Gladia one last time and then he faced the robots.

Vasilia smiled and said, "This should be interesting."

The robots paused. Vasilia said, "Get on with it."

They did not move and Vasilia turned to stare in amazement at Giskard. She did not complete the movement. Her muscles loosened and she crumpled.

Giskard caught her and seated her with her back against the wall.

He said in a muffled voice, "I need a few moments and then we will leave."

Those moments passed. Vasilia's eyes remained glazed and unfocused. Her robots remained motionless. Daneel had moved to Gladia in a single stride.

Giskard looked up and said to Vasilia's robots, "Guard your lady. Allow no one to enter until she wakes. She will waken peacefully."

Even as he spoke, Gladia stirred and Daneel helped her to her feet. She said, wondering, "Who is this woman? Whose robots— How did she—"

Giskard spoke firmly, but there was a weariness in his voice. "Lady Gladia, later. I will explain. For now, we must hasten."

And they left.

PART FIVE
EARTH

Chapter 15

The Holy World

64.

AMADIRO BIT HIS LOWER LIP and his eyes flicked in the direction of Mandamus, who seemed lost in thought.

Amadiro said defensively, "She insisted on it. She told me that only she could handle this Giskard, that only she could exert a sufficiently strong influence over him and prevent him from using these mental powers of his."

"You never said anything of this to me, Dr. Amadiro."

"I wasn't sure what there was to tell, young man. I wasn't sure she was correct."

"Are you sure now?"

"Completely. She remembers nothing of what went on—"

"So that *we* know nothing of what went on."

Amadiro nodded. "Exactly. And she remembers nothing of what she had told me earlier."

"And she's not acting?"

"I saw to it that she had an emergency electroencephalogram. There have been distinct changes from the earlier records."

"Is there a chance she will recover her memory with time?"

Amadiro shook his head bitterly. "Who can tell? But I doubt it."

Mandamus, eyes still downcast and full of thought, said, "Does it matter, then? We can take her account of Giskard as true and we know that he has the power to affect minds. That knowledge is crucial and it is now ours. —In fact, it is well that our roboticist colleague has failed. If Vasilia had gained control of that robot, how long do you suppose it would have been before you, too, would have been under her control—and I, as well, assuming she would think I was worth controlling?"

Amadiro nodded. "I suppose she might have had something like that in mind. Right now, though, it's hard to tell what she has in mind. She *seems,* superficially at least, undamaged except for the specific loss of memory— she apparently remembers everything else—but who knows how this will affect her deeper thought processes and her skill as a roboticist? That Giskard could do this to someone as skilled as she makes him an incredibly dangerous phenomenon."

"Does it occur to you, Dr. Amadiro, that the Settlers may be right in their distrust of robots?"

"It almost does, Mandamus."

Mandamus rubbed his hands together. "I assume from your depressed attitude that this whole business was not uncovered before they had time to leave Aurora."

"You assume correctly. That Settler captain has the Solarian woman and both of her robots on his ship and is heading toward Earth."

"And where does that leave us now?"

Slowly Amadiro said, "By no means defeated, it seems to me. If we complete our project, we have won—Giskard or no Giskard. And we can complete it. Whatever Giskard can do with and to emotions, he can't read thoughts. He might be able to tell when a wash of emotion crosses a human mind, or even distinguish one emotion from another, or change one to another, or induce sleep or amnesia—dull-edged things like that. He cannot be sharp, however. He cannot make out actual words or ideas."

"Are you sure of that?"

"So said Vasilia."

"She may not have known what she was talking about. She did not, after all, manage to control the robot, as she said she was sure of doing. That's not much of a testimonial to her accuracy of understanding."

"Yet I believe her in this. To actually be able to read thoughts would demand so much complexity in the positronic pathway pattern that it is totally unlikely that a child could have inserted it into the robot over twenty decades ago. It is actually far beyond even the present-day state of the art, Mandamus. Surely you must agree."

"I would certainly think it was. And they're going to Earth?"

"I'm sure of it."

"Would this woman, brought up as she was, actually go to Earth?"

"She has no choice if Giskard controls her."

"And why should Giskard want her to go to Earth? Can he know about our project? You seem to think he doesn't."

"It is possible he doesn't. His motivation for going to Earth might be nothing more than to place himself and the Solarian woman beyond our reach."

"I shouldn't think he'd fear us if he could handle Vasilia."

"A long-range weapon," said Amadiro icily, "could bring him down. His own abilities must have a limited range. They can be based on nothing other than the electromagnetic field and he must be subject to the inverse square law. So we get out of range as the intensity of his powers weaken, but he will then find that he is *not* out of range of our weapons."

Mandamus frowned and looked uneasy. "You seem to have an un-Spacer liking for violence, Dr. Amadiro. In a case like this, though, I suppose force would be permissible."

"A case like this? A robot capable of harming human beings? I should think so. We'll have to find a pretext for sending a good ship in pursuit. It wouldn't be wise to explain the actual situation—"

"No," said Mandamus emphatically. "Think of how many would wish to have personal control of such a robot."

"Which we can't allow. And which is another reason why I would look upon destruction of the robot as the safer and preferable course of action."

"You may be right," said Mandamus reluctantly, "but I don't think it wise to count on this destruction only. I must go to Earth—now. The project must be hastened to its conclusion, even if we don't dot every 'i' and cross every 't.' Once it is done, then it is *done*. Even a mind-handling robot —under *anybody's* control—will not be able to undo the deed. And if it does anything else, that, perhaps, will no longer matter."

Amadiro said, "Don't speak in the singular. I will go as well."

"You? Earth is a horrible world. I *must* go, but why you?"

"Because I must go, too. I cannot stay here any longer and wonder. You have not waited for this through a long lifetime as I have, Mandamus. You do not have the accounts to settle that I have."

65.

GLADIA WAS IN SPACE again and once again Aurora could be made out as a globe. D.G. was busy elsewhere and the entire ship had about it a vague but pervasive air of emergency, as though it were on a battle footing, as though it were being pursued or expected pursuit.

Gladia shook her head. She could think clearly; she felt well; but when her mind turned back to that time in the Institute, shortly after Amadiro had left her, a curiously pervasive unreality swept over her. There was a gap in time. One moment she had been sitting on the couch, feeling sleepy; the next there were four robots and a woman in the room who had not been there before.

She had fallen asleep, then, but there was no awareness, no memory, that she had done so. There was a gap of nonexistence.

Thinking back, she had recognized the woman after the fact. It was Vasilia Aliena—the daughter whom Gladia had replaced in the affections of Han Fastolfe. Gladia had never actually *seen* Vasilia, though she had *viewed* her on hyperwave several times. Gladia always thought of her as a distant and inimical other self. There was the vague similarity in appearance that others always commented on but that Gladia herself insisted she did not see —and there was the odd, antithetical connection with Fastolfe.

Once they were on the ship and she was alone with her robots, she asked the inevitable question. "What was Vasilia Aliena doing in the room and why was I permitted to sleep once she had arrived?"

Daneel said, "Madam Gladia, I will answer the question, since it is a matter friend Giskard would find difficult to discuss."

"Why should he find it difficult, Daneel?"

"Madam Vasilia arrived in the hope that she might persuade Giskard to enter her service."

"Away from me?" said Gladia in sharp indignation. She did not entirely like Giskard, but that made no difference. What was hers was hers. "And you allowed me to sleep while you two handled the matter by yourselves?"

"We felt, madam, that you needed your sleep badly. Then, too, Madam Vasilia ordered us to allow you to sleep. Finally, it was our opinion that Giskard would not, in any case, join her service. For all these reasons, we did not wake you."

Gladia said indignantly, "I should *hope* that Giskard would not for a moment consider leaving me. It would be illegal both by Auroran law and, more important, by the Three Laws of Robotics. —It would be a good deed to return to Aurora and have her arraigned before the Court of Claims."

"That would not be advisable at the moment, my lady."

"What was her excuse for wanting Giskard? Did she have one?"

"When she was a child, Giskard had been assigned to her."

"Legally?"

"No, madam. Dr. Fastolfe merely allowed her the use of it."

"Then she had no right to Giskard."

"We pointed that out, madam. Apparently, it was a matter of sentimental attachment on the part of Madam Vasilia."

Gladia sniffed. "Having survived the loss of Giskard since before I came to Aurora, she might well have continued as she was without going to illegal lengths to deprive me of my property." —Then, restlessly, "I should have been awakened."

Daneel said, "Madam Vasilia had four robots with her. Had you been awake and had there been harsh words between the two of you, there might have been some difficulty in having the robots work out the proper responses."

"I'd have directed the proper response, I assure you, Daneel."

"No doubt, madam. So might Madam Vasilia and she is one of the cleverest roboticists in the Galaxy."

Gladia shifted her attention to Giskard. "And you have nothing to say?"

"Only that it was better as it was, my lady."

Gladia looked thoughtfully into those faintly luminous robotic eyes, so different from Daneel's all-but-human ones, and it did seem to her that the incident wasn't very important after all. A small thing. And there were other things with which to be concerned. They were going to Earth.

Somehow she did not think of Vasilia again.

66.

"I AM CONCERNED," said Giskard in his whisper of confidentiality in which sound waves barely trembled the air. The Settler ship was receding smoothly from Aurora and, as yet, there was no pursuit. The activity onboard had settled into routine and, with almost all routines automated, there was quiet and Gladia slept naturally.

"I am concerned for Lady Gladia, friend Daneel."

Daneel understood the characteristics of Giskard's positronic circuits well enough to need no long explanation. He said, "It was necessary, friend Giskard, to adjust Lady Gladia. Had she questioned longer, she might have elicited the fact of your mental activities and adjustment would then have been more dangerous. Enough harm has already been done because Lady Vasilia discovered the fact. We do not know to whom—and to how many—she may have imparted her knowledge."

"Nevertheless," said Giskard, "I did not wish to make this adjustment. Had Lady Gladia wished to forget, it would have been a simple, no-risk adjustment. She wanted, however, with vigor and anger, to know more of the matter. She regretted not having played a greater role in it. I was forced, therefore, to break binding forces of considerable intensity."

Daneel said, "Even that was necessary, friend Giskard."

"Yet the possibility of doing harm was by no means insignificant in such a case. If you think of a binding force as a thin, elastic cord—this is a poor analogy, but I can think of no other, for what I sense in a mind has no analog outside the mind—then the ordinary inhibitions I deal with are so thin and insubstantial that they vanish when I touch them. A strong binding force, on the other hand, snaps and recoils when broken and the recoil may then break other, totally unrelated binding forces or, by whipping and coiling about other such forces, strengthen them enormously. In either case, unintended changes can be brought about in a human being's emotions and attitudes and that would be almost certain to bring about harm."

Daneel said, his voice a little louder, "Is it your impression you harmed Lady Gladia, friend Giskard?"

"I think not. I was extremely careful. I worked upon the matter during all the time you were talking to her. It was thoughtful of you to bear the brunt of the conversation and to run the risk of being caught between an inconvenient truth and an untruth. But despite all my care, friend Daneel, I took a risk and I am concerned that I was willing to take that risk. It came so close to violating the First Law that it required an extraordinary effort on my part to do it. I am sure that I would not have been able to do it—"

"Yes, friend Giskard?"

"Had you not expounded your notion of the Zeroth Law."

"You accept it, then?"

"No, I cannot. Can you? Faced with the possibility of doing harm to an individual human being or of allowing harm to come to one, could you do the harm or allow the harm in the name of abstract humanity? Think!"

"I am not sure," said Daneel, voice trembling into all but silence. Then, with an effort, "I might. The mere concept pushes at me—and at you. It helped you decide to take the risk in adjusting Lady Gladia's mind."

"Yes, it did," agreed Giskard, "and the longer we think of the Zeroth Law, the more it might help push us. Could it do so, I wonder, in more than a marginal way, however? Might it not only help us take slightly larger risks than we might ordinarily?"

"Yet I am convinced of the validity of the Zeroth Law, friend Giskard."

"So might I be if we could define what we mean by 'humanity.' "

There was a pause and Daneel said, "Did you not accept the Zeroth Law, at last, when you stopped Madam Vasilia's robots and erased from her mind the knowledge of your mental powers?"

Giskard said, "No, friend Daneel. Not really. I was tempted to accept it, but not really."

"And yet your actions—"

"Were dictated by a combination of motives. You told me of your concept of the Zeroth Law and it seemed to have a certain validity about it, but not sufficient to cancel the First Law or even to cancel Madam Vasilia's strong use of the Second Law in the orders she gave. Then, when you called my attention to the application of the Zeroth Law to psychohistory, I could feel the positronomotive force mount higher and yet it was not quite high enough to supersede the First Law or even the strong Second Law."

"Still," murmured Daneel, "you struck down Madam Vasilia, friend Giskard."

"When she ordered the robots to dismantle you, friend Daneel, and showed a clear emotion of pleasure at the prospect, your need, added to what the concept of the Zeroth Law had already done, superseded the Second Law and rivaled the First Law. It was the combination of the Zeroth Law, psychohistory, my loyalty to Lady Gladia, and your need that dictated my action."

"My need could scarcely have affected you, friend Giskard. I am only a robot and though my need could affect my own actions by the Third Law, they cannot affect yours. You destroyed the overseer on Solaria without hesitation; you should have watched my destruction without being moved to act."

"Yes, friend Daneel, and ordinarily it might have been so. However, your mention of the Zeroth Law had reduced the First Law intensity to an abnormally low value. The necessity of saving you was sufficient to cancel out what remained of it and I—acted as I did."

"No, friend Giskard. The prospect of injury to a robot should not have affected you at all. It should in no way have contributed to the overcoming of the First Law, however weak the First Law may have become."

"It is a strange thing, friend Daneel. I do not know how it came about. Perhaps it was because I have noted that you continue to think more and more like a human being, but—"

"Yes, friend Giskard?"

"At the moment when the robots advanced toward you and Lady Vasilia expressed her savage pleasure, my positronic pathway pattern re-formed in an anomalous fashion. For a moment, I thought of you—as a human being —and I reacted accordingly."

"That was wrong."

"I know that. And yet—and yet, if it were to happen again, I believe the same anomalous change would take place again."

Daneel said, "It is strange, but hearing you put it so, I find myself feeling you did the proper thing. If the situation were reversed, I almost think that I, too, would—would do the same—that I would think of you as a—a human being."

Daneel, hesitantly and slowly, put out his hand and Giskard looked at it uncertainly. Then, very slowly, he put out his own hand. The fingertips almost touched and then, little by little, each took the other's hand and clasped it—almost as though they were the friends they called each other.

67.

GLADIA LOOKED ABOUT with veiled curiosity. She was in D.G.'s cabin for the first time. It was not noticeably more luxurious than the new cabin that had been designed for her. D.G.'s cabin had a more elaborate viewing panel, to be sure, and it had a complex console of lights and contacts which, she imagined, served to keep D.G. in touch with the rest of the ship even here.

She said, "I've seen little of you since leaving Aurora, D.G."

"I'm flattered that you are aware of that," answered D.G., grinning. "And to tell you the truth, Gladia, I have been aware of it as well. With an all-male crew, you do rather stand out."

"That's not a very flattering reason for missing me. With an all-human crew, I imagine Daneel and Giskard stand out, too. Have you missed them as much as you have missed me?"

D.G. looked about. "Actually, I miss them so little it is only now that I am aware that they aren't with you. Where are they?"

"In my cabin. It seemed silly to drag them about with me inside the confines of the small world of this ship. They seemed willing to allow me to be on my own, which surprised me. —No," she corrected herself, "come to think of it, I had to order them rather sharply to stay behind before they would do so."

"Isn't that rather strange? Aurorans are never without their robots, I've been given to understand."

"What of that? Once, long ago, when I first came to Aurora, I had to learn to suffer the actual presence of human beings, something my Solarian upbringing did not prepare me for. Learning to be without my robots, occasionally, when I am among Settlers will probably be a less difficult adjustment for me than that first one was."

"Good. Very good. I must admit that I much prefer being with you without the glowing eyes of Giskard fixed on me—and better yet, without Daneel's little smile."

"He doesn't smile."

"To me, he seems to, a very insinuatingly lecherous tiny smile."

"You're mad. That's totally foreign to Daneel."

"You don't watch him the way I do. His presence is very inhibiting. It forces me to behave myself."

"Well, I should hope so."

"You needn't hope so quite that emphatically. But never mind. —Let me apologize for seeing so little of you since leaving Aurora."

"That's scarcely necessary."

"Since you brought it up, I thought it was. However, let me explain, then. We've been on battle footing. We were certain, having left as we did, that Auroran vessels would be in pursuit."

"I should think they'd be glad to be rid of a group of Settlers."

"Of course, but you're not a Settler and it might be you they would want. They were anxious enough to get you back from Baleyworld."

"They got me back. I reported to them and that was it."

"They wanted nothing more than your report?"

"No," Gladia paused and, for a moment, frowned as though something was nibbling vaguely at her memory. Whatever it was, it passed and she said indifferently, "No."

D.G. shrugged. "It doesn't entirely make sense, but they made no attempt to stop us while you and I were on Aurora nor, after that, when we boarded the ship and it prepared to leave orbit. I won't quarrel with that. It won't be long now before we make the Jump—and after that there should be nothing to worry about."

Gladia said, "Why *do* you have an all-male crew, by the way? Auroran ships always have mixed crews."

"So do Settler ships. Ordinary ones. This is a Trader vessel."

"What difference does that make?"

"Trading involves danger. It's rather a rough-and-ready life. Women on board would create problems."

"What nonsense! What problems do I create?"

"We won't argue that. Besides, it's traditional. The men wouldn't stand for it."

"How do you know?" Gladia laughed. "Have you ever tried it?"

"No. But, on the other hand, there are no long lines of women clamoring for a berth on my ship."

"I'm here. I'm enjoying it."

"You're getting special treatment—and but for your service on Solaria, there might well have been much trouble. In fact, there *was* trouble. Still, never mind." He touched one of the contacts on the console and a count-down briefly appeared. "We'll be Jumping in just about two minutes. You've never been on Earth, have you, Gladia?"

"No, of course not."

"Or seen *the* sun, not just *a* sun."

"No—although I have seen it in historical dramas on hypervision, but I imagine what they show in the dramas is not really *the* sun."

"I'm sure it isn't. If you don't mind, we'll dim the cabin lights."

The lights dimmed to nearly nothing and Gladia was aware of the star field on the viewing panel, with the stars brighter and more thickly spread than in Aurora's sky.

"Is that a telescopic view?" she asked in a hushed voice.

"Slightly. Low-power— Fifteen seconds." He counted backward. There was a shift in the star field and a bright star was now nearly centered. D.G. touched another contact and said, "We're well outside the planetary plane. Good! A little risky. We should have been farther from the Auroran star before Jumping, but we were in a slight hurry. —That's *the* sun."

"That bright star, you mean?"

"Yes. —What do you think of it?"

Gladia said, a little puzzled over what sort of response he expected, "It's bright."

He pushed another contact and the view dimmed perceptibly. "Yes—and it won't do your eyes any good if you stare at it. But it's not the brightness that counts. It's just a star—in appearance—but think of it. That was the *original* sun. That was the star whose light shone down on a planet that was the *only* planet on which human beings existed. It shone down on a planet on which human beings were slowly evolving. It shone down on a planet on which life formed billions of years ago, life that would develop into human beings. There are 300 billion stars in the Galaxy and 100 billion galaxies in the Universe and there is only one of all those stars that presided over the human birth and *that* is the star."

Gladia was about to say: "Well, *some* star had to be the star," but she thought better of it. "Very impressive," she said rather weakly.

"It's not merely impressive," said D.G., his eyes shadowed in the dimness. "There's not a Settler in the Galaxy who doesn't consider that star his own. The radiation of the stars that shine down on our various home planets is borrowed radiation—rented radiation that we make use of. There—right there—is the real radiation that gave us life. It is that star and the planet that circles it—Earth—that holds us all together in a tight bond. If we shared nothing else, we would share that light on the screen and it would be enough. —You Spacers have forgotten it and that is why you fall apart from each other and that is why you will not, in the long run, survive."

"There is room for us all, Captain," said Gladia softly.

"Yes, of course. I wouldn't do anything to *force* nonsurvival on Spacers. I just believe that that is what will happen and it might not happen if Spacers would give up their irritating certainty of superiority, their robots, and their self-absorption in long life."

"Is that how you see me, D.G.?" asked Gladia.

D.G. said, "You've had your moments. You've improved, though. I'll give you that."

"Thank you," she replied with evident irony. "And though you may find it hard to believe, Settlers have their prideful arrogance, too. But you've also improved and I'll give you that."

D.G. laughed. "With all that I'm kindly giving you and you're kindly giving me, this is liable to end as a lifelong enmity."

"Scarcely," said Gladia, laughing in her turn, and was a little surprised to find that his hand was resting on hers. —And a great deal surprised to find that she had not removed her hand.

68.

DANEEL SAID, "I am uneasy, friend Giskard, that Madam Gladia is not under our direct observation."

"That is not needful on board this ship, friend Daneel. I detect no dangerous emotions and the captain is with her at the moment. —In addition, there would be advantages to her finding it comfortable to be without us, at least on occasion, while we are all on Earth. It is possible that you and I might have to take sudden action without wishing to have her presence and safety a complicating factor."

"Then you manipulated her separation from us now?"

"Scarcely. Oddly enough, I found a strong tendency in her to imitate the Settler way of life in this respect. She has a subdued longing for independence, hampered chiefly by the feeling that she is violating Spacerhood in this. That is the best way in which I can describe it. The sensations and emotions are by no means easy to interpret, for I have never encountered it among Spacers before. So I merely loosened the Spacerhood inhibition by the merest touch."

"Will she then no longer be willing to avail herself of our services, friend Giskard? That would disturb me."

"It should not. If she should decide she wishes a life free of robots and will be happier so, it is what we will want for her, too. As it is, though, I am sure we will still be useful to her. This ship is a small and specialized habitat in which there is no great danger. She has a further feeling of security in the captain's presence and that reduces her need for us. On Earth, she will still need us, though I trust not in quite so tight a fashion as on Aurora. —As I have said, we may need greater flexibility of action once on Earth."

"Can you yet guess, then, the nature of the crisis facing Earth? Do you know what it is we will have to do?"

Giskard said, "No, friend Daneel. I do not. It is you that have the gift of understanding. Is there something, perhaps, that you see?"

Daneel remained silent for a while. Then he said, "I have had thoughts."

"What, then, are your thoughts?"

"You told me at the Robotics Institute, you remember, just before Lady Vasilia entered the room in which Madam Gladia lay sleeping, that Dr. Amadiro had had two intense flashes of anxiety. The first came at the mention of the nuclear intensifier, the second at the statement that Madam Gladia was going to Earth. It seems to me that the two must be connected. I feel that the crisis we are dealing with involves the use of a nuclear intensifier on Earth, that there is time to stop it, and that Dr. Amadiro fears that we will do just that if we go to Earth."

"Your mind tells me you are not satisfied with that thought. Why not, friend Daneel?"

"A nuclear intensifier hastens the fusion processes that happen to be already in progress, by means of a stream of W particles. I asked myself, therefore, whether Dr. Amadiro plans to use one or more nuclear intensifiers to explode the microfusion reactors that supply Earth with energy. The nuclear explosions so induced would involve destruction through heat and mechanical force, through dust and radioactive products that would be thrown into the atmosphere. Even if this did not suffice to damage Earth mortally, the destruction of Earth's energy supply would surely lead to the long-term collapse of Earth's civilization."

Giskard said somberly, "That is a horrifying thought and would seem to be an almost certain answer to the nature of the crisis we seek. Why are you not satisfied, then?"

"I have taken the liberty of using the ship's computer to obtain information concerning the planet Earth. The computer is, as one might expect on a Settler ship, rich in such information. It seems that Earth is the one human world that does not use microfusion reactors as a large-scale source of energy. It uses direct solar energy almost entirely, with solar power stations all along the geostationary orbit. There is nothing for a nuclear intensifier to do, except to destroy small devices—spaceships, occasional buildings. The damage might not be negligible, but it would not threaten Earth's existence."

"It may well be, friend Daneel, that Amadiro has some device that would destroy the solar power generators."

"If so, why did he react to the mention of nuclear intensifiers? There is no way they can serve against solar power generators."

Giskard nodded slowly. "That is a good point. And, to make another, if Dr. Amadiro was so horrified at the thought of our going to Earth, why did he make no effort to have us stopped while we were still on Aurora? Or if he only discovered our flight after we had left orbit, why did he not have an Auroran vessel intercept us before we made the Jump to Earth? Can it be that we are on a completely wrong track, that somewhere we have made a serious misstep that—"

An insistent chain of intermittent chiming sounded throughout the ship and Daneel said, "We have safely made the Jump, friend Giskard. I sensed it some minutes ago. But we have not yet reached Earth and the interception you have just mentioned has, I suspect, now come, so that we are not necessarily on the wrong track."

69.

D.G. WAS MOVED TO a perverse admiration. When the Aurorans were really moved to action, their technological polish showed. No doubt they had sent one of their newest warships, from which one could at once deduce that whatever had moved them was close to their heart.

And that ship had detected the presence of D.G.'s vessel within fifteen minutes of its appearance in normal space—and from a sizable distance, at that.

The Auroran ship was using a limited-focus hyperwave setup. The speaker's head could be seen clearly while it was at the focal spot. All else was a gray haze. If the speaker moved his head a decimeter or so from the focal spot, that went into haze as well. Sound focus was limited as well. The net result was that one saw and heard only the fundamental minimum of the enemy ship (D.G. already thought of it as the "enemy" ship), so their privacy was guarded.

D.G.'s ship also possessed a limited-focus hyperwave, but, D.G. thought enviously, it lacked the polish and elegance of the Auroran version. Of course, his own ship was not the best the Settlers could do, but even so, the Spacers were well ahead technologically. The Settlers still had catching up to do.

The Auroran head in focus was clear and so real in appearance that it looked gruesomely disembodied, so that D.G. would not have been surprised if it had dripped blood. On second glance, however, it could be made out that the neck faded into grayness just after the neckpiece of an undoubtedly well-tailored uniform began to show.

The head identified itself, with punctilious courtesy, as Commander Lisiform of the Auroran ship *Borealis*. D.G. identified himself in his turn, thrusting his chin forward so as to make certain that his beard was in the sharpest possible focus. It was his opinion that his beard lent him an air of fierceness that could not help but be daunting to a beardless and (he thought) weak-chinned Spacer.

D.G. assumed the traditional air of informality that was as irritating to a Spacer officer, as the latter's traditional arrogance was to a Settler. He said, "What is your reason for hailing me, Commander Lisiform?"

The Auroran commander had an exaggerated accent which, it was possible, he thought as formidable as D.G. considered his beard to be. D.G. felt himself to be under considerable strain as he tried to penetrate the accent and understand him.

"We believe," said Lisiform, "that you have on your ship an Auroran citizen named Gladia Solaria. Is that correct, Captain Baley?"

"Madam Gladia is on board this ship, Commander."

"Thank you, Captain. With her, so my information leads me to suppose, are two robots of Auroran manufacture, R. Daneel Olivaw and R. Giskard Reventlov. Is that correct?"

"That is correct."

"In that case, I must inform you that R. Giskard Reventlov is, at present, a dangerous device. Shortly before your ship left Auroran space with him, the said robot, Giskard, badly hurt an Auroran citizen in defiance of the Three Laws. The robot must, therefore, be dismantled and repaired."

"Are you suggesting, Commander, that we on this ship dismantle the robot?"

"No, sir, that would not do. Your people, lacking experience with robots, could not dismantle it properly and could not possibly repair it if they did."

"We might, then, simply destroy it."

"It is too valuable for that. Captain Baley, the robot is Aurora's product and Aurora's responsibility. We do not wish to be the cause of damage to the people on your ship and on the planet Earth if you land there. Consequently, we ask that it be delivered to us."

D.G. said, "Commander, I appreciate your concern. However, the robot is the legal property of Lady Gladia, who is with us. It may be that she would not consent to be parted from her robot and, while I don't want to teach you Auroran law, I believe that it would be illegal by that law to force such a parting. While my crew and I do not consider ourselves bound by Auroran law, we would not willingly be a party to helping you perform what your own government might consider to be an illegal act."

There was a suggestion of impatience in the commander's voice. "There is no question of illegality, Captain. A life-endangering malfunction in a robot supersedes the ordinary rights of an owner. Nevertheless, if there is any question of that, my ship stands ready to accept Lady Gladia and her robot Daneel, along with Giskard, the robot in question. There will then be no separation of Gladia Solaris and her robotic property until she is brought back to Aurora. The law can then take its proper course."

"It is possible, Commander, that Lady Gladia may not wish to leave my ship or to allow her property to do so."

"She has no recourse, Captain. I am legally empowered by my government to demand her—and as an Auroran citizen, she must obey."

"But I am not legally bound to deliver up anything on my ship at the demand of a foreign power. What if I choose to disregard your request?"

"In that case, Captain, I would have no choice but to consider it an unfriendly act. May I point out that we are within the sphere of the planetary system of which Earth is part. You had no hesitation in teaching me Auroran law. You will forgive me, then, if I point out that *your* people do not consider it proper to engage in hostilities within the space of this planetary system."

"I am aware of that, Commander, and I wish no hostilities, nor do I intend an unfriendly act. However, I am bound for Earth under some urgency. I lose time in this conversation and I would lose further time if I moved toward you—or waited for you to move toward me—so that we could carry through a physical transfer of Lady Gladia and her robots. I would prefer to continue onward toward Earth and formally accept all responsibility for the robot Giskard and his behavior until such time as Lady Gladia and her robots return to Aurora."

"May I make the suggestion, Captain, that you place the woman and two robots in a lifeboat and detach a member of your crew to pilot it to us? Once the woman and the two robots are delivered, we will ourselves escort the lifeboat to the immediate environs of Earth and we will compensate you adequately for your time and trouble. A Trader should not object to that."

"I don't, Commander, I don't," said D.G., smiling. "Still, the crewman detailed to pilot the lifeboat might be in great peril since he would be alone with this dangerous robot."

"Captain, if the robot's owner is firm in her control, your crewman will be in no greater danger on the lifeboat than he would be on your ship. We will compensate him for the risk."

"But if the robot can, after all, be controlled by its owner, surely it is not so dangerous that it can't be left with us."

The Commander frowned. "Captain, I trust you are not trying to play games with me. You have my request and I would like to have it honored at once."

"I presume I may consult with Lady Gladia."

"If you do so immediately. Please explain to her exactly what is involved. If, meanwhile, you try to proceed toward Earth, I shall consider that an unfriendly act and take the appropriate action. Since, as you claim, your trip toward Earth is urgent, I advise you to proceed forthwith to consult with Gladia Solaria and come to the immediate decision to cooperate with us. You will then not be too long delayed."

"I will do what I can," said D.G., wooden-faced, as he moved out of focus.

70.

"WELL?" SAID D.G. GRAVELY.

Gladia looked distressed. Automatically, she looked toward Daneel and Giskard, but they remained silent and motionless.

She said, "I don't want to return to Aurora, D.G. They can't possibly want to destroy Giskard; he is in perfect working order, I assure you. That's only a subterfuge. They want *me* for some reason. I suppose there's no way they can be stopped, though, is there?"

D.G. said, "That's an Auroran warship—and a big one. This is only a Trading vessel. We've got energy shields and they can't just destroy us at a blow, but they can wear us down eventually—quite soon, in fact—and then destroy us."

"Is there any way you can strike at them?"

"With my weapons? I'm sorry, Gladia, but their shields can take anything I can throw at them for as long as I can possibly have energy to expend. Besides—"

"Yes?"

"Well, they've just about cornered me. Somehow I thought they would try to intercept me before I Jumped, but they knew my destination and they got here first and waited for me. We're inside the Solar System—the planetary system of which Earth is part. We can't fight here. Even if I wanted to, the crew wouldn't obey me."

"Why not?"

"Call it superstition. The Solar System is holy space to us—if you want to describe it in melodramatic terms. We can't desecrate it by fighting."

Giskard said suddenly, "May I contribute to the discussion, sir?"

D.G. frowned and looked toward Gladia.

Gladia said, "Please. Let him. These robots are highly intelligent. I know you find that hard to believe, but—"

"I'll listen. I don't have to be influenced."

Giskard said, "Sir, I am certain that it *is* me that they want. I cannot allow myself to be the cause of harm to human beings. If you cannot defend yourself and are sure of destruction in a conflict with the other vessel, you have no choice but to give me up. I am sure that if you offer to let them have me, they will not seriously object if you wish to retain Lady Gladia and friend Daneel. It is the only solution."

"No," said Gladia forcefully. "You are mine and I won't give you up. I'll go with you—if the captain decides you must go—and I'll see to it they *don't* destroy you."

"May I speak as well?" said Daneel.

D.G. spread his hands in mock-despair. "Please. Everyone speak."

Daneel said, "If you decide you must give up Giskard, you must understand the consequences. I believe that Giskard thinks that if he is given up, those on the Auroran ship would do him no harm and that they will even release him. I do not believe this to be so. I believe the Aurorans are serious in thinking him to be dangerous and they may well have instructions to destroy the lifeboat as it approaches, killing whoever is on board."

"For what reason would they do that?" asked D.G.

"No Auroran has ever encountered—or even conceived—of what they call a dangerous robot. They would take no chances of taking one on board one of their vessels. —I would suggest, Captain, that you retreat. Why not Jump again, away from Earth? We are not close enough to any planetary mass to prevent that."

"Retreat? You mean run away? I can't do that."

"Well, then, you have to give us up," said Gladia with an air of resigned hopelessness.

D.G. said forcefully, "I'm not giving you up. And I'm not running away. And I can't fight."

"Then what's left?" asked Gladia.

"A fourth alternative," said D.G. "Gladia, I must ask you to remain here with your robots till I return."

71.

D.G. CONSIDERED THE DATA. There had been enough time during the conversation for the location of the Auroran vessel to be pinpointed. It was a bit farther from the sun than his own ship was and that was good. To Jump toward the sun, at this distance from it, would have been risky indeed; to Jump sideways would be, so to speak, a piece of cake in comparison. There was the chance of accident through probability deviation, but there was always that.

He had himself assured the crew that not a shot would be fired (which would do no good, in any case). Clearly, they had utter faith in Earth space protecting them as long as they didn't profane its peace by offering violence. It was pure mysticism that D.G. would have scornfully derided had he not shared the conviction himself.

He moved back into focus. It had been a fairly long wait, but there had been no signal from the other side. They had shown exemplary patience.

"Captain Baley here," he said. "I wish to speak to Commander Lisiform."

There was not much of a wait. "Commander Lisiform here. May I have your answer?"

D.G. said, "We will deliver the woman and the two robots."

"Good! A wise decision."

"And we will deliver them as quickly as we can."

"Again a wise decision."

"Thank you." D.G. gave the signal and his ship Jumped.

There was no time, no need, to hold one's breath. It was over as soon as it was begun—or, at least, the time lapse was insensible.

The word came from the pilot. "New enemy ship position fixed, Captain."

"Good," said D.G. "You know what to do."

The ship had come out of the Jump at high speed relative to the Auroran vessel and the course correction (not a great deal, it was to be hoped) was being made. Then further acceleration.

D.G. moved back into focus. "We are close, Commander, and on our way to deliver. You may fire if you choose, but our shields are up and before you can batter them down we will have reached you in order to make the delivery."

"Are you sending a lifeboat?" The commander moved out of focus.

D.G. waited and the commander was back, his face contorted. "What is this? Your ship is on a collision course."

"It seems to be, yes," said D.G. "That is the fastest way of making delivery."

"You will destroy your ship."

"And yours, too. Your ship is at least fifty times as expensive as mine, probably more. A poor exchange for Aurora."

"But you are engaging in combat in Earth space, Captain. Your customs do not allow that."

"Ah, you know our customs and you take advantage of them. —But I am not in combat. I have not fired an erg of energy and I won't. I am merely following a trajectory. That trajectory happens to intersect your position, but since I am sure you will move before the intersection movement arrives, it is clear that I intend no violence."

"Stop. Let's talk about this."

"I'm tired of talking, Commander. Shall we all say a fond farewell? If you don't move, I will be giving up perhaps four decades, with the third and fourth not so good, anyway. How many will you be giving up?" And D.G. moved out of focus and stayed out.

A beam of radiation shot out from the Auroran ship—tentative, as though to test whether the other's shields were truly up. They were.

Ships' shields would hold against electromagnetic radiation and subatomic particles, including even neutrinos, and could withstand the kinetic energy of small masses—dust particles, even meteoric gravel. The shields could not withstand larger kinetic energies, such as that of an entire ship hurtling at it with supermeteoric speed.

Even dangerous masses, if not guided—a meteoroid, for instance—could be handled. A vessel's computers would automatically veer the ship out of the way of any oncoming meteoroid that was too large for the shield to handle. That, however, would not work against a ship that could veer as its target veered. And if the Settler ship was the smaller of the two, it was also the more maneuverable.

There was only one way that the Auroran ship could avoid destruction—

D.G. watched the other ship visibly enlarging in his viewing panel and wondered if Gladia, in her cabin, knew what was going on. She must be aware of the acceleration, despite the hydraulic suspension of her cabin and the compensatory action of the pseudo-gravity field.

And then the other ship simply winked out of view, having Jumped away, and D.G., with considerable chagrin, realized he was holding his breath and that his heart was racing. Had he had no confidence in the protecting influence of Earth or in his own sure diagnosis of the situation?

D.G. spoke into the transmitter in a voice that, with iron resolution, he forced into coolness. "Well done, men! Correct course and head for Earth."

Chapter 16

The City

72

GLADIA SAID, "ARE YOU SERIOUS, D.G.? You really intended to collide with the ship?"

"Not at all," said D.G. indifferently. "I wasn't expecting to. I merely lunged at them, knowing they would retreat. Those Spacers weren't going to risk their long, wonderful lives when they could easily preserve them."

"*Those* Spacers? What cowards *they* are."

D.G. cleared his throat. "I keep forgetting you're a Spacer, Gladia."

"Yes—and I imagine you think that that is a compliment to me. What if they had been as foolish as you—if they had shown the childish madness you think of as bravery—and stayed in place? What would you have done?"

D.G. muttered, "Hit them."

"And then we would all have died."

"The transaction would have been in our favor, Gladia. One crummy old Trader ship from a Settler world for a new and advanced warship of the leading Spacer world."

D.G. tipped his chair back against the wall and put his hands behind his neck (amazing how comfortable he felt, now that it was all over). "I once saw a historical hyperdrama, in which, toward the end of a war, airplanes loaded with explosives were deliberately flown into much more expensive seaships in order to sink them. Of course, the pilot of each airplane lost his life."

"That was fiction," said Gladia. "You don't suppose civilized people do things like that in real life, do you?"

"Why not? If the cause is good enough."

"What was it, then, you felt as you plunged toward a glorious death? Exaltation? —You were hurtling all your crew toward the same death."

"They knew about it. We could do nothing else. Earth was watching."

"The people on Earth didn't even know."

"I mean it metaphorically. We were in Earth space. We could not act ignobly."

"Oh, what nonsense! And you risked my life, too."

D.G. looked down at his boots. "Would you like to hear something crazy? That was the only thing that bothered me."

"That I would die?"

"Not quite. That I would lose you. —When that ship ordered me to give you up, I knew I wouldn't—even if you asked me to. I would gladly ram them instead; they couldn't have you. And then, as I watched their ship expand in the viewscreen, I thought, 'If they don't get out of here, I'll lose her anyway,' and that's when my heart started to pound and I began to sweat. I *knew* they'd run and still the thought—" He shook his head.

Gladia frowned. "I don't understand you. You weren't worrying about my dying, but you were worried about losing me? Don't the two go together?"

"I know. I'm not saying it's rational. I thought of you rushing at the overseer to save me when you knew it could murder you with a blow. I thought of you facing the crowd at Baleyworld and talking them down when you had never even seen a crowd before. I even thought of you going to Aurora when you were a young woman and learning a new way of life— and surviving. —And it seemed to me I didn't mind dying, I just minded losing you. —You're right. It doesn't make sense."

Gladia said thoughtfully, "Have you forgotten my age? I was just about as old as I am now when you were born. When I was your age, I used to dream of your remote Ancestor. What's more, I've got an artificial hip joint. My left thumb—this one right here"—she wiggled it—"is strictly prosthetic. Some of my nerves have been rebuilt. My teeth are all implanted ceramic. And you talk as though any moment you're going to confess a transcendant passion. —For what? —For whom? —Think, D.G.! —Look at me and see me as I am!"

D.G. tilted his chair back on two legs and rubbed at his beard with an odd scraping sound. "All right. You've made me sound silly, but I'm going to keep right on. What I know about your age is that you're going to survive me and look scarcely any older when you do, so you're younger than I am, not older. Besides, I don't care if you are older. What I would like is for you to stay with me wherever I go—for all my life, if possible."

Gladia was about to speak, but D.G. intervened hastily, "Or, if it seems more convenient, for me to stay with you wherever you go—for all my life, if possible. —If it's all right with you."

Gladia said softly, "I'm a Spacer. You're a Settler."

"Who cares, Gladia? Do you?"

"I mean, there's no question of children. I've had mine."

"What difference does that make to me! There's no danger of the name Baley dying out."

"I have a task of my own. I intend to bring peace to the Galaxy."

"I'll help you."

"And your trading? Will you give up your chance to be rich?"

"We'll do some together. Just enough to keep my crew happy and to help me support you in your task as peace-bringer."

"Life will be dull for you, D.G."

"Will it? It seems to me that since you joined me it's been *too* exciting."

"And you'll probably insist on my giving up my robots."

D.G. looked distressed. "Is *that* why you've been trying to talk me out of this? I wouldn't mind your keeping the two of them—even Daneel and his small lecherous smile—but if we're going to live among Settlers—"

"Then I suppose I'll have to try to find the courage to do it."

She laughed gently and so did D.G. He held out his arms to her and she placed her hands in his.

She said, "You're mad. I'm mad. But everything has been so strange since the evening I looked up at the sky in Aurora and tried to find Solaria's sun that I suppose being mad is the only possible sane response to things."

"What you've just said isn't only mad," said D.G., "it's crazy, but that's the way I want you to be." He hesitated. "No, I'll wait. I'll shave my beard before I try to kiss you. That will lower the chances of infection."

"No, don't! I'm curious about how it might feel."

And she promptly found out.

73.

COMMANDER LISIFORM STRODE back and forth across the length of his cabin. He said, "There was no use losing the ship. No use at all."

His political adviser sat quietly in his chair. His eyes did not bother to follow the agitated and rapid to-and-fro movement of the other. "Yes, of course," he said.

"What have the barbarians to lose? They only live a few decades, in any case. Life means nothing to them."

"Yes, of course."

"Still, I've never seen or heard of a Settler ship doing that. It may be a new fanatical tactic and we have no defense against it. What if they send drone ships against us, with shields up and full momentum but no human beings aboard?"

"We might robotify our ships entirely."

"That wouldn't help. We couldn't afford to lose the ship. What we need is the shield knife they keep talking about. Something that will slice through a shield."

"Then they'll develop one, too, and we will have to devise a knife-proof shield, and so will they, and it will be a standoff again at a higher level."

"We need something completely new, then."

"Well," said the adviser, "maybe something will turn up. Your mission wasn't primarily the matter of the Solarian woman and her robots, was it? It would have been pleasant if we could have forced them out of the Settler ship, but that was secondary, wasn't it?"

"The Council isn't going to like it, just the same."

"It's *my* job to take care of that. The important fact is that Amadiro and Mandamus left the ship and are on their way to Earth in a good speedy ferry."

"Well, yes."

"And you not only distracted the Settler ship but delayed it as well. That means Amadiro and Mandamus not only left the ship unnoticed but they will be on Earth before our barbarian captain will."

"I suppose so. But what of that?"

"I wonder. If it were only Mandamus, I would dismiss the matter. He's of no consequence. But Amadiro? To abandon the political wars back home at a difficult time and come to Earth? Something absolutely crucial must be going on here."

"What?" The commander seemed annoyed that he should be so nearly —and so all-but-fatally—involved in something of which he understood nothing.

"I haven't any idea."

"Do you suppose it might be secret negotiations at the highest level for some sort of overall modification of the peace settlement Fastolfe had negotiated?"

The adviser smiled. "Peace settlement? If you think that, you don't know our Dr. Amadiro. He wouldn't travel to Earth in order to modify a clause or two in a peace settlement. What he's after is a Galaxy without Settlers and if he comes to Earth—well, all I can say is that I wouldn't like to be in the shoes of the Settler barbarians at this time."

74·

"I TRUST, FRIEND GISKARD," said Daneel, "that Madam Gladia is not uneasy at being without us. Can you tell at her distance?"

"I can detect her mind faintly but unmistakably, friend Daneel. She is with the captain and there is a distinct overlay of excitement and joy."

"Excellent, friend Giskard."

"Less excellent for myself, friend Daneel. I find myself in a state of some disorder. I have been under a great strain."

"It distresses me to hear that, friend Giskard. May I ask the reason?"

"We have been here for some time while the captain negotiated with the Auroran ship."

"Yes, but the Auroran ship is now gone, apparently, so that the captain seems to have negotiated to good effect."

"He has done so in a manner of which you were apparently not aware. I was—to an extent. Though the captain was not here with us, I had little trouble sensing his mind. It exuded overwhelming tension and suspense and underneath that a gathering and strengthening sense of loss."

"Loss, friend Giskard? Were you able to determine of what that loss might consist?"

"I cannot describe my method of analysis of such things, but the loss did not seem to be the type of loss I have in the past associated with generalities or with inanimate objects. It had the touch—that is not the word, but there is no other that fits even vaguely—of the loss of a specific person."

"Lady Gladia."

"Yes."

"That would be natural, friend Giskard. He was faced with the possibility of having to give her up to the Auroran vessel."

"It was too intense for that. Too wailing."

"Too wailing?"

"It is the only word I can think of in this connection. There was a stressful mourning associated with the sense of loss. It was not as though Lady Gladia would move elsewhere and be unavailable for that reason. That might, after all, be corrected at some future time. It was as though Lady Gladia would cease existing—would die—and be *forever* unavailable."

"He felt, then, that the Aurorans would kill her? Surely that is not possible."

"Indeed, not possible. And that is not it. I felt a thread of a sense of personal responsibility associated with the deep, deep fear of loss. I searched other minds on board ship and, putting it all together, I came to the suspicion that the captain was deliberately charging his ship into the Auroran vessel."

"That, too, is not possible, friend Giskard," said Daneel in a low voice.

"I had to accept it. My first impulse was to alter the captain's emotional makeup in such a way as to force him to change course, but I could not. His mind was so firmly set, so saturated with determination and—despite the suspense, tension, and dread of loss—so filled with confidence of success—"

"How could there be at once a dread of loss through death and a feeling of confidence of success?"

"Friend Daneel, I have given up marveling at the capacity of the human mind to maintain two opposing emotions simultaneously. I merely accept it. In this case, to have attempted to alter the captain's mind to the point of turning the ship from its course would have killed him. I could not do that."

"But if you did not, friend Giskard, scores of human beings on this ship, including Madam Gladia, and several hundreds more on the Auroran vessel would die."

"They might *not* die if the captain were correct in his feeling of confidence in success. I could not bring about one certain death to prevent many merely probable ones. There is the difficulty, friend Daneel, in your Zeroth Law. The First Law deals with specific individuals and certainties. Your Zeroth Law deals with vague groups and probabilities."

"The human beings on board these ships are not vague groups. They are many specific individuals taken together."

"Yet when I must make a decision it is the specific individual I am about to influence directly whose fate must count with me. I cannot help that."

"What was it you did do, then, friend Giskard—or were you completely helpless?"

"In my desperation, friend Daneel, I attempted to contact the commander of the Auroran vessel after a small Jump had brought him quite close to us. —I could not. The distance was too great. And yet the attempt was not altogether a failure. I did detect something, the equivalent of a faint hum. I puzzled over it a short while before realizing I was receiving the overall sensation of the minds of all the human beings on board the Auroran vessel. I had to filter out that faint hum from the much more prominent sensations arising from our own vessel—a difficult task."

Daneel said, "Nearly impossible, I should think, friend Giskard."

"As you say, nearly impossible, but I managed it with an enormous effort. However, try as I might, I could make out no individual minds. —When Madam Gladia faced the large numbers of human beings in her audience on Baleyworld, I sensed an anarchic confusion of a vast jumble of minds, but I managed to pick out individual minds here and there for a moment or two. That was not so on this occasion."

Giskard paused, as though lost in his memory of the sensation.

Daneel said, "I imagine this must be analogous to the manner in which we see individual stars even among large groups of them, when the whole is comparatively close to us. In a distant galaxy, however, we cannot make out individual stars but can see only a faintly luminous fog."

"That strikes me as a good analogy, friend Daneel. —And as I concentrated on the faint but distant hum, it seemed to me that I could detect a very dim wash of fear permeating it. I was not sure of this, but I felt I had to try to take advantage of it. I had never attempted to exert influence over anything so far away, over anything as inchoate as a mere hum—but I tried desperately to increase that fear by however small a trifle. I cannot say whether I succeeded."

"The Auroran vessel fled. You *must* have succeeded."

"Not necessarily. The vessel might have fled if I had done nothing."

Daneel seemed lost in thought. "It might. If our captain were so confident that it would flee—"

Giskard said, "On the other hand, I cannot be sure that there was a rational basis to that confidence. It seemed to me that what I detected was intermixed with a feeling of awe and reverence for Earth. The confidence I sensed was rather similar to the kind I have detected in young children toward their protectors—parental or otherwise. I had the feeling that the captain believed he could not fail in the neighborhood of Earth because of the influence of Earth. I wouldn't say the feeling was exactly irrational, but it felt nonrational, in any case."

"You are undoubtedly right in this, friend Giskard. The captain has, in our hearing, spoken of Earth, on occasion, in a reverential manner. Since Earth cannot truly influence the success of an action through any mystical influence, it is quite possible to suppose that your influence was indeed successfully exerted. And moreover—"

Giskard, his eyes glowing dimly, said, "Of what are you thinking, friend Daneel?"

"I have been thinking of the supposition that the individual human being is concrete while humanity is abstract. When you detected that faint hum from the Auroran ship, you were not detecting an individual, but a portion of humanity. Could you not, if you were at a proper distance from Earth and if the background noise were sufficiently small, detect the hum of the mental activity of Earth's human population, overall? And, extending that, can one not imagine that in the Galaxy generally there is the hum of the mental activity of all of humanity? How, then, is humanity an abstraction? It is something you can point to. Think of that in connection with the Zeroth Law and you will see that the extension of the Laws of Robotics is a justified one—justified by your own experience."

There was a long pause and finally Giskard said, slowly as though it were being dragged out of him, "You may be right, friend Daneel. —And yet, if we are landing on Earth now, with a Zeroth Law we *may* be able to use, we still don't know *how* we might use it. It seems to us, so far, that the crisis that Earth faces involves the use of a nuclear intensifier, but as far as we know, there is nothing of significance on Earth on which a nuclear intensifier can do its work. What, then, will we do on Earth?"

"I do not as yet know," said Daneel sadly.

75.

NOISE!

Gladia listened in astonishment. It didn't hurt her ears. It wasn't the sound of surface clashing on surface. It wasn't a piercing shriek, or a clamor, or a banging, or anything that could be expressed by an onomatopoetic word.

It was softer and less overwhelming, rising and falling, bearing within it an occasional irregularity—and always there.

D.G. watched her listening, cocking her head to this side and that, and said, "I call it the 'Drone of the City,' Gladia."

"Does it ever stop?"

"Never, really, but what can you expect? Haven't you ever stood in a field and heard the wind rustling the leaves, and insects stridulating, and birds calling, and water running. That never stops."

"That's different."

"No, it isn't. It's the same. The sound here is the melting together of the rumble of machinery and the various noises people make, but the principle is precisely the same as the natural nonhuman noises of a field. You're used to fields, so you don't hear the noise there. You're not used to *this,* so you hear it and probably find it annoying. Earthpeople don't hear it except on the rare occasions when they come fresh in from the countryside—and then they are very glad indeed to greet it. Tomorrow you won't hear it either."

Gladia looked about thoughtfully from their position on a small balcony. "So many buildings!"

"That's true enough. Structures in every direction—stretching outward for miles. And up—and down, too. This is not just a city, in the fashion of Aurora or Baleyworld. It is a City—capital 'C'—of the kind that exists only on Earth."

"These are the Caves of Steel," said Gladia. "I know. We're underground, aren't we?"

"Yes. Absolutely. I must tell you that it took *me* time to get used to this sort of thing the first time I visited Earth. Wherever you go in a City, it looks like a crowded city scene. Walkways and roadways and storefronts and mobs of people, with the soft and universal lights of fluorescents making everything seem bathed in soft shadowless sunshine—but it *isn't* sunshine and, up above on the surface, I don't know if the sun is really shining at the moment, or is covered by clouds, or is absent altogether, leaving this part of the world plunged in night and darkness."

"It makes the City enclosed. People breathe each other's air."

"We do anyway—on any world—anywhere."

"Not like this." She sniffed. "It smells."

"Every world smells. Every City on Earth smells differently. You'll get used to it."

"Do I want to? Why don't people suffocate?"

"Excellent ventilation."

"What happens when it breaks down?"

"It never does."

Gladia looked about again and said, "Every building seems loaded with balconies."

"It's a sign of status. Very few people have apartments facing out and if they do have one they want the advantage of it. Most Citypeople live inside windowless apartments."

Gladia shuddered, "Horrible! What's the name of this City, D.G.?"

"It's New York. It's the chief City, but not the largest. On this continent, Mexico City and Los Angeles are the largest and there are Cities larger than New York on other continents."

"What makes New York the chief City, then?"

"The usual reason. The Global Government is located here. The United Nations."

"Nations?" She pointed her finger triumphantly at D.G. "Earth was divided into several independent political units. Right?"

"Right. Dozens of them. But that was before hyperspatial travel—prehyper times. The name remains, though. That's what's wonderful about Earth. It's frozen history. Every other world is new and shallow. Only Earth is *humanity* in its essence."

D.G. said it in a hushed whisper and then retreated back into the room. It was not a large one and its furnishings were skimpy.

Gladia said, disappointed, "Why isn't there anyone about?"

D.G. laughed. "Don't worry, dear. If it's parades and attention you want, you'll have them. It's just that I asked them to leave us alone for a while. I want a little peace and rest and I imagine you do, too. As for my men, they have to berth the ship, clean it up, renew supplies, tend to their devotions—"

"Women?"

"No, that's not what I mean, though I suppose women will play a role later. By devotions, I mean that Earth still has its religions and these comfort the men somehow. Here on Earth, anyway. It seems to have more meaning here."

"Well," said Gladia half-contemptuously. "Frozen history, as you say. —Do you suppose we can get out of the building and walk about a bit?"

"Take my advice, Gladia, and don't jump into that sort of thing just now. You'll get plenty of it when the ceremonies begin."

"But that will be so formal. Could we skip the ceremonies?"

"No chance at all. Since you insisted on making yourself a heroine on Baleyworld, you'll have to be one on Earth as well. Still, the ceremonies will be through eventually. When you recover from them, we will get a guide and we'll *really* see the City."

"Will we have any trouble taking my robots with us?" She gestured toward Daneel and Giskard at the other end of the room. "I don't mind being without them when I'm with you on the ship, but if I'm going to be with crowds of strangers I'll feel more secure having them with me."

"There'll be no problem with Daneel, certainly. He's a hero in his own right. He was the Ancestor's partner and he passes for human. Giskard, who is an obvious robot, should, in theory, not be allowed inside the city borders, but they've made an exception in his case and I hope they will continue to do so. —It is too bad, in a way, that we must wait here and can't step outside."

"You say I should not be exposed to all that noise just yet," said Gladia.

"No, no. I'm not referring to the public squares and roadways. I would just like to take you out into the corridors within this particular building. There are miles and miles of them—literally—and they're a small bit of City in themselves: shopping recesses, dining halls, amusement areas, Personals, elevators, transways, and so on. There's more color and variety on one floor in one building in one City on Earth than in a whole Settler town or in a whole Spacer world."

"I should think everyone would get lost."

"Of course not. Everyone knows his own neighborhood here, as anywhere else. Even strangers need only follow the signs."

"I suppose all the walking that people are forced to do must be very good for them physically," said Gladia dubiously.

"Socially, too. There are people in the corridors at all times and the convention is that you stop to exchange words with anyone you know and that you greet even those you don't know. Nor is walking absolutely necessary. There are elevators everywhere for vertical travel. The main corridors are transways and move for horizontal travel. Outside the building, of course, there is a feeder line to the Expressway network. *That's* something. You'll get to ride it."

"I've heard of them. They have strips that you walk across and that drag you along faster and faster—or slower and slower—as you move from one to another. I couldn't do that. Don't ask me to."

"Of course you'll be able to do it," said D.G. genially. "I'll help you. If necessary, I'll carry you, but all it takes is a little practice. Among the Earthpeople, kindergarten children manage and so do old people with canes. I admit Settlers tend to be clumsy about it. I'm no miracle of grace myself, but I manage and so will you."

Gladia heaved an enormous sigh. "Well, then, I'll try if I have to. But I tell you what, D.G., dear. We *must* have a reasonably quiet room for the night. I want your 'Drone of the City' muted."

"That can be arranged, I'm sure."

"And I don't want to have to eat in the Section kitchens."

D.G. looked doubtful. "We can arrange to have food brought in, but really it would do you good to participate in the social life of Earth. I'll be with you, after all."

"Maybe after a while, D.G., but not just at first—and I want a Personal for myself."

"Oh, no, *that's* impossible. There'll be a washbasin and a toilet bowl in any room they assign us because we have status, but if you intend to do any serious showering or bathing, you'll have to follow the crowd. There'll be a woman to introduce you to the procedure and you'll be assigned a stall or whatever it is they have there. You won't be embarrassed. Settler women have to be introduced to the use of Personals every day of the year. —And you may end up enjoying it, Gladia. They tell me that the Women's Personal is a place of much activity and fun. In the Men's Personal, on the other hand, not a word is allowed spoken. Very dull."

"It's all horrible," muttered Gladia. "How do you stand the lack of privacy?"

"On a crowded world, needs must," said D.G. lightly. "What you've never had, you never miss. —Do you want any other aphorisms?"

"Not really," said Gladia.

She looked dejected and D.G. put an arm about her shoulder. "Come, it won't be as bad as you think. I promise you."

76.

IT WAS NOT EXACTLY a nightmare, but Gladia was thankful to her earlier experience on Baleyworld for having given her a preview of what was now a veritable ocean of humanity. The crowds were much larger here in New York than they had been on the Settler world, but on the other hand, she was more insulated from the herd here than she had been on the earlier occasion.

The government officials were clearly anxious to be seen with her. There was a wordless, polite struggle for a position near enough to her to be seen with her on hypervision. It isolated her, not only from the crowds on the other side of the police lines but from D.G. and from her two robots. It also subjected her to a kind of polite jostling from people who seemed to have an eye only on the camera.

She listened to what seemed innumerable speeches, all mercifully brief, without really listening. She smiled periodically, both blandly and blindly, casting the vision of her implanted teeth in all directions indiscriminately.

Gladia went by ground-car through miles of passageways at a crawl, while an uncounted ant heap lined the walkways, cheering and waving as she passed. (She wondered if ever a Spacer had received such adulation from Earthpeople and was quite confident that her own case was entirely unprecedented.)

At one point, Gladia caught sight of a distant knot of people gathered round a hypervision screen and momentarily had an undoubted glimpse of herself upon it. They were listening, she knew, to a recording of her speech on Baleyworld. Gladia wondered how many times and in how many places and before how many people it was being played now, and how many times it had been played since she gave it, and how many times it would yet be played in the future, and whether anything at all had been heard of it on the Spacer worlds.

Might she, in fact, seem a traitor to the people of Aurora and would this reception be held to be proof of it?

She might—and it might—and she was beyond caring. She had her mission of peace and reconciliation and she would follow it wherever it led without complaint—even to the unbelievable orgy of mass bathing and shrilly unconscious exhibitionism in the Women's Personal that morning. (Well, without much complaint.)

They came to one of the Expressways that D.G. had mentioned, and Gladia gazed in open horror at the endless snake of passenger cars that passed—and passed—and passed—each with its load of people who were on business that could not be postponed for the motorcade (or who simply didn't want to be bothered) and who stared solemnly at the crowds and the procession for the few moments they remained in sight.

Then the ground-car plunged downward under the Expressway, through a short tunnel that in no way differed from the passage above (the City was all tunnel), and up again on the other side.

And eventually the motorcade came to an end at a large public building that was, mercifully, more attractive than the endlessly repetitious blocks that represented the units of the City's residential section.

Within the building, there was yet another reception, during which alcoholic drinks and various hors d'oeuvres were served. Gladia fastidiously touched neither. A thousand people milled about and an endless succession of them came up to speak to Gladia. The word had apparently gone out not to offer to shake hands, but some inevitably did, and, trying not to hesitate, Gladia would briefly place two fingers on the hand and then withdraw them.

Eventually, a number of women prepared to leave for the nearest Personal and one of them performed what was obviously a social ritual and tactfully asked Gladia if she would like to accompany them. Gladia didn't, but there might be a long night ahead and it might be more embarrassing to have to interrupt it later.

Within the Personal, there was the usual excited laughing and chattering and Gladia, bowing to the exigencies of the situation and fortified by her experience that morning, made use of the facilities in a small chamber with partitions on either side, but with none in front of her.

No one seemed to mind and Gladia tried to remind herself she must adjust to local customs. At least the place was well-ventilated and seemed spotlessly clean.

Throughout, Daneel and Giskard had been ignored. This, Gladia realized, was a kindness. Robots were no longer allowed within City limits, though there were millions in the countryside without. To have made a point of the presence of Daneel and Giskard would have meant raising the legal issue that involved. It was easier to pretend, tactfully, that they weren't there.

Once the banquet began, they sat quietly at a table with D.G., not too far removed from the dais. At the dais, Gladia sat, eating sparingly and wondering if the food would give her dysentery.

D.G., perhaps not entirely pleased with his relegation to the post of keeper of the robots, kept staring restlessly in Gladia's direction and, occasionally, she lifted one hand and smiled at him.

Giskard, equally watchful of Gladia, had an opportunity to say to Daneel very quietly, under cover of the relentless and unending background clash of cutlery and babble, "Friend Daneel, these are high officials that sit here in this room. It is possible that one or more may have information of use to us."

"It is possible, friend Giskard. Can you, thanks to your abilities, guide me in this respect?"

"I cannot. The mental background yields me no specific emotional response of interest. Nor does the occasional flash among the nearest show me anything. Yet the climax of the crisis is, I am certain, approaching quickly, even as we sit here, idle."

Daneel said gravely, "I will try to do as Partner Elijah would have done and force the pace."

77.

DANEEL WAS NOT EATING. He watched the assemblage with his calm eyes and located the one he was searching for. Quietly, he rose and moved toward another table, his eyes on a woman who was managing to eat briskly and yet maintain a cheerful conversation with the man on her left. She was a stocky woman, with short hair that showed definite traces of gray. Her face, if not youthful, was pleasant.

Daneel waited for a natural break in the conversation and, when that did not come, he said with an effort, "Madam, may I interrupt?"

She looked up at him, startled and plainly displeased. "Yes," she said rather bruskly, "what is it?"

"Madam," said Daneel, "I ask your pardon for this interruption, but may I have your permission to speak with you for a time?"

She stared at him, frowning for a moment, and then her expression softened. She said, "I should guess, from your excessive politeness, that you're the robot, aren't you?"

"I am one of Madam Gladia's robots, madam."

"Yes, but you're the human one. You're R. Daneel Olivaw."

"That is my name, madam."

The woman turned to the man on her left and said, "Please excuse me. I can't very well refuse this—robot."

Her neighbor smiled uncertainly and transferred his attention to the plate before him.

The woman said to Daneel, "If you have a chair, why don't you bring it here? I will be glad to speak to you."

"Thank you, madam."

When Daneel had returned and seated himself, she said, "You are *really* R. Daneel Olivaw, aren't you?"

"That is my name, madam," said Daneel again.

"I mean the one who worked with Elijah Baley long ago. You're not a new model of the same line? You're not R. Daneel the Fourth or something like that?"

Daneel said, "There is little of me that has not been replaced in the past twenty decades—or even modernized and improved—but my positronic brain is the same as it was when I worked with Partner Elijah on three different worlds—and once on a spaceship. It has not been altered."

"Well!" She looked at him admiringly. "You're certainly a good job. If all robots were like you, I'd see no objection to them whatever. —What is it you want to talk to me about?"

"When you were introduced to Lady Gladia, madam, before we all took our seats, you were presented to her as the Undersecretary of Energy, Sophia Quintana."

"You remember well. That is my name and my office."

"Does the office refer to all of Earth or merely to the City?"

"I'm Global Undersecretary, I assure you."

"Then you are knowledgeable in the field of energetics?"

Quintana smiled. She did not seem to object to being questioned. Perhaps she thought it amusing or perhaps she found herself attracted to Daneel's air of deferential gravity or to the mere fact that a robot could question her so. In any case, she said with a smile, "I majored in energetics at the University of California and have a master's degree in it. As to how knowledgeable I still am, I'm not certain. I've spent too many years as an administrator—something that saps one's brains, I assure you."

"But you would be well acquainted with the practical aspects of Earth's present energy supply, would you not?"

"Yes. That I will admit to. Is there something you want to know about it?"

"There is something that piques my curiosity, madam."

"Curiosity? In a robot?"

Daneel bowed his head. "If a robot is complex enough, he can be aware of something within himself that seeks information. This is analogous to what I have observed to be called 'curiosity' in human beings and I take the liberty of using the same word in connection with my own feelings."

"Fair enough. What are you curious about, R. Daneel? May I call you that?"

"Yes, madam. I understand that Earth's energy supply is drawn from solar power stations in geostationary orbit in Earth's equatorial plane."

"You understand correctly."

"But are these power stations the sole energy supply of this planet?"

"No. They are the primary—but not the sole—energy supply. There is considerable use of energy from Earth's internal heat, from winds, waves, tides, flowing water, and so on. We have quite a complex mix and each variety has its advantages. Solar energy is the mainstay, however."

"You make no mention of nuclear energy, madam. Are there no uses for microfusion?"

Quintana raised her eyebrows. "Is that what you're curious about, R. Daneel?"

"Yes, madam. What is the reason for the absence of nuclear power sources on Earth?"

"They are not absent, R. Daneel. On a small scale, one comes across it. Our robots—we have many in the countryside, you know—are microfusionized. Are you, by the way?"

Daneel said, "Yes, madam."

"Then, too," she went on, "there are microfusionized machines here and there, but the total is quite trifling."

"Is it not true, Madam Quintana, that microfusion energy sources are sensitive to the action of nuclear intensifiers?"

"They certainly are. Yes, of course. The microfusion power source will blow up and I suppose that comes under the heading of being sensitive."

"Then it isn't possible for someone, using a nuclear intensifier, to seriously cripple some crucial portion of Earth's energy supply."

Quintana laughed. "No, of course not. In the first place, I don't see anyone dragging a nuclear intensifier about from place to place. They weigh tons and I don't think they can be maneuvered through and along the streets and corridors of a City. Certainly, it would be noticed if anyone tried. And then, even if a nuclear intensifier were brought into play, all it could do would be to destroy a few robots and a few machines before the thing would be discovered and stopped. There is no chance at all—zero—of our being hurt in that way. Is that the reassurance you wanted, R. Daneel?" It was almost a dismissal.

Daneel said, "There are just one or two small points I would like clarified, Madam Quintana. *Why* is there no large microfusion source on Earth? The Spacer worlds all depend on microfusion and so do all the Settler worlds. Microfusion is portable, versatile, and cheap—and doesn't require the enormous effort of maintenance, repair, and replacement that space structures do."

"And, as you said, R. Daneel, they are sensitive to nuclear intensifiers."

"And, as *you* said, Madam Quintana, nuclear intensifiers are too large and bulky to be of much use."

Quintana smiled broadly and nodded. "You are very intelligent, R. Daneel," she said. "It never occurred to me that I would ever sit at a table and carry on a discussion like this with a robot. Your Auroran roboticists are very clever—too clever—for I fear to carry on this discussion. I'd have to worry about you taking my place in the government. You know, we do have a legend about a robot named Stephen Byerley taking a high post in the government."

"That must be merely fiction, Madam Quintana," said Daneel gravely. "There are no robots in governmental posts on any of the Spacer worlds. We are merely—robots."

"I'm relieved to hear that and will therefore go on. The matter of differences in power sources has its roots in history. At the time that hyperspatial travel was developed, we had microfusion, so that people leaving Earth took microfusion power sources with them. It was necessary on spaceships and on planets, too, in the generations during which they were being adapted for human occupation. It takes many years to build an adequate complex of solar power stations—and rather than undertake such a task, the emigrants remained with microfusion. So it was with the Spacers in their time and so it is now with the Settlers.

"On Earth, however, microfusion and solar power in space were developed at roughly the same time and both were used more and more. Finally, we could make our choice and use either microfusion or solar power or, of course, both. And we chose solar power."

Daneel said, "That seems strange to me, Madam Quintana. Why not both?"

"Actually, that's not a very difficult question to answer, R. Daneel. Earth, in prehyperspatial days, had had experience with a primitive form of nuclear energy and it wasn't a happy experience. When the time came to choose between solar power and microfusion, Earthpeople saw microfusion as a form of nuclear energy and turned away from it. Other worlds, which did not have our direct experience with the primitive form of nuclear energy, had no reason to turn away from microfusion."

"May I ask what this primitive form of nuclear energy to which you refer might be, madam?"

"Uranium fission," said Quintana. "It's completely different from microfusion. Fission involves the splitting of massive nuclei, such as those of uranium. Microfusion involves the joining of light nuclei, such as those of hydrogen. They're both forms of nuclear energy, however."

"I presume that uranium would be the fuel for fission devices."

"Yes—or other massive nuclei, such as those of thorium or plutonium."

"But uranium and these others are exceedingly rare metals. Could they support a fission-using society?"

"Those elements are rare on other worlds. On Earth, they are not exactly common, but neither are they terribly rare. Uranium and thorium are widely spread in the crust in small quantities and are concentrated in a few places."

"And are there any fission-power devices on Earth now, madam?"

"No," said Quintana flatly. "Nowhere and in no fashion. Human beings would far sooner burn oil—or even wood—than fission uranium. The very word 'uranium' is taboo in polite society. You wouldn't be asking me these questions or I giving you these answers if you were a human being and an Earthman."

Daneel persisted. "But are you certain, madam? Is there no secret device that makes use of fission that, for the sake of national security—"

"No, robot," said Quintana, frowning. "I tell you—no such device. None!"

Daneel rose. "I thank you, madam, and I ask your pardon for taking your time and for probing what would seem to be a sensitive subject. With your permission, I shall leave you now."

Quintana waved a careless hand. "You're welcome, R. Daneel."

She turned again to her neighbor, secure in the knowledge that in the crowds of Earth, people never attempted to overhear a nearby conversation or, if they did, never admitted the fact. She said, "Would you imagine having a discussion on energetics with a *robot?*"

As for Daneel, he returned to his original place and said softly to Giskard, "Nothing, friend Giskard. Nothing helpful."

Then he added sadly, "Perhaps I asked the wrong questions. Partner Elijah would have asked the right ones."

Chapter 17

The Assassin

78.

SECRETARY-GENERAL EDGAR ANDREV, chief executive of Earth, was a rather tall and imposing man, clean-shaven in the Spacer style. He moved always in a measured fashion, as though on constant display, and he had a twinkling way about him as though he was always very pleased with himself. His voice was a bit too high-pitched for his body, but it fell well short of being squeaky. Without seeming obdurate, he was not easily swayed.

And he wasn't this time. "Impossible," he said firmly to D.G. "She *must* make her appearance."

"She's had a hard day, Secretary-General," said D.G. "She is not accustomed to crowds or to these surroundings. I am responsible to Baleyworld for her well-being and my personal honor is at stake."

"I appreciate your position," said Andrev, "but I represent Earth and I cannot deny Earthpeople their view of her. The corridors are filled, the hyperwave channels are ready, and I would not be able to hide her, even if I desperately wished to do so. After this—and how long can it last? Half an hour?—she can retire and she need not make another appearance till her speech tomorrow night."

"Her comfort must be cared for," said D.G., tacitly abandoning his position. "She has to be kept at some distance from the crowd."

"There will be a cordon of security guards that will give her ample breathing space. The front row of the crowd will be kept well back. They're out there now. If we don't announce that she will soon appear, there might well be disorder."

D.G. said, "It shouldn't have been arranged. It isn't safe. There are Earthpeople who aren't fond of Spacers."

The Secretary-General shrugged. "I wish you could tell me how I could possibly have kept it from being arranged. At the present moment she is a heroine and she cannot be withheld. Nor will anyone offer her anything but cheers—for the moment. But if she doesn't appear, that will change. Now, let us go."

D.G. backed away discontentedly. He caught Gladia's eye. She looked tired and more than a little unhappy.

He said, "You must, Gladia. There's no way out."

For a moment, she stared down at her hands as though wondering if they could do anything to protect her, then she straightened herself and lifted her chin—a small Spacer amid this horde of barbarians. "If I must, I must. Will you remain with me?"

"Unless they remove me physically."

"And my robots?"

D.G. hesitated. "Gladia, how will two robots be able to help you in the midst of millions of human beings?"

"I know, D.G. And I also know that I will have to do without them eventually if I am to continue this mission of mine. But not just yet, please. For the moment, I will feel safer with them, whether that makes sense or not. If these Earth officials want me to acknowledge the crowd, to smile, to wave, to do whatever it is I am supposed to do, the presence of Daneel and Giskard will comfort me. —Look, D.G., I am giving in to them on a very big thing, even though I am so uneasy that I think nothing would be so nice as to run away. Let them give in to me on this very little thing."

"I'll try," said D.G., in clear discouragement and, as he stepped toward Andrev, Giskard moved quietly with him.

A few minutes later, when Gladia, surrounded by a carefully picked contingent of officials, moved forward toward an open balcony, D.G. remained a little behind Gladia, flanked on his left by Giskard and on his right by Daneel.

The Secretary-General had said ruefully, "All right, all right. I don't know how you managed to make me agree, but all right." He rubbed his forehead, aware of a small vague ache in his right temple. For some reason he caught Giskard's eye and turned away with a stifled shudder. "But you must keep them motionless, Captain, remember. And please keep the one that *looks* like a robot as unobtrusive as you can. He makes me uneasy and I don't want people any more aware of him than they have to be."

D.G. said, "They will be looking at Gladia, Secretary-General. They will see no one else."

"I hope so," said Andrev waspishly. He paused to take a message capsule someone placed in his hand. He put it into his pocket, then walked on and didn't think of it again till they had reached the balcony.

79.

To GLADIA, IT SEEMED that each time she moved into another scene, it grew worse—more people, more noise, more confusing light, more invasion of every sense perception.

There was shouting. She could hear her own name being shouted out. With difficulty, she overcame her own tendency to retreat and become immobile. She lifted her arm and waved it and smiled and the shouting became louder. Someone began to speak, his voice booming out over the loudspeaker system, his image on a large screen high above them so that it could be visible to all the crowd. Undoubtedly, it was also visible on innumerable screens in innumerable meeting halls in every Section of every City on the planet.

Gladia sighed with relief at having someone else in the spotlight. She tried to shrink within herself and let the sound of the speaker distract the attention of the crowd.

Secretary-General Andrev, seeking cover under the voice, even as Gladia did, was rather thankful that, in giving precedence to Gladia, it had not seemed necessary for him to speak on this occasion. He suddenly remembered the message he had pocketed.

He frowned in sudden disturbance over what it might be that warranted the interruption of so important a ceremony and then experienced a reverse feeling of intense irritation over the fact that it would probably prove to be utterly unimportant.

He pressed the ball of his right thumb hard against the slight concavity designed to accept the pressure and the capsule opened. He removed the thin piece of plastipaper, read the message it contained, and then watched it crumble and fragment. He brushed away the impalpable powder that remained and gestured imperiously to D.G.

It was scarcely necessary to whisper under the conditions of the vast and continuing noise in the square.

Andrev said, "You said you encountered an Auroran war vessel within the space of the Solar System."

"Yes—and I imagine Earth's sensors detected it."

"Of course they did. You said there were no hostile actions on either side."

"No weapon was used. They demanded Madam Gladia and her robots. I refused and they left. I explained all this."

"How long did it all take?"

"Not very long. Several hours."

"You mean that Aurora sent a warship just to argue back and forth with you for a couple of hours and then leave."

D.G. shrugged. "Secretary-General, I don't know their motivations. I can only report what happened."

The Secretary-General stared at him haughtily. "But you do not report all that happened. The information of the sensors has now been thoroughly analyzed by computer and it would seem that you attacked."

"I did not fire a kilowatt of energy, sir."

"Have you considered kinetic energy? You used the ship itself as a projectile."

"So it may have seemed to them. They did not choose to withstand me and call what might have been a bluff."

"But was it a bluff?"

"It might have been."

"It seems to me, Captain, that you were ready to destroy two ships *inside the Solar System* and perhaps create a war crisis. That was a terrible chance to take."

"I did not think it would come to actual destruction and it didn't."

"But the whole process delayed you and occupied your attention."

"Yes, I suppose so, but why are you pointing this out?"

"Because our sensors did observe one thing you did not observe—or, at any rate, did not report."

"What might that be, Secretary-General?"

"It caught the launching of an orbital module, which seems to have had two human beings on board and which descended toward Earth."

The two were immersed in a world of their own. No other human being on the balcony was paying any attention to them. Only the two robots flanking D.G. were staring at them and listening.

It was at this point that the speaker ceased, his last words being, "Lady Gladia, born a Spacer on the world of Solaria, living as a Spacer on the world of Aurora, but becoming a Citizen of the Galaxy on the Settler world

of Baleyworld." He turned to her and gestured expansively, "Lady
Gladia—"

The sound of the crowd became a long, happy rumble and the many-
headed crowd became a forest of waving arms. Gladia felt a gentle hand on
her shoulder and heard a voice in her ear that said, "Please. A few words,
my lady."

Gladia said weakly, "People of Earth." The words boomed out and,
uncannily, silence fell. Gladia said again, more firmly, "People of Earth, I
stand before you a human being as you are. A bit older, I admit, so that I
lack your youth, your hopefulness, your capacity for enthusiasm. My misfortune is tempered at this moment, however, by the fact that in your presence
I feel myself catching your fire, so that the cloak of age falls away—"

Applause swelled and someone on the balcony said to someone else,
"She's making them happy they're short-lived. That Spacer woman has the
impudence of a devil."

Andrev was not paying attention. He said to D.G., "The whole episode
with you may have been a device to get those men on Earth."

D.G. said, "I had no way of knowing that. I could think of very little else
but saving Lady Gladia and my ship. Where have they landed?"

"We don't know. They have not landed in any of the City spaceports."

D.G. said, "I guess they wouldn't."

"Not that it matters," said the Secretary-General, "except to give me
passing annoyance. Over the past several years, there have been a number
of landings of this sort, though none so carefully prepared. Nothing's ever
happened and we pay no attention. Earth, after all, is an open world. It is
humanity's home and any person from any world can come and go freely—
even Spacers, if they wish."

D.G. rubbed his beard with a rasping noise. "And yet their intentions
might not be to do us any good whatever."

(Gladia was saying, "I wish you all well on this world of human origin, on
this well-packed special world, and in this marvel of a City—"and acknowledged the gathering applause with a smile and a wave as she stood there and
allowed the enthusiasm to catch—and gather.)

Andrev raised his voice, to be heard over the clamor of the crowd.
"Whatever their intentions, it can come to nothing. The peace that has
descended on Earth since the Spacers withdrew and Settlement began is
unbreakable within and without. For many decades now, the wilder spirits
among ourselves have been leaving for the Settler worlds so that a spirit
such as yours, Captain, which can dare risk the destruction of two vessels

within the space of the Solar system is not to be found on Earth. There is no substantial level of crime on Earth any longer, no violence. The security guards assigned to control this crowd have no weapons because they have no need for any."

And as he spoke, from the anonymity of the vast crowd a blaster pointed upward toward the balcony and was carefully aimed.

80.

A NUMBER OF THINGS happened at nearly the same time.

Giskard's head had turned to stare at the crowd, drawn by some sudden effect.

Daneel's eyes followed, saw the aimed blaster, and, with faster-than-human reflexes, he lunged.

The sound of the blaster rang out.

The people on the balcony froze and then broke out into loud exclamations.

D.G. seized Gladia and snatched her to one side.

The noise from the crowd erupted into a full-throated and terrifying roar.

Daneel's lunge had been directed at Giskard and he knocked the other robot down.

The shot from the blaster entered the room behind the balcony and gouged a hole out of a portion of the ceiling. A line drawn from the blaster to the hole might have passed through that portion of space occupied a second earlier by Giskard's head.

Giskard muttered as he was forced down. "Not human. A robot."

Daneel, releasing Giskard, surveyed the scene quickly. Ground level was some six meters beneath the balcony and the space below was empty. The security guards were struggling their way toward the region of upheaval within the crowd that marked the spot where the would-be assassin had stood.

Daneel vaulted over the balcony and dropped, his metal skeleton absorbing the shock easily, as a human being's would not have.

He ran toward the crowd.

Daneel had no choice. He had never encountered anything like this before. The supreme need was to reach the robot with the blaster before it was destroyed and, with that in mind, Daneel found that, for the first time in his existence, he could not stand on the niceties of preserving individual human beings from harm. He had to shake them up somewhat.

He tossed them aside, in actual fact, as he plowed into the crowd, crying out in stentorian fashion, "Make way! Make way! The person with the blaster must be questioned!"

Security guards fell in behind him and they found the "person" at last, down and somewhat battered.

Even on an Earth that prided itself on being nonviolent, an eruption of rage against an obvious murderer left its mark. The assassin had been seized, kicked, and beaten. It was only the very density of the crowd that had saved the assassin from being torn apart. The multiple assailants, getting in each other's way, succeeded in doing comparatively little.

The security guards pushed back the crowd with difficulty. On the ground near the prone robot was the blaster. Daneel ignored it.

Daneel was kneeling by the captured assassin. He said, "Can you talk?"

Bright eyes stared up at Daneel's. "I can," said the assassin in a voice that was low but quite normal otherwise.

"Are you of Auroran origin?"

The assassin did not answer.

Daneel said quickly, "I know you are. It was an unnecessary question. Where on this planet is your base?"

The assassin did not answer.

Daneel said, "Your base? Where is it? You must answer. I am ordering you to answer."

The assassin said, "You cannot order me. You are R. Daneel Olivaw. I have been told of you and I need not obey you."

Daneel looked up, touched the nearest guard, and said, "Sir, would you ask this person where his base is?"

The guard, startled, tried to speak but only a hoarse croak emerged. He swallowed in embarrassment, cleared his throat, and then barked out, "Where is your base?"

"I am forbidden to answer that question, sir," said the assassin.

"You must," said Daneel firmly. "A planetary official is asking it. —Sir, would you order him to answer it?"

The guard echoed, "I order you to answer it, prisoner."

"I am forbidden to answer that question, sir."

The guard reached downward to seize the assassin roughly by the shoulder, but Daneel said rapidly, "I would suggest that it would not be useful to offer force, sir."

Daneel looked about. Much of the clamor of the crowd had died down.

There seemed to be a tension in the air, as though a million people were waiting anxiously to see what Daneel would do.

Daneel said to the several guards who had now clustered about him and the prone assassin, "Would you clear the way for me, sirs? I must take the prisoner to Lady Gladia. It may be that she can force an answer."

"What about medical attention for the prisoner?" asked one of the guards.

"That will not be necessary, sir," said Daneel. He did not explain.

81.

"THAT THIS SHOULD HAVE HAPPENED," said Andrev tightly, his lips trembling with passion. They were in the room off the balcony and he glanced up at the hole in the ceiling that remained as mute evidence of the violence that had taken place.

Gladia said, in a voice that she strove successfully to keep from shaking, "Nothing has happened. I am unharmed. There is that hole in the ceiling that you will have to repair and perhaps some additional repairs in the room above. That's all."

Even as she spoke, she could hear people upstairs moving objects away from the hole and presumably assessing damage.

"That is *not* all," said Andrev. "It ruins our plans for your appearance tomorrow, for your major address to the planet."

"It does the opposite," said Gladia. "The planet will be the more anxious to hear me, knowing I have been the near-victim of an assassination attempt."

"But there's the chance of another attempt."

Gladia shrugged lightly. "That just makes me feel I'm on the right track. —Secretary-General Andrev, I discovered not too long ago that I have a mission in life. It did not occur to me that this mission might place me in danger, but since it does, it also occurs to me that I would *not* be in danger and *not* worth the killing if I was not striking home. If danger is a measure of my effectiveness, I am willing to risk that danger."

Giskard said, "Madam Gladia, Daneel is here with, I presume, the individual who aimed a blaster in this direction."

It was not only Daneel—carrying a relaxed, unstruggling figure—who appeared in the doorway of the room, but half a dozen security guards as well. Outside, the noise of the crowd seemed lower and more distant. It was clearly beginning to disperse and periodically one could hear the announcement over the loudspeakers: "No one has been hurt. There is no danger. Return to your homes."

Andrev waved the guards away. "Is that the one?" he asked sharply.

Daneel said, "There is no question, sir, but that this is the individual with the blaster. The weapon was near him, the people close to the scene witnessed his action, and he himself admits the deed."

Andrev stared at him in astonishment. "He's so calm. He doesn't seem human."

"He is not human, sir. He is a robot, a humanoid robot."

"But we don't have any humanoid robots on Earth. —Except you."

"This robot, Secretary-General," said Daneel, "is, like myself, of Auroran manufacture."

Gladia frowned. "But that's impossible. A robot couldn't have been ordered to assassinate me."

D.G., looking exasperated and, with a most possessive arm about Gladia's shoulder, said in an angry rumble, "An Auroran robot, specially programmed—"

"Nonsense, D.G.," said Gladia. "No way. Auroran or not, special programming or not, a robot cannot deliberately try to harm a human being it knows to be a human being. If this robot did fire the blaster in my direction, he must have missed me on purpose."

"To what end?" demanded Andrev. "Why should he miss, madam?"

"Don't you see?" said Gladia. "Whoever it was that gave the robot its orders must have felt that the *attempt* would be enough to disrupt my plans here on Earth and it was the disruption they were after. They couldn't order the robot to kill me, but they could order him to miss me—and if that was enough to disrupt the program, they would be satisfied. —Except that it won't disrupt the program. I won't allow that."

D.G. said, "Don't be a heroine, Gladia. I don't know what they'll try next and nothing—*nothing*—is worth losing you."

Gladia's eyes softened. "Thank you, D.G. I appreciate your feelings, but we *must* chance it."

Andrev pulled at his ear in perplexity. "What do we do? The knowledge that a humanoid robot used a blaster in a crowd of human beings will not be taken well by Earth's people."

"Obviously, it wouldn't," said D.G. "Therefore, let's not tell them."

"A number of people must already know—or guess—that we are dealing with a robot."

"You won't stop the rumor, Secretary-General, but there is no need to make it more than that by means of an official announcement."

Andrev said, "If Aurora is willing to go to this extreme to—"

"Not Aurora," said Gladia quickly. "Merely certain people on Aurora, certain fire-eaters. There are such bellicose extremists among the Settlers, too, I know, and probably even on Earth. Don't play into the hands of these extremists, Secretary-General. I'm appealing to the vast majority of sensible human beings on both sides and nothing must be done to weaken that appeal."

Daneel, who had been waiting patiently, finally found a pause long enough to make it possible for him to insert his comment. "Madam Gladia —sirs—it is important to find out from this robot where on this planet he is based. There may be others."

"Haven't you asked him?" said Andrev.

"I have, Secretary-General, but I am a robot. This robot is not required to answer questions put to him by another robot. Nor is he required to follow my orders."

"Well, then, *I* will ask," said Andrev.

"That may not help, sir. The robot is under stringent orders not to answer and your order to answer will probably not overcome them. You do not know the proper phraseology and intonation. Madam Gladia is an Auroran and knows how this may be done. Madam Gladia, would you inquire as to where his planetary base might be?"

Giskard said in a low voice, so that only Daneel heard him, "It may not be possible. He may have been ordered into irreversible freeze if the questioning becomes too insistent."

Daneel's head turned sharply to Giskard. He whispered, "Can you prevent that?"

"Uncertain," said Giskard. "The brain has been physically damaged by the act of firing a blaster toward human beings."

Daneel turned back to Gladia. "Madam," he said, "I would suggest you be probing, rather than brutal."

Gladia said doubtfully, "Well, I don't know." She faced the robot assassin, drew a deep breath, and, in a voice that was firm yet soft and gentle, she said, "Robot, how may I address you?"

The robot said, "I am referrred to as R. Ernett Second, madam."

"Ernett, can you tell that I am an Auroran?"

"You speak in the Auroran fashion, yet not entirely, madam."

"I was born on Solaria, but I am a Spacer who has lived for twenty decades on Aurora and I am accustomed to being served by robots. I have expected and received service from robots every day of my life since I was a small child. I have never been disappointed."

"I accept the fact, madam."

"Will you answer my questions and accept my orders, Ernett?"

"I will, madam, if they are not counteracted by a competing order."

"If I ask you the location of your base on this planet—what portion of it you count as your master's establishment—will you answer that?"

"I may not do so, madam. Nor any other question with respect to my master. Any question at all."

"Do you understand that if you do not answer I will be bitterly disappointed and that my rightful expectation of robotic service will be permanently blunted?"

"I understand, madam," said the robot faintly.

Gladia looked at Daneel. "Shall I try?"

Daneel said, "There is no choice but to try, Madam Gladia. If the effort leaves us without information, we are no worse off than now."

Gladia said, in a voice that rang with authority, "Do not inflict damage on me, Ernett, by refusing to tell me the location of your base on this planet. I order you to tell me."

The robot seemed to stiffen. His mouth opened but made no sound. It opened again and he whispered huskily, ". . . mile . . ." It opened a third time silently—and then, while the mouth remained open, the gleam went out of the robot assassin's eyes and they became flat and waxen. One arm, which had been a little raised, dropped downward.

Daneel said, "The positronic brain has frozen."

Giskard whispered to Daneel only, "Irreversible! I did my best but could not hang on."

"We have nothing," said Andrev. "We don't know where the other robots might be."

D.G. said, "It said, 'mile.' "

"I do not recognize the word," said Daneel. "It is not Galactic Standard as the language is used on Aurora. Does it have meaning on Earth?"

Andrev said, rather blankly, "He might have been trying to say 'smile' or 'Miles.' I once knew a man whose first name was Miles."

Daneel said gravely, "I do not see how either word could make sense as an answer—or part of an answer—to the question. Nor did I hear any sibilance, either before or after the sound."

An elderly Earthman, who till now had remained silent, said, with a certain appearance of diffidence, "I am under the impression a mile may be an ancient measure of distance, robot."

"How long a measure, sir?" asked Daneel.

"I do not know," said the Earthman. "Longer than a kilometer, I believe."

"It isn't used any longer, sir?"

"Not since the prehyperspatial era."

D.G. pulled at his beard and he said thoughtfully, "It's still used. At least, we have an old saying on Baleyworld that goes, 'A miss is as good as a mile.' It is used to mean that, in avoiding misfortune, avoidance by a little is as good as avoidance by a great deal. I always thought 'mile' meant 'a great deal.' If it really represents a measure of distance, I can understand the phrase better."

Gladia said, "If that is so, the assassin may have been trying to say exactly that. He may have indicated his satisfaction that a miss—his deliberately missed shot—would accomplish what he was ordered to accomplish or, perhaps, that his missed shot, doing no harm, was equivalent to his not having fired at all."

"Madam Gladia," said Daneel, "a robot of Auroran manufacture would scarcely be using phrases that might exist on Baleyworld but have certainly never been heard on Aurora. And, in his damaged condition, he would not philosophize. He was asked a question and he would only be trying to answer the question."

"Ah," said Andrev, "perhaps he *was* trying to answer. He was trying to tell us that the base was a certain distance from here, for instance. So many miles."

"In that case," said D.G., "why should he use an archaic measure of distance? No Auroran would use anything but kilometers in this connection, nor would any robot of Auroran manufacture. In fact," he went on with an edge of impatience, "the robot was rapidly sinking into total inactivity and it might have been making nothing more than random sounds. It is useless to try to extract meaning from something that doesn't contain it. —And now I want to make sure that Madam Gladia gets some rest or that she is at least moved out of this room before the rest of the ceiling comes down."

They moved out quickly and Daneel, lingering behind for a moment, said softly to Giskard, "Again we fail!"

82.

THE CITY NEVER GREW entirely quiet, but there were periods when the lights were dimmer, the noise of the ever-moving Expressways was subdued, and the endless clatter of machinery and humanity subsided just a bit. In several million apartments people slept.

Gladia got into bed in the apartment assigned to her, uncomfortable over the missing amenities that she feared might force her out into the corridors during the night.

Was it night on the surface, she wondered just before falling asleep, or was it merely an arbitrary "sleep period" fixed within this particular cave of steel, in deference to a habit developed over the hundreds of millions of years that human beings and their ancestors had lived on the surface of the land.

And then she slept.

Daneel and Giskard did not sleep. Daneel, finding there was a computer outlet in the apartment, spent an absorbed half hour learning the unfamiliar key combinations by hit-and-miss. There were no instructions of any sort available (who needs instructions for what every youngster learns in grade school?) but, fortunately, the controls, while not the same as those of Aurora, were not wholly different either. Eventually, he was able to tune into the reference section of the City library and call up the encyclopedia. Hours passed.

At the lowest depth of the humans' sleep period, Giskard said, "Friend Daneel."

Daneel looked up. "Yes, friend Giskard."

"I must ask for an explanation of your actions on the balcony."

"Friend Giskard, you looked toward the crowd. I followed your glance, saw a weapon aimed in our direction, and reacted at once."

Giskard said, "So you did, friend Daneel, and, given certain assumptions, I can understand why it was me that you lunged forward to protect. Begin with the fact that the would-be assassin was a robot. In that case, however it might be programmed, it could not aim its weapon at any human being with the intention of hitting him or her. Nor was it likely to aim its weapon at you, for you look enough like a human being to activate the First Law. Even if the robot had been told that a humanoid robot would be on the balcony, he could not be certain that you were he. Therefore, if the robot intended to destroy someone on the balcony, it could only be me—the obvious robot—and you acted at once to protect me.

"Or begin with the fact that the assassin was an Auroran—whether human or robot does not matter. Dr. Amadiro is most likely to have ordered such an attack, since he is an extremist in his anti-Earth stand and, we believe, is plotting its destruction. Dr. Amadiro, we can be reasonably certain, has learned of my special abilities from Madam Vasilia and it might be argued that he would give my destruction top priority, since he would naturally fear me more than anyone else—robot or human. Reasoning this out, it would be logical for you to act as you did to protect me. —And, indeed, had you not knocked me down, I believe the blast would have destroyed me.

"But, friend Daneel, you could not possibly have known that the assassin was a robot or that he was Auroran. I myself had only just caught the strange anomaly of a robotic brain pattern against the vast blur of human emotion when you struck me—and it was only after that, that I had the chance of informing you. Without my ability, you could only be aware that a weapon was being aimed by what you must naturally have thought of as a human being and an Earthperson. The logical target, then, was Madam Gladia, as, in fact, everyone on the balcony assumed it to be. Why, then, did you ignore Madam Gladia and protect me, instead?"

Daneel said, "Friend Giskard, consider my line of thought. The Secretary-General had said that a two-man Auroran landing module had come to Earth's surface. I assumed at once that Dr. Amadiro and Dr. Mandamus had come to Earth. For this, there could be only one reason. The plan they have, whatever its nature, is at—or very nearly at—the point of maturity. Now that you have come to Earth, friend Giskard, they have dashed here to see it carried through at once before you have a chance to stop it with your mind-adjusting powers. To make matters doubly sure, they would act to destroy you if they could. Therefore, when I saw an aimed weapon, I moved at once to force you out of the line of fire."

Giskard said, "The First Law should have forced you to move Madam Gladia out of the line of fire. No thought, no reasoning, should have altered that."

"No, friend Giskard. You are more important than Madam Gladia is. You are, in fact, more important than any human being could be at this moment. If anyone at all can stop the destruction of Earth, you can. Since I am aware of your potential service to humanity, then, when I am confronted by a choice of action, the Zeroth Law demands that I protect you ahead of anyone else."

"And you do not feel uncomfortable at your having acted in defiance of the First Law."

"No, for I acted in obedience to the overriding Zeroth Law."

"But the Zeroth Law has not been imprinted into you."

"I have accepted it as a corollary of the First Law, for how can a human being best be kept from injury, if not by ensuring that human society in general is protected and kept functioning?"

Giskard thought a while. "I see what you are trying to say, but what if—in acting to save me and, therefore, in acting to save humanity—it had turned out that I was not aimed at and that Madam Gladia was killed? How would you have felt then, friend Daneel?"

Daneel said in a low tone, "I do not know, friend Giskard. Yet, had I leaped to save Madam Gladia and had it turned out that she was, in any case, safe and that I had allowed you to be destroyed and with you, in my opinion, the future of humanity, how could I have survived that blow?"

The two stared at each other—each, for a while, lost in thought.

Giskard said finally, "That may be so, friend Daneel, but do you agree, however, that judgment is difficult in such cases?"

"I agree, friend Giskard."

"It is difficult enough, when one must choose quickly between individuals, to decide which individual may suffer—or inflict—the greater harm. To choose between an individual and humanity, when you are not sure of what aspect of humanity you are dealing with, is so difficult that the very validity of Robotic Laws comes to be suspect. As soon as humanity in the abstract is introduced, the Laws of Robotics begin to merge with the Laws of Humanics—which may not even exist."

Daneel said, "I do not understand you, friend Giskard."

"I am not surprised. I am not certain I understand myself. But consider— When we think of the humanity we must save, we think of Earthpeople and the Settlers. They are more numerous than the Spacers, more vigorous, more expansive. They show more initiative because they are less dependent on robots. They have a greater potential for biological and social evolution because they are shorter-lived, though long-lived enough to contribute great things individually."

"Yes," said Daneel, "you put it succinctly."

"And yet the Earthpeople and the Settlers seem to possess a mystical and even irrational confidence in the sanctity and inviolability of Earth. Might not this mystique be as fatal to their development as the mystiques of robots and long life that hobble the Spacers?"

"I had not thought of this," said Daneel. "I do not know."

Giskard said, "If you were as aware of minds as I am, you would have been unable to avoid thinking of this. —How does one choose?" he went on with sudden intensity. "Think of humanity as divided into two species: the Spacers, with one apparently fatal mystique, and the Earthpeople plus the Settlers, with another possibly fatal mystique. It may be that there will be other species, in the future, with even less attractive properties.

"It is not sufficient to choose, then, friend Daneel. We must be able to shape. We must shape a desirable species and then protect it, rather than finding ourselves forced to select among two or more undesirabilities. But how can we achieve the desirable unless we have psychohistory, the science I dream of and cannot attain?"

Daneel said, "I have not appreciated the difficulty, friend Giskard, of possessing the ability to sense and influence minds. Is it possible that you learn too much to allow the Three Laws of Robotics to work smoothly within you?"

"That has always been possible, friend Daneel, but not until these recent events has the possibility become actual. I know the pathway pattern that produces this mind-sensing and mind-influencing effect within me. I have studied myself carefully for decades in order that I might know it and I can pass it on to you so that you might program yourself to be like me—but I have resisted the urge to do so. It would be unkind to you. It is enough that I bear the burden."

Daneel said, "Nevertheless, friend Giskard, if ever, in your judgment, the good of humanity would require it, I would accept the burden. Indeed, by the Zeroth Law, I would be obliged to."

Giskard said, "But this discussion is useless. It seems apparent that the crisis is nearly upon us—and since we have not even managed to work out the nature of the crisis—"

Daneel interrupted. "You are wrong, there at least, friend Giskard. I now know the nature of the crisis."

83.

ONE WOULD NOT EXPECT Giskard to show surprise. His face was, of course, incapable of expression. His voice possessed modulation, so that his speech sounded human and was neither monotonous nor unpleasant. That modulation, however, was never altered by emotion in any recognizable way.

Therefore, when he said, "Are you serious?" it sounded as it would have had he expressed doubt over a remark Daneel had made concerning what the weather would be like the next day. Yet, from the manner in which his head turned toward Daneel, the way in which one hand lifted, there was no doubt that he was surprised.

Daneel said, "I am, friend Giskard."

"How did the information come to you?"

"In part, from what I was told by Madam Undersecretary Quintana at the dinner table."

"But did you not say that you had obtained nothing helpful from her, that you supposed you had asked the wrong questions?"

"So it seemed in the immediate aftermath. On further reflection, however, I found myself able to make helpful deductions from what she had said. I have been searching Earth's central encyclopedia through the computer outlet these past few hours—"

"And found your deductions confirmed?"

"Not exactly, but I found nothing that would refute them, which is perhaps the next best thing."

"But is negative evidence sufficient for certainty?"

"It is not. And therefore I am not certain. Let me tell you, however, my reasoning and if you find it faulty, say so."

"Please proceed, friend Daneel."

"Fusion power, friend Giskard, was developed on Earth before the days of hyperspatial travel and, therefore, while human beings were to be found only on the one planet, Earth. This is well known. It took a long time to develop practical controlled fusion power after the possibility had first been conceived and put on a sound scientific footing. The chief difficulty in converting the concept into practice involved the necessity of achieving a sufficiently high temperature in a sufficiently dense gas for a long enough time to bring about fusion ignition.

"And yet several decades before controlled fusion power had been established, fusion bombs had existed—these bombs representing an uncontrolled fusion reaction. But controlled or uncontrolled, fusion could not take place without an extremely high temperature in the millions of degrees. If human beings could not produce the necessary temperature for controlled fusion power, how could they do so for an uncontrolled fusion explosion?

"Madam Quintana told me that before fusion existed on Earth, there was another variety of nuclear reaction in existence—nuclear fission. Energy was derived from the splitting—or fission—of large nuclei, such as those of uranium and thorium. That, I thought, might be one way of achieving a high temperature.

"The encyclopedia I have this night been consulting gives very little information about nuclear bombs of any sort and, certainly, no real details. It is a taboo subject, I gather, and it must be so on all worlds, for I have never read of such details on Aurora either, even though such bombs still exist. It is a part of history that human beings are ashamed of, or afraid of, or both and I think this is rational. In what I did read of fusion bombs, however, I read nothing about their ignition that would have eliminated the fission bomb as the igniting mechanism. I suspect, then, that based, in part, on this negative evidence, the fission bomb was the igniting mechanism.

"But, then, how was the fission bomb ignited? Fission bombs existed before fusion bombs and if fission bombs required an ultrahigh temperature for ignition, as fusion bombs did, then there was nothing that existed before fission bombs that would supply a high enough temperature. From this, I conclude—even though the encyclopedia contained no information on the subject—that fission bombs could be ignited at relatively low temperatures, perhaps even at room temperature. There were difficulties involved, for it took several years of unremitting effort after the discovery that fission existed before the bomb was developed. Whatever those difficulties might have been, however, they did not involve the production of ultrahigh temperatures. —Your opinion of all this, friend Giskard?"

Giskard had kept his eyes steadily on Daneel throughout his explanation and he now said, "I think the structure you have built up has serious weak points, friend Daneel, and therefore may not be very trustworthy—but even if it were all perfectly sound, surely this has nothing to do with the possible forthcoming crisis that we are laboring to understand."

Daneel said, "I plead for your patience, friend Giskard, and I will continue. As it happens, both the fusion process and the fission process are expressions of the weak interactions, one of the four interactions that control all events in the Universe. Consequently, the same nuclear intensifier that will explode a fusion reactor will also explode a fission reactor.

"There is, however, a difference. Fusion takes place only at ultrahigh temperatures. The intensifier explodes the ultrahot portion of the fuel that is actively undergoing fusion, plus some of the surrounding fuel that is heated to fusion in the initial explosion—before the material is blown explosively outward and the heat is dissipated to the point where other quantities of fuel present are not ignited. Some of the fusion fuel is exploded, in other words, but a good deal—perhaps even most—is not. The explosion is powerful enough even so, of course, to destroy the fusion reactor and anything in its immediate neighborhood, such as a ship carrying the reactor.

"On the other hand, a fission reactor can operate at low temperatures, perhaps not much above the boiling point of water, perhaps even at room temperature. The effect of the nuclear intensifier, then, will be to make *all* the fission fuel go. Indeed, even if the fission reactor is *not* actively working, the intensifier will explode it. Although, gram for gram, I gather that fission fuel liberates less energy than fusion fuel, the fission reactor will produce the greater explosion because more of its fuel explodes than in the case of the fusion reactor."

Giskard nodded his head slowly and said, "All this may well be so, friend Daneel, but are there any fission power stations on Earth?"

"No, there aren't—not one. So Undersecretary Quintana seemed to indicate and the encyclopedia seems to agree. Indeed, whereas there are devices on Earth that are powered by small fusion reactors, there is nothing— nothing at all—that is powered by fission reactors, large or small."

"Then, friend Daneel, there is nothing for a nuclear intensifier to act upon. All your reasoning, even were it impeccable, ends in nothing."

Daneel said earnestly, "Not quite, friend Giskard. There remains a third type of nuclear reaction to be taken into consideration."

Giskard said, "What might that be? I cannot think of a third."

"It is not an easy thought, friend Giskard, for on the Spacer and Settler worlds, there is very little uranium and thorium in the planetary crusts and, therefore, very little in the way of obvious radioactivity. The subject is of little interest, in consequence, and is ignored by all but a few theoretical physicists. On Earth, however, as Madam Quintana pointed out to me, uranium and thorium are comparatively common, and natural radioactivity, with its ultraslow production of heat and energetic radiation, must therefore be a comparatively prominent part of the environment. That is the third type of nuclear reaction to be taken into consideration."

"In what way, friend Daneel?"

"Natural radioactivity is also an expression of the weak interaction. A nuclear intensifier that can explode a fusion reactor or a fission reactor can also accelerate natural radioactivity to the point, I presume, of exploding a section of the crust—if enough uranium or thorium is present."

Giskard stared at Daneel for a period of time without moving or speaking. Then he said softly, "You suggest, then, that it is Dr. Amadiro's plan to explode Earth's crust, destroy the planet as an abode of life, and, in this way, ensure the domination of the Galaxy by the Spacers."

Daneel nodded. "Or, if there is not enough thorium and uranium for mass explosion, the increase of radioactivity may produce excess heat that will alter the climate, and excess radiations that will produce cancer and birth defects, and these will serve the same purpose—if a bit more slowly."

Giskard said, "This is an appalling possibility. Do you think it can really be brought about?"

"Possibly. It seems to me that for several years now—just how many I do not know—humanoid robots from Aurora, such as the would-be assassin—have been on Earth. They are advanced enough for complex programming and are capable, when needed, of entering the Cities for equipment. They have, it is to be presumed, been setting up nuclear intensifiers in places where the soil is rich in uranium or thorium. Perhaps many intensifiers have been set up over the years. Dr. Amadiro and Dr. Mandamus are here now to oversee the final details and to activate the intensifiers. Presumably, they are arranging matters so that they will have time to escape before the planet is destroyed."

"In that case," said Giskard, "it is imperative that the Secretary-General be informed, that Earth's security forces be mobilized at once, that Dr. Amadiro and Dr. Mandamus be located without delay, and that they be restrained from completing their project."

Daneel said, "I do not think that can be done. The Secretary-General is very likely to refuse to believe us, thanks to the widespread mystical belief in the inviolability of the planet. You have referred to that as something that would work against humanity and I suspect that is just what it will do in this case. If his belief in the unique position of Earth is challenged, he will refuse to allow his conviction, however irrational, to be shaken and he will seek refuge by refusing to believe us.

"Then, too, even if he believed us, any preparation for counter-measures would have to go through the governmental bureaucracy and, no matter how that process was speeded, it would take far too long to serve its purpose.

"Not only that but, even if we could imagine the full resources of Earth mobilized at once, I do not think Earthpeople are adapted to locate the presence of two human beings in an enormous wilderness. The Earthpeople have lived in the Cities for many scores of decades and almost never venture beyond the City confines. I remember that well from the occasion of my first case with Elijah Baley here on Earth. And even if Earthpeople could force themselves to tramp the open spaces, they are not likely to come across the two human beings soon enough to save the situation except by the most incredible of coincidences—and that is something we cannot count upon."

Giskard said, "Settlers could easily form a search party. They are not afraid of open environments or of strange ones."

"But they would be as firmly convinced in the planet's inviolability as Earthpeople are, just as insistent on refusing to believe us, and just as unlikely to find the two human beings quickly enough to save the situation —even if they *should* believe us."

"What of Earth's robots, then?" said Giskard. "They swarm in the spaces between the Cities. Some should already be aware of human beings in their midst. They should be questioned."

Daneel said, "The human beings in their midst are expert roboticists. They would not have failed to see to it that any robots in their vicinity remain unaware of their presence. Nor, for this same reason, need they fear danger from any robots who might be part of a searching party. The party will be ordered to depart and forget. To make it worse, Earth's robots are comparatively simple models, designed for very little more than for specific tasks in growing crops, herding animals, and operating mines. They cannot easily be adapted to such a general purpose as conducting a meaningful search."

Giskard said, "You have eliminated every possible action, friend Daneel? Does anything remain?"

Daneel said, "We must find the two human beings ourselves and we must stop them—and we must do it now."

"Do you know where they are, friend Daneel?"

"I do not, friend Giskard."

"Then if it seems unlikely that an elaborate search party composed of many, many Earthpeople, or Settlers, or robots, or, I presume, all three, could succeed in finding their location in time except by the most marvelous of coincidences, how can we two do so?"

"I do not know, friend Giskard, but we must."

And Giskard said, in a voice that seemed to have an edge of harshness in its choice of words, "Necessity is not enough, friend Daneel. You have come a long way. You have worked out the existence of a crisis and, bit by bit, you have worked out its nature. And none of it serves. Here we remain, as helpless as ever to do anything about it."

Daneel said, "There remains one chance—a farfetched one, an all-but-useless one—but we have no choice except to try. Out of Amadiro's fear of you, he sent an assassin robot to destroy you and that *may* turn out to have been his mistake."

"And if that all-but-useless chance fails, friend Daneel?"

Daneel looked calmly at Giskard. "Then we are helpless, and Earth will be destroyed, and human history will dwindle to an eventual end."

Chapter 18

The Zeroth Law

84.

KELDEN AMADIRO WAS NOT HAPPY. The surface gravity of Earth was a trifle too high for his liking, the atmosphere a trifle too dense, the sound and the odor of the outdoors subtly and annoyingly different from that on Aurora, and there was no indoors that could make any pretense of being civilized.

The robots had built shelters of a sort. There were ample food supplies and there were makeshift privies that were functionally adequate but offensively inadequate in every other way.

Worst of all, though the morning was pleasant enough, it was a clear day and Earth's too-bright sun was rising. Soon the temperature would be too high, the air would be too damp, and the biting insects would appear. Amadiro had not understood, at first, why there should be small itching swellings on his arms till Mandamus explained.

Now he mumbled, as he scratched, "Dreadful! They might carry infections."

"I believe," said Mandamus with apparent indifference, "that they sometimes do. It isn't likely, however. I have lotions to relieve the discomfort and we can burn certain substances that the insects find offensive, although I find the odors offensive, too."

"Burn them," said Amadiro.

Mandamus continued, without changing tone, "And I don't want to do anything, however trifling—an odor, a bit of smoke—that would increase the chance of our being detected."

Amadiro eyed him suspiciously. "You have said, over and over, that this region is never visited by either Earthpeople or their field robots."

"That's right, but it's not a mathematical proposition. It's a sociological observation and there is always the possibility of exceptions to such observations."

Amadiro scowled. "The best road to safety lies with being done with this project. You said you'd be ready today."

"That, too, is a sociological observation, Dr. Amadiro. I *should* be ready today. I would like to be. I cannot guarantee it mathematically."

"How long before you *can* guarantee it?"

Mandamus spread his hands in a "Who knows?" gesture. "Dr. Amadiro, I am under the impression I have already explained this, but I'm willing to go through it again. It took me seven years to get this far. I have been counting on some months yet of personal observations at the fourteen different relay stations on Earth's surface. I can't do that now because we must finish before we are located and, possibly, stopped by the robot Giskard. That means I have to do my checking by communicating with our own humanoid robots at the relays. I can't trust them as I would myself. I must check and recheck their reports and it is possible that I may have to go to one or two places before I am satisfied. That would take days—perhaps a week or two."

"A week or two. Impossible! How long do you think I can endure this planet, Mandamus?"

"Sir, on one of my previous visits I stayed on this planet for nearly a year —on another, for over four months."

"And you liked it?"

"No, sir, but I had a job to do and I did it—without sparing myself." Mandamus stared coldly at Amadiro.

Amadiro flushed and said in a somewhat chastened tone, "Well, then, where do we stand?"

"I'm still weighing the reports that are coming in. We are not working with a smoothly designed laboratory-made system, you know. We have an extraordinarily heterogeneous planetary crust to deal with. Fortunately, the radioactive materials are widely spread, but in places they run perilously thin and we must place a relay in such places and leave robots in charge. If those relays are not, in every case, properly positioned and in proper order, the nuclear intensification will die out and we will have wasted all these painful years of effort on nothing. Or else, there may be a surge of localized intensification that will have the force of an explosion that will blow itself out and leave the rest of the crust unaffected. In either case, total damage would be insignificant.

"What we want, Dr. Amadiro, is to have the radioactive materials and, therefore, significantly large sections of Earth's crust grow—slowly—steadily—irreversibly"—he bit the words off as he pronounced them in spaced intervals—"more and more intensely radioactive, so that Earth becomes progressively more unlivable. The social structure of the planet will break down and the Earth, as an effective abode of humanity, will be over and done with. I take it, Dr. Amadiro, that this is what you want. It is what I described to you years ago and what you said, at that time, you wanted."

"I still do, Mandamus. Don't be a fool."

"Then bear with the discomfort, sir—or else, leave and I will carry on for whatever additional time it takes."

"No, no," muttered Amadiro. "I must be here when it's done—but I can't help being impatient. How long have you decided to allow the process to build? —I mean, once you initiate the original wave of intensification, how long before Earth becomes uninhabitable?"

"That depends on the degree of intensification I apply initially. I don't know, just yet, what degree will be required, for that depends on the overall efficiency of the relays, so I have prepared a variable control. What I want to arrange is a lapse period of ten to twenty decades."

"And if you allow a smaller lapse period?"

"The less the lapse period we allow, the more rapidly portions of the crust will grow radioactive and the more rapidly the planet will warm up and grow dangerous. And that means the less likely it will be that any significant number of its population can be removed in time."

"Does that matter?" murmured Amadiro.

Mandamus frowned. "The more rapidly the Earth deteriorates, the more likely it is that Earthpeople and Settlers will suspect a technological cause—and that we are the likely ones to receive the blame. The Settlers will then attack us with fury and, in the cause of their holy world, they will fight to extinction, provided only that they can inflict substantial harm on us. This is something we have discussed before and it seems we agreed on the matter. It would be far better to allow ample time, during which we can prepare for the worst and during which a confused Earth may assume that the slowly increasing radioactivity is some natural phenomenon they don't understand. That is something that has become more urgent today than yesterday, in my judgment."

"Is that so?" Amadiro was frowning also. "You have that sour, puritanical look that makes me sure you have found a way to place the responsibility for that on my shoulders."

"With respect, sir, that is not difficult in this case. It was unwise to send out one of our robots to destroy Giskard."

"On the contrary, it had to be done. Giskard is the only one who might destroy us."

"He must find us first—and he won't. And even if he does, we are knowledgeable roboticists. Don't you think we could handle him?"

"Indeed?" said Amadiro. "So Vasilia thought and she knew Giskard better than we—and yet *she* couldn't handle him. And somehow the warship that was to take him into charge and destroy him at a distance could not handle him. So he has now landed on Earth. One way or another, he must be destroyed."

"He has not been. There has been no report of it."

"Bad news is sometimes repressed by a prudent government—and Earth officials, though barbarians, might conceivably be prudent. And if our robot failed and was questioned, he would certainly go into irreversible block. That means we will have lost a robot, something we can afford to do, but nothing more. And if Giskard should still be at large, the more reason we have to hurry."

"If we have lost a robot, we have lost more than a robot if they manage to elicit the location of this center of operations. We ought, at least, not to have used a local robot."

"I used one that was immediately available. And he will reveal nothing. You can trust my programming, I think."

"He cannot help reveal, by his mere existence, whether frozen or not, that he is of Auroran manufacture. Earth roboticists—and there are some on this planet—will be sure of that. All the more reason to make the increase in radioactivity very slow. Enough time must pass so that Earth-people forget the incident and don't associate it with the progressive change in radioactivity. We must have ten decades at the very least, perhaps fifteen, or even twenty."

He walked away to inspect his instruments again and to re-establish contact with relays six and ten, which he still found troublesome. Amadiro looked after him with a mixture of disdain and intense dislike and muttered to himself, "Yes, but I don't have twenty more decades, or fifteen, or maybe even ten. You do—but I don't."

85.

It was early morning in New York. Giskard and Daneel assumed that from the gradual heightening of activity.

"Somewhere above and outside the City," said Giskard, "it may be dawn now. Once, in speaking to Elijah Baley twenty decades ago, I referred to Earth as the World of the Dawn. Will it continue to be so for much longer? Or has it already ceased to be that?"

"These are morbid thoughts, friend Giskard," said Daneel. "It will be better if we occupy ourselves with what must be done on this day to help keep Earth the World of the Dawn."

Gladia entered the apartment, wearing a bathrobe and slippers. Her hair was freshly dried.

"Ridiculous!" she said. "Earthwomen go through the corridors on their way to the mass Personals in the morning disheveled and slatternly. It is done on purpose, I think. It is bad manners to comb one's hair on the way to the Personal. Apparently, dishevelment to begin with enhances that well-cared-for look afterward. I should have brought a complete morning outfit with me. You should have seen the looks I got when I left with my bathrobe on. Leaving the Personal, one must be the last word. —Yes, Daneel?"

"Madam," said Daneel. "May we have a word with you?"

Gladia hesitated. "Not much of a word, Daneel. As you are probably aware, this is going to be a big day and my morning appointments begin almost at once."

"That is precisely what I wish to discuss, madam," said Daneel. "On this important day, all will go better if we are not with you."

"What?"

"The effect you would wish to have on Earthpeople would be greatly diminished if you surround yourself with robots."

"I will not be surrounded. There will be just you two. How can I do without you?"

"It is necessary that you learn to, madam. While we are with you, you are marked off as different from Earthpeople. You are made to seem afraid of them."

Gladia said, troubled, "I need *some* protection, Daneel. Remember what happened last night."

"Madam, we could not have prevented what happened last night and we could not have protected you—if that were necessary. Fortunately, you were not the target last night. The blaster bolt was aimed at Giskard's head."

"Why Giskard?"

"How could a robot aim at you or at any human being? The robot aimed at Giskard for some reason. For us to be near you, then, might but increase your danger. Remember that as the tale of last night's events spreads, even though the Earth government may try to suppress the details, there will be a rumor to the effect that it was a robot who held a blaster and fired it. That will arouse public indignation against robots—against *us*—and even against *you* if you persist in being seen with us. It would be better if you were without us."

"For how long?"

"For at least as long as your mission lasts, madam. The captain will be better able to help you in the days to come than we will be. He knows Earthpeople, he is highly thought of by them—and he thinks very highly of you, madam."

Gladia said, "Can you *tell* that he thinks very highly of me?"

"Although I am a robot, it would seem so to me. And at any time that you should wish us back, we will come back, of course—but, for now, we think that the best way we can serve and protect you is to leave you in Captain Baley's hands."

Gladia said, "I will think of it."

"In the meanwhile, madam," said Daneel, "we will see Captain Baley and find out if he agrees with us."

"Do so!" said Gladia and passed into her bedroom.

Daneel turned and spoke minimally to Giskard. "Is she willing?"

"More than willing," said Giskard. "She has always been a little restless in my presence and would not suffer unduly at my absence. For you, friend Daneel, she has ambivalent feelings. You remind her markedly of friend Jander, whose inactivation, many decades ago, was so traumatic for her. This has been a source of both attraction and repulsion to her, so it was not necessary to do much. I lessened her attraction to you and increased her strong attraction to the captain. She will do without us easily."

"Then let us find the captain," said Daneel. Together, they left the room and entered the hallway that passed by the apartment.

86.

DANEEL AND GISKARD had both been on Earth on previous occasions, Giskard the more recently. They understood the use of the computerized directory that gave them the Section, Wing, and number of the apartment to which D.G. had been assigned and they understood, further, the color codes in the hallways that led them to the proper turnings and elevators.

It was early enough for the human traffic to be light, but those human beings who passed or approached at first stared with astonishment at Giskard, then looked away with elaborate unconcern.

Giskard's steps were slightly uneven by the time they approached D.G.'s apartment door. It was not very noticeable, but it caught Daneel's attention.

He said in a low voice, "Are you in discomfort, friend Giskard?"

Giskard replied, "It has been necessary for me to wipe out astonishment, apprehension, and even attention in a number of men and women—and in one youngster, which was harder still. I had no time to make completely certain I was doing no harm."

"It was important to do so. We must not be stopped."

"I understand that, but the Zeroth Law does not work well with me. I have not your facility in that respect." He went on, as though to distract his own attention from his discomfort, "I have often noted that hyperresistance in the positronic pathways makes itself first felt in the matter of standing and walking and next in speech."

Daneel tapped the door signal. He said, "It is the same in my case, friend Giskard. Maintaining balance on two supports is difficult under the best of circumstances. Controlled imbalance, as in walking, is even more difficult. I have heard once that there were early attempts made to produce robots with four legs and two arms. They were called 'centaurs.' They worked well but were unacceptable because they were basically inhuman in appearance."

"At the moment," said Giskard, "I would appreciate four legs, friend Daneel. However, I think my discomfort is passing."

D.G. was at the door now. He looked at them with a broad smile. He then glanced in each direction along the corridor, whereupon his smile vanished and was replaced with a look of the utmost concern. "What are you doing here without Gladia? Is she—"

Daneel said, "Captain, Madam Gladia is well. She is in no danger. May we enter and explain?"

D.G. glowered as he gestured them inside. His voice gained the hectoring tone one naturally assumes toward misbehaving machines and he said, "Why have you left her alone? What circumstances could possibly permit you to leave her alone?"

Daneel said, "She is no more alone than any person is on Earth—and no more in danger. If you will question her later on the matter, I believe she will tell you that she cannot be effective here on Earth as long as she is trailed by Spacer robots. I believe she will tell you that what guidance and protection she needs should be supplied by you, rather than by robots. It is what we believe she wishes—at least for now. If, at any time, she wishes us back, she will have us."

D.G.'s face relaxed into a smile again. "She wants my protection, does she?"

"At the moment, Captain, we believe she is quite anxious for your presence, rather than for ours."

D.G.'s smile became a grin. "Who can blame her? —I'll get myself ready and go to her apartment as soon as I can."

"But first, sir—"

"Oh," said D.G., "there is a quid pro quo?"

"Yes, sir. We are anxious to discover as much as we can about the robot who fired the blaster at the balcony last night."

D.G. looked tense again. "Do you anticipate further danger for Madam Gladia?"

"None at all of that kind. The robot, last night, did not fire at Lady Gladia. Being a robot, he could not have. He fired at friend Giskard."

"Why should he have done that?"

"It is what we would like to find out. For that purpose, we wish you to call Madam Quintana, Undersecretary of Energy, and state that it would be important and would please you and the government of Baleyworld—if you would care to add that—for her to allow me to ask her a few questions on that subject. We wish you to do whatever seems best to persuade her to agree to such an interview."

"Is that all you want me to do? Persuade a reasonably important and busy official to submit to cross-examination by a robot?"

Daneel said, "Sir, she may agree if you are earnest enough in the request. In addition, since she may be located a distance away, it would be helpful if you would hire a darter on our behalf to take us there. We are, as you can imagine, in haste."

"And are those little things all?" asked D.G.

"Not quite, Captain," said Daneel. "We will need a driver and please pay him well enough so that he will consent to transport friend Giskard, who is an obvious robot. He may not mind me."

D.G. said, "I hope you realize, Daneel, that what you ask is completely unreasonable."

Daneel said, "I had hoped not, Captain. But since you tell me it is, there is nothing more to say. We have no choice, then, but to return to Madam Gladia, which will make her unhappy, for she would rather be with you."

He turned to leave, motioning Giskard to accompany him, but D.G. said, "Wait. There's a public communication contact just down the hallway. I can only try. Remain here and wait for me."

The two robots remained standing. Daneel said, "Did you have to do much, friend Giskard?"

Giskard seemed well balanced on his legs now. He said, "I was helpless. He was strongly opposed to dealing with Madam Quintana and as strongly opposed to getting us a darter. I could not have altered those feelings without damage. When, however, you suggested returning to Madam Gladia, his attitude changed suddenly and dramatically. You were anticipating that, I take it, friend Daneel?"

"I was."

"You scarcely need me, it would seem. There is more than one way of adjusting minds. However, I ended by doing something. The captain's change of mind was accompanied by a strong favorable emotion toward Madam Gladia. I took the opportunity of strengthening that."

"That is the reason you are needed. I could not have done that."

"You will be able to yet, friend Daneel. Perhaps quite soon."

D.G. returned. "Believe it or not, she will see you, Daneel. The darter and driver will be here in a moment—and the sooner you leave, the better. I will be heading toward Gladia's apartment at once."

The two robots stepped outside in the hallway to wait.

Giskard said, "He is very happy."

"So it would seem, friend Giskard," said Daneel, "but I fear the easy part is over for us. We have easily arranged to have Madam Gladia grant us leave to move about on our own. We have then, with some difficulty, persuaded the captain to make it possible for us to see the Undersecretary. With her, however, it may be that we will come to a dead end."

87.

THE DRIVER TOOK ONE LOOK at Giskard and his courage seemed to fail him. "Listen," he said to Daneel, "I was told I'd be paid double to take a robot, but robots aren't allowed in the City and I could get in plenty of trouble. Money isn't going to help me if I lose my license. Can't I just take you, mister?"

Daneel said, "I am a robot, too, sir. We are now *in* the City and that is not your fault. We are trying to get *out* of the City and you will be helping us. We are going to a high government official who, I hope, will arrange that and it is your civic duty to help us. If you refuse to take us, driver, you will be acting to keep robots *in* the City and that may be considered to be against the law."

The driver's face smoothed. He opened the door and said gruffly, "Get in!" However, he carefully closed the thick translucent partition that blocked him off from his passengers.

Daneel said quietly, "Was much required, friend Giskard?"

"Very little, friend Daneel. Your statement did most of the necessary work. It is astonishing that a collection of statements that are individually true can be used, in combination, to yield an effect that the truth should not."

"I have observed this often in human conversation, friend Giskard, even in that of normally truthful human beings. I suspect that the practice is justified in the minds of such people as serving a higher purpose."

"The Zeroth Law, you mean."

"Or the equivalent—if the human mind has such an equivalent. —Friend Giskard, you said a short while ago that I will have your powers, possibly soon. Are you preparing me for that purpose?"

"I am, friend Daneel."

"Why? May I ask that?"

"The Zeroth Law again. The passing episode of shakiness on my feet told me how vulnerable I was to the attempted use of the Zeroth Law. Before this day is over, I may have to act on the Zeroth Law to save the world and humanity and I may not be able to. In that case, you must be in position to do the job. I am preparing you, bit by bit, so that, at the desired moment, I can give you the final instructions and have it all fall into place."

"I do not see how that can be, friend Giskard."

"You will have no trouble in understanding when the time comes. I used the technique in a very small way on robots I sent to Earth in the early days before they were outlawed from the Cities and it was they who helped adjust Earth leaders to the point of approving the decision to send out Settlers."

The driver, whose darter was not on wheels but remained a centimeter or so above the ground at all times, had moved along special corridors reserved for such vehicles and had done so speedily enough to justify the name of the vehicle. He now emerged into an ordinary City corridor, which was paralleled on the moderately distant left by an Expressway. The darter, moving now much more slowly, made a left turn, swooped under the Expressway, came out on the other side, and then, a curving half-mile later, stopped before an ornate building front.

The darter door opened automatically. Daneel emerged first, waited for Giskard to follow, then handed to the driver a piece of foil he had received from D.G. The driver looked at it narrowly, then the doors closed sharply and he left speedily without a word.

88.

THERE WAS A PAUSE BEFORE the door opened in response to their signal and Daneel assumed they were being scanned. When it did open, a young woman led them gingerly into the vitals of the building. She avoided looking at Giskard, but she showed rather more than a mild curiosity in Daneel.

They found Undersecretary Quintana behind a large desk. She smiled and said, with a gaiety that seemed somewhat forced, "Two robots, unescorted by human beings. Am I safe?"

"Entirely, Madam Quintana," said Daneel gravely. "It is as unusual for us to see a human being unaccompanied by robots."

"I assure you," said Quintana, "I have my robots. I call them underlings and one of them escorted you here. I am amazed that she didn't faint at the sight of Giskard. I think she might have if she hadn't been warned and if you yourself weren't so extraordinarily interesting in appearance, Daneel. But never mind that. Captain Baley was so enormously pressing in his desire that I see you and my interest in maintaining comfortable relations with an important Settler world was such that I have agreed to the interview. However, my day remains busy even so and I will be grateful if we can dispose of this quickly. —What can I do for you?"

"Madam Quintana—" began Daneel.

"One moment. Do you sit? I saw you sitting last night, you know."

"We can sit, but it is just as comfortable for us to stand. We do not mind."

"But I do. It would not be comfortable for me to stand—and if I sit, I will get a stiff neck looking up at you. Please pull up chairs and sit down. Thank you. —Now, Daneel, what is this all about?"

"Madam Quintana," said Daneel, "you remember, I imagine, the incident of the blaster fired at the balcony last night after the banquet."

"I certainly do. What's more, I know it was a humanoid robot who held the blaster, even though we are not admitting that officially. Yet here I sit with two robots on the other side of the desk and have no protection. And one of you is humanoid, too."

"I have no blaster, madam," said Daneel, smiling.

"I trust not. —That other humanoid robot did not look at all like you, Daneel. You're rather a work of art, do you know that?"

"I am complexly programmed, madam."

"I mean, your appearance. But what about the blasting incident?"

"Madam, that robot has a base somewhere on Earth and I must know where it is. I have come from Aurora in order to find that base and prevent such incidents as may disturb the peace between our worlds. I have reason to believe—"

"*You* have come? Not the captain? Not Madam Gladia?"

"*We,* madam," said Daneel. "Giskard and I. I am in no position to tell you the whole story of how we came to have undertaken the task and there is no way in which I can tell you the name of the human being under whose instructions we work."

"Well! International espionage! How fascinating. What a pity I can't help you, but I don't know where the robot came from. I haven't any idea at all where his base might be. I don't even know why you have come to me for such information, as a matter of fact. I should have gone to the Department of Security had I been you, Daneel." She leaned toward him. "Do you have *real* skin on your face, Daneel? It's an extraordinary imitation if it isn't." She reached toward him and her hand rested delicately on his cheek. "It even feels right."

"Nevertheless, madam, it is not real skin. It does not heal of its own accord—if cut. On the other hand, a tear can easily be welded closed or a patch can even be replaced."

"Ugh," said Quintana, with a wrinkle of her nose. "But our business is over, for I can't help you as far as that blaster user is concerned. I know nothing."

Daneel said, "Madam, let me explain further. This robot may be part of a group that is interested in the early energy-producing process you described last night—fission. Assume this is so, that there are those interested in fission and in the content of uranium and thorium in the crust. What might be a convenient place for them to use as a base?"

"An old uranium mine, perhaps? I don't even know where one might be located. You must understand, Daneel, that Earth has an almost superstitious aversion to anything nuclear—to fission, in particular. You'll find almost nothing about fission in our popular works on energy and only bare essentials in technical productions for experts. Even I know very little, but then I'm an administrator, not a scientist."

Daneel said, "One more item, then, madam. We questioned the would-be assassin as to the location of his base and did so most strenuously. He was programmed to undergo permanent inactivation, a total freezing of his brain paths, in such a case—and he *did* inactivate. Before doing so, however, in his final struggle between answering and inactivation, he opened his mouth three times as though—possibly—to say three syllables, or three words, or three groups of words, or any combination of these. The second syllable, or word, or mere sound was 'mile.' Does this mean anything to you as having anything at all to do with fission?"

Slowly Quintana shook her head. "No. I can't say it does. It's certainly not a word you'll find in a dictionary of Standard Galactic. I'm sorry, Daneel. It's pleasant meeting you again, but I have a desk full of trivia to work through. You'll excuse me."

Daneel said, as though he hadn't heard her, "I was told, madam, that 'mile' might be an archaic expression that refers to some ancient unit of length, one that is possibly longer than a kilometer."

"That sounds totally irrelevant," said Quintana, "even if true. What would a robot from Aurora know about archaic expressions and ancient—" She stopped abruptly. Her eyes widened and her face lost color.

She said, "Is it possible?"

"Is what possible, madam?" asked Daneel.

"There is a place," said Quintana, half-lost in thought, "that is avoided by everyone—Earthpeople and Earth robots alike. If I wanted to be dramatic, I would say it was a place of ill omen. It is so ill-omened that it has been all but wiped out of conscious existence. It is not even included in maps. It is the quintessence of all that fission means. I remember coming across it in a very old reference film in my early days on this job. It was talked about constantly then as the site of an 'incident' that forever turned the minds of Earthpeople against fission as an energy source. The place is called Three Mile Island."

Daneel said, "An isolated place, then, absolutely isolated and free from any possible intrusion; the sort of place one would surely come across when working one's way through ancient reference material on fission and would then recognize at once as an ideal base where absolute secrecy was required; and with a three-word name of which 'mile' is the second word. That *must* be the place, madam. —Could you tell us how to get there and could you arrange some way of allowing us to leave the City and be taken to Three Mile Island or its nearest possible vicinity?"

Quintana smiled. She seemed younger when she smiled. "Clearly, if you are dealing with an interesting case of interstellar espionage, you can't afford to waste time, can you?"

"No. Indeed we cannot, madam."

"Well, then, it comes within the purview of my duties to take a look at Three Mile Island. Why don't I take you by air-car? I can handle an air-car."

"Madam, your work load—"

"No one will touch it. It will still be here when I return."

"But you would be leaving the City—"

"And if so? These are not old times. In the bad old days of Spacer domination, Earthpeople never left their Cities, it's true, but we've been moving outward and settling the Galaxy for nearly twenty decades. There are still some of the less educated who maintain the old provincial attitude, but most of us have become quite mobile. There's always the feeling, I suppose, that we might eventually join some Settler group. I myself don't intend to, but I fly my own air-car frequently and five years ago I flew to Chicago and then, eventually, flew back. —Sit here. I'll make the arrangements."

She left, very much a whirlwind.

Daneel looked after her and murmured, "Friend Giskard, that, somehow, did not seem characteristic of her. Have you done something?"

Giskard said, "A bit. It seemed to me when we entered that the young woman who showed us in was attracted by your appearance. I was certain that there had been the same factor in Madam Quintana's mind last night at the banquet, though I was too far from her and there were too many others in the room for me to be sure. Once our conversation with her began, however, the attraction was unmistakable. Little by little, I strengthened it and each time she suggested the interview might come to an end, she seemed less determined—and at no time did she seriously object to your continuing it. Finally, she suggested the air-car because, I believe, she had reached the point where she could not bear to lose the chance to be with you for a while longer."

"This may complicate matters for me," said Daneel thoughtfully.

"It is in a good cause," said Giskard. "Think of it in terms of the Zeroth Law." Somehow he gave the impression, in saying so, that he would be smiling—if his face allowed such an expression.

89.

QUINTANA DREW A SIGH OF relief as she landed the air-car on a concrete slab suitable for the purpose. Two robots approached at once for the obligatory examination of the vehicle and for repowering if necessary.

She looked out to the right, leaning across Daneel as she did so. "It is in that direction, several miles up the Susquehanna River. It's a hot day, too." She straightened, with some apparent reluctance, and smiled at Daneel. "That's the worst of leaving the City. The environment is totally uncontrolled out here. Imagine allowing it to be this hot. Don't you feel hot, Daneel?"

"I have an internal thermostat, madam, that is in good working order."

"Wonderful. I wish I did. There are no roads into this area, Daneel. Nor are there any robots to guide you, for they never enter it. Nor do I know what might be the right place within the area, which is a sizable one. We might stumble all through the area without coming upon the base, even though we passed within five hundred meters of it."

"Not 'we,' madam. It is quite necessary for you to remain here. What follows might conceivably be dangerous and, since you are without air-conditioning, the task might be more than you could easily bear, physically, even if it were not dangerous. Could you wait for us, madam? To have you do so would be important to me."

"I will wait."

"We may be some hours."

"There are facilities of various sorts here and the small City of Harrisburg is not far."

"In that case, madam, we must be on our way."

He sprang lightly from the air-car and Giskard followed him. They set off northward. It was nearly noon and the bright summer sun sparkled from the polished portions of Giskard's body.

Daneel said, "Any sign of mental activity you can detect will be those we want. There should be no one else for kilometers about."

"Are you certain that we can stop them if we encounter them, friend Daneel?"

"No, friend Giskard, I am by no means certain—but we must."

90.

LEVULAR MANDAMUS GRUNTED and looked up at Amadiro with a tight smile on his thin face.

"Amazing," he said, "and most satisfactory."

Amadiro mopped his brow and cheeks with a piece of toweling and said, "What does that mean?"

"It means that every relay station is in working order."

"Then you can initiate intensification?"

"As soon as I calculate the proper degree of W particle concentration."

"And how long will that take?"

"Fifteen minutes. Thirty."

Amadiro watched with an air of intensifying grimness on his face until Mandamus said, "All right. I have it. It's 2.72 on the arbitrary scale I have set up. That will give us fifteen decades before an upper equilibrium level will be reached that will be maintained without essential change for millions of years thereafter. And that level will make certain that, at best, Earth can maintain a few scattered groups in areas that are relatively radiation-free. We'll have only to wait and, in fifteen decades, a thoroughly disorganized group of Settler worlds will be meat for our slicing."

"I will not live fifteen more decades," said Amadiro slowly.

"My personal regrets, sir," said Mandamus dryly, "but we are now talking of Aurora and the Spacer worlds. There will be others who will carry on your task."

"You, for instance?"

"You have promised me the headship of the Institute and, as you see, I have earned it. From that political base, I may reasonably hope to become Chairman someday and I will carry through those policies that will be necessary to make certain of the final dissolution of the by-then anarchic worlds of the Settlers."

"That's pretty confident of you. What if you turn on the W particle flow and then someone else turns it down in the course of the next fifteen decades?"

"Not possible, sir. Once the device is set, an internal atomic shift will freeze it in that position. After that, the process is irreversible—no matter what happens here. The whole place may be vaporized and the crust will nevertheless continue its slow burn. I suppose it would be possible to rebuild an entirely new setup if anyone on Earth or among the Settlers can duplicate my work, but if so they can only further increase the rate of radioactivity, never decrease it. The second law of thermodynamics will see to that."

Amadiro said, "Mandamus, you say you have earned the headship. However, I'm the one to decide that, I think."

Mandamus said stiffly, "You are not, sir. With respect, the details of this process are known to me, but not to you. Those details are encoded in a place you will not find and, even if you do, it is guarded by robots who will destroy it rather than allow it to fall into your hands. You cannot gain credit for this. I can."

Amadiro said, "Nevertheless, getting my approval will hasten matters for you. If you were to wrest the headship from my unwilling hands, by whatever means, you will have a continuing opposition among other members of the Council that will hamper you through all your decades in the post. Is it just the title of head you want or the opportunity to experience all that comes of true leadership?"

Mandamus said, "Is this the time to talk politics? A moment ago, you were all impatience over the fact that I might linger fifteen minutes over my computer."

"Ah, but we are now talking about adjusting the W particle beam. You want to place it at 2.72—was that the figure?—and yet I wonder if that can be right. What is the extreme range you can handle?"

"The range goes from zero to twelve, but it is 2.72 that is required. Plus or minus 0.05—if you wish further detail. It is that which, on the basis of reports from all fourteen relays will allow a lapse of fifteen decades to equilibrium."

"Yet what I think is the correct figure is twelve."

Mandamus stared at the other in horror. "Twelve? Do you understand what that means?"

"Yes. It means we will have the Earth too radioactive to live upon in a decade or a decade and a half and we will kill a few billion Earthpeople in the process."

"*And* make certain a war with an infuriated Settler Federation. What can you want of such a holocaust?"

"I tell you again. I do not expect to live another fifteen decades and I want to live to see the destruction of Earth."

"But you would also be assuring the maiming—maiming, at the very least —of Aurora. You cannot be serious."

"But I am. I have twenty decades of defeat and humiliation to make up."

"Those decades were brought about by Han Fastolfe and Giskard—and not by Earth."

"No, they were brought about by an Earthman, Elijah Baley."

"Who has been dead for more than sixteen decades. What is the value of a moment of vengeance over a man long dead?"

"I do not want to argue the matter. I will make you an offer. The title of head at once. I will resign my post the instant we return to Aurora and nominate you in my place."

"*No.* I do not want the headship on those terms. Death to billions!"

"Billions of *Earthmen.* Well, I cannot trust you, then, to manipulate the controls properly. Show me—*me*—how to set the control instrument and *I* will take the responsibility. I will still resign my post on our return and will nominate you in my place."

"*No.* It will still mean the death of billions and who knows how many millions of Spacers as well. Dr. Amadiro, please understand that I will not do it on any terms and that you cannot do it without me. The setting mechanism is keyed to my left thumbprint."

"I ask you again."

"You cannot be sane if you ask me again despite all I have said."

"That, Mandamus, is a personal opinion of yours. I am not so insane that I have failed to send off all the local robots on one errand or another. We are alone here."

Mandamus lifted a corner of his upper lip in a sneer. "And with what do you intend to threaten me? Are you going to kill me now that there are no robots present to stop you?"

"Yes, as a matter of fact, Mandamus, I will if I have to." Amadiro produced a small-caliber blaster from a pouch at his side. "These are difficult to obtain on Earth, but not impossible—if the price is right. And I know how to use it. Please believe me when I tell you that I am perfectly willing to blow your head off right now—if you do not place your thumb on the contact and allow me to adjust the dial to twelve."

"You dare not. If I die, how will you set the dial without me?"

"Don't be an utter fool. If I blow your head off, your left thumb will remain intact. It will even be at blood temperature for a while. I will use that thumb, then set the dial as easily as I would turn on a water tap. I would prefer you alive, since your death might be wearisome to explain back on Aurora, but it would not be more wearisome than I could bear. Therefore, I give you thirty seconds to make up your mind. If you cooperate, I will still give you the headship at once. If you don't, it will all go as I wish, in any case, and you will be dead. We start now. One—two—three—"

Mandamus stared in horror at Amadiro, who continued to count and stare at him over the leveled blaster with hard, expressionless eyes.

And then Mandamus hissed, "Put the blaster away, Amadiro, or we'll both be immobilized on the plea that we must be protected from harm."

The warning came too late. Quicker than the eye could follow, an arm stretched out to seize Amadiro's wrist, paralyzing it with pressure, and the blaster was gone.

Daneel said, "I apologize for having had to inflict pain on you, Dr. Amadiro, but I cannot allow you to hold a blaster pointed at another human being."

91.

AMADIRO SAID NOTHING.

Mandamus said coldly, "You are two robots with, as far as I can see, no master in view. By default, I am your master and I order you to leave and not return. Since, as you see, there is no danger to any human being present at this moment, there is nothing to overcome your necessitated obedience to this order. Leave at once."

Daneel said, "Respectfully, sir, there is no need to hide our identities or abilities from you, since you know them already. My companion, R. Giskard Reventlov, has the ability to detect emotion. —Friend Giskard."

Giskard said, "As we approached, having detected your presence at quite a distance, I took note, Dr. Amadiro, of an overwhelming rage in your mind. In yours, Dr. Mandamus, there was extreme fear."

"The rage, if rage there was," said Mandamus, "was Dr. Amadiro's reaction to the approach of two strange robots, especially of one who was capable of meddling with the human mind and who had already badly— and perhaps permanently—damaged that of Lady Vasilia. My fear, if fear there was, was also the result of your approach. We are now in control of our emotions and there is no reason for you to interfere. We again order you to withdraw permanently."

Daneel said, "Your pardon, Dr. Mandamus, but I merely wish to ascertain that we may safely follow your orders. Was there not a blaster in Dr. Amadiro's hand when we approached—and was it not pointed at you?"

Mandamus said, "He was explaining its workings and he was about to put it away when you took it from him."

"Then shall I return it to him, sir, before I leave?"

"No," said Mandamus without a quiver, "for then you would have an excuse to remain here in order to—as you would say—protect us. Take it with you when you go and you will have no reason to return."

Daneel said, "We have reason to think that you are here in a region which human beings are not allowed to penetrate—"

"That is a custom, not a law, and one which, in any case, holds no force over us, since we are not Earthpeople. For that matter, robots are not allowed to be here, either."

"We were brought here, Dr. Mandamus, by a high official of Earth's government. We have reason to think that you are here in order to raise the level of radioactivity in Earth's crust and do grave and irreparable damage to the planet."

"Not at all—" began Mandamus.

Here Amadiro interrupted for the first time. "By what right, robot, do you cross-examine us? We are human beings who have given you an order. Follow it now!"

His tone of authority was overwhelming and Daneel quivered, while Giskard half-turned.

But Daneel said, "Your pardon, Dr. Amadiro. I do not cross-examine. I merely seek reassurance, in order that I may know that I can safely follow the order. We have reason to think that—"

"You need not repeat," said Mandamus. Then, in an aside, "Dr. Amadiro, please allow me to answer." To Daneel again, "Daneel, we are here on an anthropological mission. It is our purpose to seek the origins of various human customs that influence behavior among Spacers. These origins can be found only here on Earth and it is here, then, that we seek them."

"Do you have Earth's permission for this?"

"Seven years ago, I consulted the appropriate officials on Earth and received their permission."

Daneel said in a low voice, "Friend Giskard, what do you say?"

Giskard said, "The indications in Dr. Mandamus's mind are that what he is saying is not in accord with the situation as it is."

"He is lying, then?" said Daneel firmly.

"That is my belief," said Giskard.

Mandamus said, his calmness untouched, "That may be your belief, but belief is not certainty. You cannot disobey an order on the basis of mere belief. I know that and you know that."

Giskard said, "But in Dr. Amadiro's mind, rage is dammed only by emotional forces that are barely up to the job required of them. It is quite possible to slit those forces, so to speak, and allow the rage to pour out."

And Amadiro cried out, "Why do you fence with these things, Mandamus?"

Mandamus shouted, "Do not say a word, Amadiro! You play into their hands!"

Amadiro paid no attention. "It is demeaning and it is useless." With violent anger, he shook off Mandamus's restraining arm. "They know the truth, but what of that? —Robots, we are Spacers. More than that, we are Aurorans, from the world on which you were constructed. More than that, we are high officials on the world of Aurora and you must interpret the phrase 'human beings' in the Three Laws of Robotics as meaning Aurorans.

"If you do not obey us now, you harm us and humiliate us, so that you will be violating both the First and Second Laws. That our actions here are intended to destroy Earthmen, even large numbers of Earthmen, is true, but is, even so, utterly irrelevant. You might as well offer to refuse to obey us because we eat the meat of animals we have killed. Now that I have explained this to you, leave!"

But the last words turned into a croak. Amadiro's eyes bulged and he crumpled to the ground.

Mandamus, with a wordless cry, bent over him.

Giskard said, "Dr. Mandamus, Dr. Amadiro is not dead. He is at the moment in a coma from which he can be roused at any time. However, he will have forgotten everything in connection with this present project, nor will he ever be able to understand anything in connection with it—if, for instance, you tried to explain it. In the process of doing this—which I could not have done without his own admission that he intended to destroy large numbers of Earthmen—I may have permanently damaged other parts of his memory and his thinking processes. That I regret, but I could not help it."

Daneel said, "You see, Dr. Mandamus, some time ago, on Solaria, we encountered robots who narrowly defined human beings as Solarians only. We recognize the fact that if different robots are subject to narrow definitions of one sort or another, there can only be measureless destruction. It is useless to try to have us define human beings as Aurorans only. We define human beings as all members of the species *Homo sapiens*, which includes Earthpeople and Settlers, and we feel that the prevention of harm to human beings in groups and to humanity as a whole comes before the prevention of harm to any specific individual."

Mandamus said breathlessly, "That is not what the First Law says."

"It is what I call the Zeroth Law and it takes precedence."

"You have not been programmed in such a way."

"It is how I have programmed myself. And since I have known from the moment of our arrival here that your presence is intended for harm, you cannot order me away or keep me from harming you. The Zeroth Law takes precedence and I must save Earth. Therefore, I ask you to join me—voluntarily—in destroying these devices you have here. Otherwise, I will be forced to threaten harm to you, as Dr. Amadiro did, although I would not use a blaster."

But Mandamus said, "Wait! Wait! Hear me out. Let me explain. That Dr. Amadiro has had his mind wiped clean is a good thing. He *wanted* to destroy Earth, but I did *not* want to. That was why he held a blaster on me."

Daneel said, "It was you, however, who originated the notion, who designed and built these devices. Otherwise, Dr. Amadiro would not have had to try to force you to do anything. He would have done it himself and would not have required any help from you. Isn't that right?"

"Yes, that is right. Giskard can examine my emotions and see if I'm lying. I built these devices and I was prepared to use them, but not in the fashion Dr. Amadiro wished. Am I telling the truth?"

Daneel looked at Giskard, who said, "As nearly as I can tell, he is telling the truth."

"Of course I am," said Mandamus. "What *I* am doing is to introduce a very gradual acceleration of the natural radioactivity in the Earth's crust. There will be one hundred and fifty years during which the people of Earth can move to other worlds. It will increase the population of the present Settler worlds and increase the Settlement of additional worlds in great numbers. It will remove Earth as a huge anomalous world that forever threatens the Spacers and stultifies the Settlers. It will remove a center of mystical fervor that is holding back the Settlers. Am I telling the truth?"

Again Giskard said, "As nearly as I can tell, he is telling the truth."

"My plan, if it works out, would preserve the peace and make the Galaxy a home for Spacer and Settler alike. That is why, when I constructed this device—"

He gestured toward it, placing his left thumb on the contact, and then, lunging toward the volume control, shouted, "Freeze!"

Daneel moved toward him and stopped, frozen, right hand upraised. Giskard did not move.

Mandamus turned back, panting, "It's at 2.72. It's done. It's irreversible. Now it will be played out exactly as I intended. Nor can you bear witness against me, for you will start a war and your Zeroth Law forbids that."

He looked down at the prone body of Amadiro and said, with a cold look of contempt, "Fool! You will never know how it should have been done."

Chapter 19
Alone

92.

MANDAMUS SAID, "YOU CANNOT HARM ME NOW, robots, for nothing you do to me will alter the fate of the Earth."

"Nevertheless," said Giskard shakily, "you must not remember what you have done. You must not explain the future to the Spacers." He reached for a chair and, with a trembling hand, pulled it toward himself and sat down, as Mandamus crumpled and slid down into what seemed to be a gentle sleep.

"At the last," said Daneel in soft despair, as he looked down at the two unconscious bodies, "I failed. When it was necessary for me to seize Dr. Mandamus to prevent harm to people who were not present before my eyes, I found myself forced to follow his order and froze. The Zeroth Law did not work."

Giskard said, "No, friend Daneel, you did not fail. I prevented you. Dr. Mandamus had the urge to try to do what he did and was held back by the fear of what you would certainly do if he did try. I neutralized his fear and then I neutralized you. So Dr. Mandamus set the Earth's crust on fire, so to speak—on very slow fire."

Daneel said, "But why, friend Giskard, why?"

"Because he was telling the truth. I told you so. *He* thought he was lying. From the nature of the triumph in his mind, I am under the firm impression he felt that the consequence of the growing radioactivity would be anarchy and confusion among Earthpeople and Settlers and that the Spacers would destroy them and seize the Galaxy. But I thought the scenario he presented us to win us over was the correct one. The removal of

Earth as a large crowded world would remove a mystique I have already felt to be dangerous and would help the Settlers. They will streak outward into the Galaxy at a pace that will double and redouble and—without Earth to look back to always, without Earth to set up a god of the past—they will establish a Galactic Empire. It was necessary for us to make that possible."

He paused and, his voice weakening, he said, "Robots and Empire."

"Are you well, friend Giskard?"

"I cannot stand, but I can still talk. Listen to me. It is time for you to take on my burden. I have adjusted you for mental detection and control. You have but to listen to the final pathways as they are impressed upon yourself. Listen—"

He spoke steadily—but increasingly weakly—in language and symbols that Daneel could feel internally. Even as Daneel listened, he could feel the pathways moving and ticking into place. And when Giskard was done, there was suddenly the cool purr of Mandamus's mind impinging on his own, the unsteady thumping of Amadiro's, and the thin metallic thread of Giskard's.

Giskard said, "You must return to Madam Quintana and arrange to have these two human beings sent back to Aurora. They will not be able to harm Earth further. Then see to it that Earth's security forces seek out and inactivate the humanoid robots sent to Earth by Mandamus.

"Be careful how you use your new powers, for you are new to them and they will not be under perfect control. You will improve with time—slowly —if you are careful always to undergo self-examination with each use. Use the Zeroth Law, but not to justify needless harm to individuals. The First Law is almost as important.

"Protect Madam Gladia and Captain Baley—unobtrusively. Let them be happy together and let Madam Gladia continue with her efforts to bring peace. Help supervise, over the decades, the removal of Earthpeople from this world. And—one more thing—if I can remember— Yes—if you can— find out where the Solarians have gone. That may be—important."

Giskard's voice trailed off.

Daneel kneeled at the side of the seated Giskard and took the unresponsive metal hand in his own. He said, in an agonized whisper, "Recover, friend Giskard. Recover. What you did was right by the Zeroth Law. You have preserved as much life as possible. You have done well by humanity. Why suffer so when what you have done saves all?"

Giskard said, in a voice so distorted that the words could barely be made out, "Because I am not certain. —What if—the other view—is right—after all—and the Spacers will—triumph and then themselves decay so that—the Galaxy—will be—empty.— Good-bye, friend—Dan—"

And Giskard was silent, never to speak or move again.

Daneel rose.

He was alone—and with a Galaxy to care for.